"THE RENDIES ARE GATHERING. . . ."

The stars awoke me from the wizard's trance. The wizard stood amid a cloud of Rendies. My sister's gaze began to drift from the wizard to the wraiths. "Ylsa," I said sharply, "do not look at them." I did not know why I voiced the warning.

"Evaric, come away from there," Arvard called to me even as he tried to coax Ylsa into moving. "In here," he ordered, and we ducked under twisted limbs and into a hollow of tangled brush. "We will survive," Arvard assured me. "The Rendies have a wizard, and that must be a rare treat to them."

Almost as though the Rendies heard him, a loud wailing trill sounded and smoking, tenuous ribbons snaked through the trees and into the brush. A lacy tendril brushed my back. It stung frightfully. The tendril blackened, becoming opaque and stiff.

"You burn!" accused the Rendie as the wailing sank to a low moan. The wraith's color deepened to a steady russet, and discord made its keening voice feel harsh. "You are cruel, and I have killed for you. Fire-child, why do you burn your own?"

Cheryl J. Franklin's Magical Tales of the Taormin:

FIRE GET

FIRE LORD

FIRE LORD

Cheryl J. Franklin

DAW BOOKS, INC.
DONALD A. WOLLHEIM, PUBLISHER

1633 Broadway, New York, NY 10019

First Printing, June 1989

1 2 3 4 5 6 7 8 9

PRINTED IN THE U.S.A.

I.

Let (X,T) be a topological space.
Let S be a subset of X.
The union of S and all of its limit points is called the
closure of S.

CLOSURE

Chapter 1

Disjointed words tumbled across the screen. As though burned, Beth snatched her hand from the smooth membrane of the keypad. The surge of data ebbed into a silent, mocking glow:

LIFE EXTENSION PROJECT
STATUS REPORT #7
GENETIC RESEARCH CENTER,
IX AXIS REPUBLIC

Beth's fingers hovered above the keys which would delete the unbidden file. "A fine psychic researcher you make," she chided herself, "shuddering like a superstitious crone." She relaxed her hand deliberately and steeled herself to read the document. The brutal details of the descriptions appalled her. No such information regarding the Immortals' predecessors had emerged at the trial or appeared in any published records. The GRC personnel had exerted great care to ensure the thorough destruction of those peculiarly talented children.

Beth tapped the keypad delicately, and the flat display became blank. She brought her hands together slowly, folded her manicured fingers, and pondered the eerily pertinent data. The initial gifts of anonymous information had fascinated her, augmenting her thesis invaluably. She had attributed the data to Dr. Jonet; she had eventually dismissed her initial assessment. Jonet could not possibly anticipate her paths of research so accurately, nor could his sources be so uncannily complete. Beth considered the subject of her research and the unsettling conclusions that coalesced from her analyses. Beth Shafer Terry began to fear, and a young and cunning man, who was something nearly human, smiled viciously in the city of Sereia.

*   *   *

Jon Terry grumbled to himself as he emerged from transfer, evaded an overly zealous young woman who tried to direct him to the off-world queue, and entered the DI security scanner. His identity flashed coldly on the guard's screen; the security guard stared at the flashing name, stared at Jon, and requested a second scan. "Welcome back, Dr. Terry," said the guard stiffly, as he confirmed the computer release of the dome's exit barrier.

"Officious cretin," muttered Jon sullenly, annoyed by the unnecessary delay of dual scans. Awaiting the tram, he ignored the flustered whispers of the DI personnel who rushed around him. He studied the DI complex with its peculiar use of structural texture and color; Jon reaffirmed his loathing of that sterile gaudiness, as the tram lifted him from the port dome to the upper entry of DI technical headquarters.

"Dr. Terry, how good of you to join us." The immaculately clad man who greeted Jon looked young, which meant that he might be any age between twenty-five and eighty. "I am Derek Coggins, senior relational specialist."

"I am only here because Network threatened to terminate my research grants unless I cooperated," replied Jon bluntly.

Coggins abandoned his strained smile. "I did not favor your inclusion on the Crisis Committee, Dr. Terry." A rumpled figure shambled across the crimson lobby and tapped Coggins' shoulder. Coggins tried to recover his bland courtesy. "You know Dr. Davison?"

Jon smiled at Davison, a man of peculiarly imperfect appearance in a world dominated by genetic uniformity. "The reclusive Tom Davison emerges just to welcome me? How have you been, Tom?"

"Terrible," answered Davison, and Coggins shuffled uncomfortably. "Come talk to me after your meeting, Jon."

"Same office?"

"Have I quit yet?" retorted Davison.

Coggins interrupted crisply, "The other members of the Committee will be waiting, Dr. Terry." Davison retreated without a word to Derek Coggins. Jon stared after Davison, wondering for the first time if a crisis might actually exist.

"We are no longer able to complete transfer to Aleph 2C7."

Only a purist like Weywood would bother with the cumbersome Aleph designations. "Is that Floral Park?" asked Jon innocently. "What happened to that lawsuit they brought against DI?"

Pained expressions acknowledged Jon's bleak irony. Helen Martines, another reluctant DI recruit, replied evenly, "Network arbitrators suggested a sizable settlement in favor of Floral Park, citing the precedent of Terry versus DI."

Weywood never faltered. "Aleph 2C7 corresponds to Smithson's Well. We have been forced to reroute through Aleph F8."

"Our transfer monitors perceive Smithson's Well as topologically nonexistent." said Coggins, glaring askance at Jon. "The Smithson's Well monitors report nothing extraordinary, except that DI central no longer responds to their contacts."

"The topological flaw is obviously local," commented Dr. Martines.

"So it appears," conceded Weywood.

"You have run all of the customary tests, Dr. Weywood?" asked a dark, nervous man whose sesquipedalian name Jon had forgotten.

"The DI central monitor verifies that our equipment is functioning flawlessly."

"A flaw could exist in your verification procedures," suggested Jon.

"I designed those procedures myself," returned Weywood coldly.

Terrific, thought Jon, wondering how many other members of the Crisis Committee resented him. He slumped a little farther in his chair, bored and distinctly unimpressed with the meeting, the committee, and the few facts that had emerged in the past two hours. The eager experts like Weywood could transform even a simple problem into a subject of endless debate. Marliss and Eaton had contributed nothing intelligent; Landsian had droned interminably on about the vital need to protect the public from awareness of the crisis, which he also paradoxically insisted did not exist. Wade and Martines had asked some pertinent questions, but Coggins had waylaid every answer with a reminder of DI's technical supremacy in topological systems.

If your systems are so perfect, Jon wanted to ask, why have a few minor transfer disturbances thrown you into such a frenzy? Jon did not voice his question, because he had promised himself to maintain some small degree of diplomacy where technical issues were concerned. At the first opportunity, Jon abandoned the meeting. His marginal diplomatic restraint had worn very thin.

Tom Davison's office wallowed beneath an impressive array of technical archives and quasi-historical trash. "You escaped your committee," remarked Tom from his computer console.

"I doubt they'll miss me. I seem to have been inflicted upon an unreceptive audience."

"DI loyalists have never forgiven you. A lot of heads rolled on your account."

"Punishment of the innocent."

"Honors for the nonparticipants." Tom moved his hands over the vast control grid, which had been elaborately redesigned to his specifications. The computer responded with a scaled holographic image of the DI transfer ports. "I made this recording last night. Watch that couple enter the Culver port."

Jon sank into the chair beside Tom and leaned forward with his chin in his hands. The DI node intersected an exceptional number of Network sets, making it one of the busiest ports in connected space. Tom's matrix displayed only a small portion of the terminal building, but Jon still spent several moments distinguishing the Culver port among the opalescent arc from which radiated endless queues of travelers.

A very modish couple approached the Culver port with the indifferent confidence of habitual travelers. They stepped through the light curtain, that nonfunctional aspect of transfer mechanization which protected the untrained eye from the mind-confounding sight of topological space distortion, and they remained visible. They strode two meters into the central field, which should have been unattainable via three-dimensional passage, before disappearing into spatial distortion. The holographic image faded.

"The couple reached their destination safely," said Tom. "They fortunately asked a minimum of questions."

"Transfer ports cannot spatially translate of their own accord. Someone has altered the configuration."

Tom adjusted the projection to produce the controller in

a highly magnified rendition. The intricate arrays resembled orderly golden lace trapped in pale amber. Tom increased the magnification, and the resonator webs became distinguishable. "See any signs of tampering?"

Jon frowned. "I haven't looked at a resonator in thirty years," he began, but something about the maze of circuitry stopped him. "Has anyone modified the portal structures?"

"No one but you ever understood the DI portal structures well enough to try. You created a thing of genius, and nobody has ever found a way to improve on your design."

"That is not my logic."

"DI central insists otherwise."

Jon shook his head stubbornly. "That is not my logic," he repeated, and Tom nodded. "You're not surprised?"

"No other answer made sense to me, but I wanted to hear it from you."

"The controller adapts to natural changes," mused Jon. "But the basal structure cannot vary without a major upheaval in the projected physics of the associated set. I think we would have noticed if gravity had changed direction." Tom grunted in laughter. "Wait." Jon closed his eyes, retreating into the infinite-dimensional realm which defied physical representation. He opened his eyes just long enough to assimilate the images registered in Tom's computer; he reconstructed the mental gyrations which had produced DI's original transfer port controller. "That reflects an incipiently unstable system," he concluded with a dawning of concern. "I'm surprised that the transfer ports are functioning at all."

"They are not working very well, even within the Taormina set."

"Weywood only recounted two incidents which sounded like anything more than coordinate errors."

"Most of the facts have been declared DI-proprietary." Tom gave Jon a lugubrious glance. "You are still cleared; I verified it before I submitted your name for the Crisis Committee."

"Preservation of my clearances was one of the few concessions my lawyers gained for me."

Tom grunted. "I'd been tracking inexplicable quantum phenomena for a month when this transference problem surfaced. Seven of the ports have now stopped mapping completely. Twelve others have shifted focus. New Loring and Thess have cross-mapped. The Governor of Thess missed his birthday gala due to transfer port error, and you can believe he let DI know about it." Tom allowed the viewing matrix to fade. "We have real trouble."

Jon tapped the arm of his chair. The chair reconfigured very slowly to his straightened posture. "You need a new chair," he commented. "This one is going inflexible."

"Supply center has been promising me one for a year." The two men studied the emptiness of the viewing matrix. "If we inform Coggins and company that the controller is defective, they'll order immediate development of a replacement."

"Without analyzing the cause of the first failure."

"They'll use this incident to press funding of redundant units."

"Expensive and pointless in this type of system. Topologically connected systems must fail equivalently, and the controller of a given space must be topologically connected to any other mechanism of equivalent control. Otherwise, the system is unstable."

"What happens if an unstable system is perpetuated?"

"Cataclysm. I can see why your transfer port quanta are misbehaving."

"The problem is not localized around the transfer ports. My team has measured erratic data on a planetwide scale, extending into the upper ionosphere."

"I haven't noticed any unusual interference."

"The most severe disruptions have centered over the Axis Republics. Let me show you something else." Tom touched the view grid, and the display matrix became a two-dimensional screen. "The first column reflects occurrences of energy transfer aberrations. The second column represents incidents of abnormally high electron counts in the ionosphere."

"One-to-one correspondence?"

"Yes. My quantum aberrations follow the pattern as well."

"That's actually reassuring. As long as the energy fields react consistently, my faith in the physical laws can remain intact. We have an anomalous force in play which we haven't yet identified."

Tom murmured with uncharacteristic diffidence. "I have one more list to show you: a correlation that Weywood and the DI central system failed to check."

"The thoroughness of DI central must have deteriorated since I left here."

"Not really. They still enter new scientific developments almost as soon as they emerge, scrutinize them via the latest in intelligent algorithms, and apply extensive consistency thresholds to the resultant statistics. Unsubstantiated theories migrate to a holding file, and elements of pseudoscience are automatically purged." Tom touched the grid again, and a third list of dates appeared beside the first two. "Did you ever hear about the GRC scandal sixty-some years ago? A social worker claimed that the geneticists had illegally created and subsequently abused a group of experimental children. The Ninth Axis Governor fined the Genetic Research Center and would have prosecuted the project's administrators, except that everyone involved in the project died before the court could complete its investigation."

"Of course. The case of the 'Battered Immortals,' as the more imaginative media types called it. The GRC trial evidence is central to Beth's doctoral thesis."

"I'd forgotten: she's a psychic researcher, isn't she?" Tom became pensive for a long moment. "Well, my boy, Rob, adopted the plight of these 'forlorn' victims as evidence of the immorality of the scientific community. Rob is an anarchist at the moment. He was lecturing me on the sins of my profession and praising these 'Immortals' for their rebellion."

"I assume this discussion is leading somewhere pertinent?"

"I decided to gather some facts on my own and give Rob a good debate. I had the DI computer attach the data base of the sensationalist news media, some of which have pursued the Immortals to this day with pretty wild accusations. As soon as I attached the new data, my computer registered the third correlation to the transfer port anomalies." With quick motions across the grid, Tom added brief event descriptions to the columns of dates. "The timing of every port anomaly corresponds to an act of aggression by one of these Immortals."

"I thought the sensationalists reported such acts on the hour. How many of those aggressive actions have been authenticated?"

"All of them measure at least ninety-five percent probable. None of the other reported actions show a verification probability greater than fifty percent. Don't ask me why the legitimate news sources haven't picked up any of this."

Jon leaned back, and the chair reluctantly adapted to support him. "Maybe the Immortals perceive quantum variations as we perceive ultrasonics: with a headache. A little physical discomfort can inspire a lot of aggression."

"Maybe. Or maybe the Immortals really are bringing us to Armageddon, as the doomsayers of the anti-genetics movement would have us believe." Tom Davison's round face and tilted features always gave his expressions a puckish cast, but something woeful dominated that face today. "You want to hear how paranoid I've become? I think that the Immortals are changing the universal topologies, energy patterns, material world, and who knows what else. I think those GRC geniuses accidentally tapped a motherlode of the kind of mental powers that inspired supernatural legends throughout history. None of the original Immortals ever showed much interest in anything beyond themselves, but these later ones may have begun to look beyond private insanity and family squabbles. Don't say it, Jon—I sound as mad as an Immortal myself."

"It is quite a theory," murmured Jon vaguely. He would have ridiculed anyone but Tom Davison for proposing anything so preposterous. Tom had always been an unusually stable and sensible member of one of the most esoteric of scientific communities. "Beth did mention some peculiarity of the Immortals' projected energy. I suppose that a correlation could exist, though I have trouble believing that it poses the danger you suggest."

"If anyone can rigorously prove or disprove the topological cohesion of my theory, it's you."

Jon grimaced. "Thanks a lot for the confidence. What do you intend to do while I study aberrant psychology?"

"Prepare a closure of the transfer ports, just in case you decide to agree with me."

Jon wondered for a shocked moment if Tom Davison had spent too many years working among overly educated eccentrics. "Maybe you had better downplay your intentions, if anyone else asks."

"Don't I know it." The puckish face grew sadder.

"I shall need more data on these Immortals," said Jon slowly. "I don't suppose that anyone else has addressed their peculiarities from a topological perspective."

"The DI computer has nothing on them except the garbled media garbage I attached last week."

"I'll talk to Beth."

"You should appease your committee first."

"And waste the day talking in circles," grumbled Jon. Though Tom might sound crazy, he was not boring company. Jon sulked all the way to the meeting room, while topological improbabilities rattled his nerves.

Chapter 2

"How far do you believe the allegations regarding these Immortals you've been studying, Beth?"

"Don't tell me you're developing an interest in my work, Jon Terry. I could never stand the competition." The dog ran yapping through the room, followed closely by Kitri and her brother. "Kitri, Michael, don't run in the house!"

"What sort of data do you have on them?"

Beth became peculiarly still. "How much do you want to hear?"

Jon tilted his head, pondering his wife's sudden change of mood. He said slowly, "Everything." Beth's obvious distress bewildered him; he had not yet told her of the day's events.

"Of the original seventeen Immortals," began Beth didactically, "only two are still thought to be alive. 'Immortals' is clearly a misnomer, though the subjects' potential longevity has certainly been enhanced. The Immortals are remarkably resilient to injury and impervious to most diseases. The characteristics which enhance their longevity appear to breed true. Unfortunately, the mental instability has also been perpetuated, a situation doubtless aggravated by inbreeding."

"The mental instability is balanced by unusual mental strengths in select areas?"

"All of the original subjects demonstrated exceptional intelligence, countered by acute paranoia and (in five cases) schizophrenia. All seventeen produced consistent indications of active psychic abilities." Beth became fervent. "The problem with psychic research has always been the intermittency of the data. These bizarre products of a misguided experiment seem to offer incontrovertible evidence of the human mind's potential power. If the GRC administrators in charge of the Immortals project had concentrated less on conceal-

18

ing their crime, we might have learned enormously from these people while they were still manageable."

"Before all the administrators and technical personnel died."

"The apparent causes of the deaths ranged from heart failure to a freak fire in a laboratory. All of the deaths were explicable, albeit oddly coincidental in light of the allegations of the GRC administrators. Even the social worker who had rescued the children began to question the children's stories. Most of my data was gathered at that time, but the study was never completed. The Immortals were psychiatrically treated and released after the aborted GRC trial, and the matter was officially closed. Since the GRC administrators had been discredited on an ethical basis, it seems that no one gave their findings much analysis."

In the next room, Kitri shrieked at Michael. The children dissolved into giggles. Beth stared at the connecting door, but she made no move toward it. She continued her recital restlessly, "According to the GRC personnel associated with the Immortals project, the children demonstrated psychic talents closer to witchcraft than to any scientific category, at least in appearance. When tested, the Immortals displayed no telepathic capabilities, though subsequent events suggest that the Immortals can indeed influence the thoughts of others. They do not appear to be clairvoyant. Some psychokinetic ability has been cited, but it appears to be an incidental result of the actual psychic intent."

"Which is?"

"Manipulation of energy sources. At least, that is the theory on which I have based my thesis. The records regarding the Immortals' effects on GRC's atmospheric control center are extraordinary." Beth hesitated. "And a little frightening." Beth leaned forward and placed her hand on Jon's. "What happened at DI today?"

"Tom Davison thinks that these Immortals of yours are altering the topological structure of this world. I need access to whatever information you have." Beth's lovely face, the result of genetic control at its best, became solemnly pensive.

"The Immortals were given only standard testing when they were contained at GRC," explained Beth. "The geneticists were not equipped to run full psychic analyses. Once the children were declared psychologically cured, they had the right to refuse further testing, which they did. They matured into class C functional citizens, which meant that they could live on their own with only the most sporadic, limited supervision. Inbreeding should never have been allowed. However, the city of Sereia, where the Immortals were assigned after their creators' trial, is ridiculously protective of its citizenry."

"The Immortals don't seem to merit much protection, whatever their past misfortunes might have been."

"They are cruel, ruthless, and exceedingly dangerous. All of the deaths among them have been attributed to conflicts among themselves, and a good many would-be interviewers have disappeared over the past fifty years."

Jon nodded soberly, his fingers nervously tapping the computer console. In an explosive movement, Jon applied another test to his wife's data, hoping to see his previous results contradicted. The pattern remained uncannily consistent.

Beth said gently, "You have been running tests all night. Do you expect the answer to change?"

Jon shook his head reluctantly. "How did you acquire your initial data, Beth?"

Beth smoothed her blonde hair, recently cropped short after the fashion of the year. "Someone sent it to me anonymously."

"Do you have any idea of your benefactor's indentity?"

"Yes." Beth slid from the console. She walked to the window-wall, which currently displayed a wintry mountain scene, subdued for the waning night. "I have avoided the obvious answer."

"That you have been fed this information, just as the social worker who originally 'rescued' the Immortals from GRC received anonymous information about the Immortals' plight."

"I consider it unlikely that these genetic abominations would send their psychic histories to an insignificant doctoral student on the far side of the planet, unless they intended that I convey the information to my extraordinarily famous husband."

"Maybe so," Jon agreed, finding the ramifications distasteful in the extreme. "If these Immortals can alter physical topology at will, they could destroy all connected space."

"And they want you to know their power."

"A deliberate taunt."

"It would be psychologically congruous to their profiles."

"My God." The facts were consistent. The conclusions were inescapable. "Class C citizens do not have transfer privileges. So far, the Immortals are confined to this world." Jon drummed his fingers pensively. "Take Kitri and Michael to Inulaii. Leave this morning, while the ports are still functional. I shall try to join you this afternoon. We are not likely to return, so take whatever is most important. Take the stupid dog."

Beth did not even protest his disparagement of her prized puppy. She watched Jon transfer the night's work to light disk and erase it from the central memory. "Where are you going?" she asked him tightly.

"To DI. I need to see Tom about closing the ports."

Chapter 3

"Someone is playing games," growled Tom. He struck the view grid irritably, and an image appeared, suspended in the center of the display matrix:]∞["I've lost thirty files since I talked to you yesterday. Each emptied of everything but this symbol." Tom looked at Jon. "Did you find anything in Beth's data?"

"Yes. Courtesy of your gameplayer. I sent Beth and the kids to Inulaii."

"Eleanor is visiting her sister on New Athens. Rob refuses to go anywhere, if only because I suggested it."

"Too bad. This world could become a very unpleasant place to live."

"Are we overreacting?"

"No. We can't allow the gameplayer to define the rules."

"I have configured a closure mechanism. It's basically the same device we use to inhibit travel to inimicable habitats and previously tenanted spaces."

"Can you gain me access to the controller?"

"That depends on the reason."

Jon smiled wanly. "We cannot entrust reconfiguration to DI central, since the gameplayer has apparently claimed our computer networks."

"Can you ensure permanence of the closure?"

"I can rearrange the universe, if you can give me environmental isolation from the controller's energy fields."

"With the controller in node, I can only guarantee you about ten minutes. After that the operational distortions will begin to alter your molecular contiguity. The process does not promote longevity."

"Ten minutes should suffice to tangle a few connectors."

"We are condemning a lot of people. Maybe we should consult Coggins and company."

"We cannot wait for these Immortals to master topological transport. If we allow them to spread beyond local space, we could jeopardize the entire Network."

"You want me to implement the closure device while you sabotage the controller?"

"Yes." Listen to us, thought Jon, matter-of-factly condemning our home world to eternal isolation. Even if those we strand should revive conventional space travel, there is not a benign planet within practical reach. Neither Tom nor I have any close friends at risk, but Tom will lose a stepson, and I shall lose my home. I know a lot of people on this world, even if Beth does call me antisocial.

"The planet is self-sufficient," mused Tom, as if in answer to Jon's own doubts. "It's one of the most agreeable worlds we ever discovered. We cannot possibly evacuate the whole planet anyway. Our gameplaying friend won't wait for us to debate about who should be saved."

"We may eventually discover another solution and be able to rescue this place from whatever it has become."

Tom turned his head back to his computer. "You believe that?" he asked curiously.

"No. When I've finished with the controller, not even DI's technical wizards will be able to reassemble the open structure."

*   *   *

Beth and the kids still waited in the line for Inulaii. Beth was forcing cheerfulness, and Michael had adopted his mother's enthusiasm. Kitri looked bewildered, muddled between Michael's exuberant teasing and the strangeness of sudden change.

Jon did not speak to them. Beth saw him, but she averted her eyes quickly. Beth knew that her husband had no legal authority to close the Culver port for maintenance inspection. She kept the children's attention on the light curtain ahead of them and the window-wall simulation of Inulaii's tropical beaches beside them.

Jon felt a yank at an internal tension when he saw his family disappear through the Inulaii port. He released a tightly held breath when the controller signaled a normal transfer. He activated the entry barrier, isolating Culver port from the rest of the DI sights and sounds.

Tom had disengaged the light curtain, and he was removing his closure device from the maintenance unit that he and Jon had appropriated. Jon walked gingerly toward the dark, rippling distortion of air, which encompassed the shifted Culver port. He half expected to pass the marked entry and find himself on Culver, but the synthetic floor beneath him did not change to otherworld metal. He stepped around the Culver port, feeling queasy as he did it. The ports should have formed a continuous sphere surrounding the controller, extending even to the nulls beneath the dome's smooth floor. Walking around a disjointed port, as idly as if circling a piece of furniture, should have been impossible.

"Ten minutes, Jon." Tom was not as engrossed in setting his mechanism as he appeared.

Jon activated the protective field which was part of the maintenance uniform he had taken. The field had not been designed to defeat the controller's direct energies, but Tom had made some delicate changes. The changes, Tom had warned with disheartening candor, would almost certainly destroy the mechanism after one usage, if they lasted that long.

Jon entered the controller space, feeling decidedly relieved when his monitor's readings remained level. He walked toward the cylindrical extrusion which housed the node. Jon knew the controller's theory intimately; he was accustomed to seeing the controller itself in magnified versions, as represented on view matrices. He had seldom interacted with his creation physically. The reality of the controller was no bigger than his fist.

He breathed deeply three times to achieve some sort of steadiness, reached out his protected hand, and lifted the controller from its energy nest. He could not hear anything beyond the ports, but he could imagine the confusion which was resulting from the sudden failure of transfers all over the world. A dozen DI officials would descend on the maintenance consoles in a few minutes; it would take them some additional time to focus on the controller.

Jon inserted the force probe through the controller's outer network, adjusted the intensity and registered the coordinates that were to be fused. He extracted the probe, reversed it, plunged it back into the controller for the required instant, and restored the controller to its nest. The fields began to operate again, warping the air across the ports.

The controller had never been designed to emulate a

personality, but its complexity had necessitated a synthetic intelligence. The intricacy of the controller's fail-safe mechanisms made it self-teaching and almost capable of original thought, so carefully had it been programmed to preserve universal integrity. It certainly comprehended the alteration Jon was inflicting. Jon felt like a murderer.

"I am sorry," he whispered to the controller, the prototype for all of the topological controllers on all the Network worlds. He was beginning to feel sick. He checked his watch: seven minutes. He turned to circle again around the Culver port, but the port had shifted. It had returned to its proper location, locking him into the controller's distorted space.

A short, fidgety young man stood beside the controller. Jon tried to recall how many seconds a man could survive unprotected beside the controller-in-node. "Which port were you entering?" demanded Jon hurriedly, even as he set his monitor to scan.

"I had hoped that you would offer me more of a challenge, Dr. Terry," replied the young man sadly. "Sabotage is such a childish effort." The young man directed his fingers toward the controller with a respectful care. His fingers shifted and blurred as they neared it.

"Don't try to touch it!" cried Jon instinctively. The monitor on his wrist was recording energy contortions of alarming magnitude surrounding the young man. The controller's fields were being impaired, and the implant had not had time to complete implosion. Tom would hesitate to implement the external closure until Jon reappeared. Damn.

The young man had paused, apparently unable to touch the controller's lacy surface. "It repels unprotected flesh," recalled Jon aloud, feeling a momentary smugness for that precautionary tactic.

The young man's sharp gaze became angry and supercilious. "How little you understand, Dr. Terry. Bereft of your technological trappings, you mortals are a very primitive people," he remarked. "I mean to improve this sterile society of yours. Your controller and every world it touches will be mine, despite your feeble attempts to thwart me."

The controller space shuddered, and the energies roared. A strange expression nudged the confidence from the Immortal's face: shock and recognition. Fear surged in

Jon, who knew that an explosion of energy so near the node could dismantle the controller's hold on dimensional continuity.

Another shifted port rippled beside the controller node. Too close to the controller to be safe, thought Jon, but he edged toward it. Jon watched the Immortal carefully, but that impervious young man had concentrated all of his desperate attention on the controller. Jon calculated the odds of surviving a leap through the tantalizing port, finding them low but better than any other chance of escape. He wondered where the port would take him; he wished that he could signal Tom, but the controller's interference would overwhelm the maintenance uniform's transmitter.

Jon readied himself to risk transfer, when the port's directional reading registered negative on his monitor. "Damn, damn, damn!" he muttered, but the newcomer had already emerged: a young man whose perfect, chiseled features suggested genetic manipulation of the most elaborate kind. The newcomer was holding the controller. The controller remained in its proper place, beneath the gaze of a startled Immortal.

Jon smacked his wrist monitor, hoping to jar its readings into sense. "The DI controller has never been duplicated," he told himself, but he queried the monitor further: unidentified program overlays stabilized the active coexistence of the DI controller with a time-shift of the Taormina set. "Time transference is a cataclysmic mapping," he informed the monitor sharply, while the monitor blandly reiterated its message. "A future-shift of twenty-two thousand years?" murmured Jon, staring in wonder at the flawlessly handsome man who was the future node of the DI controller.

The Immortal cried with sudden shrill defiance. He dropped his hands upon the present controller, claiming it and tearing it from its node. Jon imagined he could hear the controller scream at the agony of strange reconfiguration inflicted by the merciless Immortal. In a shuddering of violated space, the Immortal and the captive controller vanished. Waves of topologically sundered energies stormed the stability of a broken node.

Shock destroyed the protective field of Jon's uniform. His monitor registered the commencement of molecular disruption; warning lights flashed with indifferent efficiency. The twisting and churning pulled and mutilated the fragile working mechanism of a mortal body. Jon's legs buckled. Something harsh and fiery thrust itself through Jon's head.

"Recall the pattern," commanded a compelling, sourceless voice.

The dimmed ports rekindled, skewed from their proper space. They existed here, now, and they existed there, then. *Now* was being shredded by dismembered control. Jon had a foggy view of ports rippling across waves of terrified, bewildered travelers and DI personnel. The fortunate were fully caught; others were severed by partial transfer. Nothing remained stable, except the oddly anachronistic young man who held the strands of a thousand infinities in his unprotected hand.

Jon closed his eyes against the onslaught of a world's death condemning him, a mortal who had failed at an Immortal's game. "Recall the pattern," repeated the relentless voice in his head.

Jon could see nothing but dark, broken space shot with fires of blue, gold, and green. He found himself on his feet with no recollection of how he had achieved that position. He reeled, took a step forward and tripped. Arms caught him: soft arms wearing a scent he recognized.

"Jon," whispered Beth, relief and concern flowing from her.

"We nearly lost you, despite your emergency signal," said a shaken port official, observing Jon's singed maintenance uniform with puzzlement. "What's wrong with your transfer port?"

"Everything," muttered Jon, clutching at Beth to feel her reality. He focused on the monitor grid, near which Kitri and Michael stood in uncertain silence. Jon laughed a little hysterically to see the stupid dog wrap its leash around Kitri's legs.

Jon tugged at Beth, and she steadied him as he hurried to the monitor. The monitoring personnel argued as he shoved them aside and ran his hands over their console. "Step away from the grid, sir." One of the monitor officials had run to summon the guards. The others hesitated, deferring instinctively to Jon's purloined uniform. "You have no authority on this world, sir."

Jon moved his hands once more. The view matrix became entirely dark. He took Beth's hand in his. "I think you'll find that DI transfers have become inoperable," he announced calmly.

He began to walk away from the ports. Beth held to his right arm; Michael and Kitri vied for his left. The dog strained its leash to speed their pace. Guards were gathering at the doors. There would be many questions.

"Tom's closure seems to have worked," he told Beth tersely.

"Where is Tom?"

"I don't think he transferred. The node was disconnected prematurely, which would have nullified the delay mechanism, effecting suffocation on instant of closure. Atmospheres are peculiarly sensitive to disruptions of topological spaces."

"You're rambling, Jon," said Beth with slow, taut fear. Jon squeezed her arm and fell silent, as the guards surrounded them.

RENDING

Chapter 1

Day of Rending
Year of Serii—9009
Tulea, Serii

She returned alone from Ceallagh's Tomb on the Day of Rending. Her gray eyes were cold and intense with the Power she bore. Only her hands retained any softness, as they clasped a spindle-shaped thing of amber and gold filigree. "The war is ended," she said.

"Where is Kaedric?" Abbot Medwyn asked her cautiously. The abbot's face strained for the faithful brightness which minimized his true age.

The woman delicately stroked the spindle before responding. "He destroyed Horlach." She added rather bitterly, "He conquered the unconquerable, deathless Sorcerer King to save the mortals who hate him." She lifted her eyes to meet the abbot's, and he saw for the first time how distanced her vision had grown. "No mortal host could contain that much Power."

"He is dead?" whispered the woman's dark-haired sister hopefully. Kinship had snared her in a pattern she did not understand. She blamed Lord Venkarel, as would others, and she welcomed the possibility of his death.

The golden woman with the amber spindle did not answer. She opened the hand which had been clutching the spindle most tightly, and her hand was bleeding where the filigree had cut it. She swayed slightly, and the fair-haired man who was King Astorn's Adjutant steadied her with perceptible concern. "Let me take you back to the castle, Rhianna," he urged softly. His own hand shook, for he had fought many sleepless hours against the mortal tools of their Immortal foe.

31

The golden woman responded clearly and firmly, "You and I have yet much work to do, Ineuil. The patterns have been Rent. Serii is no longer as it was. The mortal world is no longer as it was."

The King's Adjutant studied her oddly, then gave a slow nod. "Of course," he murmured to himself, "the wizard of greatest Power at time of selection—you will become the Infortiare now."

The golden woman remained silent. Her sister stared, fascination and lingering shock making her dark eyes wide. The sisters had never been friends, but it is hard to watch the familiar become strange.

"I must go pray for him," said the abbot painfully. He turned his face toward the rough path which climbed the Mountain of Tul to Ceallagh's Tomb. The path was long and very steep.

The golden woman removed her open hand from the spindle. Very fine, gray dust covered her bleeding fingers where they had rested against the spindle's surface. She pressed the fingers to her taut lips before responding, "I think the prayer will be quite as effective, Medwyn, from here."

* * *

He scanned his surroundings closely. He assessed the patterns, cleansing those he recognized, sorting those he mistrusted. "Energy and infinity," he said softly, mocking himself. "I begin to understand you, Horlach, and your obsession with mortality."

He moved carefully, for he had not lost mortal caution. Suspicion was instinctive in him, bred and trained. He had come to know himself strong in a mortal world. He accepted no such certainty in this strange environment.

The Taormin had let him glimpse the deeper Powers. It had not prepared him for the sense of personal infinity. He had not, like Horlach, prepared himself for centuries.

The patterns extended farther and deeper than he had known. His own pattern impressed him quietly, but still he did not trust his strength. He would test new Power cautiously, as had ever been his way. So he had learned Ixaxis; Ixaxis had been new to him once.

"Ixaxis plays a child's game," said a voice he knew.

"You survive," he remarked, knowing the comment idle

and uninspired. He was unsurprised by the voice, but neither had he anticipated this moment. He berated himself, yet asked smoothly, "Whom can our contest serve now?"

"As ever, Venkarel, it will serve the victor."

"What do you hope to gain?" mused the Venkarel. "I eliminated your last bond to the mortal world by destroying my own physical shell." The Venkarel revised his infinite conceptions. There were other patterns at work here; immediate analysis was imperative.

The dark, little man chuckled gleefully. The Venkarel's anger coiled within itself; the Venkarel would not yield the satisfaction of its emergence to his foe. "An interesting maneuver," remarked the Venkarel very mildly. "Commuting mortal fear and anger into energies which perpetuate themselves at mortal expense."

"As you say, it is an interesting maneuver, but is it mine?" taunted Horlach. The Venkarel knew an unaccustomed sensation: inability to grasp the fullest meanings in an opponent's words. The sensation made him deeply uneasy. "Do you know your foe, Venkarel, as well as you believe?"

"Defeat has not humbled you," commented the Venkarel dryly. "You are conquered, Horlach. I have bound you from yourself."

"You have Rent the mortal world in the process. You have freed energies older than mine so as to thwart me."

"Your sudden concern for mortal kind is most laudable."

"Mock me now, Venkarel, but you will need my aid. You said it to me: by clinging to mortality, I abrogated the advantages of infinity. You have eliminated my flaw, and you were correct. Much has become clear which I did not see before. You will begin to understand soon. You will know that you need me to complete the pattern."

"The Taormin's pattern," murmured the Venkarel, testing his answer, uncertain still of the ramifications and wary of his own doubts.

"The pattern of control," responded Horlach cryptically. "Consider it, Venkarel. I shall be waiting."

Chapter 2

Fifth Month, Year of Rending
Tulea, Serii

The King's Councillors recovered their arrogance rapidly, thought Rhianna with wry distaste. Five months of humility evidently satisfied their sense of collective guilt over Liin and the Caruillan War. It was regrettable that Princess Joli had yet to achieve legal age; she was far more adept than her father at manipulating the Council's temper.

"His Majesty recognizes Lord Aesir," announced Ineuil stiffly. It entertained Rhianna to watch Ineuil squirm in the role of peacetime Adjutant. It amused her equally to observe the grating reluctance of the Council to acknowledge the notorious Lord Arineuil dur Ven as Serii's Adjutant; wartime heroics provided dubious atonement for prior scandals.

Lord Aesir reached his point abruptly: "There have been at least a dozen more reports of these night attacks since yesterday. What do we intend to do about it?" He looked directly at Rhianna, but he was answered from all sides.

"Fables!" shouted Lord Davril. "Are we superstitious peasants?"

"Fables do not murder men and women by the score!" That was Lord Sian, a young and fiery replacement for Lord Cail, dead in the war's last hour.

"Men murder men! There must be three hundred Caruillans still in our lands."

"Caruillans cannot account for deaths in Serii's farthest corners. There is not a man here who has not received reports of these strange deaths and disappearances from his domain." Do they exclude me unintentionally, wondered Rhianna, because I am the only woman among them, or

34

have they realized that Ixaxis is immune to the Rending wraiths? "These deaths are foul deeds. Bodies are found dismembered and brutalized. Whole families have been rendered mindless."

"Servants and villagers begin to fear the night. Have you tried recently to find an inn with its doors open past dusk? Our people are being terrorized."

"It seems that the 'servants and villagers' are not alone," commented Ineuil. Rhianna noted with acrid interest the sudden silence in the room. "How many of you gentlemen have hired guards in the past month? I have heard that some members of the assassins' guild have begun to guarantee safe night passage, and they have more business than they can handle at any price."

"Certainly, we have hired extra guards. Our families are frightened." Was that Sian again? Sian's voice was not distinctive, and Rhianna could not consistently see him past the gloomy figure of her brother, Lord Dayn dur Tyntagel.

"Frightened enough to traffic openly with K'shai assassins?" demanded Ineuil.

Lord Aesir answered impatiently, "The K'shai are the only ones willing to face the night these days."

"Except for the Ixaxins," growled Dayn. It would be Dayn, sighed Rhianna to herself; of all the antagonistic Councillors, only Dayn fully acknowledged her as the Infortiare, and his belief was born chiefly of childhood fears.

"Ixaxis, too, has been visited by these creatures," responded Rhianna carefully. She had not wanted to address this subject until she better understood her data. "We have been fortunate in that the attacks have had no serious consequence among us."

Aesir shouted triumphantly, "Finally, someone admits that they are 'creatures' and not looters or stranded Caruillans."

"Of course they are 'creatures,' " seconded someone from the room's rear. "Have you not read the reports of wraiths who move without sound and appear without warning? Nothing can stop them."

"They are never seen during the day."

"Myths!"

"What of the night? The creatures penetrate a pane of glass as easily as light."

"K'shai can stop them."

"The things cannot pass through a wall of stone or a shutter of sound wood."

"There have been no incidents reported in a solid house sealed for the night."

"What does Ixaxis call these creatures?" demanded Dayn, loudly enough to dominate his fellow noblemen. He stared across the room at his sister: the deceptively frail woman who was liege of Ixaxis.

Rhianna responded reluctantly, "Creatures of the Rending. They are the legacy of Horlach—his parting gift to the mortal world."

"They are things of wizardry?" asked Sian with a trace of accusatory horror.

Why do you pretend surprise? wondered Rhianna grimly. It is the answer you have each whispered since the Rending. "They are constructs of Power abused," Rhianna countered. "They are the tools of a dead Sorcerer King."

"Tools of the cursed Venkarel," murmured someone indistinctly. Rhianna could guess the speaker's name without probing for it: Lord Gorng dur Liin, whose brother's envy had first betrayed them all to Horlach.

"You are much more open in your slander of Lord Venkarel now that he is dead," remarked Ineuil. Only Rhianna smiled appreciatively at his irony—and his support, which she suspected was on her behalf and not her husband's.

"It matters not who caused the creatures of the Rending. How do we combat them?" Dayn must have given this matter much thought, mused Rhianna; his statements sounded rehearsed.

Then she sighed in resignation, realizing it was again for her to answer. She wished she had a clever answer to give. "Accustom yourselves to a changed world," she suggested evenly.

"Is that the best that Ixaxis can recommend?" This complaint issued from several sources.

"The mortal world," said Rhianna in a soft voice, which yet penetrated the din of grumbling, "has been Rent." She was tempted to blame them: these sanctimonious men who had forced her beloved Kaedric to combat a Sorcerer King unaided. If Kaedric's weapon had been more than the mortal world could bear, it was no more than this thankless lot deserved. "Be grateful that the Rending has left anything intact. As for the Rending creatures, lock your doors, shutter your windows, and remain in your Halls at night." She was angry; she was furious. Every man in the room gave blame for the Rending to Kaedric, Lord Venkarel, who had saved all of their lives.

Rhianna saw the King's page following her at a wary distance when the Council session adjourned. The boy was one she had met, and he had not seemed a particularly fearful lad. Still, none of the pages approached the Infortiare without hesitation.

"Someone finds you daunting, my dear Infortiare," murmured Ineuil.

"I mistrust messages delivered formally."

"Perhaps our great King Astorn, having succumbed (like others we know) to your incomparable charms, seeks a discreet rendezvous."

"Your suggestion, Lord Arineuil, is as appalling as it is treasonous," she responded. They both smiled engagingly at Lord Davril, who acknowledged them in passing with a suspicious nod. "I suppose the lad's message must be accepted. It is likely another report of death or disappearance from some inexplicable cause."

"Another fat farmer carried away by Rendies?"

"Do not be so flippant about the Rending creatures, Ineuil. They pose a serious problem." A wave of dizziness possessed her, but she remained upright by dint of will.

"So I continually hear, but I stare at the stars by the hour, and I have yet to encounter worse than a chill breeze."

Rhianna's feeling of illness deepened, but she beckoned to the page and smiled at him as she accepted the parchment from his tremulous hands. A cursory glance confirmed her gloomy expectations; incidents had occurred in every domain of Serii, and reports from throughout the Alliance indicated that the Rending had spared no corner of the world. "I should think you might already have contended with enough foes beyond your measure," she told Ineuil, trying to return her attention to painless conversation.

"My dear Infortiare, your lack of confidence devastates me. My battle record compares quite impressively with that of any man but Kaedric, who can hardly be counted. If these ragtag assassins can combat your Rending creatures, then assuredly I can do as well."

"The K'shai scarcely qualify as 'ragtag.' I do concede that

you could very likely stop a Rending creature, but please, Ineuil, do not test the matter needlessly. I have already lost my husband to heroics. I should rather not lose you as well." Her head was spinning with the effort to stifle the sickness rising within her.

"You look as white as the snow on Mindar."

"Do I? I cannot think why." She adjusted her energies subtly, so the signs of her weakness would be concealed.

"You are a poor liar, Rhianna."

She touched his arm with a tentative gentleness which silenced him. "Come and talk to me this evening, Ineuil. There is something I would discuss with you." She was away from him quickly.

Ineuil would have pursued her, but a trio of Council members waylaid him with yet another demand for military action against the Rending creatures. Their arguments were absurd, but they were as difficult to elude as Rhianna was difficult to hold.

Chapter 3

Her head was bowed. A twist of the golden strands of her hair fell free of confinement; she smoothed it back into its knot. She finished reading the most recent report from Ixaxis and replaced it on her desk with meticulous care. She rose in a rush which carried her to the window. Her purpose seemed to falter, for she only stood and watched the fog. All distant views were hidden.

The glass of the wide windows was smooth and very cold. She leaned her face against the pane, then straightened guiltily and used her full sleeve to rub the mist of her breath from the glass. Mistress Amye, whose job it was to maintain the Infortiare's quarters, had labored lengthily to make the vast windows spotless. The task was largely a futile one, since the Tower stood free to absorb all of Serii's buffeting winds. Nonetheless, Rhianna was too grateful for Mistress Amye's service to criticize excessive zeal.

Mistress Amye entered just as her Lady stepped away from the window. Amye was of an age to retire to a cottage at royal expense, but she had accepted the Infortiare's service as an alternative to leaving the castle enclave. Her children thought her daft with age.

"Will there be anything else this evening, my lady?" Amye was quartered with the King's servants, which still seemed odd to her, since she was not rightly one of them any longer; but it was the Lady Rhianna's wish. Amye dismissed her children's notions that Rendies frequented the Tower at night.

"No. Thank you, Amye." The Infortiare smiled graciously.

At least, thought Amye, the Lady Rhianna is a lady born, not like *him,* her predecessor. The Lord Venkarel's origins had been nothing short of unsavory. It was birth rank that counted, right enough. See what that Venkarel person did to us. Imagine calling a man like that a Lord, indeed.

"Unbolt the lower door as you leave," commanded the Lady sharply. "I am expecting Lord Arineuil soon." The Infortiare's sudden sternness puzzled Amye a bit, but it did not do to question the moods of the nobility.

"Yes, my lady. Would you not like me to stay and escort him to you?" Amye could not sound eager. She was tired and ready for a nice cup of tea in her own room.

"That will not be necessary, Amye. Lord Arineuil is quite able to find me on his own." The Lady Rhianna's expression had a sardonic twist to it. She was such a delicate wisp of a woman that her occasional hardness always startled Amye. Perhaps, considered Amye sagely, the child is beginning to make its presence known in uncomfortable ways.

Amye had begun to suspect her Lady's state some weeks back. To Amye the pregnancy was now obvious, even though the Lady wrapped herself in voluminous black robes. It was not Amye's place to wonder about the father of the Lady Rhianna's child. Still, Lord Arineuil had certainly come and gone frequently all winter, and he had a reputation, that one, below stairs and above. There were, of course, the whispers about the Lady Rhianna and that Venkarel person, and the Lady certainly did seem to mourn his death, goodness knows why. She seemed such a polite, respectable Lady. Although, pondered Amye, she was Infortiare, and that was a queer enough thing of itself.

Muttering, Amye left the Tower. It was an odd service, she admitted to herself, tending the rooms of so nearly mythical a personage as the Infortiare. But the Tower largely tended itself; the water ran freely with never the problems of the castle proper; the lamps never sputtered and died (there was something odd about the clarity of the Infortiare's lamps, but Amye spared little thought to that sort of thing). It was an odd service, but the Lady was fair and rarely harsh.

Will she want me to tend the child? wondered Amye. Surely the father could not be the Venkarel. Surely not.

A moment's doubt made Amye shiver. She shook her head free of the bleak images of fear which she associated irresistibly with the Venkarel. A terrible man, he had been: dark and terrifying with those cold-ice eyes of his. Amye hastened from the Tower.

Chapter 4

"You have acquired too many of the devil's traits," commented Ineuil from the door of the Infortiare's study. As was usual when he alluded to the late Lord Venkarel, Ineuil spoke with a mixture of cautious disapproval and regret. The disapproval had commenced years before; the caution stemmed merely from prudence. The regret mildly puzzled even him.

"Occasional abstraction in study is scarcely a trait unique to Kaedric." Rhianna shook herself free of indignation. "I need no more quarrels, Ineuil. I spent most of the afternoon listening to Lord Gorng demand Ixaxin aid in the reconstruction of Liin."

"Demanding assistance from his family's intended victim? Gorng always did have nerve." Ineuil perched on the corner of the Infortiare's desk. "You are certainly solemn this evening."

"I am a widow, and widows mourn." Her voice was clipped, her emotions tightly bound.

Ineuil's nod was noncommittal. He leaned forward to take hold of Varina's stone, the milky pendant that Rhianna had made her badge of office. Kaedric's Power had destroyed the medallion of gold which had been the emblem of the Infortiare since Ceallagh's day. "I remember the day you found this," said Ineuil, eliciting clear surprise from Rhianna. Ineuil smiled a trifle smugly. "I caught you studying it, just as Kaedric saw you and you hid it. You, of course, could see only Kaedric." Ineuil laughed and let fall Varina's stone. It struck Rhianna's breast dully, and she clutched at the familiar weight. "I could hardly blame you for the distraction. Kaedric so rarely looked at you openly in those days that he astonished even me. I already knew that you fascinated him, but that day was when I first realized that Kaedric was actually beginning to feel love for you."

"You did not believe him capable of any warm emotion, Ineuil," Rhianna mocked. "Hindsight, I think, has contributed much to your memory."

"Then say, if you prefer, that I had concluded that Kaedric felt for you a fiercely obsessive passion. Did you know that he forbade me to see you while you healed from that battle for the Taormin? Kaedric sat with you day and night at Benthen Abbey, scarcely even allowing Abbot Medwyn to approach. Kaedric would emerge (looking like death himself), snatch a few minutes of sleep, and sequester himself with you again, never speaking a word."

"Benthen Abbey maintains vows of silence," returned Rhianna automatically.

Ineuil shrugged away her comment. "Kaedric did not mind breaking the silence when he learned your rank. He treated me to an unprecedented quantity of speech then: trying to pump me dry of information regarding the noble family of Tyntagel."

"He never told me of that," said Rhianna with the wistful gentleness she reserved for Kaedric.

"It would have been entirely uncharacteristic of him to have confessed to such a very mortal weakness as awe of the nobility."

"I think you did not hate him, Ineuil, nearly so much as you pretend."

Ineuil's grin twisted. "I care for you, my lovely Rhianna, and you possessed him from the day you found that stone." An element of bitterness appeared furtively in Ineuil's handsome face, but he recovered his careful facade of levity to ask, "You wanted to speak to me about something?"

"I am going to have a child, Ineuil." She sounded calm.

Too calm, thought Ineuil, wondering that he could still feel such envy for a dead man. "Kaedric's, of course," responded Ineuil phlegmatically.

"You take the news calmly."

"My dear Infortiare, bemoaning accomplished facts is far too tedious a pastime to tantalize my jaded senses." *As ever, dearest Rhianna, you perceive everything and nothing at all. I am seething with jealousy.*

"I wish I might expect as indifferent a reaction in other quarters." There was a hesitation in her voice: fear?

Ineuil let his expression grow pensive. "I see what you mean. Very few of Kaedric's enemies ever dared attack him openly, because dread of his Power restrained them. The same protective mechanism will not apply to his child. The fear will be all for what the child might become if allowed to mature into Power."

"And I, as Infortiare, cannot directly defend my own child without defying the laws that I am sworn to protect."

"You have a dilemma."

Rhianna's delicate features tightened. "I hoped for a more useful comment."

"Even a deceptive one, which might not be in keeping with your laws of Ceallagh and your maternal wishes?" She is admitting a need for me, thought Ineuil with twisted self-deprecation; I should be ecstatic. "Very well. My advice: tell no one that the child is Kaedric's, for a start. Few know that you married him. Attribute the guilt of fatherhood to me, if you like. You certainly cannot damage my reputation." Rhianna blushed, which made Ineuil want to laugh. "Then foster the child in some remote domain where Kaedric never made his endearing qualities known."

"Is there anywhere so remote?" asked Rhianna ruefully.

Not bloody likely, snarled Ineuil to himself. "The 'Venkarel' may be cursed across the nine continents, but not a hundred (living) men beyond Tulea and Ixaxis ever met or saw him with knowledge of who he truly was."

"It is not any physical resemblance which concerns me."

"Power? Send the child to Ixaxis. The novelty of rearing an infant might stir some stodginess from the place."

"Do you think that Ixaxis would be any safer a haven for my son than the King's castle?" There was angry bitterness in the storm-gray eyes. The black silk of her widow's gown emphasized her lack of color, making her skin seem pale as the milky stone which hung from a fine silver chain about her neck. Only her hair retained any warm color: fallow gold which seemed to gleam with a light of its own.

She is so damnably beautiful, thought Ineuil with a silent curse. Why did the confounded fates bind her to the devil? "You are the Infortiare. You command the Ixaxin Council."

"Ixaxis understands the Rending just well enough to know that Kaedric did cause it, though Horlach fashioned its evil. The same laws that forced Ixaxis to elect me will convince them to destroy a child whose Power could produce another such calamity."

"Possibly," said Ineuil with great care, "they judge rightly." He watched Rhianna very closely, knowing better than most that her anger could be as lethal as her dead husband's.

She betrayed no sign of reaction. "Kaedric grew to manhood alone," she said at last. "Unguided save by hatred."

"Ixaxis did train him."

"As best they could, which was far short of what he needed. My son will fare better."

"And become even more dangerous?"

Rhianna smiled at him so brilliantly. Does she think to hide her anguish? wondered Ineuil. She is breaking apart before my eyes. "Will you arrange the fostering for me, Ineuil? You know the way of such things, having fostered a few of your own."

It was not a difficult discovery to have made, but it irritated Ineuil that Rhianna remarked on it so coolly. "Confounded wizardess," he grumbled only half lightly, "can I hold no secrets from you?"

"Not from me, Ineuil, but I pray that you will hold one for me." Her eyes held him, or her Power did; Ineuil was never sure how much she used her wizardry to effect her will.

"Have I ever been able to deny you, Rhianna?" His tone was dry.

"I rather suspect that you have, but I think you would never betray me."

She manipulates me so well, he thought. Yldana is not the only enchantress in the family, but Rhianna is more subtle. Ineuil slid from the desk and ambled across the room. "Do you know the 'Excursis Santii'?" He pulled a book from the shelves. "It was a favorite of my Ixaxin proctor. The Santii says, 'The young hope, but the wise remember.' 'Walk through life as through the garden of your enemy.'" He flipped a few pages idly. "'Obsession's great madness is truth.'"

"Your proctor's taste in literature enchanted you?"

"Sporadically." He tapped the book's cover with respect.

"That particular volume is an obsolete almanac, I believe, but your gesture is a nicely theatrical one. Has it some significance?"

"'To give love is to withhold nothing.'" He nudged the

book back into its place on the shelf and so did not see the Infortiare blush for a second time that evening. "I shall assist you, Rhianna, in whatever mad scheme you concoct."

"Thank you, Ineuil," she whispered in a small voice.

He only nodded at her with a self-mocking grimace, before he left her to her Tower alone.

Chapter 5

Tenth Month, Year of Rending
Tulea, Serii

How did I let Yldana connive me into this? wondered Ineuil.
He appraised his dark-haired bride, busily enthralling her
usual host of admirers. She is exquisite, of course, he mused,
and she will never expect monogamy of me; the very concept of fidelity is foreign to her. Effectively, our relationship
should be no different from what it has been: physically
satisfying, emotionally uncomplicated. Marriage will appease
my family and hers. The whole practical business makes me
feel conventional, ordinary, and old.

Since Serii's Adjutant despised chronic pessimism, he began to tally extraordinary features of his wedding. Few
weddings, save of royalty, were celebrated in the castle's
grand ballroom. As Adjutant, he had been able to insist
that the royal ballroom would best appease all tempers: his
own and Lord Baerod's being of most personal concern.
Ineuil had insisted that Rhianna attend. Lord Baerod had
refused to admit Rhianna to Tyntagel Hall, where the wedding festivities would normally have been celebrated. Lord
Dayn, who represented Lord Baerod in Tulea, had argued
rather surprisingly on Rhianna's behalf, but Baerod possessed an incredible talent for obduracy. Fortunately, Baerod
favored Yldana enough to overlook her choice of husband.
Or perhaps, thought Ineuil with cynical insight, comparison
to Rhianna's selected husband makes my merely scandalous
flaws seem insignificant.

Ineuil assessed the elegant crowd. It included virtually
every prominent Seriin noble. It was a pity, he thought, that
the ballroom could no longer be kept open to the portico

after the sun had set. Without the breezes from the harbor, the ballroom became stifling. The moonlit colonnade had always offered such a useful retreat as well. The creatures of the Rending had played havoc with romantic evenings.

A servant passed, bearing a tray of replenishments for the refreshment table. Ineuil deftly exchanged his empty goblet for a filled one. He sidled away from the congratulatory crowd around Yldana, glad that wedding celebrations centered on the bride. Ineuil generally enjoyed the tribute of attention, but he would be expected to speak and think only of Yldana tonight. He had imbibed too many goblets of wine to trust his tongue to feign fidelity.

Ineuil espied Lady Liya, animatedly conversing with a portly dowager from Cam. Rhianna had been clinging to her brother's young wife for most of the evening. Ineuil displaced several conversational exchanges with an insincerely cheerful smile, so as to reach Liya's side. He was forced nearly to shout in her ear to make himself heard above the clamor. "Where is Rhianna?" he asked her, and he had to repeat his question to make himself understood.

Liya looked around abstractedly, puzzlement creasing her pretty face. She cannot possibly be so engrossed, thought Ineuil, in a conversation she cannot possibly hear. He pulled her toward a curtained wall, where the sound was somewhat muffled. He was not particularly pleased when the persistent dowager accompanied them.

"I last saw her speaking to Her Royal Highness," replied Liya, trying to balance a frown at Ineuil with an apologetic smile for the neglected dowager.

"She is not there now," contributed the dowager helpfully.

I can see that much for myself, thought Ineuil impatiently. "Lady Ruith, I am glad I found you! Yldana is so eager to thank you for your gift. Do go speak to her." He prodded the bewildered dowager into a maelstrom of milling guests.

"Arineuil, that was not Lady Ruith," amended Liya with faint concern.

"Just as well. Yldana despises Lady Ruith. Rhianna did intend to congratulate me, I trust?"

"I am sure that Rhianna is here somewhere. She cannot have gone anywhere very quickly." Liya was frowning at him more sternly. "You are not supposed to worry so much about your sister-in-law on your wedding night."

Ineuil grinned at Liya amiably and left her. He appreciated Liya's good-hearted intentions, but the Lady Liya was a trifle too proper for his tastes. Rhianna's disappearance had begun to worry him; she had appeared well enough earlier, but the child was overdue.

Ineuil edged his way across the room, successfully assuring himself that Rhianna no longer remained among the celebrants. Numerous guests accosted him, but he escaped them with glib untruths of random inspiration. A man was expected to be preoccupied on his wedding eve.

With a guileless smile, Ineuil trespassed on the royal quarters to reach the royal entrance to the Infortiare's Tower. The King's guards answered to him, after all. They might wonder at his reasons for deserting his guests, but they would not stop him.

Rhianna maintained no shimmering wizard's barrier to block the King's Way. Ineuil knocked firmly upon the stout door and was answered by a sallow slip of a girl. "My Lord Adjutant," she acknowledged him archly.

"I have an important matter to discuss with Lady Rhianna," returned Ineuil with lofty self-assurance. He had not seen the girl before, and he felt disinclined to flatter himself into her good graces. She was certainly an ugly little obstacle. It was like Rhianna to choose for staff a charmless misfit. Ineuil put his hand to the door, pressed, and met unrelenting resistance. He pondered the girl through the narrow opening: not a servant but a wizardess. "It is a matter of considerable urgency," he told her firmly.

"Lady Rhianna has retired for the evening."

"The matter cannot wait."

"I am sorry, my lord." Ineuil inserted his arm between the door and the jamb. Ceallagh's laws would hopefully prevent her from closing the door on his arm. "Please, my lord, step away. Lady Rhianna will not receive you."

"She will when she knows why I come," insisted Ineuil, trying to believe in a nonexistent cause so that the wizardess would not perceive his lie. "Kindly use some sense, young Mistress. Would I pay a social visit on my wedding night?" What kind of visit is it? Ineuil asked himself quizzically, but he suppressed the inner questioning quickly. He knew that few wizards could penetrate his carefully practiced techniques of deception, unless his concentration on the lie began to waver. He needed to persuade the girl, for her Power could deter him indefinitely.

"My Lord Adjutant, I was given strict instructions." Good, thought Ineuil, she begins to make excuses. She is beginning to believe me.

"If you do not let me enter immediately, you will answer both to me and to the Infortiare." Will I anger Rhianna too far if I badger this girl further? "Open the door!"

The girl lost the confidence of her stance. Her Power wavered. Ineuil's continued pressure against the door suddenly served to slam the door open. The metal bolt clanged against the wall as the girl jumped hastily aside. The door had struck her forcibly, but Ineuil did not concern himself about any lasting damage to a wizardess. Ixaxins could not be sorely hurt so simply.

The study door was ajar, but the room was empty of life. Ineuil began to retreat, intending to seek Rhianna's private room two floors down. A scream stopped him, shaking him deeply. The sound came from above him, where there was only one tiny room, the room which Rhianna seldom used, though it had been Kaedric's. Ineuil flung himself at the stairs and began to climb two at a time. It was a precarious mode of ascent, for the stairs were narrow and often treacherous.

"Come no closer, Ineuil!" commanded Rhianna. Her pain and panic drove into his mind, making his own muscles contract against the echo of agony. He clutched the stair's rail to keep from hurtling backward in recoil from the will which had stopped him.

A crack of light appeared above him, and a woman's silhouette filled the gap, but it was an old woman with hair of white. Another sound of incoherent pain tore through the darkness and made him shudder. "You must not stay so near to me, Ineuil," pleaded Rhianna in some shadowy recess of his head. "You are too open to my feelings." She dictated his descent with precise and absolute control, though her dreadful suffering beat against him.

She released him when he reached the study, and the sense of shared pain left him. Ineuil slumped into a chair, drained by the contact with Power desperate for ease.

"Rhianna, blast you, what is happening?" he murmured softly, but he shouted it at her in his thoughts. He felt infuriatingly helpless. It must be the child, he realized: Kaedric's child, he thought with a forceful resurgence of envy. "Lords, Kaedric, can you not spare her this? Have you not hurt her enough?"

Ineuil settled deeply into the velvet recesses of the chair. He expended several minutes in wishing that he owned more than a useless taste of Power. With such concentration as his wish could muster, he imagined Rhianna and tried to will a lessening of her anguish.

Chapter 6

Ineuil awakened near dawn, finding himself stiff from the chair's inflexible contours. He noted with a certain sour amusement that it was Kaedric's chair which he had absently selected for his fretful waiting. The old serving woman, whose entry had interrupted his restless sleep, observed him with some surprise. Her hesitation became alarm when he reached toward her, grabbed her firmly and demanded, "How is she?" with the force of fury.

The woman cringed, fear widening her pallid eyes. "Ineuil, let her go," chided a faint voice from the narrow stairs. "You are terrifying her."

Ineuil looked upon a golden-haired wraith, leaning heavily against a rather worn and twisted stair rail. She was wan in her widow's black, her fair hair lay damp and tangled around her shoulders, and her smoky eyes seemed deeply sunken in her thin face. "My beautiful Infortiare," he whispered to her. "Sight of you gives greater gladness to my impenetrable heart than you will ever credit."

Rhianna smile at him crookedly, but the slight gesture filled him with the warmth of its issuance. He became aware that he still gripped an indignant serving woman. He released her with a rueful grin, and she fled upstairs past her mistress.

"You are a stubborn woman, Rhianna, and a remarkably durable one. I hardly expected you to survive the night, let alone start the morning by berating Serii's Adjutant."

"Even my stubbornness will not much longer keep me standing." She raised her thin hand to her face in a gesture of exhaustion and suffering. "You have made the arrangements?"

Ineuil frowned. Slowly he nodded. "A wet nurse, K'shai as escort, even a genuinely dead infant." He added hurriedly, "There are always too many who really do die at birth. Are you still certain that this is what you want?"

A reedy wail floated down from the Tower's upper chamber, and Rhianna winced. "It is the only course possible," she murmured thickly. "He must be away from here tonight. I cannot conceal him from the King for more than a day."

"I shall arrange it. Your serving woman is discreet, I trust."

"Amye is a simple and honest woman. She will know that the child died, and she will be believed."

Ineuil whistled soundlessly. "Altering a mortal's memories?" But to himself: why not? Rhianna was defying Ceallagh's laws merely by bearing Kaedric's child.

"I have too much at stake to quibble over the finer points of the Ixaxin ethos," snapped Rhianna. She made an effort to straighten but ended up sinking to the stair. Ineuil reached to help her, but she glared at him dangerously.

Ineuil glowered at her in return. "There is also a young wizardess guarding your door," he reminded her. "You cannot alter her memories without tackling the entire Ixaxin Council."

"There will be no need. Lizbet is young and believes implicitly in her Infortiare." Rhianna's wryness echoed Kaedric with uncanny accuracy.

"No one else is in the Tower?"

"Only yourself, my friend." Rhianna's laugh was hurtful. "Yldana will be furious with you." Another cry sounded.

Ineuil knelt to take the Infortiare's hand gently, and this time she did not stop him. "You have an infant to tend—at least until I return."

*　　*　　*

"You married me only because you could not have Rhianna!" accused Yldana furiously. "Even on our wedding night, you run to her."

"I was concerned about her," replied Ineuil evenly.

"You obviously were not concerned about me."

"You were not in labor."

"You are not a midwife."

"I am her friend, and she has few."

"Do not try to make me feel guilty for neglecting my little

sister. She has made it very clear that she does not need help from me."

"You have never demonstrated particular eagerness to offer help."

"I was the one who warned her against Veiga's treachery. I probably saved Rhianna's life."

You probably caused her to witness her husband's death, thought Ineuil, and how much other pain have you given her? "You are a model of sisterly devotion, Yldana. You can stitch a shroud for her dead baby."

"I am not happy that she lost the child."

"Are you not?" asked Ineuil with sudden weariness. "Are you not pleased that the Venkarel's child is dead? Does it not make everything very much simpler for all of us mortal survivors?"

Yldana's anger wavered. Her face resumed the softness which could entice and deceive, but there was simple hurt in her beautiful eyes. Ineuil did not see, and the hurt in her deepened. Because it was her instinct to strike at a source of pain, Yldana remarked with cool disdain, "I have never loved any man but Hrgh, but I understood that his Power would never let him love me. Accept the second-best, Arineuil, as I have." She laughed with the shivery magic which was only mortal witchery.

What momentary madness possessed me to marry this vixen? wondered Ineuil. She is right, however. Is it some great cosmic jest which uses us? Hrgh is dead, and Rhianna might be, so obsessed she remains with Kaedric. And Yldana and I tear at each other like dyrcats, because we can neither of us have what we want.

Ineuil grinned easily. "You and I are not made for eternal devotion, Yldana, and that is the kind of love an Immortal requires. You and I will not shake history by our loves or loathings. If we are faithless to one another, it is at most a peccadillo in time."

"And we shall be faithless, Arineuil. Do not ever expect me to plead for constancy or to give it: not after this. But we do have appearances to consider."

"Rhianna is not likely to bear another child," drawled Ineuil mockingly. Rhianna remains too stubbornly loyal to a ghost, he added with silent bitterness.

"Nor shall we have another wedding night from which you can so indifferently abstain."

"I doubt that our guests were sufficiently sober to note that we left at different hours."

"Father noticed."

"Your father already despises me."

"If you were his subject, he would have you flayed for your behavior."

Ineuil shrugged. "Then I must thank whatever deity exists that I am not a Tyntagellian."

Chapter 7

He was born, and he had potent enemies, but those who would have destroyed him did not know that he existed. They believed that the Venkarel had died without heirs, and those who knew a little truth of the Rending sighed in ignorant relief at one problem's resolution in the midst of so much other calamity. Those who knew only the chaos of the Rending's effect were too occupied with new hazards to care about any but their own kin. Those very few who knew nearly the full truth, even those who had reluctantly supported the Venkarel in the final days, felt very much safer for the Venkarel's death. They would not welcome any remembrance of the Venkarel's overwhelming Power, least of all an heir.

The child was born, and he would have quickly died had the mortal enemies of his Immortal father known that he existed. The mortal world in ignorance of his nature did not choke him from itself; an infant was a weak thing, a thing perhaps to be protected, never feared. Other energies were less kind, but they would not seek death for their own. They had laid their patterns about him, and they would await him.

In the tiny chamber at the apex of the Infortiare's Tower, a weary, golden-haired woman clutched her infant and wept with guilt. The child is unnaturally quiet, she thought. It is as if he already condemns me for betrayal.

* * *

The messenger mercilessly crushed and cracked the autumn leaves beneath his boots. Serii's Crown Princess hated him for destroying so carelessly all that remained of a lost spring, though she recognized the injustice of directing the blame so narrowly.

"Word has come from the Infortiare's servant, Your Majesty," said the messenger distinctly. "The Infortiare's child was born dead." The King sighed his relief, and echoes sounded from his staff.

"Send condolences to the Lady Rhianna," ordered King Astorn.

"Hypocrite," breathed the Princess Joli, and she alone shed tears.

THOSE WHO
GO MAD

Chapter 1

Tyntagel is dreary in the fall. The sky's dark clouds spill watery souls upon the drenched and muddy earth. Leaves sag and fall into slippery splotches on cobbles and clay bricks. The clinging mists conspire to conceal the reassuring truths of solid land and stable township. When the sighs and creaks of soggy branchlets penetrate the sound of rain, careless imaginings conjure the creatures of the Rending. It is hard to be brave when the mist hides the truth, and sometimes the truth holds all the chill horror of the fears.

The night things do come. They rarely harm the cautious: those who bar their doors and shutter their windows between the dusk and dawn. This is the first lesson a toddler learns: never see a night sky. The Rending stole the stars from mortals. The night belongs to the creatures of the Rending, and they will devour your soul and body. Three kinds of people survive the Rendies' stars: wizards, K'shai, and those who go mad in the night of seeing.

My mother told me many tales of the night and the horror of Rendies. She used to read me moral lessons each evening before I slept. I always thought it unfair that I received such an inundation of those moral lessons, which were usually unpleasant, when my sister, Ylsa, received few. I was hardly a model child, but Ylsa was not much better. I blamed the discrimination on gender. Boys were always accused of wrongdoing. I only knew one boy who could dodge suspicion as well as a girl, and he was Arvard, of course.

I met Arvard shortly after my sixth birthday. I was at that time pathetically undersized, excruciatingly shy, and absolutely terrified of a bully named Miff who delighted in

tormenting me because of my appearance: I was pretty, a
loathsome situation for a young boy. Every adult visitor to
the Tyntagel Keep school avowed that Nori and I were by
far the prettiest children in Tyntagel. Nori savored every
morsel of the adulation. The attention embarrassed me to a
painful degree. I cringed as cooing mothers extolled the
fineness of my features, the richness of my hair, or the
quickly shifting color of my eyes. Several times I hacked at
the black curls I hated, but I received no less teasing with
ragged hair, and my mother beat me until I could not sit. By
age six, I had developed a thoroughly cynical perspective on
life.

They were waiting for me again. I knew they lurked just
beyond the toolshed, though I could not yet see them. I
knew even before I heard their broken whispers. I could
return to the classroom, giving Mistress Carolanne some
excuse of a forgotten paper, but Miff would only be the
harder on me for the delay. I wished there were another
way, but there was none, so I walked forward.

Miff emerged first, taunting me with a grin on his freckled
face. Denni jumped from behind the cistern to jab at my
back. "Where are you going, Evaric?" asked Denni.

"Answer him, Evaric," said Miff. "Little girls should be
polite and answer their betters."

"Say something, Evaric," said Nik.

"Can you speak, Evaric?"

Nik tried to grab me, but I wriggled free and ran. My
tormentors would not let me run toward home and momentary safety. They herded me, pressing me along the road
through the dry maple wood. The Keep wall and a gully
overgrown with briars imprisoned me. I might have twisted
my way through the briars, but I had heard that dyrcats
laired beyond the gully. I did know better than to choose a
dyrcat over Miff and his pranks.

Miff caught my arms and dragged me to the ground. He
held me against the dirt and gravel, while Denni methodi-
cally ripped the pages from my workbook, shredding those
pages to which I had devoted hours of tedious effort. I
sacrificed the dubious privilege of watching Denni, so as to
protect my eyes from Nik's barrage of acorns and pebbles.
As I turned my face, I caught a glimpse of straw-colored
hair rising from the gully.

Nik landed near me on the ground, and I saw my work-book tumble into the brush. Miff loosened his grip, and I rolled free. The owner of the straw-colored hair was pound-ing Miff with an efficient strength I envied. Nik helped Denni to rise, and the two of them raced after Miff, who had ducked his assailant and taken undignified flight.

"You've a share of enemies," commented my straw-haired savior, sucking his abraded knuckle.

He had a strange, strong accent. "You are not local," I observed, which expressed nothing of the gratitude I felt.

"Near enough. You from the village?"

"The Keep." My savior was a little taller than Miff, shorter than Denni, and heroic to my innocent eyes.

"Ta." I could not discern if disbelief, disgust, or awe prompted the boy's suddenly cautious expression, but he was plainly diffident now, which made me feel as if I had betrayed a trust. "You'd better watch yourself with those three."

"Thanks."

"Don't mention it to anyone else."

"No, I never would. Miff would deny it if I did." I stared at my own uselessly small, scratched hands, folded too tightly and nearly hidden by the woolen sleeves of a too-large sweater. Comparing them to my savior's strong fists, I be-gan to feel the worship which would carry me along for many years. "No one ever frightened Miff before."

"My sister could fight better than those three," replied this remarkable boy disparagingly, but the praise clearly pleased him. "Of course, I've frightened better fighters than them. Just a moon ago, I frightened ten of the biggest, meanest bears you ever saw—in that very wood over there."

For a fraction of a second, I believed him. I was not usually so gullible, but the boy had impressed me deeply. When I appreciated his exaggeration, my respect only in-creased. I smiled hesitantly. "Did they have teeth as long as daggers?" I asked, trying to win my savior's approval by imitating his wit.

My savior grinned broadly, and I was delighted. "Longer, and their claws were as sharp as a cat's."

"Were the bears as tall as that oak?"

"Much taller. When they walked the ground shook, and all the buds shrank back into their branches, hiding until the bears passed. How old are you?"

"Six," I replied, unconcerned by his redirection.

"So am I," responded my savior, surprising me, for he looked and acted older.

Wheels creaked, warning of an approaching cart. The face of my straw-haired savior closed into caution. "Maybe I'll see you around here again," he said, already sliding down the gully's edge. That is my first memory of Arvard: a straw-haired, six-year-old hero who saved me and slipped away from Master Cormagon's dairy cart.

We next met near the old bridge to the wild, northern woods. Arvard was looking for me, which flattered me immensely. "Anybody bother you recently?" he asked me.

I shrugged, unwilling to admit that Miff harassed me more incessantly than ever. "Miff visits my sister sometimes." Ylsa longed for Miff's approval and achieved it best by teasing me.

Arvard nodded, as if he understood my problem. Some sound of wood and wind caused him to duck beneath the bridge, but he reappeared quickly with a large, straight stick in his hand. "I'll slay your enemies with my sword," he said, brandishing the stick. He surveyed the road closely before beckoning to me. When I approached him, he informed me in a conspiratorial whisper, "The evil King Gill wants to capture me because I'm the rightful heir to the crown he stole. Do you want to be my devoted servant, who followed me into exile?"

"Exile from where?"

"The Great Kingdom, of course. You need a sword." He pried a stick from a bedraggled bush and offered it to me with solemn grandeur. "It's not as large as mine, because mine is magical, but yours is also a jeweled treasure from one of our glorious battles."

I accepted the stick uncertainly. "I think I need to hone it," I said, breaking a twig from its length.

"Good idea," agreed Arvard soberly. "I have some honing tools over here."

"Beyond the bridge?"

"It's not far," he promised me, and I trusted him implicitly. After all, he was the Lost Prince of the Great Kingdom, and I was his loyal retainer, who would follow him to the death.

We fashioned dragons from a breath of wind, and mystical cities from a beam of sunlight on a stream. We rode magical steeds, and we conquered evil Sorcerer Kings and Queens. We performed great, valorous deeds and won the gratitude of vast civilizations, but always some enemy would strike in treachery, and the Lost Prince and his servant would resume their endless journey, reliant only upon each other.

Most of my childhood years have blurred now. Most of my images of Arvard have been tainted by later memories. Only rarely can my mind recapture the unsullied innocence of those early dreams. For an instant, I am six again and Arvard is my truest friend and hero. Then my recollections race beyond those first two years, and I see the fragments of the design in which Arvard and I were already entrapped.

Chapter 2

Ninth Month, Year 9 of Rending
Mindar Wilderness, Tyntagel Domain

"Arvard! Get the wood in here! The cook fire is nearly out!" The girl who shouted was thin and gangly. She wore an undyed dress which had been made and remade several times as she grew. Even the recent addition of an odd, uneven flounce had left it too short by several inches.

She shaded her eyes from a beam of sun piercing the thick clouds and thicker trees, and she scanned the woodsy clearing for the boy. Arvard had disappeared again. "Drat him," mumbled the girl. She tied her mismatched skirt around her waist, which left only a bit of the flounce dangling taillike over her pantaloons. She crossed the yard and clambered down into the gully where the tree had fallen the previous winter. Several of the logs were already twisted with ivy, but she pulled away the stubborn tendrils, ripping bark from the wood. She gathered a bundle of logs against her bony chest. She pulled herself from the gully using her one free hand on the protruding roots of trees she recognized but could never have named.

She mumbled to herself continuously as she carried the logs to the house, which was almost indistinguishable from the trees around it. One of the trees even leaned across it, and rats sometimes dropped to the roof that way. Pa had been talking for a year about cutting away that big limb, but it hid the house so well that he would probably delay until he thought the limb a bigger danger than unfriendly eyes.

The structure of the house was wood, but ivy had fastened into every crack. The door was almost lost amid the new growth. The house was no more than thirty-five years old, for it had been built by refugees from the Venkarel's destruction of Ven, but the Mindar wilderness had made the house a part of its timeless, ancient self. The house had only two rooms: the main room, which was used for sleeping and living, and the kitchen, which was always smoky from a half-clogged chimney.

A woman, who looked older than she was, knelt before the stone fireplace in the kitchen, trying to stir the dying fire into life. "Here, Ma," said the girl, dropping the logs onto the hearth.

"The bread will be heavy as lard," muttered the old-looking woman. "Where is Arvard? He promised to stock the wood closet."

"He's off again. Likely spying on the village folk."

"Useless whelp. We ought to have left him where we found him."

The girl threw a log onto the fire. She watched flames burst from a dried leaf still holding to its shriveled stem. "Arvard's all right most of the time." She never liked to think of finding Arvard. She had not been the one to lift him from the tangle of his dead mother's torn body, but it was she who had first found that litter of Rendie victims.

She had brought her Pa. He had shown her how to leave no trace when searching for valuables, but she had not wanted to touch the mutilated bodies. The Rendies had not left much of the two men, but Pa had taken a fine sword from one and two nice daggers from the other. There had been a brand on the man with the sword, which Pa said was a K'shai assassin's marking. Pa had hacked at the brand to make it unidentifiable. No one would notice the extra damage, Pa said, considering what Rendies had already done, and it was better not to be caught stealing from dead K'shai.

Not many K'shai were caught by Rendies. Maybe, Ma had said, somebody wanted the attack to look like Rendie work. A few armed men could work as much mischief as any Rendie if circumstances were right. That was why Ma had made Pa sell the takings for so little. It was too bad; there had been a pretty necklace on the dead woman, and not much nice jewelry ever came their way. Too bad, but Ma wanted no visible ties to those dead travelers. So nothing had been kept but Arvard.

Sometimes Arvard was a nuisance, thought the girl, but he was just so full of grand plans that he forgot the simple things like stoking the fire. Arvard was clever. The girl wished she were as clever as the boy, who was not even as old as the Rending. Arvard understood things. He could make her understand things, too, when he bothered; like how to watch the moon to know when her times would come; or how to make Mitshch look at her.

She wondered if Mitshch would come with the other men tonight after the hunting. If the men had been successful, there would be good meat, and maybe Pa would dole out some of his Tonic. The Tonic would make everyone warm and friendly, and maybe Mitshch would be friendly with her.

*   *   *

Ma had locked Arvard in the wood closet, so he would remember his duties next time. The girl felt a little sorry for the boy, so she smuggled him a bit of venison. Everyone else was enjoying the Tonic in the main room, and Ma never noticed her sneaking off to the kitchen.

She lifted the iron hook to free the door. Arvard was huddled among the logs he had spent the afternoon carrying. His knees were tucked under his chin. Even so, there was hardly enough room for him to sit. "I brought you some supper, Arvard," whispered the girl.

"Thanks, Nel," he whispered in return. His face and yellow hair were all smudged by the dust from the logs, but he still looked neat and proud. "Ma hasn't forgiven me yet?"

"Give her time for another mug of the Tonic, and she'll be holding no more grudges against anyone."

"Another hour maybe?"

"Maybe. I'll let you know. I'll leave the latch undone, but I've got to close the door again. Sorry."

"That's all right, Nel. It gives me a chance to think."

Nel pushed her lank hair over her ear. She hoped Mitshch would finish talking to Pa before she returned to the main room. "What do you think about, Arvard?"

"Things. Like how to sell Con's leather pieces in the village, where they'd bring a proper price."

"We can't go to the village. The Lord's taxers would catch us for sure."

"That's why I have to think." Arvard was always patient with her, but sometimes Nel knew he was thinking her stupid. She did not mind. She knew she could never be as clever as Arvard. "Quit fussing with your hair, Nel, and twist your skirt right way around. You want Mitshch to think you're still a baby who can't keep herself straight?"

Nel adjusted her skirt in a hurry. She clasped her hands together so she could leave her hair be. "Do I look right?"

"Mitshch will think so." Arvard fastidiously cleaned his fingers of the venison's grease by wiping them on the old kerchief he always carried for that sort of purpose. He never forgot to clean that kerchief. He never forgot the tasks that mattered to him.

Nel smiled nervously. She closed the door; it stuck, and she had to push it. "Later, Arvard," she whispered against the wood. She could not hear his answer over the sounds of her father's laughter in the other room.

* * *

Arvard tried to shift. The wood closet allowed no comfortable position, but Arvard did not mind a punishment he had anticipated and earned. He had freely made the choice to spend the extra hour with his Keep friend. He did not regret his decision.

It was strange to have a friend who occupied such a different world. Pa would never understand how Arvard could enjoy the company of anyone so weak, timid, and naive. Arvard could never have explained to Pa, Wilard, Con, Ols, or Kite that imagination could matter as much to a boy as an ability to fight, hunt, and make a good taking from an unwary traveler. Arvard's foster family and their friends would despise Evaric, and Arvard agreed with them in many respects. Arvard was sure that Evaric would not have survived a moon's time in the wild lands; Evaric could not even hold his own with the puny Keep brats.

Evaric was weak, but no one listened the way Evaric did. No one else understood the things that mattered. Sometimes Arvard envied Evaric a little, because imagining and questioning were a Keep brat's privileges, rights denied to a boy like Arvard whose life consisted chiefly of struggle. The wilds' families had no time for any learning that did not contribute directly to the subjugation of a relentlessly antagonistic environment.

Arvard sighed. The closet really was uncomfortable. He wished that Nel would return.

* * *

Ma was telling a story. It was a bawdy one. Maybe Arvard would not need to wait long for Ma to forgive him.

Mitshch was looking at Nel. Nel blushed because her brothers were laughing at her. Nel was the youngest—save for Arvard, who was different—and she was the only girl. With four older brothers, she took a lot of teasing.

"Nel's looking pretty, Mitshch," said Ols slyly.

Mitshch was beginning to blush himself, which made Nel feel tingly and fine. Wilard handed her a mug, and the sip of Tonic gave the tingle an embarrassing warmth. Mitshch shifted on the bench so she could sit beside him, and she felt dizzy and hot and fine. Everything was *fine*.

A loud crash interrupted Ma's story. Ols went to check the kitchen, while everybody else sat breathless. "Nothing there," said Ols on returning.

"Must be that rotten branch breaking," said Pa. "Knew I should've trimmed it." He was trying to sound cheery about it, but everyone could see that it worried him. The limb hung over the house. Nel snuggled closer to Mitshch, who put his arm around her protectively.

"Wilard, go fetch Arvard from the kitchen," ordered Pa, and then Nel knew how worried Pa really was. Pa thought the limb would fall through the kitchen roof, and then the house would be open to the night.

"It'll be fine, Nel," Mitshch told her, and Nel began to feel better, but she kept thinking about the way the kitchen door sagged and never wanted to close soundly.

There was another great cracking and a crash of smashed and broken timbers. Wilard yelled. Mitshch ran to help him. Pa and Kite dragged the great table across the floor so as to seal off the kitchen more effectively.

Something already occupied the kitchen doorway. It was neither Wilard nor Arvard. It was gray and misty, and it was reaching for Mitshch. Nel screamed, and Ma screamed, and Pa was bleeding, and Mitshch was gone.

Everything around Nel was gray. Everything was cold and hot, and it hurt, and she was screaming at the Rendies, but it did no good. They were eating her and hurting her, and nothing was fine anymore. Nothing would ever be fine again.

Chapter 3

Keep Enclave, Tyntagel

The day had cleared despite the morning's damp promise. The wind had risen, hurtling across the snowy Mountains of Mindar, dispersing the clouds but bringing bitter cold. The wind had carried away the little snow that had fallen. The barrenness of the earth enhanced the illusion of a desolate summer heath, making our heavy woolen garb appear incongruous.

Ylsa kept searching the road and the trees, doubtless hoping that Miff would appear. I watched with equal care, hoping that Ylsa would be disappointed. "I can reach that tree before you," said Ylsa suddenly. I began to race toward the maple. "Hey," called Ylsa plaintively, but she saved the rest of her protest.

I slammed into the tree just an instant before Ylsa, despite my head start. "Cheat," Ylsa snapped at me. "Runt," she added meanly.

"Sore loser," I accused.

"Runt," repeated Ylsa. "No real boy would need to cheat against a girl."

I ran ahead of Ylsa, not wanting her to see how her accusation embarrassed me. I was still running when I heard the voice crying for help. I stopped abruptly, and Ylsa ran into me.

"Evaric is a girl," taunted Ylsa again.

"Hush!"

Ylsa frowned at me. "What?"

"Listen."

"There is nothing to hear."

"Listen!"

The wind softened. No clearer sound breathed for a full minute. The wind gathered itself in a rush which could have carried a faint cry, but it was a less tangible voice I heard. "What is it?" asked Ylsa restlessly, impatient with me, as usual.

I ignored her. I still do not know if Arvard actually called to me that day, or if imagination fulfilled itself by driving me to find him. I cast a cautious glance at the lengthening shadows. The thickets across the ravine held menacing circles of darkness, but the road lay clear of shade or specter. I headed for the old bridge, even though the day approached its end.

"Evaric," called Ylsa angrily. She gave the path toward Miff's house a wistful look, but she knew that our mother would be angry if Ylsa let me wander too far alone. Ylsa chased after me, grumbling, "Unless you come with me now, Evaric, I shall leave you."

"Then go."

"Mother will beat you if you come home late."

Some terrible trouble had assaulted my great, secret friend, and Ylsa pestered me with threats of punishment from our mother. "Will you be silent, Ylsa!" I shouted, stunning her into compliance. "Arvard!" I cried in my head, for his danger reached inside of me. I heard the screaming, felt the cold fire, and tasted misty death. There was a figure before me, but it was a man.

I stopped, for the man stood squarely in front of me. "What are you?" he demanded, staring at me fiercely. My fear became all for myself. I retreated a pace, but the stranger restrained me with a hand on my shoulder.

"Let go of my brother," said Ylsa, suddenly protective.

"I shall not harm you," said the man earnestly, and Ylsa became oddly silent. When I looked at her, she did not seem aware of me. "What domain is this?" asked the stranger, though he could not have come so near the Keep unchallenged.

Ylsa answered him woodenly, "It is Tyntagel, Master."

The man's furrowed brow cleared. "Of course," he said. "The patterns would be strong where She originated."

"You know someone in Tyntagel, sir?" asked Ylsa courteously.

"Know someone?" The stranger winced, and his next words were whiny. "I was happy as a cobbler. I was never strong enough to serve in such a circle, but they said that I was needed. The Power of the Infortiare burned through us, and then he left us, and the world writhed in anguish at the parting." His Power pushed his emotion upon me. He endangered me, and I hated him. The man stiffened. "I am mad now," he acknowledged calmly, "for I was weak, and I must now walk the Rendies' world in blindness, pursuing their paths of fear, reft of the illuminating fire of him who was Infortiare. I thought that I sensed him here, but he is dead, as I should be. Some thickening of the pattern deluded me into hope." Solemnly, the man admonished, "You really ought not to be outside at night, little Mistress, but I shall protect you this time."

I sensed deep wrongness in the wizard, a crippling more severe than any physical deformity. I wanted the wizard gone. Something sinuous began to form near the wizard. It reached toward the wizard and shuddered. "I want him gone," I whispered. Mist became thick.

"Come away," pleaded an urgent voice, which was oddly thick with accent. "He's bespelling you." I felt a tugging on my arm. The wizard rambled on obliviously of War, cobbling, and the uselessness of fire-fused hands. "Please, come away. It's very dangerous here."

"I can save you, little Mistress," promised the wizard.

"The Rendies are gathering," said the voice urgently.

"I want the wizard gone," I insisted.

"No," argued the wizard. "I am not the one who wants to hurt him." I observed that something very peculiar was occurring to the wizard's face. It had begun to bleed.

"Come away."

Several pieces of the wizard's face seemed to be missing now. It was hard to tell, for the regions not covered in blood had become foggy. Maybe I was the one who was becoming blurred.

"When did it become dark?" I demanded. Darkness spread above me, though it was less black than my room at night. The sky was dusty with lights: stars, I supposed. Adults made much of the stars. Perhaps they had some cause.

The stars awoke me from the wizard's trance. The wizard stood amid a cloud of Rendies. Ylsa's gaze began to drift from the wizard to the wraiths. "Ylsa," I said sharply, "do not look at them." I did not know why I voiced the warning.

"Evaric, come away from there." Arvard crept a little farther from the brush, warily watching the cloud of Rendies wrestle for the mad wizard. Matted with leaves, Arvard's hair still shone in the dimness. He tried to coax Ylsa into moving. "In here," ordered Arvard, looking greatly relieved when I nodded. We ducked under twisted limbs and into a hollow of tangled brush. Arvard dragged Ylsa, and she sat stiffly where he placed her. "We will survive," Arvard assured me. "The Rendies have a wizard, and that must be a rare treat to them."

Arvard settled among the damp grasses and leaves. I could see him more clearly than I would have expected. Could the moon be so bright? I wondered, recalling grown-up reminiscences. I shifted my head, and I could see the brilliant orb through the brush. "You stayed and watched us even though night came," I remarked dreamily, knowing that such a decision was indeed worthy of the noble, exiled prince who Arvard was to me.

"I couldn't tackle a wizard like he was some stupid Keep brat," snapped Arvard, and he immediately muttered an abashed, incoherent apology. I knew that he considered me a Keep brat, but I also recognized the depth and worth of his singular friendship.

"You called for help earlier," I said.

"I didn't."

A loud wailing trill made us both cover our ears, though the gesture did little good. Smoky, tenuous ribbons snaked through the trees and into the brush. A lacy tendril brushed my back. It stung frightfully. The tendril blackened, becoming opaque and stiff.

"You burn!" accused the Rendie, as the wailing sank to a low moan. The Rendie enclosed its injured member in a hastily gathered veil of frost, which it tore from its own pulsing body. The wraith's color deepened to a steady russet, and discord made its keening voice feel harsh. "You are cruel, and I have killed for you," lamented the Rendie.

"Fire-child," sighed a second Rendie in what sounded queerly like a plea, "why do you burn your own?"

I had never heard that Rendies talked. I did not relish the privilege of their conversation. "Think about something else," suggested Arvard.

"You hear them, too?" I asked him curiously.

"I don't listen to Rendies. You shouldn't either."

"Son of the Taormin," cried a Rendie softly, "come to us."

I tried to disregard the Rendie's unsettling voice. "What happened, Arvard?"

"The Rendies came," answered Arvard tersely.

"They killed your family?" Arvard and I had rarely discussed our families, for our own world of danger and great deeds had always been more real to us.

"Yah. I thought I could reach the village before dark came again, but I guess I started later than I thought."

"Fire-child," sighed an echo through my head.

I tried to shake free of the haunting voice. "Do you know anyone in the village?" I asked, clinging to the sense of my friend, someone alive, strong and familiar.

"Nah. We were a secret." Arvard's laugh was a little off-key. "Pa never wanted to tithe to the Lord, so he hid us away on the edge of the wild regions."

"Fire-child, come to us. We are not your enemy."

"You're listening to them again," accused Arvard sharply.

"No!" I retorted, but it was impossible not to listen. I touched Ylsa's cold face where a drop of the wizard's blood had hardened. I shivered.

"That's only the wizard's spell holding her a while," Arvard assured me knowledgeably; I suspected that he had become the Lost Prince again. "She's lucky. She'll not hear the Rendies through that."

I wrapped myself more tightly in my cloak. "Are you cold?" I asked Arvard, whose leather coat looked worn and thin.

Arvard shrugged. A wraith dashed through the brush in a pattern of shreds. Arvard shrank from the trailing mists.

"Only three kinds of people survive the night: wizards, K'shai, and those who go mad." I recited the warning, though I did not yet know the meaning of Rendie madness.

"Maybe wizards and K'shai know better than to listen to Rendies," replied Arvard staunchly. Arvard did not intend to let me think about fear. "The Rendies won't hurt us. The wizard satisfied them. We'll survive the night, and nobody will ever know that we saw Rendies."

I nodded, more to placate Arvard than to concur. I closed my eyes as a wraith swept past me, crying enticingly. "You can stay with us," I promised Arvard.

"Me live in a Keep house? Your family won't want my kind. The liege'll place me somewhere." The Lost Prince preferred noble exile.

"You will stay with us," I repeated firmly. I became

aware that the Rendie voices in my head had stopped. The keening continued, but it circled warily. "They are leaving."

"About time," grumbled Arvard. He did not like this game of Rendies and reality. He snuggled down among the leaves. "I feel like I've been awake forever."

"You intend to sleep out here?"

"Where can we go? Your sister's not going anywhere tonight, unless you want to try carrying her, and she'll be dyrcat-bait if we leave her."

"What could you and I do against a dyrcat?" I asked, which seemed to me a reasonable question; a dyrcat would not respect an imaginary sword. Arvard began to snore softly. I lay down, covered my face with my cloak, and slept uncomfortably.

In my nightmare, I could feel the cold presence of a wounded Rendie in limping pursuit. The Rendie's attenuated limbs twisted restlessly, constantly shifting in both color and amorphous form. The face was difficult to define; I caught glimpses which appeared variously to be a single silver eye, a multifaceted expanse like the eye of an enlarged insect, and a flash of green as deadly bright as a dyrcat's stare. The Rendie exhaled its coldness into a web, which stretched toward me. The atmosphere grew thick and strange.

The Rendie's voice trilled with an odd, melodic disharmony. "I have tasted you now, and I know you. I shall remember, as will you. It must be, for it was. Look at me," said the Rendie, and it wore the face of Arvard. The Rendie/Arvard felt pain from the burned and blackened limb, and the pain became mine. I reached for some offering within myself to ease the creature's pain. The Rendie/Arvard howled with heightened agony.

As the dream wavered, I recognized its deceptions, but it carried me on relentlessly. It was the first of many nightmares, and it was mild, though it horrified me at the time. I had survived the night, and I was neither wizard nor K'shai.

I awoke to the piercing sound of Ylsa's screams. Arvard was shaking her to rouse her, when the searchers burst upon us. The sun had crept above the trees, and the searchers were the familiar folk of Tyntagel.

"We have found them!" called someone triumphantly, and in a moment the hollow of brush became crowded.

Mother gathered Ylsa and me into her arms in a rush, but Father saw Arvard and stopped, obviously puzzled. I extricated myself from my mother's embrace with some embarrassment. "This is Arvard," I said. "He helped us last night." I would not admit to our secret friendship. "I told him he could stay with us." I poised myself for defiance. "His family was killed by Rendies."

Mother raised her head slowly from cradling Ylsa. She exchanged with Father a forbidding look composed of the night's dreadful worry. She had regained her children; she was too exhausted to deal with further complications. I took advantage of my mother's momentary weakness; I knew that my father could not deny me.

"He can stay with us," I insisted, pressing my point with a fierce determination which was rare for me in those days. "He is my friend, and he has no one else."

"We shall discuss it later, Evaric," said my father absently. Arvard gave me a guarded shrug. I took my father's hand and tugged it until he looked at me. "Arvard may come with us for now," conceded my father weakly, and I knew that I had won.

My mother's expression began to reproach Father's weakness, but Ylsa stirred. "How did you two stray so far from home?" clucked our mother, postponing the inevitable argument with our father. "You know what I told you about staying nearby."

"Mother?" asked Ylsa in bewilderment. "Where is the wizard?"

The friends and neighbors who had assisted in the search became very silent. "What wizard, Ylsa?" asked our mother cautiously.

"I saw no wizard," volunteered Arvard promptly. "Did you, Evaric?"

"Ylsa must have been dreaming, Mother. We met no one but Arvard." Both Arvard and I gazed at Mother with solemn sincerity.

"Mother," Ylsa begged, "my head hurts awfully. I cannot remember. What happened to me?"

"You have learned a lesson, I hope. The night comes quickly in the autumn," answered our mother brusquely. She watched me whisper a reassurance to Arvard, and I fell silent beneath her inspection. I think she suspected our conspiracy of silence even then, but she knew nothing of the Rendies. She thought that Arvard and I had somehow left Ylsa to face the night alone. Ylsa worried her, but she still considered me sane.

* * *

Two weeks later, the Ixaxins came to give the annual testing to all children of school age. I had never minded the testing, but an unaccountable sense of dread overcame me as I left the schoolroom. I stayed close to Arvard, who watched me with puzzled concern. Arvard was called early, for he had never previously been tested. I could not remain among my classmates without Arvard to defend me. I left the schoolyard, deliberately disobeying Mistress Carolanne's instructions.

I ducked inside the toolshed, closed the door, and pressed myself against its rough surface. My arms began to shake. I felt the cold heat of a Rendie's breath. I could feel the wraith's hunger, and feeling it made it mine. I felt soiled and evil, and I loathed myself for sharing in the Rendie violence.

I wanted to hurt them. I wanted to hurt myself, for I was part of them. I pressed the point of a nail into the flesh of my thigh and felt the heat of welling blood. The pain inflamed me.

"Fire-child," I laughed hysterically, but it was the echo of Rendie voices which made me long to crawl away like the ants into the soil. I shook for long minutes, beseeching myself to stop. A spasm of pain sprang through my skull, and I cried aloud. After a moment, the deep pain passed. Lights beat against my eyes with aching pressure, but they faded one by one. "Lords of Serii," I whispered hoarsely, wondering what horrible legacy I had reaped from my view of the night sky.

"Evaric?" called Arvard into the dark shed. "Are you in there?" Arvard peered into the shed, but I had crawled into the shadows, so he could not see me.

"Yes," I answered tightly. I clenched my teeth to keep them from chattering. I covered the bleeding wound with my hand, feeling shame for my weakness in yielding to the voices. Arvard was here; the Rendies could not claim me.

"Your name has been called, little brother. The Ixaxins want to test you next."

Lords, no. Ixaxins could not see me like this. They would see the Rendie sickness in my mind. They would know my guilt. Everyone would know my guilt.

"Get me out of it, Arvard. Make an excuse for me. Please."

"Are you sick?"

"Yes." Lords, yes.

"You want anything?" Arvard was concerned. Arvard was coming closer. I could see his silhouette against the light.

"No. Nothing. I cannot face the Ixaxins, Arvard."

"All right. Don't worry, Evaric. I'll take care of it."

I smiled a little wanly in the darkness. Arvard would take care of me again. I removed my hand from where it rested on my leg. There was no wound. There was no hurt. Even the fabric was whole. I laughed with relief. "Only three kinds of people survive the seeing of the Rendies' stars," I recited aloud, though only my own ears heard. "Wizards, K'shai, and those who go mad in the night of seeing." I did not wonder that Arvard had apparently survived unscathed; heroes were not susceptible to the afflictions of the rest of us.

"Arvard, where is Evaric?"

Arvard answered with a fine semblance of surprise. "He has gone home, Mistress Carolanne. He has already been tested."

Carolanne's surprise was not feigned. "His name is next on the list, Arvard. I thought you went to fetch him."

"Mistress Carolanne, he has already been tested. He failed and was dismissed."

"Mistress Carolanne," demanded one of the Ixaxins, appearing at the vestibule door. "We are waiting for the next candidate."

Carolanne fumbled with her papers, recalling how ashen Evaric had looked when he left the classroom. Arvard had certainly devoted himself to Evaric's protection; she wondered if Arvard realized that lying to Ixaxis was a treasonous crime. "I apologize, Master Tain. I lost my place for a moment. Arvard, will you please bring Quin to be tested."

Carolanne held her breath, waiting for the Ixaxin to perceive her falsehood.

Arvard nodded agreeably, his expression frank and cheerful. Carolanne placed a check beside Quin's name, indicating that he had been called. The Ixaxin retreated into the classroom. Beside Evaric's name, Carolanne placed the check which indicated failure of the Ixaxin test. She felt only the faintest of qualms and did not even wonder at her own calm compliance with deception. Arvard was very persuasive.

Chapter 4

Seventh Month, Year 18 of Rending

Arvard stayed, of course, and became my foster brother. He never quite lost his status as affable guest of long duration in our house, something like an orphaned cousin accepted out of family duty. He was brother to me, though not to Ylsa, and he was never son to my parents. Mother, at least, came to respect his abilities, if not his glib excuses for evading chores and due punishments. Father never gave Arvard much attention of any sort, but Father never knew how to deal with any of his children; Father was even uncomfortable with me, and he overtly favored me over Ylsa.

Arvard excelled, and I took pride in him. He won every school honor, and he claimed every festival prize without apparent effort. He protected me from Miff and the others. I protected him from criticism and loneliness. That much of the old dream persisted: we were two against the world.

When the Rendie madness claimed me, as it did too often throughout those years, Arvard lied and manipulated to conceal my ailment. Arvard succeeded, and no one guessed my affliction. My parents considered me merely weak and prone to illness; others considered me a malingerer. Only Arvard knew the truth: I spent as much of those ten years in the Rendies' world as in my own. A few teachers tried to encourage me, sure that I performed far below my capabilities; most despaired over my inattention.

They were good years, despite the Rendies. Arvard's enthusiasm for life infected me, though I viewed everything but Arvard with unalloyed cynicism. I often wondered how I managed to retain Arvard's devotion for so long, because we had never shared any trait but a taste for adventurous sagas.

Arvard and I viewed the world too incongruously to retain forever a bond as close as ours had become. My tastes were simple ones; I craved peace from madness and little else. Arvard's ambitions had no bounds. Tyntagel could not contain him, as I should have realized long before he actually departed. I suppose he stayed for my sake. When our differences finally became obvious, his cause for remaining vanished along with his old ideals.

The argument began in a small way, three years before it matured. While searching our room for some forgotten article that Arvard had borrowed from me, I discovered a letter that he had wedged between the bureau drawers. We had both begun our apprenticeship on the Keep staff that year, and Arvard had already been promoted twice. When I found the letter, I began to perceive the method of Arvard's astonishing advancement.

"Just you watch me, Evaric," gloated Arvard with a wide grin across his face. He jumped to reach the barn's loft and lifted himself to straddle the stout support beam. "I shall have Chul's own position in a year."

I never doubted that Arvard could do just as he claimed. Arvard always achieved his goals. "And after you replace Master Chul, will you seek Father's post?" I asked sardonically.

Arvard twisted his expressive face into comical disgust. "You make a little ambition sound like patricide."

I frowned into my fist. I sat amid the new hay on the barn floor. The Keep's smaller barns, such as this one, were used mostly to store feed for the Lord's horses in the adjacent mews. Arvard had selected this barn as a private retreat from the other members of the Keep staff, most of whom lunched together in a room designated for that purpose. Arvard preferred not to socialize with the other staff apprentices. He intended to direct that staff soon, and he generally behaved as if his superior rank were accomplished fact.

Arvard leaped from the beam and landed in the hay near enough to me to make me jump. He took a sandwich from the parcel that our mother had packed for our lunch. "What is the matter with you anyway? You act as gloomy as Father Guiarde. Did Nori refuse to go to the festival with you?"

"She could not refuse what was never asked of her."

"You're afraid of her."

"I dislike her."

Arvard continued as if I had not spoken. "You can't go through life believing that the things you want are unattainable." Arvard gestured emphatically, orating to a vast, unseen audience. "Decide what you want, and take it. If you want Nori, conquer her and be done with the matter. Moping never solved anything."

"I am not moping."

"You need to set goals for yourself, then pursue them. A man can claim a kingdom if he sets himself to it and works for it."

"Kingship does not appeal to me."

"After I become Keeper of Records, I shall pursue a position with access to Lord Baerod. I'll have real influence then. I can carry you with me, little brother, but you have to quit accommodating everyone. Even the pages take advantage of you."

"Should I resort to blackmail, too? I found the letter, Arvard." I withdrew it from my shirt. Arvard snatched it from my hand.

"It's my duty to reveal corruption when I find it," said Arvard defensively. "You don't think I'd actually try to profit from Irrn's misdoings."

"Why did you hide the letter?"

"I wanted to be sure before I said anything. Evaric, I found the letter by chance. What would you have had me do?"

I wanted to trust Arvard. Irrn's corruption did not dismay me; corruption inhabited every corner of the Keep. I did not want to believe that Arvard could be contaminated. "You must not use that letter."

"Why can't you ever sound so implacable at the Keep?" asked Arvard with a humorless laugh. He grimaced and offered me the incriminating missive. I tore it into shreds. Arvard muttered, "Irrn is too slippery to let such flimsy evidence bother him anyway." I did not like the wistfulness in Arvard's remark.

The bits of torn paper drifted from my hand. I began to shudder, and Arvard redirected his concern. "The Rendies?" asked Arvard quietly. I barely managed a nod. Arvard touched me cautiously. "I'll cover for you at the Keep," Arvard promised.

I did not try to answer. The madness carried me far from

the familiar barn to a place of mists and horror. There were
voices, anger, and hunger. There were Rendies, and they
desired my soul.

Arvard gathered the remains of the lunch we had shared.
His eyes shunned sight of me, caught in the Rendie spell
that never quite ended. Arvard left the barn, returning to
the Keep to tell more lies on my behalf. If I had accompanied him, it would have been I who performed the minor
errand for Master Garnett; it would have been I who met
Mistress Giena, an insignificant serving woman who had
come with Lady Yldana from Tulea for the summer.

When my agony finally ebbed, I left the barn and walked
without any particular goal. I was overdue at the Keep, but
I could not face the connivery and hypocrisy with my nerves
still raw from Rendie visions and Arvard's suspiciously un-
heroic schemes. I tried to brush the sun's heat from my neck
and smiled at my own useless gesture. The early summer
had made its presence felt throughout both Keep and village. I was both fortunate and unusual for Tyntagel, for the
sun never burned me.

The clash of swords startled me, until I realized that I had
approached the practice yard. I drew closer from idle disin-
terest in anything more pressing. Lord Buern, the noble
recipient of the lesson, struck an unenthused pose opposite
the swordmaster, Master Conierighm, a large man with
thinning hair. They argued, and Conierighm prodded Buern
into sparring. I leaned for a moment against the fence rail to
observe them.

The swordmaster drove his blunted sword against his student's chest. Buern staggered, though the blow had been
light by my inexpert reckoning. "Carelessness like that will
cost you dearly," commented Conierighm with cool contempt.

Buern straightened. "As your arrogance will cost you,
Master Conierighm."

"I teach fighting skills, not manners. I suggest that you
cultivate the latter and return when you have mastered
respect."

Lord Buern threw the dull practice sword at the swordmaster's feet. He left the practice ground proudly, but
Conierighm shook his head in disgust. I retreated a pace to
let the oak shadows better conceal me; the dry fence rail
creaked. Conierighm's head lifted.

"Come here," commanded Conierighm.

"Master Conierighm," I acknowledged, trying to imitate Arvard's confidence, and failing. I left the oak shadows reluctantly. I had no reason to fear the swordmaster, I reminded myself, but I was not convinced. I was a coward for good reason; I was a Rendie-mad young man of no particular distinction except the friendship of a remarkable brother.

I did feel surprise that I could meet the swordmaster's narrowed eyes with a level gaze. Master Conierighm had always seemed such a hugely imposing figure. I had gained my own height so recently and so rapidly that I had yet to accustom myself to the sudden diminishment of the world. After so many years of craning to see my classmates, I had not merely grown to ordinary height; I had surpassed Arvard, a transformation that I found both unexpected and disconcerting.

"I have seen you previously." Conierighm made the statement an accusation, but he was appraising me closely. I knew the look and accepted it with patience: the long hesitation as Conierighm associated a formidably tall, overly lean young man with a small, spindly boy of features so softly delicate as to appear feminine. "You are the clerk's son: the one who never leaves his brother's shadow. I suppose your brother had the wit to escape before I caught you."

"Master Conierighm, I merely paused to observe his lordship's lesson."

"Did you learn anything?" snapped Conierighm.

Some shade of Conierighm's contempt struck me as too fatuous for credibility, and my fear of him evaporated. "Not from Lord Buern," I returned wryly. I had too recently faced the demons of my mind; Conierighm's efforts to intimidate could not compete.

Conierighm almost smiled. His thin lips stretched. Appraisal, calculation: I wondered if he expected to see me crumble back into fear. "You are so eager a student," said Conierighm. "Let us see what you have learned." In a single fluid motion, he tossed me a blunted sword and he attacked.

I accepted the hurled sword from the air without thinking. Conierighm's blunt blade hit my chest and forced the breath from me. I sparred (badly), because Conierighm's blows struck uncomfortably.

Conierighm pursued me the length of the practice yard. The match was absurdly one-sided; the only sword I had ever held before that day was Arvard's ragged stick. Another of Conierighm's blows struck my shoulder heavily. I managed to block a second from my head. "Do you find great sport in beating an apprentice clerk?" I asked in as scathing a tone as I could manage between the gasps which Conierighm's blows elicited.

"A clerk would be at his duties now," retorted Conierighm.

I could hardly tell Conierighm that a spell of Rendie madness had kept me from my work. "I never claimed to be a diligent clerk." I had begun to parry a few of Conierighm's thrusts, which pleased me disproportionately. Conierighm's game bore unfavorable resemblance to Miff's bullying, but Miff had never inspired an urge to retaliate in kind. I had always shunned competition, leaving the contests to Arvard.

My incipient self-satisfaction died quickly. With a quick play of feint and stroke, the swordmaster tore the student's weapon from my hand. Conierighm's lips again narrowed into an unappealing smile. He raised his sword and lowered it with rigorous formality. "Return tomorrow," ordered Conierighm, retrieving the fallen sword as he retired to the armory.

I stared at the swordmaster's retreating back. I felt hot and abysmally sore. I felt harshly aware of the burning sun, the hard earth, and the air I labored to absorb. This was Arvard's game made real; this was solid and true, not misty with Rendie madness. The wielding of a weapon conveyed an amazing sensation of strength; slow as I was to recognize my new height, I was slower still to realize that I had matured in other ways as well. "Two hours past noon?" I called across the yard. If I raced through my mindless duties at the Keep, I felt sure that I could escape for a time without attracting notice, even without Arvard's help.

"Satisfactory," replied Conierighm without turning.

Arvard would never understand. He had virtually forgotten the game that he had invented, for he had become a man with a man's ambitions. I was still in many ways a boy, trying to cling to old dreams. Playing at swords now, when I was already apprenticed to the Keep staff, was ludicrous.

Deliberately shirking Keep duties was not the route to Arvard's much-vaunted Success.

Arvard would not approve, but Arvard need not know. It was a small secret to keep from Arvard, though it was the first. I suppose that I was trying to repay Arvard in kind for the secret that he had attempted to keep from me. Arvard's was a solemn game of the kind he had just begun to master, but I saw only that he played it without me. I was certain that Conierighm would never sustain this whim to teach a clerk for more than a single lesson. When the sword lesson ended, I fully intended to let Arvard know of it. Arvard had disappointed me, and a gesture of my own independence was the hardest punishment I could consciously give him.

*   *   *

Conierighm surprised me. Rather than teaching me a lesson in humility, as I expected him to do, he actually instructed me in combat, and he did not begin with the sword. He insisted that I must first learn to defend myself unarmed; I must develop the strength, control, and agility to counter even a superior opponent. He gave me assignments to perform on my own, and Conierighm would not hear any protest that my apprenticeship would interfere. He scorned my function as merely another of Lord Baerod's numerous apprentice clerks; inasmuch as I agreed with him, I began gradually to give priority to Conierighm's demands. My apprenticeship deteriorated, but I was viewed as merely inefficient, lazy, and irresponsible. Not even Arvard seemed to notice that I had redirected my energy, for Arvard's ambitions consumed his full interest, and I practiced with Conierighm at obscure times and places.

The Rendie madness ebbed to an affliction only of the night; I still heard Rendie voices as I slept, but the true dreams had never taken the toll of the waking terror. I was slow to correlate my improved mental state with the swordmaster's lessons. Conierighm had very subtly commenced my training as a K'shai.

By the time I realized Conierighm's intentions, I had proceeded too far to stop. I lied to myself instead, assuring myself that Conierighm's teaching would never make me an assassin, whatever Conierighm might plan. I refused to believe the truth that Conierighm would kill me himself rather than let his investment of time be wasted by my recalcitrance. He owed a favor to the K'shai, and he recruited for them as payment. In later years I came to understand why Conierighm devoted himself so thoroughly to my mastery of swordsmanship and those other skills he taught; I was the only viable candidate with whom he could hope to appease the K'shai. If he failed to please them again, as he had done several times in the years prior to my training, the K'shai had promised him death. Not even Conierighm dared contradict a K'shai.

For the sake of easing the Rendies' grasp upon me, I might have accepted Conierighm's way even if I had known what I would become. My parents ought to have apprenticed me to a butcher so as to educate me appropriately and give me warning. Death was unreal to me. I would become death's instrument before I would understand that tearing of soul from body which comprised it.

Chapter 5

Third Day, Seventh Month
Year 21 of Rending

Master Irrn sat at his great polished desk with his head low and his hands interlaced before him. His assistant, glancing through the door, thought that Master Irrn had drifted off to sleep. Master Irrn was an old man, thought the young assistant with callous satisfaction. Master Irrn would need replacement soon, and the young assistant considered himself quite the most likely candidate for the position.

Irrn watched his assistant through narrowed eyes. Irrn had a very good idea of the young man's aspirations, but Irrn was unconcerned by that sort of feeble competition. Irrn was a shrewd man. He had advised Lord Baerod on judicial matters for many years, and Irrn did not intend to relinquish that privilege.

The young assistant was of no concern, but this Arvard who had replaced Chul was another matter. Chul had never been careless, but this boy had produced enough incriminating evidence to undo years of Chul's good service, and the boy had used the data well. This Arvard had handled the matter with a delicacy worthy of Irrn himself—and Arvard had become Keeper of Records at the inconceivable age of twenty.

Irrn sighed. Thirty years ago he might have made good use of Arvard, but such an ambitious young man presented too much of a threat to an aging retainer. It was time to put a stop to Master Arvard's advancement through the Keep ranks.

Weaknesses: everyone had weaknesses. What were Arvard's flaws? Irrn had been collecting data for several months. The basic facts were not difficult to obtain. Arvard was the foster son of that ridiculous idealist, Evram, whom Lord Baerod perversely insisted on admiring; there could be no more impeccable a family in Tyntagel, even if the wife did have a reputation as a shrew. The daughter was insignificant. The natural son was more interesting; imagine that too-beautiful young man a swordsman! But swordsmanship, even practiced in secret, was an insufficient aberration for Irrn's purposes. The entire family was despicably innocuous. There was no hold to be gained in that direction.

This letter, now, was more promising. It said nothing overtly incriminating, but Mistress Giena was obviously attempting to blackmail the slippery Master Arvard. She knew or hoped she knew something which Master Arvard would not want made public. It would be interesting to observe the young man's reaction to the letter. Unfortunately, Irrn could not effect such an observation without admitting guilt over the letter's interception. No matter. Any of Irrn's agents could extract information from a perfidious serving woman in the Lady Yldana's employ. Irrn would see to it that one of his men carried Lord Baerod's messages to Tulea this month: perhaps Jorame. Jorame had always performed effectively for an adequate price. The man was more greedy than loyal, but Master Arvard was not so significant as to tempt Jorame into betrayal. Yes, Jorame would serve the purpose nicely.

Chapter 6

Eleventh Month, Year 21 of Rending

The air felt chill, though the sun burned brightly through the scattered clouds. Arvard tucked his hands into the pockets of his coat. He saw only his own feet taking strides across the ground, for his head was low in contemplation. Jorame had died in Tulea by a K'shai hand: an inconsequential event to Arvard, but Master Irrn, of all people, seemed to think that Arvard knew something of the circumstances. The lofty Master Irrn had become ridiculously, improbably accommodating; why? Mistress Giena had not responded to the last communication; why? Arvard's Power refused to appear; why?

Arvard felt a muscle twitch at his eye. He tried to smooth away the tic with his hand, but it persisted. The sense of panic had begun in small ways over the months since Arvard realized, thanks to Mistress Giena's cupidity, the truth of his heritage. The knowledge should have made him stronger; it had certainly delighted him initially. Imagine how proud Evaric would be to know that his foster brother was the only son of Lord Venkarel. Perhaps it was the need for silence that had corroded Arvard's spirit. He had not dared tell even Evaric the truth. Without mature, usable Power, even the son of Lord Venkarel was vulnerable.

Arvard could recognize his own dangerously emotional state, but he could not control it. The growing inability to master his emotions frightened him further. A wizard cannot panic, screamed Arvard in his mind. Without control, Power comprises absolute destruction. A Power which cannot be controlled must be destroyed. That is Ceallagh's law. That is the Infortiare's justice.

I need to find Evaric, thought Arvard wildly. I shall remain strong because Evaric believes that I am strong. I

have always been the strong one. I have always been the
one to protect my little brother. Evaric understands. I must
find Evaric.

Inquisitive whispers pursued Arvard as he stumbled from
his office and the Keep. Let them think me ill, he prayed.
Let them not stop and ask me why I leave my work at
mid-morning. Let Evaric be at Fielding's office or at home
and not running errands to farmers and tenants beyond the
village. Let me find Evaric quickly. Evaric will listen.

*   *   *

"Ai, Evaric," called Nori with zealous brightness. I conceded that she was a very pretty girl. I could hardly blame
her for unfortunate childhood comparisons between us. I
could blame her for her long allegiance to Miff, but Miff
had left Tyntagel over a year ago, seeking his dubious
fortune. "Are you walking to town, Evaric?" asked Nori
coyly.

Since the path connected only my family's home and
Nori's to the village, the question was absurd. I answered
stiffly, "Master Fielding asked me to collect some papers
from Master Sodaii." I glanced at the thickly growing ever-
greens lining the path, wondering who was hiding, waiting
to see Nori make a fool of me.

I began to move more quickly, but Nori matched my
pace, though it must have been uncomfortably rapid for her.
"Whom are you taking to the next festival, Evaric?"

"No one."

Nori place her hand on my arm. "You cannot go to a
festival alone, Evaric."

"My family will be there." I tried to disregard Nori's
unsettling proximity. I did not trust her. I did not particularly like her.

"Arvard has asked Vina."

Because Vina's mother was Lady Nadira's confidante, I
thought cynically. "Yes."

"Did you never think about asking a girl yourself?"

"Not really."

"Evaric." Nori stepped in front of me, forcing me either
to stop or bowl her over; I stopped. I stared over her head,
until her hands began to draw patterns on my chest. I
looked down at her reluctantly. Her smooth chestnut hair

was gathered by ribbons which drifted over her shoulders. Warmth, softness, and the scent of lavender: she was obvious in her approach, but she was difficult to ignore. "Your arms are strong," she said, as if awed. She traced the muscles.

"Arvard is stronger," I said, which was untrue.

"Arvard never makes me tremble."

I knew that I should walk away from her. I was certain that she meant only to bait me. I was entirely innocent, for I had always been too shy to court a girl formally, and the advantages of less chaste pursuits had not yet occurred to me.

"You make me tremble, Evaric."

I did desire her; the realization surprised me mildly, for I was backward in such interests. Conquer her and be done with the matter; that had been Arvard's advice, considerably in advance of any inclinations of my own. I grabbed her clumsily, having little idea of the ways of seduction. I expected resistance, which would spare me the embarrassment of trying to proceed beyond an awkward embrace. I felt her press tightly to me. She guided me, leading me to the thick autumn grasses hidden by the trees. The ground was uneven and rough. I tried to protect her from the twigs and pebbles, but she directed my hands in other ways. She had lain with other men, I decided: hardly a difficult conclusion but an astonishing revelation to me. Her lips tasted of ale, which also shocked me.

"What have you done!"

I rolled to a crouch, while Nori tried to cover herself with her shift. Arvard was not looking at her but at me. I had never seen Arvard so angry.

"How could you soil yourself with this slut!" shouted Arvard. His eyes held a wildness I did not recognize.

"Arvard . . ."

"Betrayer!" Arvard turned sharply and ran toward the village. A jutting branch tore across his cheek, leaving blood in its wake, and he did not seem to feel it.

Nori began to laugh, a sharp, shrill sound which reminded me of mockingbirds. "Your brother is jealous of me."

I stared at her, disgusted with her, with myself, and with Arvard. I retrieved my coat, while Nori pouted at me. I left her struggling to refasten her skirt.

*　　　*　　　*

I had lost all interest in the errands I had begun. I retraced my steps toward home, feeling ashamed and angry. I hoped to find the house empty, but my mother stood at the gate. "Bother," I sighed, a much milder expletive than my emotions reflected. My mother was hardly the person I wished to see at that moment.

She met me with a frown, but she did not speak to me. She walked beside me, taunting me with silence, until I stopped and faced her. "Master Fielding released me for the rest of the day," I said more defensively than I had intended. Lying did not come easily to me, though I had practiced a fair amount of it to keep secret both my madness and my lessons with Conierighm.

"Then you will be free later to accompany your father to the Ratquer mill. You can load the barley while your father discusses the discrepancy he found in the last accounting with Master Ratquer."

"Ratquer's son can load the barley. We pay them enough for it," I replied mechanically, though I thought the physical effort might eliminate some uncomfortable tension.

"Siahan works hard, as does his father. They earn their prices." My mother puckered her face: she did not believe my lie. Master Fielding would not release me from duties too often shirked. "You might do well to spend some time at the mill, Evaric. Not everyone lives as easily as we do."

"I am fortunate. My brother succeeds enough for both of us, however dubious his methods."

"You are not Arvard's shadow. He dominates you only because you encourage it," said my mother slowly. I had never previously criticized Arvard aloud, and my mother was clearly astonished.

"Domination is Arvard's life and sanity, but it is a madness in itself. Arvard calls it ambition."

"Arvard understands poverty. He does not want to face it again."

"I know," I said tersely, wanting only to end this discussion. I could still taste Nori. I could still see Arvard's shock and anger. "The patch on the roof has slipped. I had better fix it." Master Fielding would not tolerate another neglected assignment; he would terminate my apprenticeship.

I went to cut the new shingles. My mother watched me with a troubled expression. She entered the house just long enough to find her shawl and change to her walking shoes. I did not ask her destination.

She returned some two hours later. I was in the kitchen, sanding the edge of a door that had sagged and begun to stick. My mother observed me for a time in silence. I let her think I did not know that she had come. "You already finished the roof?" she asked me, though she must have seen the evidence of my work.

"You said that I should learn about working hard," I reminded her, indulging myself in a strong dose of self-pity. "Arvard wants me to abet him in his boundless ambitions. Father frowns and says nothing, and Ylsa says nothing constructive. Roofs and kitchens would seem the safest place for me to occupy myself, since none of you approves of anything I choose for myself."

"I want what is best for you, Evaric."

"Thank you, Mother. I appreciate your concern."

The bitter edge to my voice must have made her wonder. She must have known that Arvard and I would reach this point of schism eventually. She must always have expected it. "Arvard wants only to see you succeed. I think you are the only person who actually matters to him."

"So I am, Mother: the only person who matters to him, except himself. Arvard would never hurt me. Arvard is always so capable, so much in control of everyone and every situation. Since I met him, I have wanted to be like him."

My mother hesitated. She placed her roughened hand on my shoulder. "You and Arvard are very different people. It is time you found separate interests."

She put her arms around me and hugged me to her tightly. I reacted stiffly at first. My mother was so rarely demonstrative that I was startled. I grinned at her apologetically, warmed by the sympathy I did not deserve.

"You do know how to smile like an angel when you want," said my mother, pulling back to study me. "That smile could break hearts more surely than any of Arvard's schemes." She whispered, "That smile could break my heart." I did not understand her comment at the time.

"What a charming domestic scene," drawled Arvard from the entry.

My mother dropped her arms to her side, looking absurdly guilty. "What are you doing here at this hour?" she demanded of Arvard.

"It appears to be the place to gather. You are here, Mother, when I was sure I saw you entering the village church not an hour ago. My dear little brother is here, when he should be running errands for Master Fielding. Surely, at any moment, Ylsa and my honored, honorable foster father will enter as well, and the entire, tightly respectable little family will be together." Arvard's jaw was tensed. His yellow hair stood at stiff angles.

I sensed a deeper disturbance than his recent anger. Something had altered in Arvard. Perhaps it owed to his shock at seeing me with Nori; perhaps I had stopped gilding him with my own ideals. I asked him tentatively, "Did something happen at the Keep?"

Arvard answered very clearly, "Nothing happened at the Keep, little brother. Nothing happened anywhere. Nothing is all that happens." Arvard kissed our mother's forehead lightly, which made her start. "I am going to my room, dear Mother, so that you and Evaric may continue your family discussion without further interruption from the fosterling." Arvard kicked the flowered throw rug into a huddle.

Mother allowed me to follow Arvard alone up the stairs to the attic room we shared. "Are you drunk, Arvard?"

"No, little brother, I'm not drunk. Not very. I should be much more drunk than this." Arvard flung open the door to the room, and the door's handle slammed another indentation into the wall. "Where is Nori? I thought surely you would have smuggled her into your bed. Or did she tire of you already? Is she off telling stories about you to her other lovers? Can't you ever learn not to be a victim?"

I should have been kinder, but I was annoyed. I replied dryly, which aggravated Arvard the more. "Nori did not exactly attack me, Arvard."

"She degraded you, which is worse." The light caught something on the table, drawing Arvard's attention, impatiently at first; then he stared as if nothing else existed in the room. I looked to see what had distracted him, but I could see only my brother's back. "The acknowledgment has finally come," said Arvard wonderingly. "The waiting has ended."

He reached, and I saw his object of desire winking past his hand. It was crystalline, pale violet, faceted and exquisite. It did not resemble the sort of prosaic items one might expect to find in the room of any commoner. "No!" I shouted. I leaped across the narrow room, striking Arvard with a force which carried us both to the floor.

"How do you dare to touch me with the stain of a whore still on your hands?" snarled Arvard.

"Did you touch it?" I shouted urgently, too concerned by my question to notice Arvard's mood.

Arvard closed his broad hands around my throat. He seemed to savor my shock. I tried to pry his fingers loose, but Arvard tightened his grip relentlessly. "No more games," said Arvard coldly. "No more pretense. You made your choice. You shame the aspirations I would have shared with you. You have dragged at me long enough, holding me to a nothing's destiny."

I drove my fingers deeply into Arvard's side. Arvard choked and doubled, his hands releasing their hold. His eyes watered. I was on my feet, breathing hard and glaring down at my brother. "You just tried to kill me, Arvard." Arvard groaned, unable to speak or move; that was the way of the movement I had used against him. "Do you realize that I saved your life an instant ago? That elegant bauble is yadovitii, an assassin's tool." I slowed my breath but not my anger. Arvard shifted laboriously to see the crystal cluster he had mistaken for a noble gift.

"What?" Arvard was fuzzy, confused.

I informed him stiffly, "Yadovitii is one of the more exotic weapons of a K'shai, but it can be very effective when properly utilized. The crystals resemble razors in their sharpness, and they splinter very easily. The K'shai coat them with an oily, penetrating poison, which requires very minimal contact with the bloodstream to kill. I do not know what you have been doing to advance yourself to glory. I do not want to know. But you have offended someone badly—someone who can afford to hire a K'shai to eliminate you."

With a bleak abruptness, I extended my hand to Arvard, who struggled to rise from the wooden floor. It was my strength which lifted Arvard and led him to the bed; I did not like seeing Arvard helpless and uncoordinated.

"I shall go downstairs to find something to wrap around the yadovitii," I said. "Then I shall burn the poison from it, smash the crystals, and bury the shards. I suggest that you ensure that no one touches the yadovitii in my absence."

"Of course," agreed Arvard meekly. Sobriety was slowly asserting itself. He managed to roll onto his side, and he stared at me. "Miff should try to harass you now," he remarked with pallid humor.

I left him, went to the kitchen, and selected several empty grain sacks. Mother watched me curiously, as she heated water for the laundry. "Tell your brother to save the sporting practice for out-of-doors."

I answered tonelessly, "I shall tell him." She knew that Arvard and I had argued. I wondered what she would think if she knew how seriously we had fought.

"I'm sorry, little brother," said Arvard as I returned to our attic room.

"If you know who has named you as target, I suggest that you try to placate him or her. I also suggest that you request your own lodgings, since your presence here would appear to endanger all of us." I kept my voice devoid of emotion.

"I need your help, little brother."

"You have considerable authority on the staff, as you so often tell me. You might even manage to obtain a room in the Keep itself."

"I never intended to hurt you."

I wrapped the yadovitii with delicate respect. I had brought oil and rags to clean the wood of the table. I dropped the cleaning materials on the bed beside Arvard. "I am gathering the loose splinters, but be cautious when you clean. Wrap your hands, and let none of the oil soak through to your skin."

"Listen to me, Evaric."

I turned from the table. I looked not at Arvard but at a point on the wall above Arvard's head. A nail protruded; unadorned for years, it had held a wreath of leaves, until the leaves had turned to dust. Arvard and I had jointly won the wreath as a school prize not long after Arvard had become my foster brother. "I am listening, Arvard. I always listen to you. You are the one who cannot hear above the sound of your ambitions."

"Our goals differ. That does not make either of us wrong."

"Someone wants to kill you, Arvard."

"Not for anything I have done, little brother. I swear it."

"Then you do know who is responsible for this attack."

"Not who, but I think I know why." Arvard paused dramatically. "Someone has learned that I am Lord Venkarel's son."

I categorized his statement as another claim of the Lost Prince. I barely raised one brow, a lack of reaction that must have tantalized the raw violence that Arvard had suppressed. "That would explain why you continue to request Ixaxin testing at every opportunity. I assume that your startling discovery occurred approximately three years ago. Prior to that time, your interest in Power was resignedly wistful. Since then, you have devoured Ixaxin texts, when you thought I would not notice, and you have pursued every reference to Power that has been made in your hearing." I shook my head, exasperated by Arvard's latest fantasy. "You do not need to build yourself false histories to impress me or anyone else."

"I did not concoct this story, Evaric." Arvard hoisted himself upright.

"You told me once before that your father was a farmer." And I suspected strongly that he had been not a farmer but a thief and cutthroat.

"Pa was not my father. Without your help, Evaric, Lord Venkarel's enemies will have me assassinated, as they have tried to do today."

"Your imagination has always favored extravagance, Arvard. You obviously have an enemy, but you are scarcely a wizard."

"Not yet."

"Not ever." I began to gather up the bag which contained the yadovitii.

"Don't you understand, Evaric? My Power has been bound."

"I should not have thought that binding could take effect against any kin of the Venkarel's."

"Not if normal means were applied." Arvard gave his words urgency. " 'Son of the Taormin.' Do you remember, Evaric?"

I stiffened. I answered coldly, "The Rendies' chant."

"Yes!" hissed Arvard eagerly. "The Taormin binds me."

I hated the subject of Rendies. I loathed the brightness that it now brought to Arvard's face and manner. "I do not recall that the Rendies addressed you in particular."

"You did not understand them as I did," replied Arvard hurriedly. "Evaric, the Taormin is a tool of tremendous Power. I've read about it. It was the key to Horlach's dominion. That is the binding that has been used against me!"

"Arvard, we have both listened to Rendies more than anyone's sanity can fully accept." Arvard shook his head at me and laughed, though the movement was rigid and the laugh was hoarse. "I have nightmares, and you have this delusion . . ."

"It is not a delusion."

"This delusion that you are something other than what you are. You do not need to manufacture skills or strengths. You can do anything, achieve anything, become anything you wish. Can you not be satisfied with your own excellence in everything you try?"

"It is too much for you to believe, isn't it, little brother?" Arvard sounded compassionate now, as if he deeply regretted my failing.

I tried to shut away the sympathy that Arvard exuded. I tried equally to evade the pity that I felt in return. I did not want to pity Arvard, my faithful and invincible friend. Arvard had tried to choke the life from me, but I understood the potency of Rendie lies too well to withhold forgiveness. I had combated the Rendies every night and nearly as many days since that first fateful night. I knew that Rendies had corrupted my own mind and soul. I had once thought Arvard immune, but the hero had failed me in more ways than one.

"You want me to leave this house, little brother? Very well. Perhaps you're right. I have stayed too long."

"I spoke in anger."

"I know, but you were correct. I am endangering you by remaining. I can work my way to Tulea. I shall go to Ixaxis, and I shall learn everything there is to know about Rendies, wizardry, and the Taormin. I shall master my Power, and I'll find a cure for your Rendie madness. I'll prove myself to you, little brother."

I watched a squirrel steal an acorn from the tree beyond the window. I dropped my glance to the wrapped yadovitii. "How do you expect to live once your money is spent on inns and tariffs? You can hardly afford to hire K'shai Protection, and your travel will be slow and circuitous without it. Caravans are notoriously ponderous and costly."

"You might come with me," said Arvard cunningly. "You could provide Protection."

"I am not a K'shai," I replied, startled.

"You're nearly one." Arvard smirked, supremely pleased

with himself. "I know that Conierighm has been teaching you. I've seen you. You're better than he'll ever be."

"That does not qualify me to fight Rending wraiths." I was not pleased that Arvard knew my secret, though I could not feel particularly surprised. I disliked his calm assumption that I intended to fulfill Conierighm's expectations. "No matter how unbearably the Rendies haunt me, I do not intend to become an assassin simply to learn the K'shai methods of surviving the night."

Arvard leaned back on the bed. "You refuse to accompany me," he said quietly.

A quality of such loneliness shrouded Arvard that I winced. "I understand Rendie madness, Arvard. I know how real it seems, but the Rendies will destroy you if you heed them. You have no Power; you have been tested repeatedly. Only Rendie illusion makes you believe that some sorcerous conspiracy has deprived you of your heritage."

"It is not Rendie madness but truth."

"Was it truth that made you want to kill me?"

"No. I didn't. You don't understand." Arvard pushed himself along the edge of the bed and forced himself to stand. "I must go, little brother, not just from this house. You do understand that much?"

"I suppose I do." Rendie lies were inescapable.

"I shall succeed. I've finally realized what must be done."

"What shall I tell Mother and Father?"

"Nothing. Or tell them that the liege has sent me on some needful journey. It's better if no one else knows the truth. There has already been one attempt on my life. I don't want to be followed from here. You must not tell anyone what I've told you today, little brother. Promise me."

"As you wish." I felt as if part of my life were being ripped away from me.

"We'll always be brothers, Evaric. Whatever happens." Arvard reached for my arm, and I met the gesture, knowing that it signified an ending. The Rendies had claimed the Lost Prince.

Chapter 7

Arvard wasted no time. He gathered his possessions, gave me various letters of deception to deliver to the Keep, and counted his silver at least a dozen times. He sorted that which he would hide from that which he would need to pay for the first step of his intended journey, a step which would carry him farther from his destination. He meant to misdirect any pursuit by starting toward Cam and turning aside as soon as he passed the Tyntagel border.

A caravan for Cam had just left the village when Arvard bought his passage. Rather than wait a month for another caravan, Arvard chose to catch this one at the crossroads. He took the shorter route through the dense woods, a route seldom traveled, for it boasted no proper road. I accompanied Arvard, running beside him until he could grab a berth on the last wagon. I watched until the caravan disappeared beyond the trees, and I continued to watch when nothing remained to be seen.

The road was darkly ruddy with streaks of late afternoon sun through stormy clouds when I finally began my return to home. I did not have the road to myself. Another traveler was approaching from the east, though the hour had grown late and inns would soon be sealing their doors for the night. The man was large but not extraordinary. Taxes were due from the Gellan district; many strangers came to the village for a day or two, citizens who lived far from the Keep. I often passed such men on the country roads without thought, but this one attracted my notice. Wrapped in a ragged brown cloak though he was, he exuded a confidence near bravado in his gait. The man's hands were hidden in the folds of his cloak, but I did not need to see them. He was K'shai: an assassin. He had attempted to kill Arvard. Because of this man, Arvard had gone.

The conclusion filled me with a strangely secure calm. I

had no doubt of the man's identity. I had no question of what I must do. I approached the man with a smile so warm that he looked startled. The K'shai was reaching within his cloak; he reached, I was certain, for a weapon. A sword broke free of the cloak and sliced the air that my neck had occupied a moment earlier.

I had ducked and kicked, catching the K'shai behind the knees before the sword could complete its stroke. The K'shai staggered and recovered. I knew that he meant to throw his dagger while I avoided the sword. I dodged the dagger before it left my opponent's hand.

I had fastened my eyes on the K'shai brand. The brand had not been cleanly made; the sword was barely identifiable, but the significance of the seared skin was unmistakable. The brand moved quickly as the K'shai attacked, but I frustrated his deft moves.

I could feel the man change from cool professionalism to aggravated bewilderment. I could follow his thoughts as if they issued from my own mind. Every quick, strongly directed K'shai action found the target absent. The K'shai thought uneasily that it was like fighting wraiths. The killer had never faced such an elusive opponent of human kind. For a wraith, the K'shai would have known the proper forms to follow, as he knew the way to kill a man efficiently. This youth was neither one nor the other. This spindly youth, smiling so uncannily, began to alarm the powerful K'shai.

My foe's disquiet fed my calm. This game required less concentration than sparring with Conierighm, for the K'shai's intentions shone so abrasively clear to me. I found myself slowing deliberately, allowing the K'shai's blade to cut close to me, testing my own precision of evasion. It was a game: an exhilarating game. This K'shai had tried to kill Arvard; this K'shai would die.

"Feed on him, Fire-child." The voices in my head sang of blood's sweet fire. "His energy is fear, and his fear will make you strong." The K'shai lay dead with his own short sword buried in his heart. The freed energy flowed into me, expanding into heady strength, but the madness faded with the act of killing. A man's hacked flesh lay bleeding at my feet, and I had stolen the life and soul from it.

Evening would come before anyone else took this path. The Rendies would consume the assassin's remains, for they would protect their Fire-child. Only the Rendies and I would know that the voices in my head had learned to destroy.

"He tried to kill Arvard," I reminded myself, but I had lost my certainty. I wiped blood from my hand; I had murdered a man, and the man's final, agonizing incredulity would now haunt me as surely as the Rendies. I had killed, and the worst guilt of all lay in the fierce joy that I had derived from the killing. Conierighm had trained me well; the Rendies had trained me better.

* * *

"You understand," said the little man.

Grim laughter was the answer of he who had been known as the Venkarel.

The little man felt annoyance. "You require me, Venkarel."

"Your motives are so pure," responded Kaedric.

"I am selfish. I do not deny it."

"You excel at both selfishness and cruelty."

"You are arrogant."

"Shall we scatter a few more epithets across infinity, Horlach? How very productive we are become."

"We are both necessary to the stabilization of the system."

"The process which will preserve you."

"And you, Venkarel. And your precious mortal world. You must yield him to me. I am the only one who can direct what must be."

The image of Kaedric smiled with feral coldness. "You are a very accomplished deceiver, Horlach."

"You cannot exclude me, Venkarel. See what the mere attempt has done to your world."

"It has opened a gate."

"The wrong gate!"

"By your choosing."

The little man's voice became hard and deliberate. "The cause is irrelevant. The remedy is necessary. Release him to me, or nothing will survive. This is truth."

"Truth, Horlach? Half-truth at best, I think."

"You have recognized the instability. You understand that it cannot last."

"Yes, Horlach, I understand. I also understand your treacherous nature. Any remedies must be of my own devising."

"You lack the necessary knowledge."

"You lack the necessary Power."

The little man, who had been a Sorcerer King for twenty thousand years, shrieked.

"Do try to behave, Horlach, until I need you. As you have said, we are both necessary to the process." The shade of Kaedric vanished.

"Your arrogance, Venkarel, could easily destroy us," murmured Horlach in his own mind, but he felt no personal anger against his too-perceptive foe. The Venkarel was worthy.

It was the other toward whom Horlach's darkest anger burned, and the other was long dead and dust upon another world. "Wretched mortal," snarled Horlach, "you dared condemn us all." Jonathan Terry was fortunate to be dimensions removed from the little man's reach.

PATTERNS

Chapter 1

"I wrote to Ixaxis." Evram raised his head from Lord Baerod's accounts. "I wrote to Ixaxis," reiterated Terrell calmly. "I told them that our son is a latent sorcerer."

Evram blinked several times. "After all these years," asked Evram woodenly, "how could you betray him?"

"It is not I who betray him. I love him—for himself and not for memory of a Tyntagel witch. He deserves more than we can offer him."

"She will send for him when the time comes."

"How long does she intend to wait?"

"Time passes differently for Immortals."

Terrell sniffed disdainfully. "Her son has become a man, and she has not seen him since his birth. We cannot keep him forever hidden from anyone who might recognize him as the son of the Venkarel."

"Do not speak that name again!" hissed Evram furiously. He added more quietly, "Would you undo all our years of silence?"

"I am not so afraid of the Venkarel's enemies as you."

"Then you are thrice a fool." Evram rubbed his brow. "I must send word to Rhianna. Perhaps I can rectify at least a part of your mischief." Evram clenched his fists, the only sign he gave of the depth of his fury and concern. He left the room with a jerky stride, as if even motion had been stunned in him.

"It is not often I promote such strong emotion in you, Evram," said Terrell to the smooth walls of whitewashed boards. "I almost wish you would strike me. We might then understand each other a little better." She rubbed her aching hands roughly on her apron, as if the argument had soiled them irreparably. She looked up to find Ylsa watching her.

"Are you all right, Mother?" asked Ylsa hesitantly.

"Why should I be?" snapped Terrell. Ylsa's eyes acquired the glaze of tolerant hurt which made them so like Evram's and so annoying to Terrell.

"I did not mean to upset you, Mother." Ylsa withdrew softly, holding her drab green skirts close about her to keep them from rustling in any disturbing manner. She tries so hard to be a nonentity, thought Terrell. I wish she did not succeed so well.

Terrell began to clean: anything, everything. She needed distraction, because she felt less confident than she wanted to believe. She actually feared the Ixaxins far more than did Evram, because Evram's imagination did not encompass the inhumanity of Power. He had always adored his Lady Rhianna, but he respected her birth-status more than her position as Infortiare of Serii. Terrell felt nothing for the Lady Rhianna dur Tyntagel; she dreaded the Lady Rhianna dur Ixaxis. More, Terrell feared that darker shade who had also visited them on the night of choice over twenty years past. She had never confessed that strange interchange. She occasionally wondered if even the Lady Rhianna knew of it.

The Lady Rhianna had appeared first: the silvery, fragile enigma Terrell remembered. Evram had seen nothing else, for he could not bend his attention from the Lady who constituted his only dream, even when the Lady's image was only a projection of the wizardry in which Evram disbelieved. Terrell had not so much seen as sensed the other. She had faced the dark one rather than watch the blatant worship in her husband's eyes. The darkness had blurred and reformed.

She had seen the man with his ice-cold eyes and known that he appraised her. She had felt him coolly probe and categorize; she had felt her soul dissected and reconstructed in some complex file in his awareness. She had felt the danger of him. Even to her unflaggingly prosaic person, the contact had brought a nearly sensual enticement, the irredeemable fascination of the unimaginably remote.

Terrell knew the man's identity: he was Lord Venkarel. Terrell knew, as did all her world, that Lord Venkarel had died in the Rending. Terrell knew, as the rest of her world apparently did not, that the truest part of Lord Venkarel had not died. Almost, she could forgive Evram his obsession with the Lady of Ixaxis. Terrell had felt a hint of its like when the Ixaxin Lord had confronted her.

Terrell had tried to confess to Father Guiarde that the dark wizard obsessed her. She had needed to tell someone that the perilous wizard had come again. She could not speak of the matter to Evram, and to no one else could she speak. When she reached the priest, she realized that the long years of silence prevented her from trusting the church, also.

Almost a month ago, the wizard had returned in the night. Terrell and Evram had argued that evening, as they often did: herself shrill, Evram calmly reasonable but more infuriating to her because of his impenetrability. Ylsa had eaten silently, pitifully attempting to smile her parents into peace; her efforts failed. Arvard had observed them with that detached amusement of his. Evaric's comment had constituted the only unusual factor.

"Why can you never argue honestly, Father," Evaric had asked calmly, "instead of pretending that Mother originates all of your differences? We all know that you detest one another equally."

The idle remark, patently valid though Terrell found it, had caused Evram's color to drain in shock. Arvard had laughed outright, and Ylsa had looked miserable. Evram had later blamed Terrell fiercely for corrupting their son's perceptions. Terrell had laughed at the man who could ever consider Evaric innocent or incapable of penetrating the simplistic deceptions of others.

"For all his meek facade," Terrell had chuckled in sincere amusement, "he is his father's son." She had clarified wryly, "Lord Venkarel's son," and Evram had stoically marched from the room, reverting to his customary policy of avoiding unpleasantness.

Terrell had scarcely blinked (she thought) at Evram's retreating back, when the silhouette had stretched and reversed direction. Evram did not return; the figure who approached was considerably taller and leaner, more finely cast, and far more graceful of movement. His hair was dark, and his clothing carried the somber gleam of black silk. His eyes were intensely blue, but they were deeply cold.

"My Lord Venkarel," she had murmured both in horror and in awe.

"Applicability of the title has ever been questionable, but

the appellation will serve." He had smiled austerely, some trace of a daunting humor stirring in the frosty eyes. "You shall write a letter, Mistress Terrell, to Ixaxis. You shall petition Master Ertivel, who currently presides as headmaster, on behalf of my son. You shall affirm that the boy displays evidence of Power, and you shall offer your sworn testimony with full acknowledgment of the penalties accrued by perjury."

"I would be lying, my lord," she had whispered. "Your son displays no Power, and he was yearly tested by the Ixaxin representatives, as law demands for any child."

"I do comprehend Ceallagh's laws, Mistress Terrell. I yielded the greater part of my mortal life so as to preserve their hold."

"Are you not suggesting that I defy them?" Terrell had asked, accepting the impossible conversation as a nightmare's gift.

"Do not mistake my 'suggestion' for a subject of debate. You shall write the letter that I dictate."

In the nightmare, Terrell had written it without further question. She awoke in the morning with a throbbing head and a lingering thrill of terror from her dream. She had found the letter on her bureau; the hand was hers, but the formal intricacies of its legal wording had not issued from her knowledge. She recognized his precision of style and shivered. She had quickly hired a messenger to bear the letter to Ixaxis.

Chapter 2

"The lords of Serii are a rough lot," murmured the voice in her mind.

"The impenetrability of bureaucracy outweighs the aggravation of mere individuals," complained Rhianna to the voice. "I despise councils and conspiracies. I loathe enforcing my will by virtue of this Power which accident inflicted upon me. I practice deception and domination for the good of our world, as if I were some omniscient authority on what the populace of the Seriin Alliance needs and wants."

"Omniscience—or the pretence thereof—is the lot of the Infortiare."

"Perhaps Ceallagh was omniscient. I am not. I feel wretched." The usual frustrations of fools and foolish customs had grated on her severely that day. She read a missive which had been left for her and laughed bitterly. "The Ixaxin holdings in Caruil have been attacked again. Several recent recruits have deserted us."

"Infortiares have tried to tame Caruillan sorcerers for centuries, Rhianna. You have made far more progress than your predecessors."

"You effectively shredded such primitive unity as they possessed, dear husband," she returned glumly. "A sound defeat is generally quite persuasive."

"You have no intention of being consoled, have you?"

"Not the slightest." She quit her pacing and sank into the chair which her husband had once favored. It had been badly worn at that time, over twenty years ago, when she had first entered Ceallagh's Tower. It was dreadful now, but

111

she could not bear to replace it, though she had renovated most of the more dilapidated furnishings.

"You are the most confoundly obstinate woman." His unpredictable temper flared. "You have been as touchy as a dyrcat for a week, but you stubbornly pretend that a very predictable mote of political turmoil is all that concerns you. Must I coerce the truth from you?"

Rhianna smiled wanly. "Could Serii survive such an argument between us?"

He did not lighten his focus. "Not if it were a direct conflagration. We could attempt a circuitous contest in hopes of sparing the mortal world, or you might condescend to think honestly for a while."

"I need to keep some thoughts my own rather than yours," she countered a bit sharply.

"Your independence does not seem to have flagged severely in the twenty-one years since you married me," retorted her husband. The coils of his consciousness gathered, twisting and probing at her. It was a sting of rapidly directed Power. "Our son," he concluded ponderously.

"Of course, our son! He is our son, or he was once. I see him now, and he belongs wholly to Evram and Terrell." Admission deepened her depression. "Terrell has written a letter to Ixaxis." She had read it repeatedly, but she could not explain its existence. "She has sworn that Evaric is a sorcerer."

"Then you can hardly defend the claim that 'he belongs wholly to Evram and Terrell.' "

"Evaric has evidenced no Power. Terrell has perjured herself."

"Only in a technical sense," answered her husband in detached tones. "Evaric has not displayed any Power which Mistress Terrell could clearly identify, but she knows his heritage."

"He has no active Power, Kaedric. Do you think I would not have reclaimed him if he did? How can I subject him to Ixaxis—and your unforgiving enemies—when he has no defense?"

"I recall that Ineuil endured Ixaxis for almost a year, and he had neither Power nor the promise of it."

"Ineuil is a marvelous pretender, and he was obsessed with vengeance against you."

"I meant merely to remind you, dearest Rhianna, that

precedence exists for the Ixaxin acceptance of a student
without Power."

"Not when Ixaxis knows for certain of the student's lack."

"You own no such certainty about Evaric." Kaedric's
response held an untraceable element which touched Rhianna
oddly. "Evaric conceals his Power, as does your father,
even from himself."

"Evaric was tested, as my father never was. It was you
who instructed me that Ixaxin tests are infallible." Rhianna
assessed her husband's lack of response. "Or did you lead
me to that conclusion by letting me read and hear from
others that such tests could not lie? Did you want me to
accept that which you do not credit?"

Kaedric's amusement tingled with the pleasure of being
discovered. (He had ever been so, building puzzles around
that which he sincerely wished hidden, while genuinely hoping that someone would pierce the clues to his deviousness.)
"I possibly distorted the truth, but it was a slight deception.
Ixaxin testing is virtually infallible. I know of only two
individuals who have defeated it."

"You hypothesize the second," Rhianna suggested dryly.
"I assume that you were the first."

The image of Kaedric grinned wickedly in her mind. "I
cheated regularly during my early days on Ixaxis. Marga
suspected, I think, but she could never catch me at it."

"You wanted your Power to appear less than it was."

"Naturally."

"It did you little good," Rhianna murmured sweetly.
Kaedric could still infuriate her with his unnecessary secrets.

Kaedric's specter grimaced. "I overestimated the average
performance."

"If you suspected Evaric of concealing Power, why did
you not tell me until now? He must be trained."

"He will be trained."

"So you assured me at his birth. Yet I must wait to be
informed by Terrell that he has Power!"

"I could have been wrong," shrugged Kaedric.

Rhianna stared at her shadow-image of Kaedric with his
twisted smile and perceptive crystalline eyes. She was certain that Kaedric knew his own abilities too well to doubt
his judgment of Power. The coldness of a forgotten fear
began to instill its icy core within her. She knew that he was
deceiving her, and she had no idea of how or why. "If

you—and Terrell—are correct," said Rhianna coolly, though doubts of many kinds twisted mercilessly within her, "our son could be an untrained Power waiting to explode across Tyntagel." Rhianna shuddered at a muddled vision of Tyntagel oaks caught by the fires of Ven's destruction.

"Evaric is not likely to find himself in my circumstances."

"But you consider the danger sufficient to send him to Ixaxis."

"Not at all. Our son will certainly not go meekly to Ixaxis on his 'mother's' whim. He will demand explanation, and he will weigh it against the K'shai."

"The K'shai are too practical to court Ixaxin displeasure."

Kaedric murmured wryly, "The K'shai pride themselves on developing their nearly supernatural abilities out of purely mortal strength. It might be amusing to watch them discover a major Power in their midst."

"As your Infortiare, my love, I must inform you that you are displaying a complete dearth of conscience. Lord Ceallagh would not approve." Nor would she have done had she believed him serious in contemplation of creating a sorcerous assassin of their son. She implicitly trusted her husband's self-imposed, unyielding rules, which he insisted knew no moral base. She trusted enough that though she could feel him manipulating her, she did not forcibly analyze his motives as she would have done with any true opponent.

"Dear, proper Rhianna, you have always attributed too much honor to me. It is probably as well for our marriage that carnal sins are beyond my ability."

"The only major sin to which your instincts incline you, my Kaedric, is murder. It is hardly an honorable tendency, but your capacity for destruction remains undimmed and unrivaled. I certainly should never fret over the specter of infidelity. No other woman would tolerate you."

The image formed clearly: dark, expressive eyebrows raised over blue-ice eyes; lips quirked in mingled irritation and amusement; lean elegance deceptively relaxed. "I do love you unconscionably."

"What can the child of our love become," sighed Rhianna, for she desperately loved and sometimes hated Kaedric as well, "save a dangerous aberration?"

"Like his father," added Kaedric evenly. His wife touched him and his terrible burning Power gently. "Dear Rhianna, would you have loved me if the Taormin had not forced my life upon you? You never had much of a chance to choose your own way, being flung from your father to me. Is that why you endeavor so fixedly to defend Evaric from my influence?"

Rhianna protested, "It is not from you that I defend him, Kaedric, but from your enemies and mine. It was you who chose the course we have taken for him."

"When he was a child, there was cause. Now, he is nearly a man; by mortal reckoning, he is a man already. You scarcely speak of him, but you watch him secretly. You want desperately to see him without the veil of your Power, but you leave your Evram believing that you have forgotten your son."

"Our son," she amended absently.

"Our son," agreed Kaedric. His voice held an emotion that Rhianna could not name. "Evaric begins to need more than Tyntagel can give him. Even Mistress Terrell recognizes that he outgrows his fosterage. You still hesitate to interfere, though you know that continued restraint could press Evaric into the K'shai, a group of whom you deeply disapprove. Ergo, you view the alternative to restraint as the greater evil. The alternative is, of course, the environment of major Power: Evaric's, yours, and mine." Kaedric's voice sharpened critically. "You cannot prevent the eventual manifestation of Evaric's Power. You condemned him, if you choose to consider it as such, when you elected to bear my child." He added, "Do not protest falsely to spare my feelings," in anticipation of her response. "You never wanted Power beyond the bespeaking of trees, hounds, and squirrels. You gauge Evaric's feelings by your own, discounting the fact that he may not share your disdain for the trappings of authority. Darling Rhianna, I leveled half a city to escape the clutch of poverty and ignobility. You pity my childhood. You form excuses for me out of love, despite the legion of curses which enshroud my name. Almost, my dear, you have made a decent man of me by your faith, but for Evaric's sake, I must impress upon you the inaccuracies in your image of me."

"Kaedric, do you think I love only an illusion?"

"I think you do not admit that the man whom you (astonishingly enough) love is very nearly the devil his detractors paint him. I am dangerously ambitious for Power—arrogant, ruthless, conceited, and quite amoral. The Ixaxins call me a revert: a Sorcerer King born to a later age by calamity of breeding. They are half right: I am more than a Sorcerer King. My Power exceeds that of any member of our ancestral race of madmen. Their greatest flaws, however, are mine. It was purely by accident of fate that I did not destroy more than Ven. Had I matured more fully before rebelling, my outburst might well have eradicated the mortal world." He enunciated with acuter emphasis, "Though he does not yet know it, Evaric is like me, Rhianna, and like Horlach."

For a moment of utter silence, Rhianna sat altogether alone in the Infortiare's Tower. She could see the ordinary sights: the view of Tulea, the Queen's exquisitely impressive castle, the distant white blossom of Ixaxis against the blue-violet sea. Her own thin hands were spread before her on the desk which had been her husband's. The ancient books, the walls, the burnished wood had been restored since the days of his tenure, but they had known his touch more often than she. In such still moments, she missed him most deeply. Her heart and body mourned him, though her mind and Power denied that he had ever died. She could not bear to let such moments linger. She forced the tactile world to fade, and she touched her husband desperately. He took her hand with a queer deliberation and pressed to it a kiss of mist and longing. Too late, she perceived his intention. She screamed his name, but she was battering a wall which no longer barred her way.

He withdrew from her each fiber and fiery tendril of sensed spirit of himself, emptying quarters of her soul which she had not even known were his. The frozen chill curled her into herself like a sorely wounded animal. She cried his name again, and Ixaxis might have trembled had they understood her Power's desperation. For the first time since Kaedric's Power had tested her in an obscure Anxian tavern, no trace of him stirred in her deepest senses. Rhianna was again alone, as she had been until she met him. She thought of how much more alone Kaedric was, and she was horrified.

"Dear God, why?" Rhianna heard her own small voice and scarcely knew it. She clasped her hands together, for they were icy and stiff. She could feel the silence. The room smelled of ashes years gone. How many widows, she wondered, must feel their husbands die a second time?

Of all the futures, this one she had not foreseen. She

could have seen him turn from her in anger; she could have seen herself despised. She could not have believed they could be parted so completely.

Analysis was imperative. She must understand. "Whatever plan you have concocted," she whispered, "I shall be part of it, Kaedric." Nonetheless, she was torn; she had a son as well. "My Kaedric, what have you done to me?"

* * *

The little man frowned: something odd was occurring. The Venkarel had always been a clever opportunist, but where was the reason in using a tool like this wretched Terrell? Puzzlement disturbed the little man greatly.

He reviewed his analyses with adamant care. A few uncertainties were inevitable given the subject's nature, but the analytical weaknesses were exceedingly minor. The central pattern was strong, for it had been developed over centuries, and the little man had woven his own design near to the focus. He knew the outcome, for he had lived it once before. It was unfortunate that he had been so young and impatient. If he had been less quick to escape with his stolen prize, the uncertainties might have been eliminated.

The little man gathered darkness like a cloak and pondered the Venkarel's moves. "Distraction?" he mused. That would be almost too childish, for it served no purpose. Did it?

A vivid joke struck the little man, and he roared appreciatively, "Distraction!" It was sensible; it was clever. It was tortuous and like the Venkarel. It was directed against another!

The little man frowned again. "Against her?" he demanded dubiously. His puzzlement doubled; so also grew his doubts.

Chapter 3

Mountains of Mindar, Serii

The rocks had tumbled recently. The cliff still wore the red scars of wounding. The man who cursed the stones matched his stony, scarred surroundings. He limped across the littered path and sat heavily upon a flat boulder.

He drank deeply from his flask, corked it carefully, and wiped the damp residue from his mouth with a dusty sleeve. The brand on the back of his hand showed through the dirt of travel: it represented in primitive form a bloodied sword, the hilt upon his wrist, the blade extending up the middle finger, the blood dripping along the sword's length. The man was K'shai. His K'shai name was Fog, for he could assassinate and escape as elusively as his namesake.

Fog was old for an active K'shai. He had been K'shai before the Rending. He could have retired in luxury if he had ever learned to curb his drinking and his gambling, but Fog did not crave respectability. He belonged to the old K'shai. Fog was strictly an assassin. He took no partner. He fought Rendies only for the practicality of his own defense.

Fog shaded his eyes to study the landslide. Part of the path had fallen away from the mountain. He would be forced to retrace his steps. "Blasted Mindar fangs," he muttered. His quarry could be in Alvenhame before he found passage around Dwaelin. He had lost too much time in Anx. He was growing old.

He massaged his knee. The rough passage had made it sore. He had torn it years ago, but it had only begun to trouble him again lately. He tried to straighten it where he sat; the knee cracked and argued.

He heard a faint keening. As it grew louder, Fog began to grumble anew. "Blast Gnarl, he told me all the gargoyles had retreated north."

It was a nightmarish beast that flew at him in attack. Fog had fought gargoyles before. The bloated, taloned beast could not suffocate the K'shai with fear, and Fog knew its vulnerability. He knew the proper K'shai pattern. He began his sword dance stiffly, but the rhythm of it smoothed as he fended against grasping claws and slavering teeth. His sword sliced cleanly through the barbed tail.

Fog stepped aside to consider the fallen gargoyle as it gasped for death. He did not try to finish it, for he had given the lethal blow. Any further butchery would only spread the acid ichor, and severed pieces would die no more quickly than the gargoyle's writhing tail.

Fog left the creature thrashing among the rocks. He wiped his sword in the first soft dust he found. A few bits of dried grass shriveled when the ichor touched them. Fog did not sheathe his sword until he had removed all taint of the gargoyle from it.

"Worse nuisance than Rendies," he snarled as he buried the traces. He looked at the painted sky, which soon would shine with stars. He grunted and decided that it was too late to return to level ground before nightfall. The narrow cliff path would be a poor place to fight Rendies, but the gargoyle had left him too winded to succeed against a Rendie unless he had some rest. He would just have to hope that no wraiths came this night. He was growing too old, he thought again. He settled himself among the rocks.

Fog awoke from sleep before midnight, knowing the chill forewarning of a Rendie visit. He flexed his stiff knee gingerly. He folded and packed his blanket neatly, chose a stable space on which to stand, and waited with his sword and a sigh. He had fought too many Rendies not to know their habits of timing.

Two wraiths began to form, and Fog resigned himself to his final battle. He might have managed to combat one. He was too sore and tired to master both. He had grown too old for his profession.

Fog began the sword dance mechanically. The knowledge that he would fail succumbed to the hypnotic rhythms of the familiar. He moved automatically, and the Rendies did not exist. It was the secret of the pattern; it denied the Rendies even while it fought them.

A stone caught Fog's foot, and his traitorous knee buckled beneath him. His sword flew from his hand, and his mind forgot the pattern. He saw a Rendie open itself into a lightless maw. He could feel it snatch pieces of his mind. Defeated, Fog crawled to his feet and ran, knowing flight was a desperate and unlikely hope. He misjudged his direction, but he realized his mistake only as his feet slipped across the cliff's crumbling edge. He wondered idly whether he would be smashed to his death before the Rendie could devour him.

The rocks seemed to spread throughout his body. Fog felt punctured and broken. He opened one eye; the other was swollen shut. He lay upon his back at the bottom of the cliff, and there were no Rendies. Fog grinned as he spat out a broken tooth. Miraculously, he had survived. It was very hard to kill a K'shai.

Fog's satisfaction ebbed when he tried to move. He tried to shift his legs and found that they responded no more readily than the rocks which seemed to cover him. He could not lift his arms. He craned his head, expecting to see himself at least half buried. A single dagger of stone jutted from his side. The remainder of his body was skewed upon the moon-dusted dirt.

Fog's head fell back hard against the ground, but he felt little pain from the shock. He tried to wet his lips and realized that his mouth was parched. He cursed himself for botching his own death. He had always taken pride in executing his victims cleanly and quickly.

By morning the ravens began to gather. Fog shouted at them, until his voice cracked like their own. They circled him steadily, awaiting his death.

By evening, his sight had failed him. He could hear only a steady roaring, which he knew meant failure of his ears. The pain had faded, but Fog did not welcome the easing. He knew it was a precursor of death, and resentment against death had been building in him during his paralyzed hours.

"I can preserve you." The voice filled his head, and no other senses remained to distract from it.

"What are you?" whispered Fog. He saw death as an absolute, an inevitable prospect, especially for a man of his profession, but it was a phenomenon he found exceedingly disagreeable. He did not believe in salvation of any kind, but Fog would bargain with God or devil to save himself. He began to feel eager.

"Immortal," answered the voice.

"You will preserve my life?" demanded Fog. "What does it cost me?" There was a price on everything.

"Your soul, of course," replied the voice dryly.

"Preserve me!" said Fog with nearly a laugh. He had no qualms about bargaining away a thing in which he disbelieved.

"You will be physically whole. The world will generally perceive no change in you, but you will not be as you have been. From time to time," warned the voice carefully, *"you will become an extension of myself."*

"Word the contract as you will."

"Your choice will not be irrevocable," said the voice slowly. *"True death will remain an option."*

"What are you? A devil with a conscience?"

The voice chuckled softly. *"Something of the sort."*

"I am dying, blast you. Quit wasting time."

The voice did not respond, and Fog began to despair. He began to curse himself for believing his own nightmare, and he cursed the nightmare for being unreal. He cursed his body for failing him at last. He cursed the dead gargoyle, who had exhausted him, and the Rendies, who had driven him to fall. With a final gasp, Fog cursed the Rending which had released both Rendies and gargoyles into the inhabited lands. Fog's heart stopped, sputtered, and began to beat strongly again. The body of the K'shai called Fog began to heal.

* * *

"Venkarel has deceived you from the beginning," whispered a dim, nearly unnoticed voice in her mind.

Rhianna stiffened. Her Power flared. She scanned for other Power and found no source. She found nothing, and the voice did not return. Slowly, she relaxed into her chair, but her eyes were troubled and her Power wary.

Chapter 4

Tyntagel

I lay in my bed and stared at the fastened shutters, the solid walls, the heavy door of oak, which in any case led only to the rest of the well-sealed house. I feared to move, feared to seek my parents or my sister, feared to know or not to know what I might or might not find. Rendies had entered, despite the solidity of walls and wood. Arvard had gone, and nothing remained to divide me from the bitter night.

I arose and dressed slowly. I took from the bureau the small knife that Arvard had given me five years before. I had no better reason for taking it than the fact that it comforted me.

I opened the room's door and met the prosaic aroma of bacon. Ylsa yelled from the kitchen, "Evaric, are you planning to eat breakfast?"

I walked down the stairs, employing all of Conierighm's lessons in cautious, silent movement. I trusted nothing I saw and nothing I felt. I paused at the base of the stairs, studying the walls, rugs, and chairs. Grimly, I inspected the charcoal sketches of Tyntagel Keep, which hung in oak frames upon the wall. Suspiciously, I searched them for some skewed image which would betray them as imposters, visions of a Rendie dream from which I might yet wake.

I entered the kitchen. My breakfast sat cooling on the table. All other places had been cleared. "I thought you had decided to sleep all day," grumbled Ylsa, who was scrubbing the tiles of the floor. "Father has already gone to the Keep, and Mother went early to the market."

I lifted a piece of cold bacon from my waiting plate and stared at it. I replaced it carefully. I could not eat. Not after yesterday. Not after last night.

"Mother wants you to fix that loose fence rail before you go to the Keep this morning," said Ylsa as she worked.

I nodded without hearing her. "Do you ever have nightmares, Ylsa?"

Ylsa stopped moving. "Sometimes," she conceded wanly. She began to scrub again at a furious pace. "You had better hurry if you intend to eat your breakfast, finish your chores, and reach the Keep on time for work. Father will not plead with Master Fielding for you again."

"I misplaced my appetite." I opened the door and breathed slowly of the cold air.

"Will you close the door before you freeze me!"

"Sorry, Ylsa." I stepped outside into the drizzle and closed the door behind me.

*   *   *

"Your performance disappoints me," said Conierighm with disdain. He withdrew his weapon from its position at my throat, deliberately drawing the blade across my jaw.

I blinked at the unexpected cut, annoyed by Conierighm's ruthless disregard for any hurt that did not kill or maim me. "Your point, Master Conierighm," I replied stiffly.

"The winning point, Master Evaric." Conierighm's thin smiled reappeared. "At least you accept the unpleasant consequences of inattention."

Conierighm had developed an unfortunate tendency to gloat each time he scored against me. I told him coldly, "I could have killed you a dozen times today."

"Generosity does not constitute victory." Conierighm forestalled my wordless retreat. "There is a man you must meet. He will be here tonight. Come after sunset."

I answered over my shoulder, "I have no interest in your nameless strangers, Master Conierighm."

"The K'shai need not explain themselves to insolent little boys," sneered Conierighm. "Or perhaps it is the night that you fear to face?"

I regarded Conierighm without response. I had faced the night before, and Conierighm knew it; Conierighm knew nothing near the whole of it. I vaulted over the low fence rather than elbow past Conierighm to reach the gate.

For two hours I sorted records, carried Master Fielding's

ledgers as he made his rounds, transcribed the lists of taxes paid and owed, and wondered if I looked to be a murderer. I received a few questions regarding Arvard's sudden errand; I lied consistently, saying that I knew nothing of his mission's nature, and no one troubled to question me twice.

For three hours I updated family rolls with the recent birth and death reports. I carried boxes for Master Croft, fetched ink for Master Ban, and listened to a recital of Master Garnett's health complaints. Master Fielding berated me at some length for inattentiveness, while I wondered if anyone had actually died yesterday on a lonely road at dusk; I was not sure if Rendie madness had goaded me to slay a man, or if Rendie madness had merely made me believe that the murder had been done. I smiled, apologized to Master Fielding, and took orders. Arvard had gone, and I had killed, and Rendies had entered a solid, sealed room, but the people of Tyntagel Keep saw only that Evaric was dreaming again and never would amount to anything. I left early.

I walked home slowly, berating myself for allowing Arvard to depart. Arvard had supported me through years of harassment and Rendie madness. I had abandoned him the first time he asked for my help.

Someone had again knocked the loose rail from the fence, and I replaced it, absently recalling that my mother had asked me to repair it more permanently. I glanced at the ground near me, searching for a suitable wedge to keep the rail in place. I knelt and dug my fingers into the soil, bringing up nothing but recollection of the last digging I had done. "Why trouble to use yadovitii against someone as unprotected as Arvard?" It rankled me that I had no palatable answer. There was no sense in attempting a yadovitii kill, unless the assassin had good reason to maintain distance from the victim. Someone considered Arvard a dangerous target.

Arvard might win every festival contest in Tyntagel, but he could not present a threat to a K'shai. Someone thought otherwise. Someone believed Arvard's fantastic theory. Someone believed that Arvard was the son of a dead Infortiare.

I entered the house diffidently, preparing myself for confrontation and more lies about Arvard's errand. I strode directly to the kitchen, peered into the laundry room, and frowned because my mother was not at her usual tasks. I went to my father's study and found it empty as well. It was early yet for Ylsa to be home from the Keep, but I checked her room mechanically. Save for myself, the house was empty.

I had no reason to expect to find my father or sister at home. My mother could be in the town on one of the ladies' errands. Too many explanations contended, and none of them deserved disquiet. It was only the shadow of last night's dream, I thought uneasily, and the troublesome uncertainties about yesterday. I curled my fingers restlessly, wishing for one of Conierighm's swords.

"You do not need a weapon, Master Evaric."

I wheeled at the voice, furious with myself for not having heard the speaker approach. Recalling Conierighm's lessons with deliberation, I gathered my energies into the center of myself, relaxing and subtly readying muscles for attack.

"Master Conierighm has trained you well." The speaker smiled slightly. He was a thin man of indeterminate age. The sharp-featured face was pale; the hands were empty, and no blade hung at his side. I stared and wondered, speculatively appraising the potential hazard.

"You were not sent by Master Conierighm."

"No, indeed." The man paused. "You do not know who I am?" he asked slowly.

I felt oddly suspicious that the question contained a test: not Conierighm's test; not the test of a K'shai. It was another kind of test, a darker one. "I do not know you, nor do I know why I find you alone in my parents' house." I filled my voice with the sort of bellicose indignation that Miff had often favored. The man's cheek tightened infinitesimally. I felt my own tension ease, knowing that I had failed the man's examination.

The man became direct. "My name is Ragon. Your mother sent for me. I gather that she did not tell you."

"Where is she?" I demanded.

"Elsewhere. I prefer to meet candidates alone."

"Candidates for what?" I asked with heavy irony, refusing to accept the truth I sensed but did not understand. "Or is that something else which I am supposed already to know?"

"It is all a part of the same." Ragon's scrutiny became puzzled. "I must admit that you present me with a novel—and rather awkward—situation. It might be best to await your parents' return. Still . . ." Ragon appeared intense but increasingly dubious. "You have truly no idea of my identity."

The Rendie dreams had always been worst before the Ixaxins came. "I suggest that you consider your plottings more carefully if you intend to make a habit of this sort of unexplained intrusion. I have another engagement." I needed to escape before the Rendie madness overtook my careful control. I did not trust my marginal sanity in the presence of an Ixaxin, especially after yesterday's events.

I could not depart. I frowned, feeling more irritated than angry. I could not direct my limbs to carry me.

"It saves trouble," commented Ragon evenly, "which your ignorance might bring upon both of us." Ragon seated himself in the chair which was customarily my father's. "As you must finally have begun to realize, I am a wizard. Currently, I am assigned to escort recruits to Ixaxis. I generally take groups of five or six, but I made a special journey for you." Ragon's voice held a trace of disapproval. "You apparently earned attention from someone of importance."

Lords, I thought, he has confused me with Arvard. It was not my own madness that the Ixaxins pursued but Arvard's. "I am not a wizard, Master Ragon."

"Obviously, you are not a wizard. You are untrained. Therefore, you are at best a sorcerer. Evidently, you are also a latent. Surprising," mused Ragon. "The Scholars do not generally exert such effort to recruit latents."

"I have no Power, latent or otherwise."

"You are the son of Evram and Terrell, liege-bound to Lord Baerod dur Tyntagel?" It was not voiced as a serious question, and I did not answer it. "Your mother has sworn that you show Power. Do you say that she perjured herself?"

It was my mother who answered, arriving at the door and meeting my incredulous glance with defiant implacability. "You have arrived much earlier than I expected, wizard. I have had no opportunity to discuss this matter with my son."

"I hope, Mistress Terrell, that you have not brought me here without just cause," warned Ragon. "The Infortiare does not treat deception lightly." Ragon stood, a solemn, menacing symbol of a guild more deadly than the K'shai. He said curtly, as he left, "Discuss quickly, Mistress Terrell. Your son and I have a journey before us, and I should prefer to leave before night." The door closed softly.

I breathed slowly, wondering why I alone seemed unable to accept Arvard as a sorcerer. "What have you done?"

"What was necessary," answered my mother tersely. She was unsteady; the wizard's appearance had obviously frightened her.

"Necessary for whom? For Arvard? Did he tell you that he had Power?" If Ixaxis believed, then the Venkarel's enemies would be certain; Arvard would be the target of more than one K'shai attack. Arvard would need more Protection than he could afford, and he would be unprepared and overly confident. "You sent Ixaxis a letter of lies."

"Forget about Arvard for once."

I would not listen; I did not want to hear what she was telling me. "Forget? Arvard is my brother, and I intend to Protect him against Ixaxis, against you, against whatever enemies he may accrue." I grew harsh. "Arvard may have gone to Ixaxis already, but I want any talk about his specious Power ended here. Such talk has already made him a target of attack. I shall tell the wizard that a mistake was made. He believes that I am the sorcerer; I shall tell him that I deceived you, never expecting my joke to carry so far. I shall tell him anything to be rid of him, but I shall not let Arvard's delusion return with Master Ragon to Ixaxis. You see, Mother, Arvard asked for my help, and I shall give it to him, albeit belatedly."

"You will not hold to your intentions," said my mother sternly. "Your father will not allow it."

I laughed. Because, of course, I did not yet realize that the father of whom she spoke was not Evram of Tyntagel Keep.

* * *

Strange, thought Ragon, the candidate shows no sign of Power. Yet, the orders came quite clearly; Master Amardi even intimated that the Infortiare herself had confirmed the candidacy. There is something odd about that young man, but I should not have considered him a likely Ixaxin.

Ragon stared thoughtfully at the cloudy sky and the massed green of Tyntagel's ever-present oaks. Ragon belonged still to the student class himself, though he had devoted many years to Ixaxin studies. He no longer expected to win a Scholar's white robes; his Power sufficed only for the level he had reached. Unlike many others of his ilk, Ragon had not left Ixaxis upon realizing that he could advance no further in the ranks of the Wizards' Guild. Ixaxis was home. Ixaxis was the only home for Ragon, for Ragon had been born in Ven.

He had come from a wealthy family, though they had no claim to noble kinship. Ragon had visited them once yearly during the first fifteen years of his Ixaxin education, an extravagance of time and travel in which few of his fellow students indulged. Ragon's mother had been enormously proud when he gained senior status, though wizardry had not been popular among her circle. Ragon's father had smiled and nodded, as if no doubt could have ever existed that Ragon would pass the senior level examination.

Ragon missed them: his parents, his sisters, his cousins, uncles and aunts. He wondered why thought of them had suddenly come to him so keenly. The greatest part of his sorrow had surely faded with the passing years, and he seldom thought of it now. Tyntagel affected him badly; even the trees brood here, he thought. He recited a silent litany of control to still his disquiet.

He turned to find the candidate, Evaric, approaching him. The mother stood clearly visible at the window, but she did not follow her son. "Master Ragon," said the young man distinctly. Why is his voice familiar? wondered the wizard. "Unless you intend to take residence here, I suggest that you return to your Guild and inform them that I am not what they seek."

The youth is too confident, thought Ragon; Ixaxis will teach him humility at least. Ragon contemplated holding the candidate again by Power, but the feeling crossed him that another demonstration of strength would only antagonize the candidate further. As Evaric started down the road toward the village, Ragon fell into place beside him.

The candidate seemed unconcerned. "This is not the route to Ixaxis," he remarked. Ragon merely smiled.

* * *

The wizard would not leave me. I was doubly dismayed by the unwelcome company and the concern that someone might mention Arvard in the wizard's hearing. I deliberately led Ragon to a disreputable tavern, where a member of the Keep staff would not likely be acknowledged.

I drank little, but I forced myself to linger over the tavern's bitter ale. My pose of a brashly indifferent youth, annoyed by an old man's company, demanded effort and concentration. The unpleasant ale helped my focus, as did a mildly vindictive enjoyment of the wizard's evident distaste for his environs. The wizard did not speak, and I did not encourage him. My mind was busy with schemes; Arvard would be proud, I thought wryly.

*   *   *

Observing the oddly unresponsive candidate, Ragon felt strangely apprehensive. There was something icily inhuman, Ragon decided, about the unconcerned way this young man courted the danger of a wizard's anger. The candidate seemed too intelligent for bravado. Something troubled was stirring in the young man's silver-gray eyes, and Ragon doubted it was merely superstitious fear of a wizard's mild disfavor.

*   *   *

Conierighm's cottage masqueraded as a peaceful, stone-walled haven from the encroaching night. Warm light spilled from the window, not yet shuttered against darkness. The gardener had trimmed the hedges into well-ordered boxes; no stray limbs cast those inexplicably active shadows.

The pair of us who silently approached the house did not suffer from the delusion of peace. I knew better what to expect from the visit, but Ragon held the imperturbability of trained Power. I rapped sharply upon the moss-green door.

Conierighm pursed his lips in a vain attempt to conceal his satisfaction at seeing me on his doorstep. I entered without invitation, and Conierighm closed the door without remarking that I seemed to cast dual shadows. Conierighm placed a sword in my hand and motioned me to enter the salon alone.

The salon was stark, for Conierighm had stripped it of its plaster moldings and flowered rugs, and he had painted even the plank floor with untempered white. He had left intact only the iron candelabrum suspended from the far wall. The K'shai stood before it, his face shadowed, his back protected, his sword lightly held but readied. He was a professional.

The sword rose to meet mine in salute. We both began to move in a careful arc, neither presenting to the other more access than required. Our swords met first with slow, deliberate grace. They met again and rang clearly, for they were true, hammered steel, and they were deadly. I moved to meet the K'shai's swift lunge. I parried and attacked. The K'shai circled and feinted. I countered.

We proceeded carefully through the first form. It was a practiced pattern and a relatively simple one, but absolute precision of execution was mandatory for acceptance. The next form followed; the motions grew more complex. With the sixth form, the steps began to quicken into a flickering of motion. The tenth form incorporated the element of unexpectedness. The subtleties and surprises of the twelfth form generally killed those candidates who lacked such concentration as could defeat a Rendie. Only twelve forms were required for acceptance. We completed fifteen; no higher form was taught to one who was not K'shai.

A final ringing of swords: I began to feel again. "You are not unworthy," commented the K'shai, and he waited for me to speak the ritual plea. I could feel Conierighm's triumph—and his envy. He fancied himself superior to a K'shai in skills of arms: he would never admit that he feared the night.

I feared more than Conierighm ever would comprehend, but my fears were no worse beneath the stars than behind my bedroom walls. If I became K'shai, I would confound the wizard who trailed me. I could Protect Arvard, as I deemed necessary, even against Ixaxis. Perhaps I would be freed of dreams. I need not be assassin, I assured myself; I could not be assassin.

"My worth cannot yet be measured," I said, cursing my own weak words.

"I hear," the K'shai answered evenly. "Seek us before the year passes, and we shall hear you again."

The K'shai's expression became guarded. His sword aimed at a dark, detached shadow. "Face us, wizard," ordered the K'shai, and his voice coarsened, reft of stiff formulas. "You have no place here."

Conierighm entered the room slowly, cautiously inspect-

ing the corner toward which the K'shai addressed himself.
Ragon did not stand among us, and then his gray figure
became clearly present. "I do not often meet K'shai," remarked Ragon mildly.

"We are not fond of wizards."

"You have offered your Choice to one who is promised to
us."

The K'shai's attention broadened to encompass me. "Is
this a true claim? Are you a sorcerer?"

Conierighm and I replied in unison, "No."

"Yes!" asserted Ragon, though he looked doubtful. "His
sword burns more brightly than yours, K'shai." Ragon seemed
bewildered by his own words. "It is an extension of his
Power."

The sword I held began to glow dimly. It brightened, blue
fire coiling vividly along its length. The nimbus appeared to
radiate from my fingers. I raised the hand so as to better
observe the illusion. The sword-light streamed from my
blade, flickering in a sardonic mockery of the fifteenth form
of the K'shai.

The fire began to touch the room. Across the walls, the
twining tracery began to etch fiery runnels. Both Conierighm
and the K'shai began to beat at the sparks, which appeared
to relish the conflict: an army of malicious imps with a
potent sting.

"You are a madman," said the K'shai to Ragon fiercely.
"What do you hope to prove by your tricks?"

"This is not my Power," Ragon answered weakly, but
only I believed him. "Would I wear student gray if I could
control something like this?" The wizard shouted at me,
"Sheathe the sword before you destroy us!"

I lowered my arm and concealed the blade to its hilt. The
fire faded. The room cooled, as if a winter's draft had
suddenly chilled it.

The K'shai spoke into the silence. "To what weapons
have you trained your apprentice, Conierighm?"

I pushed past Conierighm. The swordmaster grabbed my
arm and walked with me, whispering sharp words which I
did not hear. I jerked away from Conierighm's clutching
questions. Though it was fully night, I drew the bolt from
the heavy door and flung myself from the house. I threw
Conierighm's sword beneath the manicured shrubs.

                    *   *   *

The K'shai and the wizard faced each other in the empty white room. "Do you realize how much Power it takes to control fire in that manner?" whispered Ragon. "Not just to start it—any novice can do that—but to mold it, color it, pattern it, investing every spark with apparently independent will? Only once before have I seen anything like this done, save by Rendies, and that was an act of him who became Infortiare."

"Venkarel?" demanded the K'shai gruffly.

Ragon assented. "I was a student with him. He rarely used his Power openly in those days, but I saw him angered once."

"I saw him defeat Lord Hrgh dur Liin at the Challenge," commented the K'shai, as if he understood Ragon's allusion fully. If he witnessed the Challenge, thought Ragon, he probably does.

*   *   *

I followed the road away from the Keep and the Keep enclave. Above me, darker branches bowed against the dark sky. Nothing else moved. Tyntagel had withdrawn for the night behind its stout shutters and strong barriers of wood and stone. I let my long strides turn into a loping run.

Something dimly visible drifted beside me, but I disregarded it. It floated before me, and I circled to avoid it. It coalesced into a thing of weaving limbs and amorphous tendrils. "Come with me, Fire-child," it begged.

"Damn you!" I cried at it.

Another joined the first wraith, adding its mellifluous singing to the other's plea. "Son of the Taormin," whispered a third into my ear. I brushed it away angrily: a useless gesture against a thing of no substance.

"Come with us, Fire-child."

"You belong with us, Fire-child. You are the son of the Taormin, and one world cannot contain you."

"I am the son of Evram and Terrell!"

"You are the son of the Taormin. Come with us. You will have greatness among us, for we can teach you the way of your gift."

"I want nothing among you or from you. I want none of your tricks to help me. You tainted my sword with your spells, you damnable creatures of hell."

"You belong with us, Fire-child."

"Come with us, and we shall have all worlds and all energies. You are the Taormin's son. Come with us, and understand. Feed with us, and be strong."

"Come with us. Come with us."

"Away from me!" I roared. The wraiths shrieked and winked from sight. They were not usually so accommodating.

"Nuisances, nothing but nuisances." I wheeled to face the latest speaker. I saw a man with a sword, assorted knives, and leather armor. The man raised his fist in a haphazard greeting; the back of his hand had been branded with the bloodied-sword emblem of the K'shai. "Rendies bother you often?"

"Only at night," I responded flatly.

The K'shai croaked a chuckle. "The problem is you listen to them. Never listen to a Rendie. Never look at them. Never acknowledge them."

"Only fight them?"

"Only follow the patterns. If you follow the patterns, the Rendies do not exist."

"Who are you?"

The man considered. "Call me Fog."

"You are K'shai."

"I am your instructor."

"As what?"

"K'shai." Fog squinted at me through the darkness. "You are the one who wanted to be K'shai?"

K'shai did not read minds; that was a wizard's trick. One K'shai tested and offered. Another claimed. Was that their method? I had already declined to give answer once.

"The assassination attempt was not directed at your foster brother."

"How did you know of the attack?" I snapped. Fool, I told myself, he knew because he was K'shai.

"I never use yadovitii myself—too unpredictable." Fog's voice thickened, but it became sharp again. "But Stone always was lazy about research. He did not expect you to recognize the yadovitii. A K'shai should never underestimate a target, especially when the target has been labeled dangerous. The attack was aimed at you, of course."

"At me?"

"A man of Tyntagel, a Master Jorame, was sent to Tulea to learn something about your foster brother. Master Jorame tried to market the knowledge he acquired to Lord Gorng dur Liin.''

"Jorame is dead." Fog's smile was chill and informative. "What kind of knowledge?"

"That the Venkarel had a son, who lived in Tyntagel as the son of Evram and Terrell."

Arvard actually was Lord Venkarel's son. It was impossible. It did not matter. "Jorame did not specify which son?"

"There was some confusion," agreed Fog. "You are the target."

"If I believe you . . ."

"You do."

Yes, I believed him, though I had no sound reason to do so. "If I believe you," I repeated carefully, "then I cannot accept your offer of training. A target cannot become K'shai."

"If a target eliminates the assassin, then he is no longer a target. You did eliminate him?"

Did I? "I intended to Protect my brother."

"You will not help anyone by remaining here, performing menial chores for Lord Baerod's clerical staff. We should leave before dawn."

He gave me no true choice; he had maneuvered me too effectively to the brink of madness, that I might know the threat and resist it. I repeated my internal debate on the subject of K'shai, but I could have saved myself the effort. Either I accompanied Fog, or I acquiesced to the Rendies' way. "I must deliver a message."

"Delays can be costly."

"It will not take long."

Fog nodded. He matched my pace easily. "Fire," he said: slowly, as if tasting the word.

"What?"

"Fire: it is a good name. It will be your K'shai name."

I accorded him a sharp look of sudden suspicion. "I thought you said never to listen to Rendies."

"Rendies?" he asked, his scarred face becoming innocent and stupid. "What have Rendies to do with your name?"

"Nothing," I replied gruffly. "I think I might prefer another name."

"No. You get no choice of name. You need never use it." Fog shook his head. "It is a good name, though. I knew a K'shai named Spit. He had cause to hate the name. Always used it. Most do. Pride. It is not easy to earn your name." I stopped before my parents' home. "Nice," commented Fog.

"I shall need only a few minutes."

Fog sat against the fence, which creaked reluctantly at the weight. "Bring a better coat, if you have one. Too bad you threw away the sword. We shall have to find you another."

I exhaled through clenched teeth, but I only muttered, "Right," and entered my home for the last time.

I studied my sister's sleeping face by the light of the single candle I carried. Her face had been with me always: square, a little sad, only rarely pretty. I lifted a stray brown tendril from her forehead and laid it gently in place.

Ylsa stirred and gasped when she realized she was not alone. "What do you want?" she asked me roughly. She drew away from me and set her jaw in mulish distrust.

I smiled tightly. "I want two favors."

"In the middle of the night?"

"First, I want you to tell our parents that I have left. I am K'shai."

"K'shai!" I had shocked Ylsa into a moment of concern, but she recovered quickly. She did not yet believe me.

"Tell them yourself," she growled sleepily. "Father is likely still at work downstairs. He never sleeps much anymore."

"I know. But he might try to delay me."

"Write him a note."

"I prefer that you tell him."

"Why?"

Because a note was too impersonal, and I could not face the crushing disappointment and horror in my parents' eyes. "Because it fulfills the proper order of things," I said evenly. "You will rejoice to see me gone. I am offering you a chance to participate in gaining your wish."

Ylsa narrowed her eyes, probably suspecting some jest of Arvard's planning played at her expense. "What is the second favor?"

"I want you to memorize a message for Arvard. If he returns, you will repeat it to him—only to him—exactly as I tell it to you. You have always had a knack for reciting."

"If he returns?"

"He may not."

Ylsa twisted her dark braid contemplatively, then she

raised her head sharply. "You really mean to leave? Without waiting to see Arvard yourself?"

"Yes."

Ylsa stared at me. Arvard and I had always been too close, excluding Ylsa and making her bitter against us, but she was my sister. Worry had snagged her. "You cannot leave in the middle of the night anyway. Why not go to sleep now? We can talk about this in the morning."

"I am K'shai, Ylsa." I am not sure why I wanted Ylsa to believe; perhaps I still resented old taunts. I forced Ylsa to see me as K'shai; Conierighm had taught me the tricks of attitude, and I had a few less tangible resources as well.

"Tell me the message," said Ylsa slowly, and I knew that I had made her fear me, whose weakness she had always despised.

"That which we buried between us came for me. The sender will leave with me. A wizard named Ragon is similarly misinformed about the son of Evram and Terrell, but you must make your own decision about him and his kind. Be cautious, Arvard. Be well."

Chapter 5

Like the namesake of my self-proclaimed K'shai instructor, I faded from Tyntagel and into a K'shai's world of chill Rendies and remorseless death. As I would tell Lyriel years later, none of my K'shai indoctrination seemed to constitute reality. I walked too close to the core of a vast design, and proximity made me blind.

*   *   *

The dawn in Tyntagel came cold and damp. Conierighm sat alone in bitter, resentful despair; he had not slept, for he had failed again to fulfill a pledge to the K'shai, and no one escaped K'shai revenge. Evram sat alone in his study, reproaching himself for failure. Ylsa stood at her window, feeling guilty for her sense of freedom and of gladness; she wondered if it were too late for her to become a person, released at last from the shadows of her exceptional brothers.

Terrell kissed the worn jacket that Evaric had laid across a kitchen chair. She carried it to the attic room that Evaric had shared with Arvard. She closed the door, gently touching the gouged wall. She had never cured either boy of opening that door too energetically.

The wizard, Ragon, walked the empty roads of the early morning at a somber pace. He passed the Tyntagel outer wall by the main gate; the guards nodded curtly at his letter of passage. Less than a mile from the gate, a man broke fast beside the road.

"The journey to Ixaxis must be long and lonely," remarked the man. He was the K'shai who had tested Evaric's sword.

"You travel alone," returned Ragon.

"I am K'shai." The man raised his branded fist, then

137

lowered his open hand. "I had a partner, but he died recently."

"I am a wizard," answered Ragon, "and accustomed to solitude." Ragon glanced at the K'shai, who shrugged indifferently. "But your company is welcome. Not," added Ragon, "on a paid basis, of course. A poor wizard can scarcely afford the services of a K'shai."

"I am called Summer," volunteered the K'shai gruffly.

"Ragon. Why Summer?"

"We do not explain."

"Sorry."

"You did not help the boy?" asked Summer after a moment.

"I did nothing," answered Ragon, willingly sharing his uneasiness.

"Was it the boy himself?"

"Someone thinks he has Power. Important people want him in Ixaxis."

"He cannot be K'shai then."

"He has refused to be Ixaxin."

They sat for some minutes in a mutually acceptable silence. "I wonder where he went," mused Summer.

"I cannot sense a trace of him."

"He is a dangerous swordsman."

"He may be dangerous in other ways as well."

"He could have become a superior K'shai."

I wonder, thought Ragon glumly, if Ixaxis will as easily accept the loss of its candidate.

Chapter 6

Fourth Month, Year 22 of Rending
Benthen Abbey, Serii

Rhianna entered the aged gate of Benthen Abbey and grew wistful at the sight of the orderly gardens in which she once had worked. The silent figures in brown robes and heavy cowls could have been the same as those she remembered. The gardens had not changed. The seedlings of spring emerged shyly from the soil, and Rhianna longed to go and whisper encouragement to them. She chastised a rabbit for coveting the new growth. The rabbit fled in terror; Rhianna had not meant to frighten him so deeply.

Twenty years had wrought too much of a transformation. Rhianna had become Infortiare, and those whom she had briefly known as fond friends perceived her now as the symbol of a discordant order. Rhianna had altered inwardly, while they had aged in body. She had joined a species apart. She had become Kaedric.

Rhianna curtailed a familiar cycle of painful memory, but her contentment had escaped her. Power disrupted peace. Benthen Abbey could not welcome a wizardess. Only for Medwyn had they admitted her. Abbot Medwyn was dying.

He was so frail! All the strength of life within her could not help him. His hair had lost all color. His cheeks were sunken, and his eyes were shadowed. He smiled when he saw Rhianna, and she smiled in return, but bright tears clouded her sight.

"How lovely you look, Rhianna," he told her, for the vows of silence did not bind the abbot.

"I am travel-worn and tousled."

"You did not journey all the way from Tulea just to see a feeble-witted old man?"

"Feeble-witted? I wish that certain Lords of Serii had wits as stout as yours."

"That could be a twisted compliment."

"You are quite right, dear Medwyn. Too many members of our nobility have no wits at all. Yours, however, are as sturdy as the stone of these walls."

"Unlike the rest of me."

"You abuse yourself with overwork," Rhianna accused him sternly, though she knew that he had been completely invalided for over two months.

"I do hate being coddled."

"It is justice, Medwyn, for all of the unpalatable cures you have inflicted on others."

His eyes twinkled almost as of old. "Did you come here to insult my cures?"

"Never. They are too successful. I simply wanted to see you. We have had so little time to visit in recent years."

"Your duties have kept you busy, Rhianna."

"Even the Infortiare deserves an occasional holiday with old friends."

Medwyn grew suddenly solemn, and the awful gray of his face seemed the more pernicious. "Old friends," he mused. "I have had the oddest notion, Rhianna," he said slowly, but his eyes held a trace of their old bright perception. "I have thought several times that Kaedric was here—not as memory or even spirit of the dead—but as a living man. I have felt that terrible force of him as keenly as the day he stood beside me in the rubble of Ven, and I have heard him speak." The weakness of Medwyn's smile bit deeply into Rhianna's heart. "Do I sound feeble-witted now?" he asked lightly, despite the effort speech cost him.

Rhianna shook her head jerkily, before she could bring herself to answer. "Never you, dear Medwyn. You always see more clearly than those of us who think in suspicious circles." She touched his hand gently, feeling the veins pulse erratically.

"Then tell me the truth now, Rhianna." Medwyn's hand returned her grip weakly.

I might conquer kings or change a world, thought Rhianna desperately, but I cannot keep a good and gentle man from the gate of death. "Kaedric lives," she said simply, though she was not certain that she spoke truthfully.

Some tautness left Medwyn's wrinkled face, and his hand relaxed. "I felt it rightly then."

Rhianna finished quietly, "His son lives, also."

Medwyn's eyes sought hers. He murmured, "No, that had not occurred to me. I had not thought you would lie to me about that."

"I never wished to lie to you," insisted Rhianna emphatically, but her fierceness faded quickly. "Not to you. Not to anyone. He is my son also, whom I held only for the briefest of days. I sometimes forget that he is mine as well as Kaedric's, because it is as Kaedric's son that he is both endangered and dangerous."

"You are hardly insignificant in your own right, Rhianna."

"I am only Kaedric's echo, Medwyn." Guiltily, she set aside the haze of her private tauntings. "Well enough, you have the truth now: all my awful secrets."

"I could wish you had confessed it earlier. I am asea with questions, and I can barely whisper a one of them." He spoke through a wheeze of labored breath. He shifted as if to rise.

Rhianna's concern sharpened, and she stilled him. "You ought to be sleeping. I shall be here in the morning, and questions kept so long will keep a little longer."

"Rhianna, dear child, I may not wake again."

"It has been many years since anyone called me 'child,' " she told him with a laugh, but she considered him soberly. She knew that he indeed would sleep but once more.

"Tell me, Rhianna, for yourself if not for me."

"My child has been raised as the son of other, safer parents. He knows nothing of me or of his father, and the ignorance has allowed him a childhood I could never have provided him." Rhianna tried to soften Medwyn's disquiet, but Power had no place in Benthen Abbey, and she had forgotten any other way.

"There is more to tell."

"He has shown no trace of Power."

"Is it possible that he has none?"

"Even a latent generally displays some trace by this age, and he has been tested thoroughly." She did not consider her response a falsehood; her own misgivings were built not of fact but of speculation and Kaedric's misleading truths.

"It is time you reclaimed him, Rhianna."

"I am rather a lot to inflict upon anyone without warning." And I fear him and what he will think of me.

Medwyn barely managed to smile. "The child of such parents should be strong enough for the shock." He hesitated. "What of Kaedric?"

"I have lost him. He chose me once, but he never learned to trust."

"Did you, Rhianna?"

She did not answer, and then there was no need. Medwyn died so gently. Between one breath and the next, his deeply good spirit escaped her. "Dear Medwyn," she whispered. She kissed his parchment cheek. She no longer had reason to hide her tears, but they could only well within her. She had hidden so much for so long.

Chapter 7

Tyntagel

How absurd it all seemed in retrospect, thought Rhianna
sadly. Could I have ever been so innocent? What an overly
educated idiot I was, and what a blindly obstinate fool was
my liege-father, sanctimoniously playing censor to the laws
of King and Ceallagh! Yet, if her father's coldness had not
pressed her into rebellion, she might never have known
Kaedric. Horlach would have claimed his prey. Or Kaedric
would have won and lost humanity. In either outcome, a
Sorcerer King would now command Serii.

Instead, Serii had acquired an incipient Sorcerer Queen
pining for her ghostly liege and consort. She struggled harder
daily to remember that greater Power did not convey greater
wisdom. I am Rhianna still, she reminded herself, though I
can mold minds and destinies according to my whim. I am
no more fit to rule a world than was that silly girl who
sought seclusion in the Dwaelin Wood.

She had even sundered Evram from his Terrell, never
knowing it until her return to Tyntagel after so many years
and so much change. In the twenty intervening years, she
had reached lightly to her oaks; she had dared risk no
nearer observation of her son than the dim sense garnered
by the stolid trees. She did not forget that time moved more
rapidly for mortal humans, but she did allow the remembrance to slip behind her fear of dislodging the precarious
serenity of her son's existence. At her return after so long
an absence, fear of her son supplanted even her fear for
him.

The Keep had not changed greatly, but the village had
spread a bit, and the familiar faces with which her memory
still peopled it had gone. Rhianna did not know this place or
these people. Which of these Tyntagel strangers would re-

call the face of their liege-lord's youngest daughter, whom
they all had shunned as a suspected sorceress? It had always
been easy to tell their eyes not to see, their ears not to hear,
their minds not to know. It had ever been easy to walk
unobserved in Tyntagel.

Rhianna knew the cottage where her son had been reared.
It had belonged to Evram's family, most of whom save
Evram and a brother in Hamley had died of a fever years
before. The cottage looked quite as pristine as Rhianna
recalled it, but it sagged a bit more along the eaves. She
recognized with a start the small woman hanging laundry in
the yard. This was Terrell, the woman whom her son knew
as mother. Terrell looked old to Rhianna, but then Queen
Joli had been a child when last Rhianna saw Mistress Terrell.

Terrell had only looked up at her for an instant, and
Terrell's politely expectant expression became icy. "My lady,"
she acknowledged stiffly. "It has been a long time since you
deigned to visit us."

"Too long, I know." She daunted Rhianna, this woman
who had raised her son.

"You are not what I expected," said Terrell shortly. She
sounded disappointed.

"What did you expect?" Rhianna asked.

Terrell shrugged. "You are not that impressive in person.
I anticipated more of the Infortiare."

"You knew my appearance."

"Of course. You do not change." Terrell made the accusation a plural, despising all of wizardry.

"Not externally."

"Inside? I would not know of that. I only know you as a
woman who cares little for her only son."

"Then you know nothing," retorted Rhianna sharply. "I
am sorry," she apologized after a pause.

"You need not be. I have long wanted to meet you again.
How old were you when we last met in flesh?"

"Twenty-three."

"So, we are the same age. Who would know it to see us?
I certainly cannot say that my rival had no cause for victory."

"We have never been rivals."

"I raised your child. My husband loves you." Terrell
smirked in self-deprecating fashion. "I know that you never
encouraged his love. You did not need his love, only his
devotion. Why are you here?"

"I came to see my son."

Terrell's expression tightened. "You come too late. He is gone. The wizard did not tell you?"

"What wizard?" demanded Rhianna, feeling unwanted currents snatch at her.

"Master Ragon: the man your Ixaxins sent for Evaric."

"I never told them of your letter," said Rhianna hollowly. "I gave no order to Ixaxis in Evaric's regard."

"Then you are even less omnipotent than I believed. Your own Guild has secrets from you."

Kaedric, thought Rhianna with a pang, are you manipulating me still? Terrell's words explained so much: why Rhianna had been unable to sense her son since autumn; why Master Ertivel had become so preoccupied of late with the accuracy of testing latents. Terrell's explanations explained nothing. "Evaric accompanied Master Ragon?"

"Evaric went with the K'shai. That is all I know of it." Terrell turned her back to the Infortiare, but she glared over her shoulder to add, "Evram knows nothing more of Evaric than I have told you, but I do not doubt he would be elated to see you."

Rhianna heard nothing beyond the word of abomination: K'shai. "Evaric has become a K'shai assassin?" she whispered, believing only because Terrell's despondency proclaimed the truth with vehemence.

Terrell paused at the gleaming door of her home, a small house which looked warm and innocent; the house hid its secrets well. "Arvard might know more," admitted Terrell stiffly, conceding the information.

"The other boy whom you fostered?"

"Evaric's brother," said Terrell sternly, and Rhianna knew herself chastised. "How can you know so little of us?"

"Where may I find Arvard?"

"He has also gone. I do not know where. But you are the omnipotent one."

Terrell made Rhianna feel insignificant, as she had always felt in her father's wizard-hating domain. "Do not mock me, Mistress Terrell," said Rhianna coldly. The two women stared at one another: a tired once-governess and a woman who could raze cities with a wisp of thought. Terrell's gaze held steadiest.

*   *   *

"Venkarel lied to you, Rhianna."

Rhianna whirled to seek the source of the velvet voice, but only Terrell's distant figure stood behind her. Rhianna willed herself to calm. She searched for patterns of Power and found no trace of any near her but her own. She resumed her course, her expression set in cold anger.

"Venkarel has stolen your son from you." Rhianna did not pause nor acknowledge the voice. *"Venkarel persuaded you to forsake your child, so that Venkarel could mold the boy as tool. Venkarel used you, for he needed the child that only a wizardess of major Power could provide for him. It was Venkarel who manipulated Terrell; you sensed it in her, as in her letter. You know that I speak truly; you recognize his twisted, ruthless way. Venkarel has used you and discarded you. He will use and discard your son. Protect your son, Rhianna. Retrieve and protect your son."*

Rhianna stopped, pressed her hands to her ears, and shouted in her Power, *"Stop!"* The sourceless voice fell silent, but the echo of it would not fade.

Chapter 8

First Month, Year 23 of Rending
Ixaxis and Tulea

Arvard cursed the retreating ferry beneath his frosted breath. The sea was as gray as the sky, and the two figures on the ferry faded into the general gloom. Even the island appeared dim on that day, and it had never seemed so distant to Arvard.

He had reduced all of his goals to the single determination of attaining Ixaxis. It had not been easy, working his way across the domains, paying for his passage from village to village by hard labor. He still had his small, secret hoard of silver bound close to his skin, but he did not want to spend that fund until all other options had been exhausted. As perhaps was now the case. But he had no more goals toward which to apply either money or effort. He had reached Ixaxis, and Ixaxis had refused him.

Arvard felt quite as much numb shock as hot anger. Despite all the failed Ixaxin tests, he had been so sure that the Ixaxin scholars—not the lesser wizards who traveled to the domains—would recognize him for what he was. When his feet first touched the chalky Ixaxin shore, he had known triumph. A wizard had led him by long stairs up the cliffs. Three other candidates, who had traveled with Arvard on the ferry, were taken by other wizards in other directions.

Arvard had gazed at Ixaxis' white stone buildings with proprietary pride. Gray-robed students had observed him, and he had known himself to be the greatest among them. Arvard's quiet escort had taken him to a simple office filled with ordinary furnishings and extraordinary history. The wizard had indicated one of the room's several chairs, and Arvard had accepted the position with gracious delight.

"Master Arvard," acknowledged a man who wore robes as white as his hair. Arvard had not heard the wizard enter, nor had he seen where the first wizard had gone. Arvard nodded; this silent coming and going was an effective means of conveying superiority. Arvard wondered how many of the carved panels concealed doors; Tyntagel Keep held similar secrets, or so Arvard had always heard.

"I am Arvard. You have read my letter."

The wizard pursed wrinkled lips. "You stated that your parents both were wizards, but you failed to name them."

Arvard spread both of his broad hands apologetically. "It would be indelicate of me to supply such names. Unfortunately, my parents were not wed. I would not make mention of them at all if they were not pertinent to my immediate situation."

"Indeed." The elderly scholar folded his hands and assumed a dignified stance directly before Arvard. Though the wizard, old as he must be to show his age so clearly, was obviously the physical inferior of the young man in the chair, the Ixaxin managed still to convey his own strength.

The mystique of Ixaxis, thought Arvard admiringly, is more than Ixaxin Power. I must cultivate that attitude of invincibility. "I have spent years studying such texts of wizardry as I could obtain," remarked Arvard, establishing a tone of equality with the wizard. Arvard did not mean to begin his Ixaxin career as a subordinate. "I look forward to exploring your library."

"You have no Power, Master Arvard."

Arvard's jaw tightened fractionally. "I explained in my letter to you. My Power was bound, but I have recently begun to feel it growing in me." Arvard had not told the Ixaxins about the Rendies, whose supplicating voices had vanished with the distance to Ixaxis. Let the Ixaxins wonder about the nature of his Power. He would summon Rendies for them when they were ready to understand.

"You have no Power. Master Laning will return you to the ferry." A young wizard emerged from somewhere indefinite and grasped Arvard's arm firmly.

"Please accompany me, Master Arvard."

"You have not even tested me!" said Arvard, abandoning his composure. An irresistible compulsion to depart enveloped him. These wizards dared to use Power against him. Arvard contemplated direly vengeful plots, but he was bitterly unable to resist the decision of Ixaxis. Arvard trailed the young wizard out of the fine, ancient building, back to the cliffs, the beach, and the ferry. The ferryman still waited, patient and unsurprised. There was no sign of the other candidates. The ferryman and the young wizard, who had begun to look bored, returned Arvard alone to the mainland.

Arvard's fingers found a piece of Ixaxin chalk in his coat pocket. The passage up the cliff had dislodged many such fragments. Arvard threw it to the earth and ground it into powder with the heel of his boot. He turned his back on the sight of Ixaxis and began the hike to the main road.

There were many carts and carriages on the road, which connected the walled city of the Queen to the main harbor of Tulea. Arvard had bypassed the main city in his haste to reach Ixaxis; he had worked at the docks for over two months, waiting for Ixaxis to grant him an appointment, and impatience had made the time a torment. His urgency was gone with his sense of purpose. He paid a kesne to ride on a wagon loaded with candles. The driver made some desultory attempts at conversation, but Arvard did not encourage the man.

The chandler journeyed only to the inner harbor region. Arvard changed transport twice more to reach the great marketplace of Tulea. From there he walked to the gated enclave of Serii's lower nobility. Guards watched closely to keep him from proceeding farther. Arvard did not stay long near the center of Seriin wealth and authority. A little distance gave a clearer view of the castle and the Infortiare's Tower, if he felt the need for a reminder of what was owed to him and denied him.

Arvard took an inexpensive room and accepted a badly paying job cleaning carriages. He had no resources in Tulea. Return to Tyntagel? There was nothing for him there either, except Evaric, who had disbelieved. Arvard had wanted to return in triumph of which Evaric would be proud.

How could Ixaxis deny him? Arvard studied his distorted reflection in the carriage's brass siding. The Ixaxins were wrong, or they had deliberately lied to him. Either way, the obstacle could be overcome. Anger had made him briefly forget the inevitability of his destiny.

Arvard's resilience began to reassert itself. "Jerk," he told himself sternly, "did you expect it to be easy? You must work for what you want in this world." He laughed at his reflection and began to polish the brass of the carriage with renewed vigor and a satisfied whistle. He would succeed. He would find a way of approaching the Infortiare directly. He could contact that greedy serving woman, Mistress Giena. Arvard would return to Evaric as a man with whom kings reckoned. Arvard did miss Evaric sorely.

"That is a fine rig," remarked a well-dressed man entering the carriage house. "Is it for hire?"

Arvard felt expansive. "Master Fraileen would be the one to see in that regard, but I think you will find that your needs can be accommodated. Would you care to inspect the carriage?"

The man nodded and approached. He began to clamber into the carriage. His foot slipped on the step. Arvard extended his arm to save the man from falling. The shock of a sharp puncture made Arvard recoil from the man's weight. The man's face blurred as it bent over Arvard, and there was darkness.

"Has he not roused yet? If you gave him an excessive dose, Sandhig, your family will mourn."

"He is rousing, my lord."

Lord Gorng dur Liin waved aside the medic and the guardsmen. Lord Gorng had already studied Arvard closely, steeling himself to seek a resemblance to the devil he remembered too well: the devil who had once been his brother's insignificant friend, who had brought death to Gorng's brother and father, who had destroyed Veiga's mind, and whom Gorng would never forget and never forgive for the endless evils inflicted on magnificent, maimed Liin. This yellow-haired young man's cheeks were too bland with flesh, the nose was too wide and the mouth was too full; the body was muscular but too broad. Arvard's eyes fluttered, and Gorng saw the dark hazel of their color; the Lord of Liin began to feel secure again. This was not the Venkarel reborn; this was only a young man, and the might of Liin had nothing to fear.

Gorng waved to the Caruillan sorceress for whose service he had paid extravagantly. "Test him, Limora," murmured Gorng. "Question him." Gorng would not repeat his siblings' mistake of underestimating the Venkarel; no hint of the Venkarel's taint could be dismissed without investigation and appropriate action.

The sorceress raised her arms dramatically. The fabric of her sleeves made a winglike web of russet shot with blue. The russet matched her hair, which flowed long. She drew her fingers softly along Arvard's face, but her touch left bruises in its wake. Arvard's body shuddered. The sorceress held his mind.

Questions, there were so many questions. Who are you? Why did you travel to Ixaxis? What do you know of a Tulean serving woman named Giena and a Tyntagellian messenger named Jorame? Did you always live in Tyntagel? Did your foster parents ever speak of the Infortiare?

"He does not know that the serving woman is dead, my lord. He does not know that Jorame killed her and sold her information to you. He believes that he is Lord Venkarel's son. He has no Power, but Power has touched him. The stain of it is deep and buried beneath confusion and misinformation. I shall injure him permanently if I probe to identify the source of the Power."

"Probe, Mistress Limora. His value lies only in the information he can supply."

"As you command, my lord." She spread her hands one atop the other and laid them both across Arvard's face. She pressed, and the skin of his face rippled from the force. She spoke distantly. "Infants. Two of them. One suckles at his mother's breast. The one who is apart reaches for warmth and touches the infant who is not his kin. All are parted, but Power does not forget."

Her voice became shrill. "Rendies are everywhere, stealing my soul. Nel, is that you? Run from them. Find the brightness, the warmth, the safety. Help me, please, Evaric, my little brother." The sorceress gathered her hands into the web of her robe. "That is the key, my lord: the brother, the other infant."

Gorng frowned. "Explain yourself."

"A bonding, built of the brother's latent Power, exists between them. The patterns of their lives are twisted together. This one," said Limora, pointing at Arvard, "belonged to the wet nurse, who was slain by Rending creatures." A faint furrow appeared on the sorceress' brow. "The other child evidently learned to transfer a large part of his own Power to his brother, as a means of concealing the Power from Ixaxis. Understandably, this one became confused. Until leaving Tyntagel, this one served as his brother's channel." Limora turned to the Lord of Liin. "The other is the Infortiare's son."

Gorng's muscles tightened; his breath seemed to become constricted. "So there was truth in the serving woman's story, albeit misdirected."

"Your investment has not been wasted," returned the sorceress without irony.

Gorng examined Arvard's strained, unconscious face. "Is he still usable?"

"Possibly, if I bind the broken pieces of his mind. He was stronger than I anticipated. Traces of Rendie madness gave him some immunity, as did his delusion of Power. Anyone who knew him, however, will soon recognize that he has been altered."

"Then he must not encounter anyone who knew him, until he can ensnare the devil's whelp and destroy him for me." Gorng pensively fingered the brocade of his vest. "Keep him unconscious for the moment. I must determine the proper influence to place upon him."

*　　*　　*

The little man asked irritably, "Where do you hide, Venkarel? What is your scheme?" Horlach pulled at a few strands of Power, searching but seeing nothing he did not know. "Concealment avails you nothing. In the end, you will need me. Only I know how to use him, as he must be used."

Chapter 9

Third Month, Year 28 of Rending
Infortiare's Tower, Tulea

"Kaedric, what have you wrought!" demanded Rhianna, and it was less a question than an accusation, for she knew that he twined his devious deceptions with relentless purpose. She ran from the Queen's chamber, startling even the Queen's expectations of her. Anger battled hope. After the years of ceaseless searching, Rhianna had ample cause for intense emotion, but she could not explain even to Queen Joli what she had so laboriously sought.

Rhianna sank into the chair which had been his. She whispered to the empty room, "My Kaedric, what have you done?" Seeking her son, she had found an instant of her husband's dreadful force. She had felt the terrible burning by which his Power destroyed. He had shrouded his Power immediately, and now there was again a cold void.

She needed Abbot Medwyn's counsel. She needed advice from the man who had tried to tame the boy, Kaedric, and who had tried to instill a soul in the man, Lord Venkarel. Rhianna missed Medwyn acutely.

She considered seeking Ineuil, but she did not want to see Yldana. Rhianna still envied her sister. She could perceive Yldana more clearly than of old and understood Yldana a little better, but the sisters had never learned to be friends. Rhianna envied her Ineuil, though Rhianna had refused him.

I could have loved Ineuil, thought Rhianna wanly, had I never met Kaedric. Knowing Kaedric, whose lesser weaknesses all were flayed from him in childhood, she could accept no gentler love. She loved Kaedric, as she could never love any other. When she hated him, the emotion seared her.

Rhianna rose and climbed the narrow stairs to the Tower's pinnacle. She seldom entered it anymore. It was the room she had shared with Kaedric for a single night, and it had been his room. It was the room in which Evaric had been born. Rhianna pressed the central stone below the embrasure and twisted the Power she had woven around it. The wall-stone softened into a milky echo of the stone around her neck, and Rhianna drew the light into her hand.

Rhianna had installed the vault herself, carefully expending insignificant Power over months of slow effort. She had not even told the Ixaxin elders of its creation. During the last twenty-five years, she had opened it only once.

The spindle's amber glow never dimmed. Rhianna touched the traces of gray ash on its filigree with tender distress. She had never cleaned the ash from its surface; she had forgotten.

She took the Taormin in her hands with delicate respect, and the old pulsing began immediately. She had never used it alone, though she knew the way of its intricate coils. Always, Kaedric had led her, when it had been Horlach's. When Kaedric took it, the need to use it had gone, and she had hidden it, abetting Kaedric's deception of the world: she had pretended that the Taormin's Power had been destroyed with Horlach and Kaedric himself.

Rhianna sat on the edge of the bed, closed her eyes, and turned inward. The dizzying webs blinded her for a moment, but she eluded their grasp and began to follow the remembered path. The way was smoother than she had recalled, and it was brighter. She could glimpse a few distant, dark corners of the old tangle, but Kaedric had permeated the central domain. The Taormin held more Power than it had ever known with the deathless Sorcerer King who had so long ordered it.

It tempted her. Its enticements had increased with its Power, or Rhianna had grown more vulnerable to the Taormin's peculiar allure. The energy fed her, until she felt almost euphoric with strength. She could have spread herself across its coils and become truly omnipotent.

"It only feels that way in the beginning," commented her husband calmly. Rhianna focused on him hungrily, while he equably recalled to her the perilous nature of the tool she

courted. *"It is the nature of infinity,"* he continued, *"to be always incomplete."*

"Like us?"

"At present."

"You left me," accused Rhianna, and her voice trembled.

"You found me," answered Kaedric with infuriating irony.

"After seven years of searching, and still I cannot reach you. I might be searching yet, had you not scattered your Power across the Alliance."

"I did generate a rather more spectacular display than I had intended. These Rending wraiths are rather a nuisance at times."

"You rattled every sorcerer in Serii."

"I have grown careless."

"Kaedric, why have you raised this wall between us?"

"Now it is you who forget the lessons of the novitiate: do not delve into another wizard's secrets."

"Only you consider secrets so essential."

"You imperil yourself, my dearest." He moved away from her, but Rhianna clung to his Power's pattern.

"You cannot elude me again so easily, my beloved."

"Do not press me, Rhianna."

"Then make me understand."

He denied her firmly, and when she tried to reach him, he threw at her a tangle of the Taormin's web. Such twisting skeins of energy could kill or capture for eternity, but Rhianna took the strands and kept her own pattern. She followed him, though it was a treacherous path, and she did not know why he led her upon it. He could not conceal himself within the whole, for she knew his patterns too well; they were a part of herself.

He wove Rhianna deeply in the Taormin, and all of it spoke of Kaedric. No great knots of Horlach's making existed here, save one. It was a dim but intricate snarl. Intent on Kaedric, Rhianna did not study it until a span of it struck her, and she knew it.

Had Kaedric led her to this choice? He must have recognized, as she did, the image of a major Power bound against itself. He surely knew that she could follow only one pattern: his or the other's.

Rhianna's hesitation sufficed for Kaedric to elude her. Feeling betrayed, she traced the bound pattern deftly, but it extended into a thickened mass of ancient chaos. Was this

Horlach's final jest? The shackles conformed to an unfamiliar design, but it was a potent one.

She could not free Evaric of the devious webs, for they spun into the Taormin's deepest parts. It was a clever trap, even for Horlach. Rhianna could easily become ensnared herself; she retreated very cautiously.

When she again felt the Taormin as only a thing of filigree in her hands, she allowed herself to despair. She hid the tool of terrible Power in her simple vault, hating it. She hated Horlach, for he had maimed her son. Kaedric's secretive schemings angered her nearly as much.

She opened the window, the highest in Tulea, and let the wind from Tul's Mountain chill her. She could visualize Ceallagh's tomb in the pass between the peaks. Horlach had died there; perhaps her husband had died there, also. They had Rent the world between them.

Evaric lived, as Rhianna did. Though Horlach had wrought great mischief, Evaric remained her son. He was not yet a mad Immortal, despite Horlach's intentions and the elusive, other patterns which Rhianna could indefinably sense. Evram and Terrell had reared and loved her son. He was K'shai, but at least he functioned in the mortal world. Rhianna did not know her son, but she would find him. She knew his pattern now.

Chapter 10

Fifth Month, Year 29 of Rending

Ineuil did not age, mused Rhianna. More sorcerous blood stirred in him than he admitted. He remained much as she saw him first in Dwaelin Wood, though responsibilities had clenched their relentless teeth in his careless attitude. He had accepted the position as Adjutant solely because of a desperate time, but he had fulfilled the role well enough. He had appointed deputies to handle all the peacetime tasks he found so tedious. Extreme delegation of authority had afforded him a sense of freedom from work's confining nature, else he would not have so long retained the distinguished post. Nonetheless, his was a marginal acceptance; he was, after all, the ultimate military authority in Serii after the Queen, a position of undeniable responsibility.

Marriage had not greatly affected him. His relationship with Yldana could be termed at best tempestuous, but their marriage had produced four children, three of whom were most probably of Ineuil's siring. Governesses preserved Ineuil and Yldana from the throes of parenthood, allowing them to share a relationship more akin to that of occasional paramours than husband and wife. It appeared to suit them, though Rhianna detected on occasions an underlying discontent beneath the couple's insouciant sophistication.

Ineuil bowed to Rhianna with exaggerated courtesy before draping himself haphazardly over an armchair. "The Infortiare has summoned the Adjutant," he announced grandly, "and he is here to serve her." He folded his arms. "What the devil is so important that you officially request my presence?"

Rhianna answered him quietly, "I have located my son."

Ineuil cocked his head. His green eyes gained a contemplative cast. "Where is he?"

"On a ship headed for Ardasia."

Ineuil shook his head. "The land of religious fanatics and barbarians. He could hardly have traveled farther from you if he tried. Or did he try?"

"He still does not know of me."

"Or of Kaedric?" Rhianna answered with silence. Ineuil said cynically, "I have no official jurisdiction in Ardasia, my dearest Rhianna, and your own influence in that country is at best insubstantial."

"Official methods have no place in my intentions, Ineuil. I shall not lose my son again." As I may have lost Kaedric, she thought with a stab of hurt, unless my most tenuous suspicions prove true. "I am going to Ardasia."

"It will be a lengthy journey."

"I am not so very indispensable at court these days." And there may be vital need for me beside my son, if I have analyzed correctly.

"Does Her Majesty know?"

"She will agree."

Ineuil grimaced, frowned, and darted at Rhianna, "Why is he bound for Ardasia? If you tell me that he has become a pilgrim, I shall know that he is not Kaedric's offspring."

"K'shai often journey to Ardasia. That country employs many Protectors."

"And many assassins. I shall never accustom myself to the concept of an Immortal K'shai."

"I should not like to be entirely alone in Ardasia," continued Rhianna, studiously avoiding further comment about the abhorred K'shai. "The marriage of Princess Lilyan to Prince Stal would provide you with a reasonable cause for the journey."

"And you?"

"I shall travel in my own way."

"Yldana will still suspect indiscretion," Ineuil remarked dryly. "But I have been respectable far too long. Do you realize, my lovely Infortiare, that we have not traveled together since the Venture?"

"I have rarely left Tulea, save for visits to Ixaxis, in the past three decades." She sounded wistful. "Between duty and bondage first to Tyntagel and then to Ixaxis, I have traveled little."

"You did not particularly savor your journeying, as I recall."

"It was the freest time I have ever known."

"Following Kaedric?" scoffed Ineuil. "He owned you from the moment you joined the Venture."

"He owned me before that," admitted Rhianna wanly. The imprisonment had been of her own choice. She did not try to explain to Ineuil; she wished that she had told Kaedric.

"You have some plan beyond merely sailing to Ardasia?" demanded Ineuil, suddenly cheerful. "It is a sizable continent, I believe."

"It is largely uninhabitable, however."

"So are Serii's northern reaches, but I should not like to search their entirety."

"You are not the one who will be searching."

"And you are less constrained than most by mortal probabilities?"

"Knowledge is itself a potent weapon against chance."

"Quoting Kaedric again," he remarked idly. Rhianna frowned slightly, but the accusation was true. "Ah, well," Ineuil continued briskly, "at least you are planning with your brain and not your despair."

"Concentrate on your own rusty skills, Lord Arineuil," returned Rhianna tartly.

"Is that the command of a Venture Leader?"

"I fear the Rending creatures have rendered Ventures nearly obsolete. The K'shai claim to be the only mortals who master the night."

"Do you think the K'shai might try to recruit me if they knew I had survived Rendies?" asked Ineuil impishly.

Rhianna shook her head at him sternly, but she was subtly pleased: the prospect of adventure had ensnared him. She had not wanted to use other persuasion. "It will require considerable effort to make of you a credible pilgrim."

"You are not a likely candidate yourself, my dear Infortiare."

Rhianna took a dark shawl from the chair and pulled it close about her face. She cast her gaze to the floor and let her posture soften into something humble and timid. "Have you never met such a pilgrim? Who would know me from one?"

Ineuil studied her critically. "Possible, I suppose, but do you intend to prate of the holy Shrine and the end of our evil world? I might manage it," he mused, "but I think you are too sincerely religious to vilify your faith."

"I shall be a reticent pilgrim."

"A nonexistent breed!"

"No longer," retorted Rhianna firmly. Ineuil merely smirked.

Chapter 11

Tenth Month, Year 29 of Rending
Serii and Ardasia

Rhianna dressed in somber gray and black robes of sturdy, common cotton, as befit a pilgrim woman of limited means. She had packed her satchel carefully, ensuring that nothing in it betokened too much of wealth or proud origin. She studied her reflection critically, adjusting her demeanor and her bearing until the image became a stranger: someone helpless, someone mortal. By Power she could alter the visions others gleaned of her, but her act demanded that she fix in her mind a solid personality that she could wear like a reliable cloak.

"If I am wrong," she whispered to the image in her mirror. She closed her eyes, unwilling to complete the thought. If she erred, she betrayed her love, the son she did not know, and the world she feared to know too well. She waited for the silent voice, both frightened and relieved that it did not come. "Your chosen path is not an easy one to follow, my Kaedric."

She checked her desk for the hundredth time. She had left complete instructions for every conceivable crisis, and Master Amardi was well qualified to attend the more ordinary matters of Power. Queen Joli had assured her (with mischievous persistence) that Serii could survive a few months without its Infortiare. Ineuil had taken ship to Ardasia over a month ago. There remained no more justification for delay. There were no more excuses.

"Let it be the right answer," she prayed. She took her satchel in one hand and clasped an amber spindle in the other. Had anyone been present to observe the Infortiare in her Tower, a brief rippling glow might have been seen where she had stood and then vanished.

*   *   *

Idle blue-green swells lapped at the ships and docks, the water's noise unheard above the human din. Fruits and fish of kinds not seen beyond Ardasia's rich coast spread bright colors, making mosaics of the open-air shops beneath the breeze-blown sky. Clay brick dwellings, adorned with bits of colored glass and anarchic images, lined the sandy streets. Sultry heat discouraged most daily traffic from any roof more substantial than a square of colored canvas, but the night demanded walls even in Ardas.

Men and women jostled and cheated one another with equable good humor. Only the very youngest children decked the open schools, squares of land distinguished by rough benches and the gathering of youth; the marketplace taught the subjects of greatest interest to Ardasians, who generally cared more for a clever bargain than for the easy life purportedly promised by formal education. Even the Ardasian clothing shouted strangeness to the foreigners spilling from the ships, for there were men uncovered above the waist, and there were women with arms and ankles bare.

Rhianna tasted the strangely rich, hot moisture of Ardasian summer. The trees feel me, she mused, though they have not met my like before. The newness held a thrill of unanticipated clarity, but it told her the full strangeness of this place. Those who were natives knew no Power here, neither as sincere memory nor as buried truth. No seeds of Power lingered in the Ardasians who were pure of lineage. Rhianna understood now the frustration of those Ixaxins whom she had stationed here. How eerie was the feeling of this matter-minded country! Wella, she thought determinedly, it is time Ardasia learned to face the world.

II.

Let (X,T) be a topological space.

Let p be an element of the set X.

Let S be a subset of X.

If each open set containing p intersects S in at least one point distinct from p, then p is a *limit point* of S with respect to the topological space (X,T).

LYRIEL

Chapter 1

Tenth Month, Year 29 of Rending
Ardas, Ardasia

Rubi's Troupe made no claims to any particular prosperity; they roved and performed throughout the three seasons, and they struggled to survive each summer in the seaport city of Ardas, when Ardasia's summer heat made inland travel impractical. Traveling companies such as Rubi's Troupe had been common during Rubi's youth; the cost of travel had grown high since the Rending. Only the K'shai would guarantee traveling Protection with any certainty, and their monopoly enabled the K'shai to command outrageous prices. Very few wanderers owned Rubi's will to persevere. Very few K'shai could be coaxed as easily as Key into an attitude akin to loyalty.

Worry furrowed Rubi's brow; she shook her head with aggravation at her own concern. "Denz!" Rubi gestured wildly at a bit of dropped scenery. Denz retrieved it with a grumble. "Denz!" she called again. This time she waved at him to collar the two boys who were trying for a glimpse at Alisa: Beauteous Alisa, the posters proclaimed her. Exasperating Alisa, amended Rubi to herself: pretending that Rubi's requests conflicted with Alisa's lofty standards, when it was only laziness that prevented Alisa from complying. Troupe of thieves, Alisa said, flinging names like a blasted pilgrim. If anyone else could be paid as erratically to draw customers so well, the Alisa would learn a lesson or two in respect. It really was too bad that Lyriel had displayed so little inclination to perform regularly since Silf left.

"We need more money for the jerked beef, Rubi," said Taf, a spare man near Rubi's age, who had inspired Rubi to create the Troupe all those years ago. Once, Rubi had

167

hoped that Taf would love her for providing him a focus for his talents. Rubi had hoped to pry Taf from his precious Silf.

Well, thought Rubi ruefully, Silf had gone. After years of jealousy and contention, Rubi had seen her rival vanquished, and nothing had changed. The old Silf, the dancer who had drawn more adulation than Alisa, the Silf whom a reckless and defiantly optimistic young conjuror named Taf had loved sincerely, still held the tired Taf who now remained. If Taf felt nothing for the coldly righteous Silf, shipbuilder's wife in Diarmon, the fact held no consolation for Rubi.

Taf loves only the past, thought Rubi sourly. He loves the Silf who was warm and free and forgiving. He pines for the naive pre-Rending Ardasia that did not weigh a conjuror against bearers of Power and the creatures of the night. He rues the Taf who expected good from the world. Taf has the past, and I have the Troupe, and neither of us remembers how to care deeply for anything.

"I thought you found a deal," Rubi muttered to him, as she ransacked her purse.

"A pilgrim company interrupted the bargaining. They claimed the lot was stolen property." Taf shrugged.

"You let a few pilgrims best you? Taf, you are growing soft. Why do I pay you?"

"You do not pay me, Rubi dear. Haggling in the market-place is purely a gesture of my good heart, and pilgrims make it no great pleasure. This latest Shrine Keeper of theirs has bought every supply and service in Ardas."

"This whole city is pilgrim-mad. Any luck replacing Kaya?"

"Let the Alisa do the stitching," retorted Taf. "She does little enough else."

"There must be an unemployed seamstress somewhere in Ardas."

"Not one who is willing to travel with a barely solvent troupe of players. They can earn more from the temples, stitching pilgrim robes and Shrine cloths, and it costs them a fraction of the effort."

"If the task were easy, I would not need your skills to accomplish it." Rubi let her hand rub tentatively against Taf's narrow shoulders. Taf grunted, and Rubi allowed her hand to fall to her side. "If you cannot find a seamstress for us," snapped Rubi, "how shall I expect you to find us new K'shai?"

"Rubi dear," said Taf with his usual gloom, "am I arguing with you?"

"So." Rubi wished she could forget: about Silf, about Taf, about Key's death and the urgent need to replace the dead K'shai. "So either find us a seamstress or persuade your daughter to add another duty to her list." Rubi stabbed her finger toward the darkly graceful young woman who so hauntingly resembled Silf.

Taf snorted. "You have seen Lyriel's stitchery."

"She can benefit from the practice," retorted Rubi sharply, but she felt a bit of guilt for the jab at Lyriel. The daughter did not merit the legacy of Silf's effect on Rubi. Rubi recalled Taf and Lyriel on the day of Silf's departure, father and daughter turning pain to fury: each had blamed the other for the loss they shared, and neither had ever relented enough to apologize. They rarely acknowledged their kinship now, and they argued almost every time they talked. Still, the bond was there, unspoken; neither would desert the other. Like Taf and me, thought Rubi, dependent upon one another but too proud or too embarrassed to allow ourselves the solace of mutually acknowledged weaknesses.

* * *

"A seamstress," grumbled Taf to himself. "Why do we need a seamstress, Rubi dear, when we have no K'shai?" Taf had not asked the question of Rubi; she could not confront the prospect of the Troupe's ending. She preferred to pretend that no problem existed. Taf's own gloomy expectations would only anger her.

"Do you think, Rubi dear, that I mind less than you the thought of disbanding your precious Troupe?" What did Rubi think he would do without the Troupe? Settle in Diarmon with Silf and her jealous shipbuilder? A fine place that would be for an embittered conjuror, whose peculiarly Ardasian art had been essentially obsolete for a quarter of a century. "Ask Lyriel the likelihood of my choosing such a course," snapped Taf. Lyriel had never spared him the fire of her opinions on his "abandonment" of Silf.

"Our daughter has a temper in her," mused Taf absently, as if Silf were returned to hear him. "She scolds me more than ever you did, Silf girl. She thinks she must take your place in protecting me from myself. Well, she is young—as young as we ever allowed her to be.

"You had reason enough to leave me, Silf girl. I could never blame you for wanting to be free of me. But how could you leave Lyriel? You knew she could not stay with you in Diarmon; you knew she would feel obliged to come with me, to save me (as she thinks) from too much self-destruction. Silf girl, you consigned your daughter to all the things you hate. You consigned her to Rubi, who makes a slave of her. You consigned her to my thieving ways. Lyriel deserves better. She has always deserved better than you and I could give her." Taf frowned at himself for straying too near to emotions he had interred the day Silf left. "Past is past and best forgotten," he muttered.

Taf espied his goal and relaxed his scowl. The temple's tiny garden constituted one of the few shaded, uncrowded retreats in Ardas. Since the pilgrims seldom used it, Taf had claimed it as a refuge of his own. He squeezed through the iron fence surrounding it. (He would never have considered entering by the gate.) The garden held a prior occupant: a pilgrim woman too lost in some private and desolate sorrow to notice Taf. She occupied the half-rotted bench beneath the bao tree. She sat motionless, her satchel tucked neatly beside her.

Taf's scowl returned, but the delicious coolness of the shade enticed him to remain. The woman gazed into the leaves above her, as if to find within them some long-departed, secretive happiness. Something in her unspoken pain appealed to a deep empathy buried beneath any normal awareness Taf might have acknowledged.

A history for her seemed to rush at him. Raised in some tight little village, the sort where everyone knew every shadow and scandal of every other life, she had spent her pitifully hoarded funds on the sea voyage to Ardas, not realizing that the Shrine lay many miles from the coast. Like so many naive pilgrims, she had nothing left to her once a few Ardasian merchants had cheated her, and she had not come within leagues of her goal. She would be lucky to earn enough for her return voyage. Even if she knew enough to plead for temple charity, she might wait months before the temple bureaucracy could attend her case.

Taf scratched his head and indulged in a momentary hesitation. He felt reluctant to believe his fabricated history, but the woman did have the meager look of poverty. A woman in such miserable circumstances might be grateful for any employment of honest kind, and she would not know what wages to expect. If she stitched even as badly as Lyriel, she would satisfy Rubi. Taf absorbed her despairing posture and felt a qualm, but he rarely allowed conscience to interfere with business.

Taf circled the bao tree, approached and sat near the woman as if unaware of her existence. He heaved an overtly emphatic sigh; he had long ago concluded that few of these pilgrims, stupid innocents that they were, could be expected to discern a subtle approach. He muttered quite distinctly, "Good copper to pay, and none to earn it." Taf's second sigh contained a substantial dose of distress.

After a long and silent minute, Taf ventured to raise his head and look about him dolefully. The woman was gazing at him without much expression. Dull-witted, thought Taf regretfully, but what does Rubi expect with the little she is willing to expend? Rubi ought to be glad if I find a seamstress at all, even a dim one. "Hello," said Taf with enough awkwardness to convey embarrassment. "I had not realized anyone else was here. I thought I knew everyone who used this garden. Are you newly come to Ardas?"

Taf had barely hoped for a response. When the woman spoke, her voice surprised him: Though her manner reeked of timidity, something almost compelling underlay her cautious whisper. "I arrived two days ago."

The woman sounded younger than Taf had expected. All that ridiculous yardage concealed her age effectively. "Bound for the Shrine, are you?"

The woman did not smile, but the sorrow about her retreated a pace behind interest. "It is a costly journey," she remarked. She fixed on Taf a gaze of certain intensity. She had remarkable eyes. She might be rather beautiful, observed Taf impersonally, if she donned something less grim than pilgrim drab.

Taf groaned with sympathy. "Between the K'shai and the supply merchants' extortion, even those of us who have been making the journey for years find it more difficult to manage every season."

Perhaps the woman reached some obscure judgment, for she became as innocently eager as Taf could wish. "You have been to the Shrine?" she demanded with such persuasive awe that Taf nearly forgot his own cynical view of pseudo-religious folderol. "If you knew how I have dreamed of attaining it! I have traveled so far, only to be defeated at the last. When I bought pilgrimage, I never imagined that my purchase would leave me so far from my goal."

To his amazement, Taf found himself almost bemused by the mousy pilgrim woman in her black and somber draperies. The deep sorrow he had imagined in her had been vanquished or veiled, if it had existed at all. Taf knew a moment's suspicion, but the woman was a foreigner and a pilgrim as well. No pilgrim could decently feign a feeling or disguise it. No foreigner ever matched an Ardasian in the business of deception. "Indeed, I have seen the Shrine. I am employed by a traveling troupe of players, and our itinerary takes us to D'hai each year."

"Each year?" breathed the woman. "How wondrous for you!"

Taf fixed his gaze on the woman's gray eyes as an artful ploy, but he found himself so fascinated by the storm-dark depths that he garbled his intended lines, demanding simply, "Do you sew?"

The woman blushed lightly, though Taf imagined for a moment that the light itself grew rose-colored around her. "My needlecraft is no less fair than another woman's."

"Our troupe needs a seamstress. You could travel to D'hai with us. Our troupe is known, and I with it, if you would verify my sincerity of intention." Not that any Ardasian who knows us would give the truth to a pilgrim, thought Taf, but the claim of sincerity generally gives a good impression.

Have I spoken too quickly and befuddled her? wondered Taf, but the woman replied, "I shall bring you answer, Master Taf, this evening."

She gathered her satchel, rose, and disappeared into the arbor which led to the temple, leaving Taf to stare agape. "What an odd bird she is," he muttered. He felt outwitted, for his mark had escaped him, and he had not even anticipated the attempt. He disregarded her final promise; it was just the sort of equivocation he expected of a pilgrim, who never would give a forthright refusal if a lie would serve. No Ardasian would use a lie to so little purpose.

Taf grumbled to himself as he left the garden, the pleasures of which had for the moment been destroyed for him.

"It was not even a good lie," he grunted under his breath, "for she never let me tell her where to find me again. She never asked the wages!" The final consideration seemed almost an affront to Taf's basic tenets. He laid the crime against the whole of foreign interlopers, none of whom had ever mastered the rudiments of decent business dealings. Having once again justified to himself his loathing for humanity, especially in its non-Ardasian form, Taf began to whistle a soundless tune of contentment, as he jostled through the heated crowd and returned to Rubi's Troupe.

Chapter 2

Same day, a few hours earlier

Occasionally, in lonely moods, I weigh the future against the past, and I wonder that a jealous scheme against my mother should have come to shape my life. I remember the Troupe as Rubi first formed it. We numbered ten: Rubi, Taf, Silf and I, Kays and Vila, Diafe, Lu, Bin, and Arious. Taf and Silf had partnered with Rubi (and Broh, who left us) for three years or more, when Rubi discovered the six unemployed performers who would join us to become the first Rubi's Troupe.

Pitiful survivors of a once-prosperous company, the six had been rendered nearly witless by the calamity of a Rendie attack. Rubi extolled the potential of the Rendie-broken company to Taf and Silf, as I sat quietly forgotten in the corner, celebrating my fifth birthday with sand-cakes and Sanston, my sole childhood friend. I recall the evening clearly, for Diafe arrived to introduce me to the terrible Rendie madness that had warped him and his companions. The morbid fears of those half-mad players exacerbated all the terrors that a child's imagination could produce.

From the first, the players talked volubly to me, whom they regarded with the intermittently tolerant amusement of childless adults. They assumed that I did not understand, because I answered their more dire tales with the solemn promise that Sanston could protect them if they asked. I believed in Sanston utterly; perhaps I did imagine him, but I can visualize him still, though he left me years ago and relinquished my Protection to the K'shai.

All things change: Key never yielded to me a more sensible nugget from the K'shai philosophy. I would have had the words scribed above his grave, but K'shai do not mark their tombs. I found it tragically ironic that a man who had defeated scores of Rendies should die of the bite of a tiny, timid wind-snake. As Key had said, all things change; death comprised simply another transition. Nonetheless, I missed him. For a K'shai, Key had been an exceptionally decent man.

Rate abandoned us, of course, to seek a new K'shai partner and a more lucrative contract. The new Shrine Keeper had established a policy of so overpaying for services that we Ardasians could scarcely compete. Rate had never shared Key's unlikely sense of loyalty to the Troupe.

I paused to kick a stone. The back streets of early dawn stood empty, else my stone would have struck an argument. I almost regretted the lack of a human target. My nervous temper wanted an outlet badly, and Taf had been too preoccupied for weeks to listen to me rant; I never dared speak freely to anyone else in the Troupe, for Rubi expected me to appease the Troupe members, not befriend them.

I twisted through the alleys to the warehouse that we leased. I could hear the dim rattle of vendors staking their posts in the market. I considered detouring through their midst for distraction, but Rubi's Troupe awaited too many uncertain exchanges; we had placed large orders to supply the Troupe, and the time of payment and receipt approached quickly. Taf would devise a way of reneging, if he could not resolve our lack of K'shai, but we would retain few friends among the merchants. Too many of our suppliers already suspected our intentions.

I stopped at sight of a long and unfamiliar shadow. The hour was too early for the debt collectors to ply their humorless work, and Taf had not committed any recent thefts, so far as I knew. Nonetheless, I poised my hand on the knife at my waist, and I waited in uneasy silence.

The shadow's source turned the corner suddenly; a brightly polished sword extended from his hand as easily as if the blade comprised a natural appendage. The young man scanned me in an instant, and his caution melted into a smile so beguiling that I scarcely noticed his arsenal of weapons or the foreign cut of his leather coat. I did manage to recognize that his skin was too fair and fine, his hair too uniformly dark to have survived life-long beneath Ardasian sun.

I leaned against the wall in the pose that Rubi calls sultry. I volunteered, "If you are seeking the marketplace, go through that alley, right twice and left." Foreigners often strayed among the streets of Ardas, and I seldom wasted courtesy on them; few of them would acknowledge an Ardasian woman for any moral purpose. Very few of them proffered smiles of overwhelming warmth and vividness.

"I appreciate the directions," he said in a clear voice, richly colored with the elegance of a Seriin accent. He studied me with a softly curious gaze, while I concluded that I had never seen a more handsome man. "I am actually seeking a woman rather than a marketplace." I raised my brows at him, and he flushed. "A Mistress Rubi," he explained hastily. "Do you by any chance know which warehouse she leases?"

"Indeed, I know it." Yielding unnecessary information to a stranger can bring trouble, but the potential value to the Troupe of such a man merited the risk. "I am Lyriel; I work for her. Are you an actor?"

"No," he laughed with a peculiar acerbity. He raised his left arm, bent and taut, the hand clenched, the brand at my eye level. "I am K'shai," he murmured with some embarrassment, presumably augmented by my dumbfounded stare; I had never before failed to recognize a K'shai. "I am truly K'shai," he assured me, as if I could doubt him; no sane man would forge a K'shai's bloodied sword from wrist to fingertip.

"Of course," I answered hollowly. I might mourn Key, who had Protected me for most of my life, but I categorized all other K'shai as somewhat less estimable than the fungus which rotted the wall beside me.

"I am older than I appear." He sounded apologetic, which was absurd. I wondered wildly if he also apologized to those whom he slaughtered in his vile profession.

I straightened, and I fingered my knife. I responded coldly, "If you want employment, our terms are these: Protection for the duration of our season, fall through spring, at the rate of eleven silvers a week plus room, keep, and performance passes. The value of the total exceeds standard, and our schedule will allow you considerable free time during our city-stays."

"Actually," he remarked with more embarrassment, "the

Guild's current rate for Protection is seventeen silvers a week, exclusive of other benefits. You will not hire K'shai for less, and you are not likely to hire others at all just now. The Shrine Keeper offers thirty silvers a week for pilgrim Protection."

"Then why are you not escorting pilgrims?" I snapped. I did not need to hear from him about the Shrine Keeper's offer.

His smile twisted ruefully. "I have reasons to avoid the Shrine Keeper's employ."

"If you plan to fulfill an assassin's contract while Protecting, look elsewhere for your customers."

"I have no contracts pending," he assured me. He exuded sincerity and the rare sort of strength that inspires implicit confidence. I remained wise enough to recognize the potential hazard of his charm and gain caution from it; however, I could not concoct any reasonable argument against him nor any good reason to seek one. This unlikely K'shai offered life itself, though I hoped he did not know the Troupe's desperation.

"You have a partner?" I asked him.

"His name is Fog."

"You have not yet told me your name. We shall require references."

"Captain Tarl of the *Sea Dancer* will supply whatever information you need. I use my birth name, Evaric."

His eyes resembled the shadows on the shifting ocean: dark and light and elusive. His smile might seem open and warm, but the eyes evaded me. I looked at the branded hand and again at the secretive eyes. "You do have a K'shai name?"

"Naturally," he replied with undaunted coolness. I continued to gaze at him expectantly, and he admitted with a grimace, "Fire. The name tends to convey wrong impressions when called loudly, and I prefer to avoid causing unnecessary panic."

"Reasonable," I conceded, still a little suspicious; no one has ever accused me of susceptibility to casual influence, however appealing. "I shall take you to Rubi," I told him rigidly.

"I did not mean to inconvenience you, Mistress Lyriel."

His Seriin courtesy disconcerted me. Taf had taught me to

equate such gentle speech with either hypocrisy or foreign weakness, and I could not mold either characteristic to the form of an assassin. "It is not a favor, K'shai." I began to feel grateful, after all, that he was K'shai and displayed his iniquitous nature openly. "How many assassinations have you completed?" I asked him chattily. He regarded me very oddly, as well he might, and he did not answer, which was just as well. Had I received any response short of mass genocide, I might have forgiven him even for being K'shai.

Chapter 3

The grand procession of a royal wedding through the streets of Ardas made the crowded city all the more congested. The members of the procession enjoyed the protection of their guards and servants, but onlookers faced considerable risk. Ardas' usual noise and furor turned to chaos, and thieves emerged to ply their eager trade with near impunity. Other questionable professions derived equal advantage from the occasion.

Serii's Adjutant enjoyed a prominent position in the festivities, but at some point between the palace and the cathedral, those regal visitors who had ridden behind him observed that Lord Arineuil dur Ven had evidently shifted his position in the train. Since Lord Arineuil had already caused his Ardasian hosts enormous consternation by refusing to comply with set schedules and safe itineraries, his disappearance from the parade generated limited concern. Lord Arineuil had exasperated his hosts, and they considered him deserving of any misfortune he accrued by his disregard of prudent warnings.

* * *

"These wretched bumpkins have the most tiresome conceit," complained Ineuil from the garden bench of the Ardas villa he had let. "Inasmuch as I am Seriin, they assure me that I could not survive for an instant unescorted in their city. They speak for me, act for me, watch me like a jealous lover—I am quite sure that they would attempt to think for me, as well, if they could discover any means by which to manage it. What are you trying to do to that tree, Rhianna? It languishes hopelessly beyond aesthetic redemption even by you."

Rhianna withdrew her hand from the strange Ardasian

tree that seemed to grow indiscriminately with no sensible design of trunk and branch. "I am trying, Ineuil, to understand it. The Ardasian people are not the country's only living things to feel an insular disdain for other sorts."

"How anyone could take pride in anything in this beastly climate, I shall never comprehend."

Rhianna gazed at the vivid aqua ocean; it met the cliff below her in streaks of snowy foam. "The weather will grow milder soon."

Ineuil folded his arms to sulk, but he abandoned the pose quickly and reached for the fan of plaited palm. He waved the fan in restless affectation. "Have you made any progress in your search?" he asked her idly. Rhianna did not answer. Ineuil snapped into stillness heavy as the humid air, "You have found him."

"I have found him."

"Where?"

"At an inn, one of those dreadful native places in the city's central district. A traveling company of players has employed him for Protection."

"Have you spoken to him?"

"Not yet. I have only glimpsed him once, as he entered the inn with the young woman who hired him. I have sensed him, though. That barrier has gone. I wonder why . . ." She fell silent again, gazing inward. When she continued, her voice retained a whisper's hush. "He is haunted."

"By you?" asked Ineuil with a cynic's whimsy.

"By me, by his own Power, by Rendies, by . . . too many things of dire kind. I carried him when I stood beside Kaedric at the Rending's broken gate, and Evaric was tangled like the Rending creatures in a place that is neither this world nor any other. By that dormant Power in him, he is as much a Rending creature as any chill wraith. Ineuil, he is a lethal promise waiting for its time. He frightens me."

Considerate of you to join the rest of us, thought Ineuil, now that regret can serve no purpose. "Do you mean to speak to him or not?" demanded Ineuil with some impatience.

Rhianna looked sharply at the lounging lord of Ven. "I shall observe him for a time. I shall accompany the troupe with which he travels. I shall not hold you here, Ineuil." She finished meekly, "If you wish to return to Serii now, I shall not stop you."

"My lovely, temperamental wizardess, I have no intention

of sitting idly among my stuffy peers, while you gallivant across the world. I resigned myself long ago to an absolute dread of your infant prodigy, just as I accepted dread of his father as the normal course for my life. Some men like to shun the objects of their greatest fear; I prefer to watch those objects closely."

Rhianna inclined her head. A breeze caught at her hair. "The company that has hired Evaric is known as Rubi's Troupe. Their route is well established. You should have no trouble in pursuing them."

Lords, thought Ineuil, cursing his own credulity. She never doubted that I would remain. She has been manipulating me this past hour. Is she even conscious of the spell she weaves? "Kaedric's shadow," murmured Ineuil bitterly, quoting Rhianna's own description of herself. Rhianna closed her eyes but did not reply. "I begin to feel a considerable sympathy for these awful Ardasians after all."

Chapter 4

Rubi allowed me little leisure during the summer's final flurry; we had delayed too many tasks, until K'shai were found. Exhaustion claimed me. Of all the Troupe members, only Noryne offered to help me, and against my better judgment, I accepted. Fatigue would make me sharp, and Noryne was far too sensitive. She would make me feel guilty.

We sat together in the warehouse, sorting costumes and props. Noryne's red-gold hair had been braided tightly and pinned close to her head for rehearsal, making her look even younger than usual. She held one of the oldest gowns, shook it cautiously, and wrinkled her freckled nose at the resultant cloud of dust. "Have you ever seen a Rendie, Lyriel?"

I dropped a skirt into a pool of wrinkles. "Yes." I felt cold, though the heat made incense of our perfumes. "So have you. Do you not remember?" Few of us did remember the Rendies' visitations and the mesmerizing battle/dance of the K'shai. Key had told me once that my facility for recalling Rendies, augmented by my dancer's training, could make me a promising candidate for the K'shai. The intended compliment had appalled me, and I had not liked discussing my ability since then.

"I always remember," murmured Noryne, surprising me a little. Her eyes were wide and serious. "The memory frightens me even in daylight: I expect every swirl of smoke to become a wraith's breath seeking me. I can better understand a man who lives by killing men than a man who can face a Rendie unafraid. You know about so many things, Lyriel, more than anyone else I ever met. Are the K'shai human, do you think?"

"They are not lizards, Noryne, though they may be equally quick and unpredictable. Key died just as painfully as any other victim of wind-snake venom."

Noryne flushed, hurt by my careless acknowledgment of

Key's death, and I felt guilty once again, though I had mourned Key more than any K'shai deserved. Noryne said softly, "They say a wizard can die, too, if he is stricken unaware. But wizards are not quite human, are they?"

"I would not know about wizards. I never met one."

"There is an Ixaxin school here in Ardas."

"Foreigners."

"Not always."

"Always," I answered impatiently. "Any Ardasian who traffics willingly with foreigners, whether they are wizards, pilgrims, or K'shai, has no right to claim his citizenship."

Noryne bowed her head meekly. "You are angry with me now. I am sorry I made you angry. I used always to anger my foster mother with my questions, and she used to tell me that Rendies would seek me for angering her."

"I am not angry," I insisted, but Noryne would not look at me. "Anyway," I continued, trying for conciliation, "you have K'shai to Protect you, whether you anger me or not."

"They are new K'shai, strange K'shai. Why did Key die?"

"It was his time. It was his privilege."

Noryne stared at me long and curiously. "Privilege of death," she mused, as if she had never thought before of death as gift. "Is it kinder than the gift of life?"

"That depends on the life and how it has been used."

"What of a life not yet given?"

I shrugged. "That depends largely on the giver."

Noryne inhaled deeply. "I carry a life in me, Lyriel," she whispered in a hurried breath, "I carry Zakari's child."

"Zakari is pledged to Alisa," I replied blankly, stunned not by Zakari's infidelity but by Noryne's concession to it.

"Alisa hurts him so much," said Noryne, pleading for the forgiveness she could not give herself. She continued with such misery in her voice that I cringed, "I have not told him. I have not told Rubi either. Will she be angry?"

"Noryne," I said despairingly, wondering what I could possibly tell her that would not hurt her the more. "How can you even consider raising a child, when you can barely support yourself? Zakari will not help you, and Rubi is not a great believer in charity."

"She lets Solomai's children travel with us, and you were raised in the Troupe."

"Solomai's children are performers in their own rights, and Solomai is a wagoner with much more time to spare for them than you could give. Rubi tolerated me only for Taf's sake, and I was born into a simpler world: Ardasia did not yet understand the Venkarel's Rendies." I was saying too much, but my tongue raced ahead of my more sensible thoughts. "You fear Rendies even in a darkened room, Noryne. How could you condemn your child to face the night with only a wagon's flimsy canvas for visible defense?" Noryne had begun to cry. I handed her a scrap of linen from the fabric supply. She rubbed it across her damp cheeks, achieving little good.

"Tell me what to do, Lyriel," she pleaded.

I rubbed my temples. "Let me think about it." Rubi would not be easily swayed, much as she preferred to leave matters of the Troupe's personnel to my judgment. "Rubi will explode." She would call me sentimental and pilgrim-hearted, and I would be forced to threaten, deceive, and cajole her.

Noryne smiled amid her tears. "You will calm her. She respects you, Lyriel, and she values you, as I value you. I never thought to have such a friend as you." I grimaced at her.

After Noryne departed, I spent a discouraging hour trying various solutions in my mind and abandoning all of them. The suggestion of a new burden on the Troupe could have been better timed. Key's death and the aggressive policies of the new Shrine Keeper had left us barely solvent.

I did not hear the K'shai enter. "Mistress Lyriel?" he called, emerging like a wraith from the dusky shadows of stacked crates and shrouded furnishings.

I jumped and spilled an open tin of beads across the floor. The beads clattered to a stop, leaving an awkward silence. I realized that I was staring at him, so I knelt to gather the worthless, tarnished beads. "Blast," I muttered, as one of the beads skittered away from me.

Evaric retrieved it, offering it to me courteously. "I apologize for startling you."

I snatched the bead from his hand. "You wanted something, K'shai?"

The openness in his expression vanished. His smile tightened and twisted. The transformation was unsettling, for it made him look like a true K'shai: a man who would do murder with remorseless efficiency for anyone who could afford his price. "Mistress Rubi indicated that you maintain the lists of inventory and personnel," he said with strict formality. "I should like copies of each. Fog and I like to establish the specifics of our responsibilities, so as to eliminate possible misunderstandings."

I stood and studied him squarely; it was a mistake, for close inspection only made him look better and just as dangerous. "Do you write?" I demanded, determined not to yield unnecessary advantage. Few literate K'shai sought work from impoverished Ardasian troupes.

"I write, Mistress Lyriel," he assured me very solemnly. A trace of laughter sparked in his shimmery eyes for just an instant.

"Then the lists are yours, as soon as you write them. Personally, I have never seen much purpose in wasting paper on such fleeting facts, and I am trained to memorize." I explained deliberately, "Lines and such for the plays."

"Tell me," he said shortly, and he leaned against a cracked bureau as if anticipating a lengthy stay. He elaborated too carefully, "I shall, of course, require your signature—or whatever mark you use for legal documents."

I did not dignify his cynical witticism with a reply. I returned to my task of sorting costumes and began to recite, "As of today, Rubi's Troupe consists of thirteen players—sixteen if you count Solomai's children—eight wagoners, one cook, one master of property, Taf, Rubi, myself, and two K'shai. . . ."

I was forced to credit the K'shai yet again. He listened attentively. When he returned with the promised list, written in a strong, swift script, it was complete to the last packet of pins.

Evaric placed the document before me. I set it aside deliberately after a single glance. "I shall attend to it later, K'shai," I remarked without looking at him. I had progressed from the costumes to the scripts, and I meant to finish my task before dusk demanded my return to the inn. I wanted this K'shai to understand that I would not rush to do his bidding.

"Tomorrow will suffice," he asserted calmly, managing to sound only quietly polite.

I could not even dent his Seriin chivalry, which, perversely, discouraged me. I sat and glowered after he had gone. The Troupe had not promised a more troublesome season since Broh deserted Rubi. "If you had any sense," I told myself, "you would follow Broh's example."

*   *   *

Taf looked as glum as I felt when we met in the dying light of day. We entered the inn together and the innkeeper growled at us as he bolted the vestibule's inner door against the night. Taf helped himself to the tankards of ale, and I claimed a table in the corner farthest from Alisa and her following. Noryne was not in sight, nor was Rubi, and the rest of the Troupe sojourned elsewhere. Taf brought the ale; the innkeeper's boy brought us fruit and twice-cooked beef, and for a time we devoted ourselves to the meal.

"Luck with the seamstress?" I asked when we had finished all but the ale.

Taf grunted, which usually meant no. "Pilgrim," he snarled.

"Poor Taf," I murmured. "Can she sew decently?"

"Should I know? She could not fare worse with a needle than you."

"When should I have studied stitchery? During performances? While persuading Denz to work another season on half pay? While writing plays that we can perform between licenses? While bribing some Tanist's minion to ignore your latest thieving?"

"Trouble with Alisa?" asked Taf glumly.

"Not yet," I grumbled in return. Alisa and Zakari were playing draughts in seemingly good humor. Judging by Miria's giggles, Alisa appeared to be winning, likely with Zakari's cooperation. Alisa was distractedly twisting a long curl around her finger. She was pretty, and her dearth of any concept of financial sense let us keep her in the Troupe by guile, when she could have achieved much more success elsewhere; she was lazy and temperamental, and I disliked her heartily. "Have you talked to the K'shai yet?"

"I discussed our route with Fog. He seems a sensible man."

From Taf, sensibleness amounted to high praise. "What of the other one?"

Taf shrugged. "Foreign."

"So is Fog," I suggested wryly, but I understood the distinction: Taf approved of Fog; Taf disapproved of Evaric.

Since Taf disapproves of nearly everyone, the latter comment signified very little.

Taf nodded toward the stair, and I turned my head to follow his glance. "Mistress Anni, the pilgrim," he explained.

"Not very distinctive. Why is she staying here?"

"Coincidence."

"This is an odd place for a pilgrim to choose."

"Odd," grunted Taf, rolling his eyes.

I looked at Taf sharply. "Are you sure about her?"

"No."

The pilgrim woman was trying unsuccessfully to attract the attention of the innkeeper. "What does Rubi think of her?"

"You know Rubi: The Troupe is All."

I darted another glance. "Only a pilgrim would suffocate willingly in all those depressing draperies. What do you suspect of her?"

Taf's hands rippled, and he cradled a kesne in his palm. The engraved wreath of the Alliance gleamed brightly on it. Taf tightened and released his fingers, and the copper coin lay dull and twisted.

"Balmy?" I asked.

"At least," he answered.

"Harmlessly so, I trust."

"She looks weaker than water," he muttered.

"She looks helpless." The innkeeper maintained a deliberate preoccupation with other customers, and the pilgrim woman had yet to gain supper. "Invite her over here, Taf," I suggested, "or she may starve before the season starts." I held no fondness for foreigners, especially pilgrims, but I tried to know the Troupe members.

Taf's expression said that I was as daft as the seamstress if I thought to make him share table with a pilgrim, but he did rise to rescue the hapless woman. When he returned with her, he wore his poorest imitation of amiability. "Mistress Anni," I said with sufficient warmth to compensate for Taf's sullenness. "I am Lyriel. Taf tells me that you have agreed to be our seamstress. We are pleased to have you with us." I disliked the way her hood shielded her eyes; I like to measure honesty from a full expression.

"It is gracious of you to say it," murmured Mistress Anni precisely. She was a mild, gray-shrouded figure of indeterminate age and nondescript character. She was pleasant, polite, and so self-effacing that she almost failed to exist. Why did she disturb me? I answered myself: because she is not a whole person. I could not quite decide what my conclusion meant, but it seemed appropriate to her.

Taf muttered something about finding the woman some supper, and he left us. Taf has never been one to waste effort in cultivating people to no profit; deceptions of character, which he enacts exceptionally well when he wishes, do not amuse him. I did not expect to see him again that evening.

"Have you been long in Ardasia?" I asked the seamstress, observing the delicacy with which she seated herself on the bench.

"Not long," she replied. The innkeeper's boy brought her a bowl of the stew's dregs, let it thud upon the table and splatter her, and slapped a broken loaf upon the board beside the bowl. "Thank you, young Master," said the woman graciously.

"The service here is not always dependable," I murmured, quietly conspiratorial in my lie. The service simply reflected the prevalent Ardasian attitude toward foreign clientele.

"I have encountered worse," responded the seamstress with a faint smile.

"Tulean hospitality must be worse than I had thought."

"You have an excellent ear for accents."

"Training," I answered confidently, though I had done little more than guess the seamstress' origin.

"You serve Mistress Rubi's Troupe as actress?" Most pilgrims disparaged our profession as frivolous and licentious, but Mistress Anni's question was respectful; my opinion of her increased.

"I am nominally a dancer, but I serve the Troupe as needed. I seem to find fewer opportunities to perform with every season. Other obligations have a way of taking precedence."

"Then you have traveled with Mistress Rubi's Troupe previously."

"All my life."

"The night has never troubled you?"

She intoned the question oddly, though she did not appear to be affected personally by the prospect. She reflected the pilgrim folly that holy pilgrimage granted immunity from

Rendies. Most pilgrims professed it; few believed it enough to travel the night alone. "We have K'shai to Protect us," I responded evenly.

"Of course." She seemed a decent sort for a pilgrim. Taf's comment about her peculiar character appeared excessive; she struck me as simply misplaced. She did not belong in Ardasia; no pilgrim ever really did belong here. I began to regale Mistress Anni with inconsequential chatter, while she consumed the stew with poorly disguised distaste.

I forgot the pilgrim woman momentarily when Evaric arrived. The Alisa rose, gushed, and drew him directly to her side. It was no great surprise that the K'shai displayed a ready appreciation for Alisa's welcome. I could see Zakari seethe, as Alisa and Miria both frothed with enthusiasm. The potential development of another complication disturbed me.

Mistress Anni had followed the direction of my stare, and she studied the vivacious group fixedly. I realized with some amusement that the seamstress watched only the K'shai. "Alisa is fierce competition for us mortal women," I remarked, nodding toward the group. Anni returned her steady gaze to me with the slow reluctance of thick honey. "The curly-headed blonde," I explained, "who is deftly sinking her claws into our new K'shai, is touted professionally as the Beauteous Alisa. She is our Troupe's leading actress. The rather handsome man sulking beside her is Zakari, our leading actor, and the fidgety woman with the child-fine, auburn hair is Miria, another of our actresses. The bored young men just leaving are two more actors: Minaro and Rayn. The K'shai calls himself Evaric. It is not a K'shai name." I shrugged. "But he does not seem concerned by that fact."

"Some men need not the artifice of a thing's name to mitigate evidence of humanity." Her comment was odd; something intense in her way of speaking it nearly rendered me speechless—no easy task. Anni proceeded quite naturally, "I merely hypothesize. K'shai do take such pride in appearing uncanny."

I laughed a little awkwardly. "You sound like Noryne, another of our actresses. She also suspects K'shai of being inhuman."

"You disagree?" asked Anni softly.

"Not altogether. They do live by killing."

"The assassin's trade is reprehensible but quite human."

"You are the one who spoke of K'shai mitigating humanity."

"By selecting names of artifice. It is pretense, illusion: That is the K'shai way."

"They do not slay Rendies by illusion," I insisted.

"On the contrary, illusion is precisely what the K'shai wield. The true K'shai survive the night because they are as remote from the creatures of the Rending as is a street-witch from a major Power."

She was certainly Seriin, I thought; they are all obsessed with their Ixaxin wizards. "Is there such a thing as a K'shai who is not true?" I mocked.

"He has no K'shai name."

Had we been discussing Evaric all this time? "He does not use a K'shai name, but he is certainly K'shai. Look at his hand!"

"A brand marks the skin, not the man."

"What do you think he is, if not K'shai?" Why did I expect anything sensible from a pilgrim?

"I do wish that I knew," she murmured almost wistfully. So, I thought with a certain sympathy, he affected even a pilgrim woman; the familiarity of Anni's reaction made me feel more kindly toward her.

Rubi summoned me to the upper floor with a shout, distinctive and loud even above the din of the common room. "Rubi has ways of making her wishes known," I muttered to Anni. A summons at this hour would surely mean a late night of working. "If anyone gives you trouble, Anni, refer them to me."

"Thank you, Mistress Lyriel. You are kind." Perhaps Anni's courtesy was mechanical, but I felt suddenly sure that she meant it warmly. I smiled at her as I left, deciding that Taf's comment about her oddness merely reflected Taf's usual surliness.

Anni remained alone at the table, observing the K'shai. I glimpsed her still there two hours later, and I think she had not moved at all. Miria had gone, and Zakari sulked by the wall. Alisa entertained Evaric to the apparent exclusion of the world. I grumbled a few unpleasant thoughts and returned to Rubi and Taf.

Chapter 5

"What do we still need?" demanded Rubi.

I gave her my tally. "Sandals, gilt paint, oats, dried fish." Taf made a terrible face; he loathes fish, which is why we always ran short of it. "A cooking pot to replace the one Solomai threw at the sand wolf last spring, another load of flour."

"How much flour can you possibly need?" complained Taf.

"Weevils infested the last two bags we opened."

"We have made do with worse."

"Not if I had a choice about it!"

"You think the flour comes to us for free?"

"Rubi asked what we need, and we need flour."

"It will only become infested like the other."

"Buy the flour, Taf," ordered Rubi.

I continued my interrupted recital, while Taf grumbled. "Paper, a new harness. We could use some nails."

"Denz again."

"He wants more than nails."

"Better iron prices inland." I only shrugged at that: Taf was probably right.

Rubi slapped her hands onto the broad plank table between us. "We are in fair shape."

"We leave in two days," commented Taf with a severely dampening humor.

"Will there be a problem?" asked Rubi. She has always excelled at portraying ingenuousness; the ploy relates to her fleshy, soft face and the trick she has of smoothing any intelligence from her expression.

"A problem?" demanded Taf indignantly. When Rubi continued to exude blankness, Taf sank into gloom. "I suppose I can manage, if Lyriel procures the fish and flour."

I took my turn at indignation. "I have enough to occupy me already, thank you."

"You want the supplies."

"We need the supplies."

"Then help acquire them."

"In two days? At the prices we can pay?"

"You expect me to obtain them for you!" Taf was gloating now.

"You are the conjurer, Taf." And if he were not kept busy during the remaining two days, he would certainly manage to cause some sort of trouble. Taf liked to depart Ardas each year with a flair, which meant that we spent each spring bribing our way back into the city's good graces.

"Give him the help he asks, Lyriel," commanded Rubi.

"Blasted conjurer," I growled. Taf came close to looking smug.

I was still grumbling when I reached the fish market a good two hours into the morning. The leering Bethiin sailor who lurked everywhere I turned did not improve my mood. He was not shopping for fish. Several of the merchants who knew me snickered and made snide comments. I snapped back at them.

"Taf has you doing the buying again?" commented Kikula, a vendor with whom I have dealt frequently. She is a rotund woman with a temper nearly as notorious as mine.

"You know how Taf feels about dried fish."

"Good for me that Rubi disagrees with him. Your Troupe brings some of my biggest sales," laughed Kikula, and we began the serious bargaining. Since we knew each other's measure well, we completed a sound exchange in little more than an hour. To my intense irritation, the Bethiin had not left.

"You belong to Rubi's Troupe?" he asked. Kikula and I had made no secret of our delivery arrangements.

I remarked mildly, "Not interested, Bethiin."

Kikula laughed uproariously at the Bethiin's blush. He persisted, "Your Troupe hired the K'shai from our ship."

He had acquired a portion of my interest. "Why did you replace them?" The Bethiin carried enough salt and herbs to equip a ship fully, which meant a return voyage soon. A lengthy voyage would require K'shai.

The Bethiin looked so eager when I addressed him that I

nearly pitied him. "Oh," he stammered. "No choice. They left us." He confirmed the story I had heard from the ship's captain. I dismissed him again. "I could tell you about them," he offered uncertainly, when I continued to ignore him. He obviously lacked experience in the type of transaction he hoped to complete, and his approach was accordingly clumsy.

"Still not interested," I replied firmly. These foreigners cherished persistent misconceptions about Ardasian morality.

"There are things you ought to know before you travel with them," insisted the Bethiin nuisance. He came closer to me than I liked. "Some of us were glad to see the last of those K'shai."

"Why?" I asked him sharply.

Kikula mumbled under her breath, "I would be glad to see the last of all foreigners," and I approved her sentiment heartily, as the Bethiin pushed his unappealing face close to my ear.

I pondered the advantages of driving my sandal's heel hard upon his bare toes. He whispered nervously, "They are not like any K'shai I ever met before."

"You have doubtless established a large acquaintance among K'shai during your extensive career as a common galley boy," I suggested scornfully.

He backed up a pace to a more comfortable distance, which constituted his most sensible action so far. "Maybe I am a galley boy," he sulked, "but I know wrongness when I see it. Even a K'shai does not talk to Rendies."

"What did you say?"

The Bethiin smirked. "He talked to the accursed Rendies—conversed with them—a dozen of us heard it. Ask Captain Tarl of the *Sea Dancer* if you doubt me."

"Captain Tarl said the K'shai gave excellent service." Why did I waste my time on this fool of a foreigner, who only wanted attention?

"So they did. But we never saw more Rendies than this trip brought. They came in dozens every night. K'shai fight Rendies. This pair attracts them like flies to carrion." A spitefulness in the Bethiin's voice might have represented envy. "Captain feared to tell you the whole of it, for dread of what those two would do to him."

Fear of K'shai was plausible, even likely, but no one talked to Rendies. Few even recalled their coming. The

Bethiin was a fool seeking attention via a farfetched story. Kikula pointed at the young pest with one of the dried eels that she usually waves at customers. "He does tell a good yarn," she said to me with an approving nod.

"Ask anyone from the ship," persisted the Bethiin, "or ask the K'shai why soot covered the deck the morning after a storm. What sort of fire burns in the rain?" His voice had grown loud, gaining him an audience.

"Rendies assume odd forms."

"Other incidents occurred. I saw . . ." He began to cough. When he stopped, he only stared at Kikula's strings of fish.

"What did you see?" I did wonder, even if the man was an obvious fool.

"How much do you want for the dried salt tuna?" he asked equably.

I hushed Kikula with a peremptory wave. "What did you see the K'shai do?"

"Could I see the third string from the end, please?"

He refused to acknowledge me again. Kikula shrugged at me and began to haggle with him. By that time, I felt inclined to scar the man's back with my dagger, but I decided he did not merit the trouble. At least he had stopped following me, so I could buy the flour without further annoyance.

*   *   *

Fog reached for his glass, found it empty, and shouted at the tavern keeper. "I told you to keep my glass filled!" The tavern keeper looked fearfully at Fog and Evaric.

Evaric said quietly, "I asked him not to serve you any more."

Fog's hand reached for his partner's throat. Evaric did not evade the larger man's attack, and Fog allowed his hand to fall. "You are a good partner, boy."

"Come outside with me, Fog. You need the fresh air."

Fog shuddered. "Did I tell you I was dead once?"

"You are alive now, and we have a job of Protection to fulfill."

"You saw what happened on the ship. The Rendies killed me again, and I burned them. How can a man burn the blasted Rendies?"

How? wondered Evaric, but he severed the questioning

thought. The Rendies had nearly claimed him that time, and Fog had saved his life and soul—again. "Outside, Fog," persisted Evaric gently. "You will feel better when you are sober." Because K'shai control would suppress this talk of death and devils. Sober, Fog would again become an ordinary K'shai: like me, thought Evaric, a man who denies his haunts.

Evaric watched his partner and wondered grimly if he saw his own tormented future. Not even a K'shai could deny haunts forever.

Chapter 6

Afternoon arrived in all its heat before I returned to the inn, where nearly half of Ardas' constabulary awaited me. One of the least popular men in Ardas demanded, "Mistress Lyriel?" as if we had never met.

"You know my name, Harbing," I replied with dry discouragement. Taf, could you not have waited until tomorrow? By tomorrow, of course, the fish would have been delivered, and Taf hates fish.

Harbing's partner, Shober, scuffed at the sand and said, "We need to talk to you, Mistress Lyriel."

"You have a charge against me?"

"I could find a dozen," grunted Harbing, exaggerating by at least a factor of three.

"About your father," continued Shober, as if he had never been interrupted.

One of the constables shouted, for Taf had appeared briefly at the end of the twisting street; most of the officials deserted me. Harbing ought to have known better than to waste energy on one of Taf's meticulously unlawful jests; Harbing had failed repeatedly to hold Taf on any number of charges.

"What did he do this time?" I muttered to Shober.

"He snatched the purses of three Seriin nobles, directly in view of their private guards." Shober nodded in appreciation. "I never saw a cleaner bit of work. Taf is an artist, Lyriel."

"Then why do you detect him so often?" Taf's remarkable talents no longer enraptured me. I had paid too many officials (including Shober) too dearly and too often for the privilege of Taf's continued freedom; too many of the officials preferred a more personal currency than copper or silver.

"You know how Taf enjoys an audience. He warned us in advance."

"I pay you to tell me such things before half of Ardas is on his trail. You owe me, Shober."

"Complain to Taf, not to me. He informed Harbing directly. What could I do?"

"Make it right, Shober, or I shall tell Harbing a few facts about you." I left Shober glowering and ran to find Rubi. I yelled, "Harbing," at her and continued my hasty course.

Locating the K'shai entailed a deal more persistence. One of the innkeeper's sons finally directed me to a tavern (a common commodity in Ardas) with solid walls (an exceedingly uncommon encumbrance for an Ardas establishment with no sleeping rooms). The tavern's owner catered to foreigners, who knew no better than to bake indoors while the sun heated the day. I had expected more sense from Master Evaric.

The stifling tavern held only three customers: a drunken pilgrim preaching to an empty chair, and at a table in the far corner, Evaric and a man whom I presumed to be Fog. The two K'shai conferred softly, but I would have wagered that they argued.

"We must leave now," I told them tersely.

I drew them both from some distant realm. Evaric nodded without expression. Fog informed me with care, "You ought not to have come here." He spoke with peculiar precision for a man who sat amid so many emptied tankards.

"It is her city," remarked Evaric with sardonic wisdom. "This is Mistress Lyriel, Fog, the young woman of whom I told you."

"I recall," mused Fog. "She persuaded you to accept K'shai minimum." I had not thought his eyes were pale when I looked at him initially, but old fires and older vices had veiled the room with deceptive smoke. "The heiress of the mortal strain fulfills the pattern: how poetically appropriate." I wondered if Fog had encountered too many Rendies to keep his sanity. "She has arrived prematurely, however." Fog's remote assurance rang like a dire warning.

"A day early," I agreed. "Circumstances have advanced our schedule. Please come immediately."

Fog ignored my injunction, though he stared at me with disquieting care. Fog appeared old for an active K'shai; he looked as battle-scarred as any K'shai I had ever seen.

When he spoke again, his voice slurred: "Careful, girl. The devil has taken note of you!" An uncanny expression stole across his battered face: calculating, sardonic, and rueful all at once. For an instant, Fog resembled an extremely wealthy and powerful Tanist I had once met; both men shared an element of unspoken assurance that made my skin crawl.

Everything about the conversation struck me as peculiar. In the bar's dim interior, I convinced myself that Fog's eyes were a very pale blue in his scarred brown face. In the daylight, the eyes looked dark, almost black. Fog's voice coarsened, and I began to think that he might actually be as drunk as I had expected initially.

The sunlight warmed Evaric's smile. He smiled so easily; his eyes remained hard and secretive. "Pay no mind to Fog, Mistress Lyriel. He does enjoy your Ardasian liquors." Evaric's effortless charm nearly succeeded in allaying my suspicions, until I concluded that distraction was his intention. I was not sure exactly what I should suspect of these K'shai, but they certainly constituted an unconventional pair, whether they talked to Rendies, affected sporadic madness, or merely made a fool of me.

I left the K'shai to Rubi's frantic orders. The single constable we passed ignored us; he was Shober's man. I headed for the stable in search of Solomai. The voices of the Troupe's preparations for departure reached me dimly. "Solomai!" I called, hearing movement from the stable's darkness. I received no answer. I turned my back to the row of lightless stalls, most of which loomed empty this time of day.

My shoulder felt the clench of harsh fingers from behind me. I tried to reach my knife, but the man gripped my wrist. His hand wore the bloodied-sword brand. "Be calm, Mistress," he hissed, "I only mean to speak to you."

"What do you want, K'shai?" I whispered hoarsely.

"You require Protection. I seek to serve you."

Why? I demanded in silent alarm; a month ago, we could not hire K'shai at any price. Aloud, I said, "We have already hired Protection. You may have seen them. We passed this way together a few minutes ago. Let me call them. They will speak for themselves."

"You need Protection."

"We have already hired K'shai," I repeated in frustration. "We require no others. We cannot afford more."

"I am called Straw. You will remember me." I nodded stiffly.

"We cannot pay you."

"You need Protection."

Are you a Protector, Straw, or an assassin? Whom have you been hired to kill? And why are you talking to me? "When we need new Protection, I shall remember you, Straw." The noncommittal concession seemed to appease him. He relaxed his grasp.

"I shall be near," he promised me ominously.

"Thank you," I murmured, because I feared to offend him. Straw stared at me. I would have welcomed even Harbing's appearance at that moment. "I must go now," I said, and I moved very slowly toward the stable door. Straw did not speak; neither did he stop me.

The Troupe departed Ardas within the hour. Taf met us beyond the city's edge. I did not tell him of my strange K'shai encounter. Taf was too busy gloating over the artistry of his thieving escapade. At least Solomai had managed to load the dried fish.

Chapter 7

The freedom of early autumn was a glorious release after the long summer of Ardas crowds and cacophony. The villages along the northern coasts smelled of uniformity (in a literal sense: they all reeked of rotting fish), but we stayed in none long enough to become unduly bored. We arrived, the sun rose, we performed, the sun set, we traveled and slept; by the next day another shore village welcomed us. The inland times were easier on the mules and the wagoners, and they did spare us from the nightly stars, but even a week in a single city left me restless and anxious to depart.

Diarmon saw the first of our protracted stays. We would remain for a full week, preparing for the journey inland. Equipped with several resident troupes, Diarmon did not encourage us to provide multiple performances. Rubi accepted the burden of the Troupe's own keep in Diarmon, as in no other city but Ardas, for two reasons: Diarmon preceded one of the most arduous stretches of our season's journey, and Taf insisted that I spend some time each year with Silf. It was his sole quirk of fatherly concern, and Rubi hated it. My obligatory visit to Silf's shipbuilder did not particularly enchant me either, but dread of it comprised a healthier obsession than Rendies or K'shai.

Anticipation of renewing old wounds made me too restless to sit through our first day's play. I abandoned my privileged position in the audience, and a dozen less fortunate viewers crowded forward to vie for my tree-shaded bench. I aggravated two rows of the audience unnecessarily, simply to avoid Rubi. She was frowning fiercely at the play's weak rendition; its leading members blossomed with apathy. I would rewrite the roles, but I refused to entrap myself intentionally in the midst of Rubi's fury, Alisa's inevitable tantrum, and Zakari's self-pitying whines.

Evaric leaned near the theater gate, apparently observing

play, players, and passersby with equal allotments of amused equanimity. The dappled shadow and light danced around him. Even the hot Ardasian sun adored him, gleaming off golden arms below rolled sleeves. I wondered cynically if he practiced posing, like an actor.

"Walking out on a performance?" he asked me with a studied smile. "What will Mistress Rubi say?"

"That the Alisa demonstrates the professionalism of a cabbage. That you are goading Zakari into a jealous frenzy, which has made him forget acting altogether."

The smile disappeared. "I am goading Zakari?"

"That the three of you had better come to an agreement soon, or I shall revise the script to eliminate both Alisa and Zakari, and I shall charge the loss of revenue against your contract."

One dark brow rose curiously. "You wrote the play?" Not a word did he give about placating Zakari or settling his position with Alisa one way or another.

"Of course I wrote the play," I snapped at him. "It saves on performance fees, and we must save all we can so as to hire K'shai Protection." I swept close past him. He moved so nimbly that his unaffected elegance did not suffer. He ought to have been on the stage. He could have drawn audiences without uttering a line.

I selected a suitably tasteless costume for my visit to Silf and her shipbuilder. Since the shipbuilder's family chose to perceive the members of Rubi's Troupe as brassy and ignorant, I cultivated the expected attitude to emphasize every difference between the shipbuilder's world and my own. If the ploy failed to jeopardize Silf's own position with the shipbuilder, it still underlined her alienism to Diarmon. I wanted her to remember.

The shipbuilder's manservant frowned when I arrived, but he knew me. He escorted me to the parlor and into the disappointing presence of the shipbuilder's two pale, prim, and myopic daughters. Both girls affected the high-collared, voluminously encompassing gowns of foreign fashion, ridiculous in the Ardasian climate. The girls differed a few years in age, but I never bothered to distinguish them by names.

"Your mother will return soon," announced the first very properly. The inspection she gave me was less gracious.

"Father and she are visiting Tanist Melhar," added the

other with a trace of deliberate snobbery. "We are pleased to see you again, Lyriel." I flashed an insincere smile and said nothing; the best enjoyment I ever derived from the sisters came of letting them squirm in my company.

The younger girl asked, "Did you see the royal visitors when you were in Ardas?"

"No." I had been unable to see past the crowds in front of me, save for a brief glimpse of Serii's Adjutant escaping the parade, but I felt no inclination to elaborate for the sake of the shipbuilder's daughters.

"I heard that the procession was wonderfully elaborate. Queen Marylne sent the finest of everything for her daughter's entourage."

"Stal must be terribly pleased. All of the Bethiin princesses are reputed to be quite stunning, and Lilyan is supposed to be by far the prettiest." The sisters scattered royal names like familiar friends. I doubted they addressed even their dear Tanist so intimately in his presence. The foreign custom of formal speech had so far eluded the sisters' mastery.

"Did you hear that King Nion has authorized five more Ixaxin schools? Father expects one of the schools to be established in Diarmon."

"Have you ever visited an Ixaxin school, Lyriel?" asked the oldest sister, but she did not await a response. I have never understood why the shipbuilder's daughters consider me sheltered as well as ignorant, since I am far more traveled than anyone else they are likely to meet, save Silf. "An Ixaxin visited Tanist Melhar last winter. The Ixaxin actually took the farrier's son away to Ardas."

"Surely the farrier's son cannot be a sorcerer. He is such an untidy boy."

"Even Ixaxins must make mistakes."

Boredom made me murmur, "They made one at least: They named the Venkarel as Infortiare, which brought the Rending upon us. Had Ixaxis elected Lord Hrgh dur Liin, as anticipated, we might not need assassins to escort us through the night." The sisters were staring at me as if a none-too-clever parrot had suddenly mastered its first word. "Of course, the present Infortiare insists that the Venkarel curbed the Rending's effect from the total destruction that might have resulted, but Lady Rhianna does have a vested interest in preserving the illusion of her position's inviolability."

Since the shipbuilder's daughters could not possibly acknowledge that I knew something more than they of history, they settled on expressions of tolerant disbelief. Silf and her shipbuilder arrived in the midst of the reciprocated disparagement. "A united family," beamed the shipbuilder, "is a reverence to a man's proud little kingdom." The shipbuilder's impromptu speeches unflaggingly betrayed him as a fool.

His daughters pecked his papery cheeks. He offered me the same opportunity, doubtless thinking his gesture a generous one; I pretended not to understand. I had no intention of according him the coy tribute he expected of a daughter. Silf knew my reluctance. She came to me, sweeping forward in her unwieldy skirts with a grace that broke my heart. She took my hands and held them. I wanted to beg her to leave with me on the instant, return to Taf and me and the world in which we three belonged. "Rubi sends her regards," I told her cruelly.

Silf blinked, her long, dark lashes rising slowly. "How is your father?" she asked a little hoarsely. The shipbuilder and his daughters retreated discreetly, closing the door on us to give us privacy and a dearth of breathable air.

"As well as ever," I returned stiffly. "You could see him."

"Taf would not wish it," she answered, releasing me with a sigh. She had coiled her beautiful black hair in a tightly bound knot, and the effect aged her.

"You mean that your shipbuilder would not wish it."

"His name is Marlund," amended Silf wearily. "He is a good man, Lyriel."

"He is a fool."

"Because he does not know how to steal, cheat, and lie as deftly as Taf?"

"You never minded when you loved Taf."

"I knew nothing else. I have taken most of a lifetime to realize that there is a better way to live: an honest way among honest, open people."

"Honesty is an overrated commodity."

Silf shook her head delicately. "I wish you would stay here long enough to understand what you scorn. Marlund would welcome you as a daughter. Peliia and Olna would be your sisters and your friends if you would accept them. You could be free of the scrounging and starving and wondering when your father will be caught and hanged."

"No one catches Taf unless he wishes it," I remarked, as

inspected the dozens of dusty little porcelain dolls cluttering the tea table. Every one of them bore the mark of an importer; the shipbuilder's daughters liked exotic toys.

"Even Taf will slip some day. Someone will catch him, or someone will catch you concealing his crimes and Rubi's. You have a right to a life of your own, Lyriel."

"With you and your shipbuilder?" I scoffed.

"You could be schooled properly instead of snatching at any morsel of neglected lore you find. You would meet good, intelligent people. I know how you detest the stupidity of those you coddle for the sake of 'The Troupe.' "

"Your shipbuilder exudes intellect." The ridiculous sleeve of my costume slipped from my shoulder, and I replaced it irritably. Silf and I no longer shared anything but a frustrated yearning to make each other understand. I began to count the room's baubles so as to stifle my unruly temper. "I think I had better leave."

"Will you not dine with us?" asked Silf, now hurt and desperate.

"I must discuss some revisions with Rubi."

"Tomorrow?"

"I do not belong here, Silf. Neither do you."

"Rubi is consuming your soul as surely as a Rendie," Silf muttered bitterly. "Like Taf: you become empty and cold."

"Rubi did not steal Taf from you. You threw him at her—and me with him." I flung open the door and nearly choked on the influx of cooler air. The shipbuilder and his daughters shuffled awkwardly in their own entry hall, every inch of which had contributed to some foreigner's profits. I waved at them flippantly, disregarded Silf's attempts to detain me, and stormed outside just as the disapproving man-servant reached the door with undignified haste.

I scattered venomous thoughts against the shipbuilder's sprawling lawns. Staffs of servants pumped water endlessly, but the lawns wore a parched look. Such lawns were a Seriin fashion. They had no place in Ardasian soil and climate.

Even the newly cobbled street discouraged me, though it represented a more practical affectation of foreign ways. Hard dirt and sand had always served Diarmon well. The heavy rainstorms, which churned the streets to mud, came

asier when I reached the older, less reputable own. The stained beggar who accosted me carried a strong, unpleasant reek, but he was thoroughly Ardasian. I flipped him an iron kesne out of respect for the tradition of his trade. I ignored the flock of other beggars who materialized at my gesture, reaching out their hands in supplication and trying to grab at my arms. Respect for tradition did not make me a fool; the beggars likely enjoyed more wealth than I would ever achieve.

Chapter 8

The man who shuffled through the crowd did not belong among the Troupe's performers or admirers. He pressed uncomfortably between the enthused youths who cast petals before the Beauteous Alisa. The man's age lay between the old and the young. He wore a comfortable paunch. His face glistened from exertion in the sun. He was soft, unaccustomed to the streets.

Lyriel saw him briefly and knew him for one of the shipbuilder's ilk. She wondered why he walked alone in the dusty streets around Diarmon's oldest inn; he was misplaced, making him an obvious target for a clever pickpocket. Taf could easily have freed him of the bulging purse which showed a faint outline beneath his tunic. Lyriel could have stolen it herself, but neither she nor Taf stole in Diarmon out of deference to Silf.

The man moved away from the Troupe, and Lyriel lost sight of him. Near the inn's entry, the man saw the two K'shai, whose presence discouraged trouble far more effectively than did the constables with their bright, brass-decorated scabbards. Dark leather concealed the K'shai weapons, but K'shai hands brandished fiercer blades.

The man hesitated near the K'shai. When he was beside them he dropped his gaze and began to turn away. When he looked again into the milling crowd, he reconsidered. He mumbled his words to the K'shai. "I need to talk to you."

"Then talk," suggested Fog easily.

"Not here!" returned the man, appalled.

Evaric's silver-blue eyes became vaguely disdainful. Fog snarled, "Inside, south hall, third door."

"Five minutes," added Evaric. The man sputtered an agreement.

"I can pay whatever you ask," said the man.

"What is the job?"

"There is a man who has wronged me."

"You want him killed," commented Evaric mildly.

The man could not complete a nod, but all K'shai were accustomed to such uncertain customers, who were laden equally with vindictiveness and guilt. "I can tell you where to find him," offered the man. "'In the early morning, there is no one near. . . .'"

"When we accept a job, it is we who decide how to execute it," said Evaric quellingly.

The man fingered his collar. "I only meant. . . ."

"To help," finished Evaric sardonically.

"Perhaps I . . . I should begin again. My name is. . . ."

"We do not need your name," interrupted Fog. "Why did you come to us? We are already employed."

"What?" The man was growing ever more frightened. "Your Guild-mate sent me to you. He said that you. . . ."

"Which Guild-mate?" asked Evaric.

"A scarred man. He came to me. I thought you would. . . ."

"What name did he give you?"

"What name?" asked the man helplessly. "Straw. Yes, that was it: Straw."

Evaric said pensively, "I have no interest in the contract." To Fog, he added, "It is yours, if you want it."

"Empty your purse," Fog ordered the man.

With shaking hands, the man obeyed. Evaric inspected the mound of silver which the man poured upon the table. Evaric sorted from it the few small coppers. He dropped the coppers back into the man's leather purse and pushed the silver across the table to Fog. "Describe the target," Fog said shortly, "in detail."

"You accept the commission?" The man was looking at his silver, unsure now of the worth of his jealousy.

"I shall take this," Fog said, spreading his fingers across the silver, "as retainer for my trouble. If, upon assessing the target, I elect to decline, then I shall return to you one half of this sum. If, however, I decide to complete the contract, then I shall expect twice this much again. Are the terms agreeable?"

"Twice again as much? That is more than a year's savings!"

"Are the terms agreeable?" repeated Fog patiently.

"I cannot afford so much."

"Then why do you waste my time?"

"Accept or decline," said Evaric sharply. "K'shai do not dicker over trifles."

The man gave the silver another hungry glance, but his eyes were caught instead by the branded sword on Evaric's hand. "The man, the target, is young," he began, nodding shakily toward Evaric, "about your age. . . ."

"How many K'shai have you killed without telling me, Fog? How many times have you forestalled my death at the hands of our Guild-mates?"

"A man Protects his partner."

"Against his own Guild? The K'shai do not accept me, Fog, though they branded me, took my vows, and claimed my soul. What am I, Fog?"

"K'shai. You have sworn it."

"Straw is challenging us," said Evaric hollowly.

"Then we shall accept his challenge," replied Fog evenly.

"By assassinating some pathetic youth, whose misfortune it is to be disliked by a man of wealth?"

"The youth sounds noxious from all descriptions."

"Is that why you accepted the contract?"

"The price is good."

"Of course, the price is good." Evaric rubbed at his eyes. "And we are K'shai, and K'shai accept contracts, and refusal to accept a good contract is impossible for any good K'shai. Straw has certainly become a generous benefactor. How long shall we let him live, Fog? If we kill him in Diarmon, we could bury him with Coal; the grave would still be soft. Is that a practical, K'shai solution to the problem, Fog?"

"Go to sleep, boy. The nights will grow long soon enough."

*   *   *

The stars shone. The wind sighed warning. A man and woman stood in the lee of Diarmon's oldest inn. "This is a desolate, uncivilized place," murmured the man, who was the more restless of the pair.

"There is a beauty to it," returned the woman softly.

"Can you actually approve of a place with such a paucity of trees?"

The woman smiled, though her expression was difficult to

discern in the darkness. "The country has a beauty of its own, but I would not choose it for myself."

"You seem to have adapted well: the little pilgrim seamstress, all in gray, earning her pittance, striving to attain the Shrine. You do know that they are cheating you unconscionably?"

Reminded of her role, she began to gather her hood around her face, but she stopped and shook it free. "I do not need their gold," she replied a bit pridefully.

"Copper, darling Rhianna. You must quit thinking in such affluent terms."

"Or I shall be discovered? Ineuil, these people would not recognize Power if it consumed them. They are more blind than Tyntagellians."

"What about your son?" Ineuil asked darkly.

"He does not see me."

"By your choice?"

"I have not used Power."

"Neither have you made yourself known to him."

"He is not an easily approachable young man. He has become very much a K'shai."

"You traveled halfway around the world to find him."

"And I have inflicted a like journey upon you."

"I have admittedly visited more hospitable climes: cleaner ones, at any rate." Serii's Adjutant stirred the ubiquitous dust with his foot. "How long do you intend to maintain this charade of yours?"

"Until I understand what I must do." She raised a supplicating hand. "Can you bear with me a bit longer, Ineuil?"

Ineuil took her hand and kissed it gently. "Since you ask me, yes. I can bear your pilgrimage, even if I am bound to the company of the most tedious, uneducated, unimaginative assortment of individuals ever inflicted upon my patience."

Rhianna's lips twitched in amusement. "Are they all men?"

"I am portraying a pilgrim, my dear Rhianna, in which tiresome species Ardasian women have no interest."

"You are a far better friend than I deserve, making such sacrifices for me."

"But pilgrimages end in D'hai," continued Ineuil with scarcely a pause. "If you have not acted by that time, then you may as well resign yourself to eternal indecision."

She pulled her hand from his, for he had held it throughout his speech. She stood straight and regal, and she answered him evenly, "I shall not leave D'hai without resolving my position with my son."

"Then we shall meet again before the Shrine."

"You are leaving?" Fear and questioning spilled from her, even as she waved and a Rendie fled in terror.

Ineuil shivered inadvertently at the wraith's wake of fear, though he had defeated enough Rendies himself to impress a K'shai. "I can shadow you inconspicuously along the coast, where I may travel alone, but to journey inland I need Ardasians who know the land. I have paid a fortune in bribes just to join a merchant train, which travels faster than pilgrims. Unless you have reconsidered letting me accompany your little Troupe. . . ."

"No. I become myself too quickly when you are with me." She looked away and back to him reluctantly. "It is better, as you propose, that we meet in D'hai. Then I shall have the time I need."

"He is your son, Rhianna."

"He resembles Kaedric greatly," she said wistfully.

"That should not daunt you." Ineuil was sardonic.

"He is both lighter and darker than Kaedric. He has been twisted."

"'If you tell me that he is more a fiend than his father, then I shall never sleep peacefully again." Ineuil took both of her hands and kissed them. "I shall await you breathlessly, my lovely Infortiare."

"Hush!"

"In D'hai," he finished.

"In D'hai," she echoed distantly.

Chapter 9

The rare luxury of a morning without urgency helped revive me. I stayed late abed more for reason of conscious self-indulgence than for any need of extra rest. I left the inn with a sigh of pleasure for the thought of immersing my sorrows in the Archives, Diarmon's chief redeeming feature. The Archives purportedly contain every scrap of Ardasian lore extant. They actually lack a few governing documents, which are held by the king in Ardas, but I have never minded the gap.

Tabok waved to me as I passed the marketplace. Taf stood with him, haggling over the price of dried beans, but Taf does not acknowledge extraneous events when a bargain is to be made. I paused to pursue some idle bargaining of my own. I began to denigrate an opaline brooch, though it was a beautiful piece and far beyond my means. The proprietor retaliated with enthusiasm.

A distinctively familiar hand dropped a ridiculous sum of silver on the proprietor's counter. Evaric grabbed both the brooch and my arm, and he wafted me along the street in complete disregard for my very vocal protest. It would have served him right if I had screamed for help, but I thought better of the notion. Even constables tend to give wide berth to a man with sword both at his side and emblazoned on his hand.

"What do you think you are doing?" I asked him indignantly.

"Accelerating your shopping," he returned evenly. He had abandoned his Seriin jerkin in favor of a light tunic. He could have been Ardasian, save for the arsenal of blades he wore and the brand, which nothing could disguise. "You Ardasians waste an unconscionable amount of time."

"You paid five times what the brooch is worth," I informed him coldly.

"I paid less than a tenth of the marked price," he protested. I sniffed contemptuously; foreigners had no sense for business. Evaric shook his head, remarking, "I must remember to take you with me the next time I need to make a purchase in this extortionate country of yours."

"Were you listening to us?" I demanded suspiciously. I did not like being spied upon by a K'shai, even an unorthodox one. It reminded me too keenly of a stable in Ardas and a menacing man called Straw.

"I cannot assume credit for such a miracle of attentiveness. Ardasian bargaining far exceeds the comprehension of a mere Seriin." He drew me into the shade of a cafe's striped awning. The tables all were occupied, until Evaric smiled meaningfully at a pair of youths who lingered over an emptied carafe. The boys departed hastily, and Evaric pushed me into one of the vacated chairs. He seated himself in the other. When he had commanded wine for us both, he continued his remarks as if they had not been interrupted. "I did not listen to your bargaining, but I did watch you—a much more rewarding pastime."

"Save your Seriin chivalry for Alisa." I was becoming somewhat less exasperated. The wine was both expensive and good. The flattery did not hurt. I was still not pleased with the K'shai's insolence, but his attention was headier than the wine. "What do you want?" I asked him.

"Entry to the Archives," he responded succinctly. "You are a licensed playwright, which means that you have access privileges."

"Any temple can give you the history of the Shrine, and that is all the Ardasian history any foreigner needs." The cafe's proprietor was watching us and whispering to the serving girl. If they recognized me from previous visits, they might well lodge a complaint against Rubi's Troupe, for the obvious presence of a K'shai was steadily driving away the customers.

"The temples do not sate a harmless appetite for ancient records. Respectful admittance to the greatest of Ardasian libraries is surely not an excessive request."

"You are a foreigner," I stated. A very curious foreigner, I added to myself; why should a K'shai wish to see the Archives?

"Your license permits you an escort."

"Does it?"

"Yes. It does. As I am sure you already know." He was suppressing annoyance with an effort. "Naturally, I shall recompense you for your trouble."

"What makes you think you can afford me?"

"What makes you think that I cannot?" His branded hand gripped my wrist. With his other hand, he counted twenty kelni into my palm. The coins felt hot from his handling. "I could buy my own license for less, but bribing Ardasians tries my patience." His eyes, which looked gray today, criticized me. "I shall not try to bargain with you," he said, as if bargaining were an indecent occupation.

"Just as well. I bargain only for what I desire."

He spread his branded hand flat against the marble table, which was not a very subtle way of reminding me of what he represented. "Is admittance to the Archives really so much to ask?"

"From a foreigner, yes."

"You sound like Taf, despising anyone who is not Ardasian."

"I am a dutiful daughter."

"Taf is your father," said Evaric with the rigid cadence of revelation.

"You thought I was his Toy?"

Evaric began to shake his head, then resorted to a shrug. "I could not identify the relationship as an emotional one."

"The mistake is common." I never discussed Taf with anyone. Stop it, Lyriel, before you make a fool of yourself over a blasted K'shai. I finished weakly, "Taf and I actually have very little in common."

Evaric volunteered quietly, "I never had much in common with my parents either."

"I always pictured K'shai as disgruntled orphans."

"Perhaps disgruntled," he replied with half a smile, "but not necessarily as a result of childhood deprivation. You would be pressed to find a more sound and stable family than mine."

"All the worse," I snapped, angry again; he did not even attempt to make excuse for his profession. I tried to leave the table, but Evaric pushed me back into place almost before I moved.

"Mistress Lyriel," he said very seriously, "I am attempting to declare a truce."

"Are we at war?"

"So it would appear, though I am unsure of the cause."

"How many men have you assassinated?"

"Is that your reason for snarling at me constantly?"

"Do I need a better one?"

"Since you employ me as Protection, yes. There are many reasons for a man to become K'shai. Inasmuch as you know nothing of mine, I think your judgment against me is rather premature."

"A K'shai kills. There is nothing else to understand."

"Seven."

"What?" I did not want to hear him; I did not want to know him. I could not avert my eyes from him.

"I have assassinated seven men. I have rejected a hundred contracts. I became K'shai because of a nightmare involving Rendies."

"You commit murder professionally for the sake of a nightmare? What sort of reason is that? You are not the first to have nightmares about Rendies. The rest of us do not become assassins."

"I have only killed those who allowed me no choice."

"By whose judgment? Yours alone?"

"Yes. Mine alone." For a moment, he gave me the oddest impression of explosively conflicting forces tightly bound, and then he was only a rueful man of unconscious charm who was trying very hard to be patient with me. "Mistress Lyriel, will you please permit me to enter the Archives with you?"

The shriveled woman who tends the Archives always looks as dusty as her charge. She knows me, but she never acknowledges our acquaintance save by admitting me without question. I think she resents the rare intrusions upon her isolation; not many Ardasians read well, and visitors to the Archives are accordingly few. The woman had fought my first entrance to her domain bitterly; admittedly, few five-year-olds own licenses to anything. I had pleaded for mine, until Taf procured it in a card game. My license had become more extensive and more legitimate since that time, but it was recorded still in its original format: Lyriel, Silf's daughter, of Ardas.

The woman opened the great door to me grudgingly. When she noticed Evaric, she tried to push the door closed again. Evaric forestalled her with an effortless motion. "He accompanies me," I assured the woman firmly. When she failed to alter her defensive stance, I added impatiently, "License twenty-six. The record of it occupies the third drawer in the second cabinet, fifth aisle from the south wall."

"He is K'shai," argued the woman in a papery voice.

"He is in my employ, and I choose to authorize his admittance in my company. The sooner we enter, the sooner we shall depart." She considered my words, and Evaric smiled at her. She let us enter, shuffled into her office, and slammed the door loudly.

Evaric gave a low whistle, which was not for the benefit of the caretaker. "Is there any method to all of this?" he asked me.

"Not much," I responded truthfully. The enormity of the Archives made research among them a highly experimental art. Rows of polished marble shelves contained the random contributions of crates dispatched through the years from the king's palace. Great chests of rusting iron cluttered the aisles, enhancing the impression of total chaos. I had no idea of how one would begin efficiently to seek a particular topic, but that was Evaric's problem and not mine.

While Evaric inspected an upper shelf of one of the few hardwood cabinets, I headed for one of my favorite corners. I pried open the shutters to air the room. I doubted they had been open since my last visit. The overturned crate, which I sometimes used as a stepladder, lay beneath the window, as I had left it two years earlier. The Archives changed so little. They belonged to me more than anything I actually owned.

Several minutes elapsed before Evaric found me. "What do you charge for a clue?" he asked me dryly. The bindings of leather and old cloth muffled his clear, soft voice. I enjoyed seeing him at a loss. I think he did not share my appreciation.

"In what regard?" I replied innocently.

"In regard to this random maze of Ardasian illogic."

"Sorry K'shai. I cannot help you." I turned a page idly. "Unless you tell me what you are trying to find."

He hesitated longer than my simple statement of fact warranted. I abandoned my abstracted pose to verify that he had not evaporated into K'shai illusion. "I have an interest in ancient history," he breathed slowly.

"Choose any tome that crumbles," I suggested.

"Your advice falls short of adequate."

"So also does your stated objective. 'Ancient history' covers nearly everything in this room."

"If I did provide you with a more specific topic, could you find its reference in all of this?"

"Why must you K'shai convert everything into a mystery? If you tell me the topic, I shall tell you whether I can help you."

He walked a few paces away from me and melted into a long shadow. I shaded my eyes from the window's light so as to see him. He scanned the spines of a row of assorted diaries, several of which I had found useful, none of which bore any title or other identifying mark. He answered me over his shoulder. "There was a thing which came to Serii some few thousands of years ago. One tale reports that it originated in Ardasia."

"Has this thing a name?"

"Taormin." He threw the word at me as if it carried a vile flavor.

"You do mean ancient history."

His stare struck me even from the shadow. He tilted his head so that his black shock of hair brushed the pale frost-blue of his embroidered collar. "You know of it?"

"The Taormin was taken from Ardasia by the Sorcerer King of Serii. We never forget a thief nor that which has been stolen from us." I replied tartly, but I was pondering uneasily how I might extricate myself from a K'shai's anger. The colorless intensity of Evaric's eyes reminded me of wraith-glow.

He asked carefully, "What else do you know of this thing?"

"Why do you care? It was stolen millennia ago."

"I have reasons."

"K'shai secrets?"

"Personal reasons."

"Why should I abet a K'shai's furtive intrigue?"

His laugh cut short my question. Something quiet fell from him. The K'shai's long fingers curled into the flesh of my shoulders. He twisted me and held me; I waited for my bones to snap. He whispered to me, "I could persuade you, Mistress Lyriel." He released me. I whirled across the room and faced him with my dagger in my hand. "What do you intend to do with *that?*" he asked reasonably.

It was a fair question to which I had no satisfactory answer. "I am leaving, Seriin. Find someone else to guide you through the Archives."

"And you will never know why a K'shai cares enough about ancient Ardasian history to travel halfway across the world, seek a contract to Protect at half of what he could earn from pilgrims, and tolerate more outright rudeness from a bad-tempered dancer/playwright than anyone should sensibly accept."

I sheathed my dagger, keeping suspicious watch over the maddening K'shai. "If you intended to answer me, what was the purpose of your K'shai coercion?"

"You may consider it a whim."

"You are the most aggravating man I have ever met."

"The adjective is mutually applicable," he said amiably. I did not trust his change of mood. I kept my responding smile cautious and cynical. "I have a foster brother." He was selecting his words very carefully, which made me wonder how much truth he intended to impart. "We have been separated for a number of years. I believe he may have come to Ardasia so as to research the Taormin. If I study it equally, I may be able to locate him."

"Why does your brother care about the Taormin?"

"Rendie madness often results in inexplicable obsessions."

"Your brother survived a Rendie attack?"

"Yes, when he was very young." I would have given much to read Evaric's thoughts at that moment.

"You were separated when you became K'shai?"

"Before that."

I was accomplishing nothing by prolonging Evaric's tense evasion of total truth. More pertinently, he was hurting, and a particularly foolish notion had begun to tell me that I might enjoy comforting him. "Enough," I said. "I have better things to do than pry your family history from you word by word." I led him to a cache of rejected relics from the king's own collection. "Workbooks of the royal children," I explained. "Be forewarned: Ardasian rulers have never achieved note for scholastic excellence." I selected one of the more intact books and handed another to Evaric. He bestowed a doubtful inspection on both the book and me, but he began to scan the mildewed pages.

An hour's perusal of the exercises of our king's ancestors taught me chiefly to appreciate the Archive's cool walls. "What event signified the end of the Ardasian Republic?" Evaric asked me unexpectedly.

I accorded him a suitably unenthused response, "The first drought of spring."

"An equally irrelevant answer did not amuse the tutor of this young prince. The tutor wrote a scathing commentary on the student's inattentiveness to lessons. He also wrote an answer to the question I just quoted: 'The Ardasian Republic dissolved when the theft of the D'hai Control by the Sorcerer King of Serii made the Ardasian interior uninhabitable.' "

"That makes no sense," I argued. "The Ardasian interior is as it has always been: inhospitable but bearable."

"An Ardasian never forgets that which has been stolen from him," Evaric reminded me. I would not have wagered my coppers on the truth of his leap of logic, but he made his conclusion sound like a well-established fact. "How many significant items did a Sorcerer King of Serii steal from Ardasia?" he asked defensively, though I had not expressed my doubts.

"One, two, perhaps a hundred. The Taormin's theft occurred ten thousand years ago or more."

"Much more like twenty thousand years, I think, but the prince and tutor who scribed this parchment lived in this millennium. They still remembered the theft."

"So the Taormin may once have controlled something in D'hai. What do you intend," I asked with what I considered rather saintly patience, "to do with this wealth of information? Pray at the Shrine for enlightenment?"

His shell of quiet reserve hardened. "How long have pilgrims journeyed to D'hai?"

"The Rending inspired them in droves. Before the Rending, the journey was too easy to feel holy. No one traveled to D'hai but a few 'inspired' lunatics and the usual assortment of merchants."

"Pilgrims claim that the Shrine is ancient."

"It is probably as old as they claim. An ancient, ruined city lies not far from inhabited D'hai."

"You have never heard anything else connecting D'hai with a Sorcerer King's theft?" He continued before I could vent my exasperation, "No, I realize that you have already answered. Perhaps I shall find something more in these awful workbooks." He grimaced, then bestowed on me one of his devastating smiles. "Thank you, Lyriel."

I wished that he had not dropped his Seriin-incessant honorific from my name. The suggestion of familiarity gave me a dizzy sensation. "It is no more than I would do for anyone who offered to cripple me," I said sweetly.

He had the decency to look abashed at the reminder. "I do apologize for alarming you."

"May I consider myself safe from further K'shai whim?"

"For the moment," he returned soberly. He might have reassured me more.

Chapter 10

"The young woman who admitted him to the Archives: Who is she?"

"The caretaker records her as Lyriel, Silf's daughter."

"You followed her." Of course.

"She is a member of the troupe of traveling players whom the target contracted to Protect."

"Their association is not solely professional?"

"The target was seen to buy her a gift of some value. She is attractive, and the target appears interested."

The first man became contemplative. "You have more data?"

"A Guild-mate, a man named Coal, requested verification of a Seriin K'shai, recently operating in Ardasia."

A frown appeared. "Coal knows of the target?"

"No." The answer came uncertainly. "No," said the K'shai more strongly. "Coal questioned the authenticity of the other, the target's partner."

"Why?"

"Unknown."

"Discover the reasons."

"I tried. Coal was to meet me in Ardas. He never arrived. His partner could provide only limited information: Coal had been negotiating a Protection contract with a Captain Tarl of the *Sea Dancer*, the Bethiin ship that brought the target to Ardasia. Coal has disappeared."

Deliberation, puzzlement, and suspicion vied. "Is the disappearance related?"

"Highly probable. Coal had no significant local enemies, and his disappearance would not be the first in connection with the target. The target is a dangerous man. So is his partner."

"You assured me, Circle, that you could handle them both. You claimed to be your Guild's finest assassin."

"I can handle them. I shall handle them. I am more cautious than an ordinary Protector like Coal. I am also better informed."

"Thanks to the Shrine Keeper. Remember that."

"Of course." Nods were exchanged between the two professionals, each adept in his field and fully aware of his own strengths and lacks. The K'shai killed; the Shrine priest arranged Shrine miracles. Each man garnered a most satisfactory livelihood from his expertise. "The woman?" asked the K'shai shortly.

"I do not want the target attached to any natives. These people are clannish. It could provide complications."

"I prefer that she survive, until I understand her significance to the target. It will be easy to eliminate her."

"As you wish." The hesitation was brief. "It is unfortunate that Coal did not convey to you his source of doubt. I dislike unknowns."

"Where one is falsely K'shai . . ."

"The other also? No." The slightest of superior smiles appeared. "You did not wish to believe that even one man could be falsely K'shai. Would you suspect another? And beyond him, another still who gave training to a false K'shai? Would you suspect your whole Guild?"

"'No!" The K'shai's response was fierce and vicious.

The Shrine priest gave a placating flutter of his white hand. "Fog is known to your Guild. His description has been authenticated by the Shrine Keeper's Seriin sponsor. Fog is K'shai: the false one's tool, but true K'shai, nonetheless."

"Why does your Shrine Keeper interest himself in K'shai justice?"

"As I have told you, the Shrine Keeper serves justice in all things."

"And this great Seriin Lord who finances the Shrine Keeper's contracts?"

"The devoted are many."

*   *   *

The seamstress gazed beseechingly over the load of fabrics in her arms, as she struggled to reach the handle of the door to the attic workroom. The innkeeper's youngest daughter moved to open the door for her. "They never do give you a bit of rest, do they?" asked the girl in sympathy. The

Troupe players intimidated the girl, but the seamstress was both foreign and subservient. The girl felt easy with her.

"I never knew a single garment could be altered so many times," replied the seamstress with a rueful sigh.

The innkeeper's daughter, bored with her own chores, leaned against the door jamb and settled herself eagerly to gossip of the rarefied beings who were Actors and Actresses with Rubi's Troupe. The girl enjoyed a lengthy talk. She would be puzzled, however, when she realized later that she could not recall the precise subject of the conversation, nor could she seem to recall where and when the conversation had occurred.

Rhianna closed the workroom door, having set a misty dream upon the troublesome daughter of the innkeeper. Rhianna spread the fabrics on the large table that Taf had commandeered for her. She frowned, and fabric fell from the lines that she drew upon it with her mind. She sighed, and the threads twisted and rewove themselves to her orders. She held her hands before her, and bleeding marks as of a needle's too frequent imprint appeared to mar her fine fingers; she fastened the illusion in her mind and then released it.

She sat and drew from a purse against her skin a potent thing of filigree and amber. She barriered the tiny workroom with a web of burning Power. She closed her eyes and walked into another realm.

She walked the Taormin's ways more surely now. She could see the vistas beyond the central pattern. She could see the veil of darkness where the vistas ended unnaturally. She could see the rent in the veil.

She stood on a path of fire, staring at the tortuous tangle of energy that crossed the rent. The fiercest part of the tangle extended beyond the bleak curtain; the tangle's bright fibers blurred the broken edges of the dark and tattered veil.

"I did not cause this thing," said the little man, who came to stand behind her.

"Horlach?" she asked quietly.

The little man inclined his head. *"At your service, Lady Rhianna."*

Rhianna smiled crookedly. *"I doubt that very much,"* she murmured. She nodded toward the dark veil. *"The curtain does not conform to the patterns. What is it?"*

"It was called a closure by the mortal who configured it. It is the imprisoner of our world."

"And of my son," added Rhianna dryly. *"A mortal constructed it?"*

"A mortal," agreed Horlach. *"He created the Taormin."*

"A most remarkable mortal," Rhianna mused.

With care and great caution, she freed a single fiery fragment of the tangle. Released, the strand snapped free of the rent. The rent shifted, and a trickle of inky darkness spilled into the Taormin's bright plain. Rhianna recoiled. The little man laughed, but he, too, felt fear. *"You perceive,"* said the little man, *"that the problem is not a simple one. The son you carried at the instant of Rending has become the Taormin's single stabilizing force, but he is himself unstable."*

"Where is Kaedric?" asked Rhianna, hating the need to ask, hating especially to ask of this dark and evil being.

"If you do not know, how should I? I am weak now. My great Power has been stripped from me."

"You still walk this world freely."

"By Venkarel's leave. He is too cunning to discard a tool while he has yet a use for it."

"I doubt the value of so treacherous a tool as yourself, Horlach."

Horlach gestured again to the tangle and the veil. *"This was not my doing,"* he repeated.

"You wield even honesty as a weapon of deceit," said Rhianna with scorn.

The little man spread his hands. *"Why should I deceive you now? I am vanquished and helpless."*

"Why else should you have sought me here, save in hope of some gain for yourself?"

"I am trapped in this desolate place between worlds, perhaps for eternity. Is it so hard for you to believe that I am lonely?"

"You have chosen to remain. You fear to abdicate control of your spirit. Do not expect me to pity you for refusing death."

"You understand little, Lady Rhianna. I cannot choose; the Venkarel has chosen for me. It is he who has sacrificed his natural life for the sake of his ambition. I assure you: I would never have chosen to abandon my mortal bonds for any cause. You know how I fought to regain that life, though achieving it would have cost me the greatest part of my Power. It is the Venkarel who has chosen Power over life."

"You allowed him no alternative," said Rhianna tightly.

"For the instant only: Yes, for that instant of Rending, he required more than flesh could hold. But he has gained such Power now as you do not comprehend. He could resume his mortal life: the Power for it is within him."

"He would not steal another's life, as you would have done."

"He would do and will do exactly as he wishes. He plays his game alone, as always, and supremacy of his own strength is all that matters to him. You know him. You know his own fear: that he might be weak and used again as in his child-hood. You know that he would do anything to ensure his own protection. For all his Power, he remains the frightened, lethal child of Ven, and his fear will destroy you, your son, and your world. I speak truly, Lady Rhianna; your Power knows."

"Stop!" commanded Rhianna sharply. She averted her sight from Horlach, the veil, and the tangle; she stared fixedly at the pattern she had woven for herself. *"I shall not heed such nonsense."* It was too hard to disbelieve that Kaedric had abandoned her, when she felt so dreadfully alone.

"Only I can help you save your son," said Horlach avidly. *"Lend me your Power, and I shall free him now. I shall not betray you. Now, Rhianna! Reach to me that I may save him."*

Rhianna tore herself free of the Taormin's world, racing through the deadly maze of energies. She threw herself into the saner world, the simpler world, where only one pattern ruled while day's light shone. She breathed heavily, as if she had run in truth, and she wrapped the Taormin into its silken shroud with trembling fingers.

She gathered the costumes into her arms. She draped herself in gray illusions. Her exhaustion was not feigned.

Chapter 11

I visited Silf once more before we left Diarmon. "Where is your shipbuilder?" I asked her caustically. I wanted only to assure myself that he would not enter unannounced.

Silf, knowing the purpose of my question, still answered carefully, "Marlund is with his cousin. The poor woman has lost her eldest son."

"How careless of her."

Silf rebuked me, "The boy is dead, Lyriel."

"So is the brother I never met, but I cannot mourn him very deeply."

"You are callous, Lyriel." I could see Silf's indignant pose hesitate and ebb. She became conspiratorial. "The boy was involved with Janeb's wife, and Janeb is a jealous man." Silf would never have made such a remark in her shipbuilder's hearing, for he disapproved of gossip. Our conversation became suddenly easy, as it had been of old.

"You think this Janeb killed the boy?" I did not care about strangers, but if Silf (my Silf) knew them, then they mattered.

"Janeb?" Silf laughed a little scornfully. "He could not kill a calf, if it were not tied and held for him. This job was a professional one: very clean and quick."

"K'shai," I whispered, my heart feeling leaden for no good reason at all.

Silf caught my mood. "The boy was no great loss. He would have been hanged before this if his father had been less wealthy." Silf paused. "He collected nasty secrets against people."

"You?" I demanded, startled out of my gloom.

"He tried. Once." She smiled wickedly—like Silf of old, who could stand up to anyone—and I loved her, but our brief rapport tumbled back into silence.

"We are leaving tomorrow," I told her, feeling terrible.

"I have scarcely seen you," she said wistfully.

"You could come with us." I was pleading, which was foolish. I knew her answer would only hurt me.

"No, Lyriel."

"You could at least come and speak with Taf."

"Lyriel, let us not argue."

"What else are you willing to do but argue?" I asked her. "You will not even try to understand Taf."

"Has Taf ever tried to understand me? Have you? I am your mother, Lyriel, not an ogre. Have you forgotten how we used to laugh together? We used to enjoy just talking to one another."

"I remember." All of the porcelain dolls were smiling. I wanted to smash their mocking happiness.

"Will you stay for supper?" She knew I would decline.

"I have too much to do before departing."

Silf shook her head at my feeble excuse. "I hope you have a prosperous season," she remarked distantly.

"Thank you. Please, do not summon that beastly servant. I prefer to open doors for myself." We did not embrace on parting. Neither of us wanted to face the other's useless tears.

*   *   *

I never allow the Troupe to see me cry. I walked for two hours, arriving late at the beach south of the Diarmon harbor. I would be caught by the night if I did not hurry, but I was not ready to face anyone who knew me. Some outskirt family could profit by my carelessness tonight. I sat on the sand and let the tide creep to my feet. The waves were mild. If they covered me, they would feel gentle and warm.

I paid for a night's shelter with a family of six who shared a crowded cottage. They were poor enough to welcome my coppers, if not my presence. I slept on the bare sand floor between the two youngest daughters, one of whom snored. I heard no Rendies wail outside the heavy, plaited frond shutters. It was the soundest night's sleep I had known since Ardas, even if I did dream about a lover who became a Rendie in my arms.

"Where have you been?" Rubi screeched at me in welcome the next morning. "We were ready to leave an hour ago!"

The Troupe members were still rushing to check final

loads, so I knew that Rubi exaggerated. I waved her an acknowledgment and went to clear my room. "Rubi is frothing," whispered Noryne to me in hasty passing on the stairs.

"You know the schedule," growled Taf when he saw me.

"I set the blasted schedule," I informed him in retort. "I can change it." We traveled mostly at night in any case, for the inland sun could be brutal between oases, and night travel was more efficient between villages. "We have ten days before we are due in Samth," I shouted through my room's door. "We need only six days to cross the Aadi by the Merchants' Route. You can spare me one miserable hour. If you were not such a stubborn, accursed fool, Taf, you would go see Silf yourself. But no, she left, and far be it from you ever to go and tell her that you miss her. Are you listening to me, Taf?" I was beginning to cry again. I raised my head to see Evaric at my door, looking startled. "What do you want?" I asked him gruffly, dropping my head quickly when I realized that he could see my tears. Crying twice in two days: blast Taf and Silf both.

"Mistress Rubi," said Evaric tonelessly, "asked me to carry your trunk to the wagon."

Blast Rubi, she would choose to send the K'shai. "I know how to call someone to load a trunk," I yelled at him.

"Perhaps I should return when you finish packing." He was looking at my ill-fitting costume with a sort of quirkily sympathetic expression, which made me want to scream.

Anyone less quick than a K'shai would have been struck by the door when I slammed it. I promised myself to strangle the Alisa if I discovered she had told Evaric about Silf. When it occurred to me that I had just shouted a great many of my private concerns across the inn, I began to curse myself.

I changed my clothes, threw the costume into my trunk with loathing, opened the door, and found the K'shai waiting quietly, leaning against the wall as if altogether unconcerned by all the flurry of last minute rushing around him. "Take it," I ordered him sharply.

He was clever enough not to speak or even show his confoundedly charming smile. If he had done either, I really would have screamed. He lifted the awkward trunk lightly and followed me to the wagon without word or expression of any kind.

We left Diarmon over twenty minutes later. Rubi had

forgotten to pay one of her young men. I failed pointedly to accuse her of delaying us.

We followed a shorter, quicker route than pilgrims used to reach the southern cities; it was a desolate way. We gave no performances between Diarmon and Samth, for no intervening settlements existed. Nothing substantial survived long in that barren land, called the Aadi.

The Aadi deserved the night. Stars emblazoned the sky, and the sand's slow dunes stretched against the wind. The trails shifted with the sand; not a hundred Ardasians knew the secret ways of crossing. Where Taf learned, I never heard, but he had taught me all the songs he knew of the Aadi and the ancient markers. I would never be lost on the Aadi, which spared me from the greatest fear the Aadi could convey. Occasionally, I even made a point of riding alone past some ridge of sand and standing free from sight or sound of any person; I danced for the joy of solitude, imagining for a time that I owed no one any debt of love or caring, imagining that I could be as free and starkly pure as the ageless, empty sand. I never stayed alone in the desert for long.

Three days from Diarmon, we encountered a train of merchants out of Samth. We spent an awkward day together, crossing tempers at the single well, but conflicts ebbed with the waning afternoon. Tabok and the merchants' cook began to prepare something of a feast. Rubi dismissed the players from rehearsal, and all of us began to gather around the three large fires, where bubbling stews and grain cakes scented the desert air.

I supped with the merchant father, a man named Chalas, because Rubi had told me to entertain him and keep Taf from robbing him too obviously. She had taken charge of the son, who looked like he might have preferred to be left to the attentions of his Toy, a pretty girl with a vacuous expression. Chalas was not bad company, until something started him on the topic of his standing in the cotton market. I applauded inwardly when Rayn brought out his gitar and sent Solomai's youngest boy to draw me into a dance.

At barely eight years old, Zel could not manage the traditional partner dances, but we improvised our own and seemed to please our audience. Miria and Tana joined us, and we began a simple round. When Zakari and Minaro joined, the dance became more serious. Zel yielded his place to Kodelh, and Silvia dragged Jaon into the circle. Kriisa began to dance with her brother, Lotin, though she watched my partner more than her own; Kriisa had developed a youthful passion for Kodelh, much to Solomai's dismay.

"We need a sixth couple, Eolh!" Eolh was the only male player not yet dancing or playing an instrument.

"Alisa," I called cheerfully.

Alisa gave a smooth imitation of eagerness as she rose with Eolh; it was her best performance of the season. She had always danced poorly. The audience of merchants and half-drunk wagoners would never notice points of skill, but Alisa and I knew her lack. I enjoyed an unkind hope that a handsome K'shai might recognize her inadequacy as well.

"May your eyes rot," Alisa whispered to me as we spun past each other in the intricate steps.

I could not retort, because the dance carried me away. Kodelh was not much older than Lotin, but he was strong enough to lift me, and he controlled his energy in easy cadence with Rayn's staccato strings, Sama's drum, and Bethali's chimes. We began a more exotic dance, which required deeper concentration.

The light turned ruddy, but we who danced did not notice. The flame spread unnatural fingers, searching angrily for better fuel than a ring of timber. The fire caught the Toy's flimsy skirt, and her merchant patron battered at the flame with hasty surprise.

The ache of cold wraith-glow pierced us, who had forgotten that night approached. We stopped abruptly in the dance. Kodelh's hands still gripped my waist. The merchants' K'shai had already begun their own dance: slow, fierce, and very different from our frivolous act.

Most of the expressions around me already grew blank. Kodelh's hand slipped from me as he sank to the ground. I sat beside him, compelled not by Rendie spell but by longing for the reassurance of mortal warmth.

We had no time to reach the wagons with their false suggestions of safety. No wagon of sufficient substance to deter a Rendie could be drawn practically across the sands and rough roads of Ardasia, but even insubstantial canvas gave better comfort than the smallness of the K'shai steel that saved us. The K'shai themselves seemed tiny against the wraith things they fought.

A Rendie's loose form coalesced from blurred nothingness and drifted around one of the merchants' K'shai. A second wraith gathered its undulating limbs around the merchants' other K'shai, a man only a fraction less massive than his partner but dwarfed by his terrible foe. The K'shai dance neared lightning's likeness; the Rendies spun deeper into the pattern's tight circle. Sometimes a Rendie would vanish on the touch of a K'shai's silvered sword, though not even the sharpest steel should have reasonably injured a phantasm; a K'shai must believe that he can kill, Key had told me, despite any contradiction imparted by logic. A fractional doubt would open the K'shai to Rendie soul-stealing. To kill a Rendie, said Key, demanded no more than perfect strength, quickness, endurance, concentration, and good fortune; I had never gauged the weight of truth in Key's facetious comment.

A cloud of Rendies barred my view of Evaric, for they swirled around him thickly. I had never seen so many Rendies gathered at one place and time, and I had seen the chilling K'shai game too frequently. Fog stood apart, observing the cloud with an air of almost detached appraisal. He strolled into the Rendies' midst, and the wraith things stretched away from him and from Evaric. Evaric's sword flashed briefly, striking sparks and erasing an entire Rendie sphere; the Rendies' shrieks might have curdled the sand.

Evaric saluted Fog with an ironic flourish. Fog raised his own sword in bland response. Our two K'shai commenced a more orthodox pattern, but I had the feeling that theirs was a performance no more real than my seduction of Kodelh in the dance. The Rendies wove in dreadful cycles against the merchants' K'shai. They floated away from Fog as if his proximity terrified them. They spun around Evaric as if his presence tantalized them. I shuddered and pressed closer to Kodelh, but I could not feel him. I could not feel anything.

Those of us whom the K'shai had Protected stirred from trance and shook to discover the sky still dark. The aftermath of the Rendie contact had left me with an aching at the base of my skull and a burning blur of vision. I saw Alisa rouse herself, fling herself upon Evaric, and burrow into his grasp. Since Alisa was one who never recalled anything past a Rendie's first appearance, I found her urgent trembling for her Protector's arms irritatingly opportunistic. I rather wished that her ploy had occurred to me.

* * *

Rhianna stood before the Taormin's rent, observing the bleak trickle of dark energy that emerged. The trickle had increased; it was a slight change, but she did not doubt its existence or its source.

"You see," remarked Horlach, *"how fragile is the fabric. The Taormin amplifies Power; it also magnifies the repercussions of ignorance."*

In some small, unwary corner of herself, Rhianna derived a faint gladness of Horlach's presence. He was evil: vile and rotted. He repulsed her, but he represented kindred in a sense that only Kaedric might have understood entirely. *"I wonder, Horlach, if you know the Taormin as well as you pretend. Kaedric did take it from you."*

"He has also left it to me—and to you, Lady Rhianna. He has left it and you and all ties to your mortal world. He has defined his own infinity elsewhere; I shall not pretend to any knowledge akin to his in that arena. I do suggest that any remedy for the Rending must be yours and mine to devise, for only you and I now walk here, where the rent is tangible. You cannot depend upon your Venkarel to resolve this battle for you; he has gone from your very universe, and he will not return."

"Do not think to lure me into trusting you above him, Horlach. If Kaedric has left me irrevocably, he had good reason, and I love him no whit less for it."

"I vie not for your love, Lady Rhianna, but for your understanding of the magnitude of the horror that approaches us."

"Persuade me of your trustworthiness," Rhianna said dryly.

"How shall I overcome this prejudice you have against me? By some token word of honesty? I have told you the only crucial truth: aid me with your Power, or nothing will survive."

"A 'token word' would be more likely to allay my doubts than blatant lies and shifting 'truths.' I am not so mesmerized by the Taormin that I grow witless within it."

"You maintain your pattern well, Lady Rhianna, as I

should expect of one trained by the Venkarel. Hence, I shall grant you your token: the greatest present danger to your son is that very guild with which he affiliates himself. The K'shai deal with Rending creatures by denying fear, that substance for which a Rending creature hungers above all else. The K'shai are served well by their simplistic conceit, but your son is menaced by it. In denying his fear, he taps the subtle harmony between himself and those he fights. He facilitates the Rending creatures' entry into the mortal world. He accelerates the coming of catastrophe."

"How would you propose that I discourage my son in his vocation?"

"Remove his K'shai partner, and other, more imminent interests will take precedence."

"Remove Fog?" mocked Rhianna. "You mean, I suppose, that I should murder him by my Power."

"He is himself a murderer, and he destroys your son."

"I am not an executioner."

"You are the Infortiare, whose duty it is to preserve the mortal world from the destructive use of Power. Your son is a sorcerer, and the K'shai encourage him to be destructive. Which do you rank most highly, Lady Rhianna: your duty as Infortiare or the pretty sensibilities of your sheltered rearing? The survival of your world and all its peoples? Or the survival of a coarse, ignorant brute whose sole purpose is to kill and spend the profit on his base and fleshly pleasures?"

"You weary me, Horlach, with your pious talk, when you are the chief destroyer of these many ages. Your token truth is like you, and it merits nothing." Rhianna spoke with stern grandeur and authority, and Horlach fled from her wrath.

Alone, Rhianna felt small again. Surreptitiously, she turned her Power to a study of Fog, but the K'shai was shallow and unenlightening; a deeper probe would injure him. With a sigh of resignation, Rhianna departed the Taormin and returned to the Aadi by night. When she noted that the Rending creatures had attacked the Troupe viciously in her Power's absence, she berated herself soundly for losing time to Horlach's practiced sophistry.

Chapter 12

Arahinos had few visitors, being largely overlooked in favor of the larger cities, Samth and Destin to the north and Mikolaii to the west. Only the Arahinos copper mine kept the supply merchants coming year after year. The houses lined a single street, if the erratic path among the houses merited such a name. The houses were all stone, for wood was scarce, and the doors and shutters were beaten out of the native copper. We presented our play at the Gathering Place, a ring of stone benches surrounding a patch of desert. Our portable stage always looked its grandest in Arahinos.

We had performed annually in Arahinos for as long as we had been a troupe. The citizens of Arahinos could not pay us as well as some of our patrons, but they always greeted our arrival with enthusiasm. They opened their best houses to us, since Arahinos lacked an inn to accommodate us, and the residents scattered with their relatives for the duration of our stay.

We had true friends in Arahinos. My own favorite was Grenz, an old and nearly crippled miner, who was much the canniest inhabitant of the town. He sought me when we arrived, and I ran to greet him eagerly, but he remained unwontedly solemn. "You have new K'shai," he remarked.

I followed the direction of his glance. Fog had emerged from one of the houses near the Gathering Place. Fog evidently sensed my contemplation, for he turned abruptly and faced me. Fog's wearily sardonic expression never varied greatly, but I fancied it held something near to an amused challenge. For a hurried, shadowy instant, I could have sworn that his eyes glowed as they had that one time in Ardas. I answered Grenz absently, "Yes. Key met a wind-snake outside Patricum."

"Nasty things, wind-snakes," muttered Grenz. After a moment, he added, "Are you in trouble, girl?"

"No," I replied, startled. "Why?"

"Someone in your company is a target."

"Not possible," I murmured, as I tried to set aside my horror and assess Grenz' statement calmly. "You think Rubi and Taf attract the caliber of enemies who can finance K'shai retaliation? Now, if you start seeing irate merchants from Ardas, let me know without delay."

"I never would worry about you holding your own against any merchant."

"Did you ever know me to involve myself in any trouble I could not handle?"

Grenz grunted, and he grinned very briefly. "You have a slippery way with you, girl, and I never doubted it, but a K'shai, all armed for killing, is not the kind of trouble to be avoided by clever words and quick wits. The K'shai earn their fees, and this one has been watching the road from the bluffs for the last week. No one in Arahinos ever afforded a K'shai." Having made his inarguable statement, Grenz left me. My eyes returned reluctantly to Fog, who was now studying the Gathering Place for some obscure purpose of his own.

"My partner interests you, Mistress Lyriel?" Blast him, he moved so quietly.

"I have no interest in any K'shai, Master Evaric." I mocked his Seriin formal tone.

"You have made that very clear, Mistress Lyriel."

Looking up at him, at his smoky blue-silver eyes, was like staring too long at the sun-bright sea. When I blinked and found him gone, the rest of the world was dark and dull by comparison.

"Kriisa's red dress in the first act is too bold," shouted Rubi into my distraction. "Have the seamstress make her something more in keeping with the character. We need it by morning."

I responded automatically, "Anni is already altering the costumes for the chorus of serving women. Which takes precedence?"

"All of them—and tell her to replace the braid on Minaro's cloak. It should be gold not gray."

"She is new at costuming, Rubi."

"If she cannot handle the job, hire someone else!" Rubi could reduce tea with a Tanist to a trivial accomplishment, so long as the deed was another's. I abandoned my useless fretting over K'shai and cryptic warnings as I went to assign Anni an impossible task.

By the time night had fallen, all of my suppressed worry had reemerged in full, and I could not sleep. I shifted uneasily, trying to find some comfortable position. My bed was but a thin mattress laid flat on the stone floor. The mattress was filled with straw, and the straw had been packed into lumps. Every lump seemed to prod me with fiendish ingenuity.

I almost fell off the mattress' edge when I heard the door creak. It was only a door to the rest of the small house, I reminded myself firmly; the girl whose room I occupied had been very proud of that door, for interior rooms in Arahinos were generally divided by no more than curtains. This house boasted true rooms: four of them, built of stone and furnished with copper wares and straw-stuffed cushions. It was the most substantial house in Arahinos, which was why Rubi had claimed one of the rooms for herself.

The door creaked again. A midnight inspiration to change a script had probably claimed Rubi's small sense of courtesy. The uncertain construction of the house could have caused the door to shift on its own. Any number of harmless reasons existed for a sound of copper hinges whining.

And footsteps. Blast, there were footsteps. I should open my eyes instead of cowering under a linen sheet which had failed even to hide the mattress lumps. Rubi would have spoken by now; Taf would never wake me in the night save in emergency. Who occupied the fourth room? I could not think. The footsteps were dragging, and a sound of raspy, labored breathing accompanied them.

Who else had stayed in this house? The fourth room was the kitchen. Rubi had assigned someone to it: the seamstress? The pilgrim woman would never enter my room uninvited.

Why had I laid my dagger on the table across the room? It was a tiny room, but I could not reach the table in a single move. I occupied an insignificant room with a stone floor being crossed by someone who had entered the house from the night: someone who had not feared Rendies. Would a K'shai kill quickly?

"Lyriel?" The voice was hesitant and soft. It exuded pain. I threw the sheet from my head and sat upright rapidly.

"Sands of the Aadi, Noryne, you scared ten years from me." I heard the raggedness of her breath more clearly. "What are you doing here?" She had been assigned to a house on the other side of town, and it was night. "How did you come here?" I fumbled for the oil lamp, found it, and dropped the match. "Blast."

"I was with Zakari." Who was quartered across the street. And it was night.

I found and lit the match and wished I had not retrieved it. Noryne's wrist dangled limply. Her skirt was streaked and spattered with blood. "Zakari did this to you?" I asked her softly. The bloodstain on her skirt was still spreading. I jerked at the sheet to free myself.

"Alisa has left him." Noryne held remarkably steady, but I tried to support her. Her poor hand was dark with suffused bleeding. The bones were awry, jutting against the skin.

"So he beats you." I could too easily picture Zakari hitting her once in anger, hitting again in frustration, continuing because Noryne would not stop him. She would weep inwardly and cherish the pain along with her guilt over things she imagined to be wrong. She had been beaten often before she left her pilgrim fostering.

I made her lie on the bed. She winced at trying to sink down to the level of it. The lumpy mattress must have been cruel to those bruises. I studied the streaks of blood and her injured hand. "I am going to bring Anni here." I hoped it really was Anni in the kitchen, and I hoped that Anni knew more of healing than how to prepare an herbal restorative, such as she had made for several members of the Troupe. Maybe she could only be kind, but that alone would be better help than Rubi could give. "Stay put!"

All of the rooms opened to a single hall. Noryne's arrival would not have penetrated Taf's drunken depression, and Rubi sleeps like the dead unless she is inspired. I found Anni awake, seated on a braided sleeping rug, leaning against the kitchen's inner wall. She was much more composed about midnight intrusions than I.

"How much do you know of healing?" I asked her.

"I have assisted healers many times." She reached for her cloak. Pilgrim prudery, I thought with irritation. "Take me to her, Lyriel."

Noryne whispered as we entered. "He was so lonely. He

was so unhappy. He needed to talk to someone. I only meant to listen. I only wanted to help him."

Anni had moved to the tiny copper table, where she used water from the ewer to concoct an acridly odorous paste. "Keep her quiet," said the seamstress firmly, which was good advice but a difficult act to implement.

Noryne cried restlessly. "He said that Alisa had betrayed him. He asked me if I knew what it was like to love someone so much that nothing else mattered, not truth, not life, not even happiness. I told him that I did understand. I told him that I loved him. He struck me."

Anni brought the paste and a goblet of herbed wine. She coaxed the goblet to Noryne's swollen lips. "No more talk, Noryne," ordered Anni gently.

"I have lost my child," continued Noryne despite the order.

"You cannot lose what you never had," I grumbled, thinking that the child's loss was the only good to come of this night's doings. The look that Anni gave me scorched the words from my tongue.

Anni's murmur to Noryne was all gentleness. "I shall set your wrist, Noryne. I shall hold the pain away from you, but you must try to help me. You must remain still and quiet. The procedure will take only a moment, and then you will sleep." While she spoke, Anni wrenched Noryne's protruding bones into their proper places. She bound the wrist with a splint and a layer of her herbal paste.

"Brainless little fool," I muttered at Noryne, who fell into a heavy slumber even as Anni had promised.

"For loving the wrong man? Or for wanting his child?"

"Both."

"She does not regret the love."

"She is a fool."

Anni and I shared the floor of the tiny room through the remainder of the night. Noryne stirred only once. She called to me. "Lyriel, you will not blame him, will you? Promise me that you will not blame Zakari."

She would not be silenced until I gave her my promise, though it goaded me to do it. When Noryne had extracted a like promise from Anni, she pleaded with us not to let Rubi know of Zakari's part in the night's events. Only after we had both agreed did Noryne sink again into uncannily silent sleep.

"How badly is she hurt?" I asked Anni in a muffled breath full of thwarted anger and pity.

"Badly, but she will mend. It is not easy to do lasting damage to a sorceress."

"A sorceress?" I hissed.

"Her Power is suppressed and immature, but she has begun to recognize it. She needs training, before her uncontrolled empathy causes her to repeat her folly with Master Zakari or another." Anni turned her face to me thoughtfully. The dim lamplight made an aura of her hair. Without the concealing pilgrim hood, she looked both younger and older.

I recalled Taf's perception of oddness about Anni. "You are a sorceress."

She did not speak at first. When she did respond, she spoke with a sigh. "I am a wizardess, Lyriel. My presence has certainly contributed to the awakening of Noryne's Power. That is the way of Power. It acts upon its own kind, often forcibly. I suspect that Noryne has been largely sheltered from Power's influence until recently."

"Noryne asked me about Ixaxins before we left Ardas." And I had told her that Ixaxin schools were for foreigners and not for Ardasians to consider; some day I might learn not to issue my opinions so indiscriminately.

"Perhaps other Power than mine affected her in Ardas. It is a populous city." Anni was distant.

I had never met an Ixaxin previously, as far as I knew. I felt vaguely that I should hate Anni for her unusual, unsuspected talent; resentment, at the least, composed the conventional attitude. Foreigners described Ixaxins as monstrous, but this was Anni, who was kind. She also sewed superbly, and I could no more match her stitchery than I could do—whatever a wizardess did. I could not seem to envy her either skill.

Her admission did augment my interest in her. A hundred questions jostled in my head. "Rendies avoid you who have Power?"

"The Rending creatures find Power unpalatable. It has a corrosive effect on them, but it also fascinates them. They do not avoid it; they avoid direct contact with it."

For a moment, I was too busy observing Anni to respond.

A certain bright, hard depth of clarity, which was new, emerged from her. Something soft and humble, expected of a pilgrim, had gone from her. She was very finely boned and delicate, quite lovely in an oddly esoteric way. I usually noticed such things immediately. Anni wore a stone around her neck; it was almost a moonstone, such as were sometimes found on shores near Diarmon, but her stone was larger and more changeable in the light. I had the suspicion that I was seeing a part of what a wizardess was: whatever she chose to appear to be. "Power fascinates the Rendies?" I mused curiously. "Do you mean that it might actually attract them?"

"Incidents have been recorded."

My next question formed itself, for I was not aware of thinking it. "Can a sorcerer become K'shai?"

The lamp flickered, flared, and subsided. The flame cast darting shadows across Anni's face. She did not want to answer me. All of her visible emotion over Noryne closed in upon itself, and she became cold. I had never seen anyone more thoroughly controlled. I derived a rather horrible and incomprehensible satisfaction from the transformation.

"A man is born to Power, or he is not," replied Anni rigidly. "He may choose to become K'shai, or he may not. By Ceallagh's law, a sorcerer of any significant Power must be trained and made a wizard. The K'shai Guild would not knowingly accept such a man. No one in your Troupe's employ has utilized active Power since I joined you, Lyriel." Noryne moved again. "We are disturbing her with our talk," said Anni.

"It must be nearly morning."

"Soon."

"Not soon enough," I muttered. I closed my eyes, but I did not sleep.

*   *   *

Rhianna's anger made her Power burn; it seared the Taormin's plain, and the patterns near her shifted in alarm. *"Hear me, Horlach,"* she cried across the plain. *"I recognize your handiwork. 'Can a sorcerer become K'shai?' indeed. I do thank you for the warning: I had not considered the value you might place on such a tool as Lyriel. I have sealed her from you now. If I find that you have wrought your mischief in other quarters, I shall be less forgiving. I can punish you, Horlach, in a most unpleasant manner."*

"Threats are unbecoming, Lady Rhianna. Why do you blame me for the girl's words? Would I risk your anger for the trivial amusement of prodding the girl's subconscious doubts into expression?"

"She was influenced. She does not comprehend Power sufficiently well to formulate the connection for herself."

"I did not influence her, Lady Rhianna. You blame me unjustly. Test me. You will sense truth in me."

Rhianna hesitated before the confident taunt, but she issued the probe of Power. "So," she acknowledged stiffly. "I have wronged you. I apologize." Horlach thanked her graciously. Rhianna trusted him less than ever.

Chapter 13

Too many worries beset me. After informing Rubi firmly that the cause of Noryne's accident had best remain unspecified, I went in search of our young K'shai. Since Arahinos could not stable all of our animals, our K'shai would have spent the night Protecting. Evaric would not have slept yet, which I hoped would make him more vulnerable and not more difficult. I could not sit and sensibly await his convenience.

I did feel briefly guilty when I found him quartered near the Gathering Place, condemned to seek sleep while two loudly enthused Arahinos matrons gossiped in the kitchen. The women became more excited when I appeared, but I only nodded to them. I tried each of the curtained alcoves before locating Evaric. He jumped to his feet as I entered, looking abruptly relieved when he identified his visitor. I wondered whom he had expected; his sword was in his hand.

He raised the sword. "I ought to use this on you for waking me." To my relief, he laid the sword carefully on the stone ledge which served as table. "I have not had a pleasant night, Mistress Lyriel. Please forgive my brusqueness."

"Are you a target?" I asked him bluntly.

"Yes," he replied with a directness that disarmed me completely.

"Why did you not warn us when we hired you?" I had not wanted it to sound like a plea.

Evaric regarded me soberly. "You asked only if I sought to complete any conflicting contracts while in service to you. You did not ask if I were the subject of any such contracts."

"You quibble over semantics," I retorted.

"If I had told you, would it have mattered? You needed K'shai desperately. You would have hired anyone at that point."

I could lose myself just in watching him. "K'shai do not hunt K'shai," I said. He began to reach toward me and stopped. I could not remember what I had meant to say. "Branded with fire," I murmured, staring fixedly at his strong and slender hand. "K'shai initiation must be painful."

He rubbed at the brand with his other hand and shrugged. "I barely remember. None of it seemed very real."

"How long ago?"

"Seven years." The outer door slammed. I could hear Minaro offering arrogant advice on acting. "It seemed a small enough sacrifice at the time, all considered."

"And now?"

"Perspectives change." He was rueful.

"You are an assassin." I was shouting it at myself. "Whether you have killed seven men or seven hundred."

"Eight. As of last night. Fog is burying him. Master Straw, I believe: the K'shai who pursued me from Ardas. Reveal that to your Troupe, if you like." Only cynical bitterness remained in his smile now.

And I had worried about Evaric. I left him hurriedly, so that he would not see how miserably sickened I felt.

* * *

Noryne felt the emptiness within her more keenly than the pain. The quilt still showed the traces of blood, though Lyriel had tried to clean it. The skirt was ruined.

What was the use of anything? Life gave nothing but hurt. It hurt too much. Noryne could not bear more hurt. Please, she prayed, let me die now; let me go into nothingness.

It would hurt to take the knife and run it across her wrists. But that was the way it was done; she had heard of it from the pilgrims, who called it sin. But all that she had done was sin. This sin would end the rest. It would be better to die than to live more evils.

The knife was not very sharp. It would hurt a little more, but it would yield the end of hurting. She had only to place it so—she could scarcely feel the blade's edge. When she pressed it, the blood would spill. She should cover the rug with her shawl.

Noryne placed the knife on the table with reverent care. It was kind of Lyriel to have brought Noryne's trunk here; Lyriel had always been kind. Noryne smiled faintly. She selected the oldest shawl first, then replaced it in favor of the newer one. She touched the finely woven fabric, remem-

bering how proud she had been to wear it. The colors were
soft and muted like the sands in shadow. She folded the
fingers of her sound hand around the handle of the knife.

"Stop it!" commanded Lyriel from the door. She snatched
the knife from Noryne's grasp. "What are you trying to
do?" shouted Lyriel angrily, her dark eyes brimming with
frightened tears. "Condemn me to play your roles for the
rest of the season?"

"Please, Lyriel." Noryne shared Lyriel's fear, and the
anguish spread. "Please," whispered Noryne. She reached
weakly for the knife; it came to her hand.

"No!" Lyriel strode to the door. "Anni!" she called
urgently.

Anni appeared, wrapped in pilgrim gray but looking golden.
"She will survive, Lyriel. Power will not allow her any other
course." Anni touched Lyriel's arm, and Lyriel's terrible
urgency ebbed into a quiet echo of Anni's calm. "My satchel
is in the kitchen. Please bring it to me." Lyriel obeyed
without hesitation. "She fears for you, Noryne," said Anni.
"She thinks you meant to use the knife against yourself."

"I did, Anni. I must."

"You cannot. You must understand that death solves
nothing. It is not an end but a gate, and whatever sorrows
or joys you bear will follow you. Your Power lets you see
the lesser gates and comprehend them. There does exist a
final gate of peace, but you will not reach it by your suicide."

"I cannot escape." The beautiful promise of endless darkness ran from her.

"You will heal, Noryne. I shall teach you."

Noryne felt Anni's deep strength and thought of trees; it
was a strange comparison for a daughter of the desert to
make. Noryne felt Lyriel's more distant worry. She tried to
feel Zakari, and she felt nothing.

"He is hollow, Noryne. You love an illusion."

"I have lost my child. I have only illusion left."

"You have Power, Noryne. You have permitted it to use
you by accepting its contradictory advice. You must not
trust your Power blindly. Your Power will seek madness.
Master it, Noryne!"

Noryne twisted the lovely, soft shawl. The knife clattered
on the floor.

Chapter 14

Taf has never liked Tanists. They are wealthy, and Taf considers them miserly for failing to convey their wealth to him. The Tanist of Mikolaii is particularly wealthy, which alone should have warned Rubi against performing in that city.

I knew as soon as I saw the Tanist's servants carting the workers' wages to the Tanist's mill. All of that lovely, shiny silver parading past the theater: no wonder Taf had disappeared before the second act. "Taf is at his art again," I whispered to Solomai. "Tell Rubi to plan accordingly."

I raced along the sandy street toward the Tanist's mill. I reached the wage cart in time to see Taf, pretending intoxication, stumble in front of it. The cart's drivers stopped and cursed him, but he sat in the road and cooed absurdly at their mules. One of the cart's guards dismounted, grumbling, and pulled Taf from the cart's path. Taf tripped and struck the side of the cart.

"I wonder how much silver you claimed with that little maneuver," I muttered to myself, wondering how I could prevent him from claiming more. I walked toward Taf and the guards. "So there you are," I said with loud disgust. "Drunk again," I grumbled, taking Taf's arm. Taf glared at me as I stole a full pouch of silver from his coat; replacing it on the cart would be difficult, because Taf would not cooperate.

"Let go of me," snapped Taf, which was warning. "Who are you, girl?" Sands, I thought, he had done it again: notified the constables of his own impending crime.

They arrived before I could react. The pouch of silver felt suddenly heavy, held tightly beneath my arm and hidden chiefly by misdirection. I backed away from Taf. It was I who had possession of the silver and the guilt by implication; explanations would achieve only the amusement of the

244

constables and guards. I exchanged one desperate glance with Taf and ran. Taf would maintain his role of innocent drunk, and no evidence existed by which to detain him, so long as they did not catch me with the silver.

I ran through the streets. The constables pursued me. I could outpace them for a time, for I could choose the path to suit myself, and I could slip through cracks and holes that they must circumvent.

I wished I were more familiar with Mikolaii. I had no safe goal. I stashed the silver beneath a scrubby weed, for I expected to be caught. I dodged into an alley and faced a high block wall. I turned, and two winded constables stood determinedly before me.

I gave them my most dazzling smile. "Lovely day for a run," I remarked brightly. They did not appear to be amused.

A barbed, black disk spun through the air in a deadly whir and embedded itself in the wall beside the oldest constable's neck. Both constables ducked, as a second disk flew between them. I dodged the disks and darted between the men, gambling that the source of the disks had aimed to miss. I was inexpressibly relieved to see Evaric.

He jerked me behind the wall that had concealed him. "Meet me at the stables at dusk," he told me hurriedly. "We can leave the city by night and rejoin the Troupe in Walier." He cast another disk; it cut the shoulder of the constable who had come nearest. "Go!" Evaric hissed at me, and I obeyed.

I did not dare approach any member of the Troupe too closely. I did reach the wagon that I shared with Taf, and I folded the spare canvas in the fashion that signaled my status. I spent the remainder of the afternoon hiding inside an empty cistern and counting the silver, which I had retrieved. The silver did not constitute enough to merit the risk that Taf had taken; as usual, it was the hazard of the undertaking that had enticed him.

Near dusk, I emerged cautiously. I could see the stables and a few straggling visitors confining their steeds for the night. I waited. The shadows of evening stretched. The stable doors had been closed and barred, and all sensible folk were safely hidden behind solid walls. I crossed the stable yard and found no Evaric. I tried the stable door, but the bar had been locked in place, and I had no tools with which to breach the lock. I leaned against the stable wall and watched the sun vanish.

Something darted across the darkened sky, and I almost screamed from fright. I shut my eyes very tightly, wondering with a pang how K'shai first learned to abide the night. I began silently to recite all the roles of our most current play; I visualized every gesture, and I forced the emotions of the characters to dominate my own stark terror. The knot within me loosened, and I dared to reopen my outer senses.

Evaric had strung my dappled mare behind his roan. He was leading them from the stable. The horses were not eager, but my mare nuzzled me for reassurance and reward. She politely accepted a bit of dried apple from Evaric.

Evaric handed me the reins of his roan, while he resecured the stable door behind him. "I was beginning to think you had forgotten me," I told him a bit indignantly.

"I have had you in sight since the sun set," he replied, sounding distinctly less than pleased.

"Did you tell Rubi that we would meet the Troupe in Walier?"

"Yes." He was curt.

"Thank you for your assistance earlier. How did you happen to find me?"

"I sensed you," he answered, and since I did not understand, I abandoned talk and attended my horse.

The air stung me with unusual cold as we rode. The sky burned clear, and the stars were so numerous that they blurred into hazy bands. The moon rose after midnight, and its brilliance cast eerie patterns in our way. The clatter of hooves sputtered loudly across the road's broken paving.

Near dawn, we passed the dry stream bed which marked Mikolaii's boundary. The lands between domains are subject to any law that cares to enter them, but we had run the horses most of the night. We had little shelter but a good five hours' margin against pursuit. Evaric allowed a rest of half that time, then he forced us to travel again.

"I hardly think that Mikolaii's constabulary will bother to chase me this far," I grumbled.

"My job, Mistress Lyriel, is to Protect you," answered Evaric coolly. "I intend to employ all reasonable precautions." He still rode bare-headed, though the sun had begun to sear the morning. His dark hair looked fiery where the light touched it, and his expression suggested an inner drive exceeding K'shai duty to Protect. His leanness and K'shai grace would certainly make him compelling on the stage. I caught myself; I did not intend to fall again into the trap of forgetting what he represented.

"Sorry to inconvenience you this way," I tried.

He shrugged indifferently. "I am well paid for it."

Indeed you are, I thought. "Alisa will be desolate without you," I said irritably. I disliked being treated like unpleasant portage.

"Probably," he returned with detached arrogance. I attempted no more conversation; I did not require the approbation of a K'shai.

We stopped for brief intervals throughout the day, but Evaric pressed us to a rapid pace. In late afternoon, I rebelled. The sweltering sun alone would have deterred any sane individual, and we had come within sight of Walier's outlying hillocks. We could let the heat of the day pass and still reach Walier before full night. I sat, refusing to budge. Evaric looked inclined to load me onto horseback with the luggage, but he leashed his irritation. Rubi paid him, but I had employed him.

I awoke to a darkness broken by the crackle of firelight. After all his haste to proceed, Evaric had allowed me to sleep into the night. Perhaps, I mused, he was endeavoring to make a point, but I did not intend to be more sparing of criticism for that reason. No decent professional should allow annoyance to supercede sense.

I sat upright rather stiffly. My eyes felt heavy with sleep, as if I had been awakened unnaturally from a deep, long slumber. I could not seem to focus clearly; a milky blur coated the world. I turned my head slightly, for I could see the night peripherally. It was not my eyes which lacked clarity.

The K'shai sat as he had sat before I slept, but the Rendies danced around him. This resembled no K'shai dance; this constituted a gathering, and it was Rendies who designed it. They had surely claimed Evaric's soul, for I had never seen so many Rendies collected. They numbered more than had beset us on the long road from Diarmon, and we had met them then with four K'shai. You will have leisure, my clever instincts informed me, to regret Evaric when you have secured your own escape; still, it hurt to feel the loss of him. Such a pointless waste, I told myself severely.

"Accept your kindred, Fire-child. You belong among us. You cannot close us away, for we are within your essence."

The voice made my pulse freeze, for it was inhuman and seditious. It was relentless and irresistible. It craved a soul.

The Rendies had no interest in me. Other quarry had obsessed them. The Rendies were as besotted as Alisa, who would not care for the character of her rivals.

Evaric was conversing with Rendies, as even a K'shai ought not to be able to do. I apologized inwardly to the Bethiin sailor, who had tried to warn me. I could only comprehend a fraction of the Rendies' moanings, but Evaric's words penetrated indelibly. In fact, he said little, merely cycling through the same words endlessly. "I am of *this* world. I am Evaric, son of Evram and Terrell. My father serves Lord Baerod. I am of Tyntagel. I am of Serii. I am neither wizard nor sorcerer, and I have no Power. I am K'shai, and no world exists but the world of my day."

The Rendies called to him, reached to him, caressed him with vaporous tendrils, though the effect seemed to pain them. They pleaded with him, and he cycled through his litany again. The horrid spectacle enthralled me: before me played a caricature of a Desperate Man.

Less than an hour passed. The Rendies thinned, as if blown by a fanciful wind, and then they vanished. I blinked, expecting Evaric to shift or disappear like his unearthly counterparts. I did not perceive for several moments the violent trembling of the K'shai.

I rose very slowly and approached him cautiously. Even in the fading firelight, I could see that his face had grown as pale as the moon. His ailment did not stir me to pity; his ailment was too wildly fierce and dreadful, like the Rendies or the K'shai himself. I touched his clenched hand gingerly and found it bitterly cold. He looked at me with madness in his deep eyes.

"They have gone?" he demanded tonelessly, but a hard precision in his voice terrified me.

"Yes," I answered with a single drawn nod. He seemed to breathe anew. He continued to shudder. I gathered a blanket from the ground and drew it around his shoulders, feeling helpless and ineffective. Some people find all illness intimidating; I find it daunting only in the strong.

"Lyriel," whispered Evaric questioningly. His strangely silver eyes seemed to search for my face.

"Let me heat some food for you," I offered. He trembled like a man who had starved for a week. Meat might strengthen him.

His quickness of reaction had not suffered impairment. He snatched my arm in an instant and detained me beside him with all of a warrior's unyielding force. "Talk to me," he ordered harshly. I detest being commanded, but desperation still shrouded him.

"Of what?"

"Anything."

"Let go of my arm," I said softly, and he obeyed. I stared into his haunted eyes, trying to think clearly. It was difficult not to be drawn into oblivion by those eyes. "First act," I began, because specific words did not seem to matter. "A small farm. An old man sits beside the fire. His wife enters: 'Has Dreke returned?' she asks. 'Not yet,' answers the old man. Woman: 'Late, late, always late when the harvest nears.' Old man: 'It has ever been so.'"

So I recited, as I can do for endless hours. I played all of the roles: queens, paupers, tarts, and innocents. My career's lengthiest performance had an audience of one, but he was utterly attentive. I recited, until dawn freed my audience from his trance. He closed his eyes and relaxed the stiff posture that he had maintained for hours. I let my tired voice grate into silence.

"We should reach Walier before noon," he remarked heavily. He reopened his eyes and gave me a crooked half-grin. "Which of us is the Protector?"

"The constables of Mikolaii begin to seem a very insignificant sort of foe." Everything had begun to seem insignificant to me, except this man who had shared the night with me.

"Simpler, at least, than my foes." He drew his hands through his dark hair. "I do apologize, Mistress Lyriel, for having subjected you to my private little nightmares. I had hoped I was free of them." He was so very polite, so very remote; he might have been apologizing for a sneeze.

"This has happened to you before?" I demanded, feeling shocked despite my memory of the Bethiin's warning. Evaric had always exuded such self-assured sanity; I could scarcely believe that the Rendies had spoken to him prior to this eerie night. Perhaps I had believed Alisa's exaggerated portrait of him; perhaps I had measured him by the imperfect likes of Zakari. A rapport with Rendies might not qualify as a flaw in character; it seemed more akin to a physical disorder; it did not, however, convey perfection.

"They have not claimed me uncontrollably since I left Tyntagel," he answered at last.

"You have conversed with them often? When did you discover this peculiar talent?"

"We shall not reach Walier before noon if I tell you." He regarded me quizzically, beginning to rebuild his invincible facade.

I took cheese and bread from a saddlebag and offered half to Evaric. He accepted it quietly from my hand; his own hand still trembled very slightly. "Nothing beckons me in Walier," I said, assuming my most receptive manner. I doubted that Evaric trusted me excessively, but those who are troubled deeply seldom require much urging to relate their woes.

"When I was quite young, my sister and I strayed intemperately far from home one evening." He smiled apologetically. "I strayed actually. Ylsa, my sister, was merely endeavoring to dissuade me from straying farther. We encountered a wizard."

Evaric stopped, so I prompted him, "Wizards are not uncommon in Serii, are they?"

"I think wizards are not particularly common anywhere except Ixaxis, but it is true that Serii has more than her share overall. In Tyntagel, however, they are nearly as rare as in Ardasia, because the Lord of Tyntagel disapproves of Power."

"But you and your sister met one."

"He was not much of a wizard. He was quite mad. He held us in the open woodland until nightfall. That was when I discovered my peculiar effect on Rendies."

"That they talk to you?"

He averted his face from me before he answered. "They summon me. They occasionally obey me. They killed the wizard for me."

I had listened to more comforting confessions. "How old were you?" I do not know why his age seemed to matter. I do not particularly favor murder at any age.

"Old enough to know what I was doing." When he smiled,

he looked a little bit inhuman, both divinity and fiend combined. "My sister remembers nothing of that night, but she learned to hate me from it."

I could imagine a little girl's reaction to the sight of Rendies devouring a wizard at her brother's behest. I was a grown woman of what could charitably be called worldly character, and the passive company of Rendies had certainly unsettled me. "I suppose she had her reasons," I commented dryly.

"Perhaps she believed the Rendies," returned Evaric with quirky self-mockery. "My brother believed, and he went mad of it."

"What did they say?" I asked pragmatically, recognizing the K'shai's bitter eagerness to shock me. At the same time, I suspected, he must hope that I would accept the admission calmly: there was a hunger in him, which tightened around me, for there was no other visible focus for him but the brilliant sky and the open dunes of sand. Look at me, Alisa, I thought spitefully: your irresistible gentleman friend desires my approval. I presumed that his hunger was not for myself, but I did not care; I held more of his true attention than Alisa had ever achieved.

"They call me kindred, Fire-child, and Rending-born," he said carefully. "They call me son of the Taormin. I asked you of the Taormin, if you recall."

"I recall." My exquisite K'shai, what connection have you to an expensive artifact out of Ardasian legend? "Am I likely to forget an offer to dismantle my person?"

"You might. You apparently garner trouble enough."

"I should have thought so until now, but you exceed my skill, Seriin."

He laughed with a fey abandon that made me shiver. "Until I came to Ardasia, I cherished a sense of mystery about the Taormin. It had been named by Rendies! How could it be a mortal thing? When I asked you of it first, I never thought to hear such answer as you gave: of course you had heard of it. Every educated Ardasian has heard of it, although it has presumably lain in Serii for many thousands of years, and very few Seriins know of its existence."

"We Ardasians have perfected stealing from each other," I remarked with cynical honesty. "We are not accustomed to being outwitted at our own game, even by a Sorcerer King."

"Yet you remember so little more than that: the Taormin was stolen from Ardasia by a Sorcerer King. You do not know what the object was or is. You do not know why it was stolen or from whom. For all you know," said Evaric accusingly, "some Ardasian may well have stolen the Taormin in the first place."

"Likely enough, but I was not the thief," I protested; we were heading for an argument. "What have you to do with the Taormin?" I asked, straining my patience to avoid another clash with him.

"Not a thing more than you already know," he answered irritably. He threw a pebble across the sand as if it were a weapon aimed at an unseen enemy.

"Then the Rendies' words mean nothing," I declared firmly. Evaric did not answer me. He threw another pebble, and it whistled against the air. "You think they do mean something?"

"My brother—my foster brother—devised a theory, which I derided at the time he first told me of it." Evaric said flatly, "Both my brother and I were born just over nine months from the Rending."

"So were many others," I reminded him.

"Others do not speak to Rendies," he continued.

"Perhaps they do and, like you, choose not to admit it freely." Evaric shook his head impatiently. Wrong tactic, I told myself. "Were you ever tested for Power?" I shattered my target completely.

"Every Ixaxin test confirmed that I have no Power," asserted Evaric viciously.

I held no particular opinions about Power, but Evaric's own beliefs fairly shouted at me. "The tests were wrong," I said solemnly.

For a moment, I feared that he might strike me. He clenched his fists and studied me intently, as if he observed me for the first time. "Ixaxin tests never err," he said.

"And the Shrine can heal all the world's ills," I scoffed. His scrutiny might have made me self-conscious, if I were not inured to thorough appraisals of every sort. "Have you ever been troubled by any signs of Power other than the whispers of your night friends?"

"Sometimes I hear other whispers as well: stray thoughts from a stranger, the intentions of an opponent, the life force of an animal or a tree. Conierighm, my swordmaster, used to say that I possessed the swordsman's instincts, because I always fought ahead of his next move. I never told him that my quickness came not from instinct. As we fought, I knew his thoughts. It used to be rare and faint, but lately I have begun to perceive thoughts more frequently." Wonderful notion, I mused ironically: a K'shai who reads minds. The possibilities appalled me, and I put a firm clamp on my reaction. "I only read thoughts when I am under substantial stress," said Evaric with a faint smile, which left me wondering if he had read me.

I knew of very few people who hated me enough to hire an assassin of Evaric's caliber, even if they could afford him, but the errant fear struck me that someone might have hired our own K'shai to wreak some vengeance upon me. I dismissed the idea immediately, disgusted with myself for fashioning phantoms to fear. K'shai, wizards, sorcerers: they are part of the world. Even a wind-snake can kill, but fretting over the remote possibility of meeting one wastes energy to no purpose.

"You could always petition the Infortiare for Ixaxin training despite the tests. Cite your conversations with Rendies as due cause," I suggested, because it seemed the obvious recommendation. "You might even discover that Ixaxis considers talking to Rendies a common, curable affliction."

"A sorcerer cannot be K'shai." He stood and began to gather the blankets and utensils into bundles. "Walier awaits us," he added with twisted tightness. I helped him complete the packing, thinking uncomfortably of the question I had asked involuntarily of Anni.

Chapter 15

We reached Walier at a little past noon, the unkindest hour of the day for what is basically a very dirty, very disagreeable waystation for pilgrims. Walier did not come into existence for the purpose of bilking pilgrims, but it had put its strategic location to good use. Walier sat atop the largest subterranean reservoir between Ardas and the Shrine.

The city was crowded with pilgrim tours. The one inn which catered to Ardasian natives did not expect Rubi's Troupe for another two days. I was compelled both to bribe the innkeeper and to assure him that my K'shai escort would view the establishment with displeasure if we were not accommodated. After paying the bribe, I was able to secure only a single room, but it was the room that Rubi generally claimed for herself. It was large, airy, and well furnished, and it nearly compensated for the innkeeper's earlier churlishness.

Evaric returned from stabling the horses and nodded approvingly at the room. "Comfortable," he remarked, planting himself in the armchair to watch me complete my selective unpacking.

"Master Lund is bringing a cot for you," I said coldly, daring his foreign notions to find depravity in common economic sense.

"I had not intended to sleep here, unless your father has antagonized the authorities of Walier as well as Mikolaii. The stables will suit me quite adequately."

His bland amusement made me feel like some idiotically prudish pilgrim. I pondered the cost of replacing the inn's glass pitcher and decided that it was a nominal price for the satisfaction it would afford me. I hefted it toward Evaric's head in a fluid motion. It was a good throw, which deserved to hit its mark. Only a K'shai would be so aggravating as to catch the fragile pitcher midair and not even crush it between his hands.

"Have you always been so even-tempered, Mistress Lyriel?" he asked sardonically. He placed the pitcher on the side table.

"Miserable Seriin."

"Thank you," he returned ironically. "As a K'shai in your employ, I shall naturally stay if that is your wish. However, I should warn you that my nightmares are quite as likely to appear in this room as in the middle of the open desert."

Not even a K'shai should face such nightmares alone. "You are being paid to Protect me, Master Evaric, and you can hardly do that effectively from the stable." I snapped at him, because I did not want him to interpret my demand as either personal concession or desire. He was paid only to Protect me from Rendies, of course, but I saw no point in discussing the contract's specifics.

From the suddenly contemplative way he regarded me, I decided that he knew precisely why I had asked him to remain. His silence made me distinctly uncomfortable. I asked him irritably, "Why are you staring at me?"

"I was wondering why you risk your life to defend him."

"Whom?"

"Your father. He wants to be caught."

"Taf never knows what he wants, except the things he cannot have."

"He does not want to see you punished in his stead."

I stood and straightened my skirt's folds. "I think it must be time for dinner. Master Lund likes to serve early and leave the night for drinking and other pastimes of profit to him."

"Why is it so impossible for you to admit to loving your own father?"

"My feelings are my own, K'shai, and not for you to ponder."

"What you did for me last night," said Evaric slowly, "must have been very difficult for you. I know of no one else who would have done such a thing for me."

"How else should I have reacted? Should I have thrown myself to the Rendies' mercy?"

"You entrusted yourself to my mercy, when I was too lost in Rendie madness to recognize a friend. You faced me, and you faced my nightmares without fear or thought for yourself."

I met his eyes. The shadows made them blue and silver in turn. I forgot the angry words that I had meant to use. "I am not so brave, K'shai, nor so selfless. I assure you that I feared every moment. I acted in unsullied self-interest."

He shook his head in solemn denial. "If you had feared for yourself, the Rendies would have taken you," he assured me. "They spared you, because you were Protecting their Fire-child. Not even my brother ever defended me so valiantly."

"Sands," I muttered from embarrassment. "You make me sound like a holy icon." He smiled. I recited silent lays and did not allow a thought about him to creep into my mind. Those clear eyes appeared uncomfortably keen.

Once the Troupe arrived (with an unrepentant Taf), I evicted Evaric from the spacious room that I henceforth claimed alone. A man who kept company with Rendies could foster notions at least as uncomfortable as Alisa's envy. Evaric had not been revisited by his nightmares to my knowledge, but I was not sure that he had slept either. I had wakened several times to see him in the lamp's dimmed light. He stared sightlessly at the ceiling. I hoped that Fog could Protect him.

Freed of the burden of concern for the safety of myself and my K'shai Protector, I should have felt relief. The unlikely K'shai had terrified me more than once; he nearly always infuriated me. I hoped he did not realize how deeply and remorselessly he affected me. I kept imagining our play with myself as the bewitching heroine and Evaric as the determined suitor. "Addlepated," I told myself and decided to investigate the Taormin.

The temples do not care for Ardasian heathens such as myself, but a properly worded plea for enlightenment disarms them completely. The priests allowed me to enter the reading room, though I attracted several disapproving stares. I had dressed as simply and modestly as I deemed practical and bearable; I could not bring myself to stifle neck, arms, and ankles in stiff, dark cloth merely for the sake of some idly curious research.

Most of the temple books dealt strictly with the Shrine, the purported miracle of its discovery a few centuries before the Rending, and the reawakening of its Believers subsequent to the Rending. The first recorded miracle was the salvation of one Zarid, an exiled lord. Ardasia exiled or executed most of its noble families at about that time, so such displaced lords were not uncommon in our history. Zarid had wandered in the desert until he collapsed from starvation and exhaustion before a white and polished obelisk near the great, ruined city of D'hai. He swore that a vision came to him there, cast upon him a glowing aura, restored him, and showed him Truth. He returned to his former holdings and impressed a fair number of citizens with his new humility before he was again escorted from civilization. Whether Zarid's first followers pursued faith in the miraculous properties of an obelisk or showed habitual loyalty to a former liege, they did follow. The pilgrim scorn of D'hai natives has always amused me, since the ancestors of those D'hai Ardasians made pilgrimage to Zarid's Shrine long before any foreigner thought to do so.

I touched the Shrine once and nearly started a pilgrim riot. It is a rather remarkable structure, though it stands not much taller than twice a man. It withstands all weathers, but its surface yields to gentle pressure: It is neither stone nor metal. Pilgrims cite even the substance of the Shrine as holy, disregarding the fact that an entire city of the same material lies an hour's ride to the east. A few enterprising Ardasians have tried hacking off pieces of the old D'hai, but the stuff cannot be cleanly carved or shaped; it serves no profitable purpose, and the effort is uncomfortable.

The temple books equally deemphasized both the settlers who joined Zarid and the very ancient, very curiously preserved ruins of the oldest D'hai of all. The temples only occasionally acknowledge that three D'hais exist: one peopled by Ardasians, one by pilgrims, and one by imagination's haunts. I had been told that creatures like Rendies populated old D'hai even before the Rending. I could not confirm the story, but ancient D'hai was most assuredly an unsettling place. The temples had never resolved conflicting opinions of D'hai as both unapproachably sacred and irredeemably blasted by retribution for old evils.

In a less impassioned text than most of those that the temple issued, I found some data on the first D'hai. The book's author admitted that the Shrine's origins had been lost, that the Shrine had physical counterparts in the ancient city, and that a cataclysm of enormous proportions had decimated its creators and left the city deserted until Zarid's rediscovery. The author compared the cataclysm to a localized Rending, and he attributed both events to the unbridled Power of wizardry.

It was a reasonably rational, literate text. I paid the temple officer a kelne for its loan, exited the clay brick temple, and found Evaric awaiting me. My heart made itself felt in most disconcerting fashion.

"Have recent events actually turned you religious, Mistress Lyriel?" he asked me sardonically. Pilgrims were staring at him, armed as he was with swords and deadliness. "I fully expected the temple to shatter from shock at your entrance."

"Are you doubting the purity of my soul?"

"Far less than I doubt the purity of your actions. Innocents need not suffer the Protection of a K'shai in daylight."

"Did Rubi tell you to follow me?"

"She expressed a concern that you might repeat your Mikolaii escapade. I volunteered myself as Protector, having some experience in that vocation."

"Considering the nature of your admirers, I think I may be safer alone."

"Each time I think you might be learning civility, you prove me wrong. Mistress Lyriel, what is it about me that so effectively awakens the worst in your temperament?"

"Ask Alisa," I replied sourly. "She surely knows all that there is to know about you by now." With perhaps one crucial exception, I thought: I did not think Alisa would care for visiting Rendies.

"Are you jealous?" asked Evaric quizzically.

I laughed at him, even as I placed my hand on his shoulder and allowed my other hand to travel around his neck. His arms enclosed me with a fierce hunger that made my teasing gesture reel into something much more intense. I allowed his kiss to linger, but when our lips parted, I whispered to him, "Remember this moment, K'shai. It holds the only kiss you shall ever win from me."

"I never expected to win this one," he murmured, and I flushed at realizing how easily I could entice him further. He would be the first man I had loved for myself and not for the sake of saving Taf's neck from the gallows; he would also be by far the most complex man I had ever besotted. I extricated myself from his embrace and resumed my interrupted course. I could not switch affections as lightly as Alisa; I would want this man to stay with me, and how long could service to Rubi's Troupe satisfy a sorcerous K'shai?

"Your sojourn into pilgrim piety did not last long," commented Evaric with only a trace of huskiness beneath his casual tone. "We have thoroughly shocked every pilgrim in sight."

I tried to match his cool demeanor. "All the better cause for them to reform me."

"Lyriel, I do believe that you are beyond any pilgrim salvation. Perhaps that is in part why you appeal to me."

"Only wizards and K'shai are irredeemable, say the pilgrims."

"Then my profession should please you reciprocally."

"A pilgrim might condemn you for both categories," I suggested. His smile tightened. I waved at him the slim book I still carried. "Ancient D'hai."

"I appreciate your taste in literature," he remarked idly enough, but he regarded the book so avidly that I drew him to the first wide, shaded stone of comparable cleanliness. Seated in the dappled protection of an acacia, I opened the book to the section I had begun to read. "It falls somewhat short of complete," he said. Disappointment marked him. " 'Traditional Ardasian lore holds that the ancient city of D'hai fell to the Sorcerer King Horlach, who stole from it that object of unholy Power later called the Taormin, which Horlach subsequently used to conquer many lands.' "

I turned a page. "There is a bit more. 'Despite common opinion, ancient D'hai exhibits no proven evidence of active evil. The theory that the evil of D'hai was consolidated into that single object of Power is supported by the Taormin's violent history and the contrasting holiness of the Shrine.' " I was not so sure of ancient D'hai's innocuousness, but I saw no reason to mention my own opinions in that regard.

"Consolidated evil: I have known a few who labeled me so."

I ignored his self-mockery, since I could not identify its source as either bitter or vain. "A footnote says that the Taormin has been secured in a Seriin abbey since Horlach's demise. Are there any abbeys in Tyntagel?"

"No. The nearest would be Benthen, but that lies miles from where I was born."

"Son of the Taormin," I mused. "No abbess attended your mother at your birth?"

"Benthen is run by an abbot." Evaric caught a falling leaf, which had been gnawed from its bough by a greedy locust. "You are reaching too far for explanations, Lyriel."

"How can you sound so certain? You confessed to not knowing the Rendies' meanings. Do you prefer to find unpleasant explanations? You could rationalize nearly any crime by laying blame on a Rendie's words. Is that what you want? Balm for a guilty conscience?"

"I am not sure I have a conscience any longer." He said it with a searching glance, awaiting my reaction. "I can concoct a fair semblance of apology for expedience, but it is almost always specious. I am an ideal K'shai in that respect. I had to become a K'shai to realize how well the profession actually suits me."

Reorganizing my thinking kept me unresponsive for several minutes. "Many people would envy you," I said, wondering how far I believed him and how far he believed himself. The Sorcerer Kings reputedly suffered—or enjoyed—imperviousness to sense of right or wrong, and I supposed that such a trait could resurface as easily as Power. "You seem to commit few transgressions for a man to whom they do not matter."

"The practicality of reward and punishment still serve, and I frequently experience the pain of those around me."

"Then the opinions of others do matter to you."

"Insofar as they dictate my pleasures and convenience. Your opinions, for instance, are beginning to hold considerable weight."

"Expect no reward," I snapped, but I wondered. "Why do Rendies concern you so much if you cannot feel evil in them? Do they harm you?"

"They offer me adulation, not harm, if I follow them, but their shadowy world does not appeal to me. They are incomplete, as I am, though they do not perceive it. I do not shun them so much for their 'evil' as for their determination to keep me incomplete."

"Hence, you pursue the significance of their ramblings."

"I am very eager to reach D'hai."

"You expect to find your brother there?"

"Perhaps."

"Is he a pilgrim?"

"Of a sort."

"A pilgrim will not acknowledge a K'shai." Evaric shrugged and did not reply. I stirred the dust with my sandal. "The city may disappoint you."

"I think not."

"The Taormin is in Serii."

"No one there acknowledges it."

"What will you do in D'hai?"

"Learn, I hope."

* * *

As I lay abed that night, I tried to visualize a mental framework without a conscience to support it. Much as my own inconvenienced me, it did so in a reassuringly constant fashion. I liked to know when I defied my sense of right, imperfectly though my ethos might accord with the moralities of others. I took for granted the awareness of good and its counterpart, even among K'shai. The shades between were malleable, functioning by circumstance, surroundings and suggestion, but I expected everyone to own definitive opinions. Even Zakari had a conscience of a sort, though he had scarcely enough wits to know it. Whatever we did with the knowledge, we were bound together by the innate recognition that some common mores exist. Lack of that shared secret made a man inhuman. Did it make him wrong?

Philosophy made me wakeful. I lit the lamp and opened the borrowed temple book. I read it thoroughly, but it did not comfort me. Too many questions remained unanswered. I had an idea of where I might find answer to some of them.

I burst into Anni's room. "Do Ixaxins understand Rendies?" I asked her. Even at this absurd hour, she was awake, embroidering a tunic, and she did not look up from her work.

"To a certain extent," she responded calmly.

Her coolness deflated my nervous eagerness, leaving me only my urgent fear and hopelessness. I would not be discouraged. "What are the Rendies?"

"Energy. Manifestations of the Power of a tortured man."

"The Venkarel?"

"No!" She cast the tunic from her, rose, and swept across the room. The rush of her pilgrim robes crackled like a fire. She held a storm in her eyes. I am as tall as Anni, but she seemed to stand above me; it was illusion, but it was effective. "The Rending," she informed me quellingly, "resulted from the attack of a Sorcerer King on a man who refused to be a pawn. The Sorcerer King was Horlach. The man was Lord Venkarel. If Lord Venkarel had submitted to Horlach, he would have lived, and this precious, fragile world of ours would have belonged to a Sorcerer King. There is not one man or woman or child upon this world whose life is not owed to that Lord Venkarel whose name you dare to speak with scorn. There has never been a greater man, nor one more unjustly maligned."

Hers was a personal ferocity. She had to be older than she appeared. "Did you know him?" I was sure that she had known him well. How did a wizardess who had known a legend come to be a seamstress for a bedraggled troupe of Ardasian players?

Anni dwindled and became a humble pilgrim all in soft, gray sorrow. "I knew him."

The daughters of Silf's shipbuilder would have asked a thousand impertinent questions, since Anni was only a seamstress and therefore unworthy of privacy in their view. I could not think of one question which was not tainted by ignorance. "Educate me." My request startled her. "Or do Ixaxins hoard knowledge for themselves alone?"

She shook her head faintly. "Most mortals seem to prefer ignorance."

"I do not. Teach me about the Rending."

We both moved warily. We sat opposite each other, distanced by the full length of the room. Anni was softly hesitant. I was leery of her deliberately mysterious Power, and I was tired of treading among secretive, unfamiliar ways. Slowly, Anni began to speak.

"When Ceallagh and Tul conquered Horlach, they destroyed his mortal body. They took his greatest tool of Power, and they bound him from it. They did not—could not—destroy Horlach's Power and essence. They could only confine him and try to ensure that he never regained a means of acting upon the mortal, material world.

"Ceallagh's laws were designed to control Power. Any Power which could not be controlled would be destroyed before maturity."

Gingerly, I said, "I have heard that many Ixaxins think

the Venkarel—Lord Venkarel—ought to have been so destroyed."

Anni fingered her odd pendant. "There are some who question the wisdom of preserving him, but there was never a choice to be made. By the time his Power was recognized, Kaedric, Lord Venkarel, was much too strong to be destroyed by Ixaxin will."

"So they named him their Infortiare instead."

"They had no other option. Nor did he." She closed her eyes. "Horlach waited thousands of years for a Power akin to his own to be born. Only such a Power could give him life again in the material world. By its existence, such a Power gave him a beacon to follow back from full binding. Horlach expended many lives to gain that Power for himself. Horlach failed, because Kaedric destroyed his own mortal bonds to thwart him. The Rending was an unavoidable outcome of the direct clash between two Powers of such magnitude."

"The Venkarel committed suicide?"

"In a sense. It was the only way he could preserve this world at all. The Rending was an insignificant thing in comparison to complete cataclysm or complete subjugation."

"Rendies have never seemed insignificant to me."

"They are Horlach's creatures, fashioned after his own fears, drawn to this world by his Power."

"Are they intelligent?"

Anni reopened her haunted eyes. "They are self-aware. They have purpose. Yes, you could call them intelligent."

"So a man could conceivably communicate with them."

"Only if he had great Power and his own pattern resembled theirs to such a degree that he could survive as well in their world as in this one." She stopped mid-sentence and whispered, "Who?"

"It was just an idle question."

"Who inspired the 'idle' question?"

I felt as if a pin were jabbing me inside my head. It was an uncomfortable sensation. "Evaric." The pin was gone. "I had not meant to tell you."

Anni smiled crookedly. "I know, but it is well that you did. Please leave now." She made it sound like an edict.

I bristled, remarking, "You give orders as if you were bred to it."

"I did not intend to sound peremptory, Lyriel. I do require some time alone. For Evaric's sake, I must assess the patterns."

"What does a pilgrim care about a K'shai?" I was not jealous of her interest. Not quite.

"He is endangered. Please go, Lyriel. And tell no one else about Evaric's ability!"

She closed her eyes, and she was gone. I was alone in the room with a half-stitched tunic and an empty chair. At least, I seemed to be alone. These uncomfortable foreigners had me doubting my own senses. "Taf would give a lot to master that trick," I said. I left, because there seemed to be no point in sitting idle in an empty room and conversing with the furniture.

Chapter 16

Pilgrims, unnatural beings of gray shadows and black sorrows, stained the landscape, which should have been as pristine and golden as the sun in the hard sky. I hated D'hai. I hated what pilgrims had made of it. The oldest D'hai loomed as a distant smudge against the hills, a reminder of abominations more pervasive than the pilgrim city.

I could only tolerate Ardasian D'hai by restricting my vision to my immediate surroundings. The Ardasians who made D'hai their home remained privately unhampered by the sober public mores they assumed to trade with pilgrims in the other, newer quarter of the city. "Why must solemnity consume the pious?" I asked rhetorically, as we rode through the outer fringe of the Shrine Keeper's realm.

Anni answered, for I rode beside Solomai's wagon. "You invert the order, Lyriel. It is the solemnity, the deep sorrow, which very often masquerades as religious devotion. That sort of holy calling flares hot and expires. Those of deepest faith are serene and joyful."

"D'hai must attract only the first kind," I returned acridly. I would not have spoken aloud initially if I had recalled the pilgrim seamstress' proximity. I did not want a pilgrim's lecture.

"The truly devout do not need reassurance from the Shrine."

"What? Do you deny the Shrine's miraculous powers?"

"You are a cynic, Lyriel. Since you share your father's agility in using human nature to mislead by implication, your cynicism is not surprising, but there is worth also to be found. I wish you could have known Medwyn," she mused.

"A man whose piety would cheer me immeasurably?" I grumbled. Solomai maintained a stoic study of the mules, but her lips twitched with amusement.

"Perhaps," responded Anni remotely. "He was a very good man, the best I have ever known." More quickly—and with an embarrassed flush—she added, "He was the abbot of Benthen for many years."

"I have heard the name Benthen elsewhere recently," I remarked in absentminded perplexity. When I recalled the elusive origin, I regretted speaking, but I decided that secrets did not sate curiosity. "From Evaric." I wanted to see Anni react; she became devoid of all expression. "He was born near Benthen, I believe."

Solomai asked slyly, "Does Alisa know how much time that K'shai has been spending with you?"

"Not from me," I answered crisply.

"Has he told you much about his childhood?" asked Anni. She looked dreamy and introspective.

"A little," I told her. "He was raised in Tyntagel. Do you know it?"

"I know it," she responded. "I also lived there as a child."

"I thought you came from Tulea."

"Tulea is my home now."

As I formulated a means of interrogating her further, our train of wagons stopped. I rode forward to join Rubi and Taf. A balding and stoop-shouldered temple official led the deputation of pilgrims who had halted us. Rubi silenced me before I could speak a word. "You are Mistress Rubi?" the Shrine priest asked her—quite unnecessarily, since her name and image loomed from great posters at her wagon's sides.

"Are you the Shrine Keeper?" retorted Rubi facetiously.

The fussy little pilgrim who accompanied the priest announced, "The Shrine Keeper does not soil himself with the company of nonbelievers." I heard some snickering from among the passersby, but the issuer seemed disinclined to be identified.

"Enough, Master Curamon," said the priest; his forehead wrinkled when he talked. "Please understand, Mistress Rubi, that we dislike interfering in the pastimes of the local villagers. However, since tomorrow commemorates the miraculous healing of Lord Zarid, you must delay your performances for a few days."

"Our schedules are fixed," I informed him.

"However," interposed Rubi, "under such exceptional

circumstances, we shall alter our plans, of course." I stared at her in wonder.

"I am gratified, Mistress Rubi. Tanist Firo assured me that you would be cooperative. If you would care to join our ceremony, you are welcome." The priest departed as regally as he could manage with his wake of followers bobbing behind him like so many plump ducklings.

"Have you lost your mind?" I asked Rubi. "Accommodating a pilgrim?"

Rubi muttered, "Tanist Firo promised to revoke our license unless we cooperate fully with the Shrine Keeper; I received the message as we entered town."

"I wonder what hold the Shrine Keeper has found," I murmured.

"Any of a hundred would serve with Firo," muttered Taf.

"What does it matter?" asked Rubi impatiently. "We can better afford to bend our schedule than to lose Firo's good will. Tell the players, Lyriel."

Both Rubi and Taf glared at me, as if I had instigated the Shrine Keeper's arrogant authority. "If we are to begin bowing to the Shrine Keeper," I grumbled, "we may as well don black robes and worship the Shrine."

"Lyriel," repeated Rubi sternly, "inform the players."

Chapter 17

The Shrine Keeper's enforced delay of our performances did not please any of us, but we realized quickly that we were not the only ones afflicted. Every native I met grumbled about the Shrine Keeper's arrogance and the presumptuous way he had assumed the rule of D'hai in recent months. The problem was largely self-inflicted: If any of the D'hai natives had been willing to sacrifice the Shrine Keeper's silver, the pilgrim populace could have been rendered entirely helpless. One of the attributes I admired most about Vale, our innkeeper, was his refusal to cater to the pilgrim crowd. He did not suffer greatly for his selectivity, but his token effort counted for something.

I had felt uncertain as to how Vale would respond to Anni's presence among us, but he accepted her indifferently as a member of the Troupe; we were long-established customers. I had also begun to wonder about Anni herself for more reasons than her avowed Power. She had reached D'hai, which must have meant the completion of her long pilgrimage. Though we held her contract for the full season, and we had not paid her nearly enough for her to purchase a return journey to Ardas, a pilgrim had privileges in D'hai. If she chose to desert us, we could do nothing legally to stop her, and the Shrine Keeper's intolerance would make even illegal methods unlikely to succeed. Rubi assured me that our pilgrim seamstress would be too naive to know the methods, and Taf agreed. I did not mention that our pilgrim seamstress was also a wizardess who struck me as anything but naive; Rubi and Taf would have thought me daft.

Anni did visit the Shrine the first day, but her interest struck me as academic rather than religious. Noryne accompanied her, guiding her through the pilgrim D'hai which had once been Noryne's home. D'hai had always depressed Noryne with bitter memories, but no dangerous melancholy appeared to envelop her now. Anni's cures evidently served more than body.

Wrapped in a depression of my own, I left the common room soon after supper. I sought the room that Anni shared with Noryne. I had a vague goal of resuming the conversation that the Shrine Keeper's edict had interrupted, but I wanted chiefly to avoid Evaric, who seemed to muddle me more each time we met.

The seamstress' room was larger than mine, but it was crowded with furniture. Aside from the two beds, the room held a stone-topped worktable, chairs, trunks, and motley odd pieces of broken ceramic. Except when Rubi's Troupe claimed it, Vale used the room for storage and repair. Anni had spread fabric across much of the table. She was pinning facing to the finer fabric. I think her fingers could never be still; they were more restless than Taf's, though to more legitimate purpose. Noryne was engrossed in forming laborious letters on a sheet of yellowed paper.

"How is Alisa's cloak progressing?" I asked Anni, for I had no better excuse for coming.

"It is nearly completed," she responded equably.

I seated myself (without invitation) on the edge of the nearest bed. "Are you writing us a new play, Noryne?"

Noryne shook her head with faint embarrassment. "Anni has been teaching me to read."

I might not have chosen a pilgrim wizardess as the ideal instructor for the impressionable Noryne, but at least Anni had managed to overcome Noryne's confused notion that literacy endangered the soul. "Anni, how do you find the time?"

"Noryne learns quickly." I received the distinct impression that Anni preferred not to speak of Noryne's lessons. "How long do you expect the performances to be delayed?" asked Anni, dodging neatly into one of my least favorite topics of the moment.

"Our obstacle is a pilgrim holiday, not an Ardasian one. You should know the details better than I."

Anni replied vaguely, "I have quite lost track of the days."

"Time is easily forgotten in the desert," whispered Noryne. "When we travel the vast lands, I sometimes wonder if the world will not be centuries removed from us before we see a city again. It must have been terrible for you, Lyriel: cross-

ing the desert without the Troupe." Her eyes held concern
for me, and her voice was compassionate. Even if her reasons were wrong, I needed the warmth.

"Evaric kept the desert from me."

"He frightens me." Noryne folded her thin hands on the
smooth, cold stone of the table. The scar still showed, but
the injured wrist had healed remarkably quickly. "He is
more vast and terrible than the desert. He is like the Rendies
he fights."

Anni's fingers poised. "What do you sense in him,
Noryne?" It was an urgent question, asked with potent
calm.

"Danger, conflict, turmoil." Noryne's eyes became eerily
distant. I think neither woman recalled that I remained in
the room. "Change."

"Change within him or because of him?"

"The first. Or both. I cannot be sure. Must I reach
further, Anni? He frightens me so much."

"I do understand, Noryne, but the fear will not fade if
you turn from it. You are not endangered. He will not
perceive you."

"I cannot sense any more. Something stops me."

"What stops you?"

"A wall. It is dark and very cold." Noryne began to
shiver. Her skin actually became white; her freckles took a
purplish tinge.

I began to wonder what sort of herbs Anni had used in
her treatment of Noryne's ailments. "Noryne," I began.
Anni hushed me imperiously. I must have been too stunned
to disobey, because argument never occurred to me.

"The wall spreads," continued Noryne, shaking now less
steadily but more strongly. "It conceals. There is something
within, and it beats against the darkness. It stretches and
throbs. It will burst soon and encompass us." She was
almost screaming.

"Stop," commanded Anni, and Noryne became still. "Turn
from the darkness. What do you see?"

"Fire. Fire everywhere."

"Can you discern its origin?"

"It is everywhere."

"It has an origin." Now Anni was desperately shaken and
unsure in her insistence.

"Infinity."

"Infinity, yes." Anni was impatient. "It has a focus. Approach the fire."

"I shall burn!"

"Where is the origin?"

"There is fire, and there is darkness. They meet in distortion. There is nothing more. I am sorry, Anni."

"You are doing well, Noryne," said Anni, but she was disappointed. "Can you still sense Evaric?"

"Only through the darkness. He confuses me."

I interrupted, "Confusion is not a crime."

Anni said very slowly, "You defend him?"

"He belongs to the Troupe," I replied.

Noryne murmured from her disquieting trance, "You hold so much love and warmth in you, Lyriel, and you barricade it out of fear of bleeding again from your heart, as Silf's loss made you bleed. The K'shai has sketched a crack in the barricade, and you are terrified that he will break your clever, worldly shell and discover you."

I scoffed, "A K'shai? I would sooner love a sand-hog."

Noryne mused wistfully, "Many of us love unwisely."

"Lyriel is quite right, Noryne," said Anni sternly, but I had the oddest impression that she was weeping for me. "Caring for a K'shai would be sheerest madness."

Noryne's comments had made me scornful. Anni's words made me feel perversely inclined to crumble into tears. A light rap sounded at the door. I rushed to open it, enormously grateful for the interruption.

I expected to find Solomai or Rubi at the door. The sight of a stranger startled me; that he was a pilgrim made me wonder the more. Anni reached past me to draw him into the room.

"You found me quickly," she told him warmly.

"Our days apart have seemed endless enough." He had a strong and vibrant voice.

Noryne asked, "Is this your cousin, Anni?" His attitude did not strike me as cousinly, but Noryne had apparently been better informed than I, for Anni nodded in agreement.

"Circumstances forced us to travel different routes," explained Anni for my benefit.

Anni's cousin bowed. "I am Ineuil," he informed me. He repeated the bow in Noryne's direction. His broad smile seemed more appreciative than pious.

"Lyriel," I answered him tersely. "And this is Noryne."

There was something familiar about him. He did not resemble Anni, though he was equally as fair in coloring. His features were sufficiently distinctive that I doubted I could have confused him with any other. No, I had seen him elsewhere. He perturbed me. "You parted ways in Ardas?" I asked him cordially.

"We parted much too long ago," was his insouciant response, which hardly constituted an answer. "I have been touring this country of yours in the company of some most unpleasant gentlemen of the merchanting persuasion. I do think that Anni has had the better arrangement."

"Her 'arrangement' has not ended," I mentioned innocently. "Unless you share your cousin's talent for stitching, Master Ineuil, I fear that it is she who must fulfill the rest of her contract." I said it lightly, as if in jest.

Ineuil answered with equal brightness. "Anni's talents far exceed mine in many subjects, not least of which is her present profession."

Anni offered me a more direct reassurance, "I shall not forsake my obligations to you, Lyriel."

"Anni has always been a great proponent of duty," murmured her cousin. The look she gave him was sharp, which intrigued me.

"Did Vale supply you a room, Master Ineuil?" asked Noryne. If I had not known her guilelessness, I might have thought Noryne deliberately diffusing an argument of wills. I made note to observe Noryne more carefully. Anni had certainly helped her outlook, but I began to wonder how much Anni and Power had altered Noryne's perspectives.

"I have quarters," returned the peculiar pilgrim gentleman.

I could evade an answer better than most, but this Ineuil seemed unable to speak directly at all. He rang even less true as a pilgrim than Anni. He wore the robes, and he was foreign. He was no more a Shrine worshiper than Taf.

*   *   *

"These people have no concept of Power," said Rhianna. "The girl, Noryne, is an obvious sorceress, and no one in this country appears cognizant of the fact. Ignorance has done the girl great harm. I only hope that she has not been permanently impaired."

"What of the other girl who was here earlier?" asked Ineuil pensively.

"Lyriel?" asked Rhianna, startled. "Her heritage is entirely Ardasian, entirely innocent of any Power beyond the fully mortal kinds: a sporadic type of empathy, a limited resistance to the Rending creatures' spells. She is not a sorceress."

"I had thought as much, but I wondered," remarked Ineuil mildly. "I observed her at supper. She could not keep her eyes away from your son."

"Evaric appears to have that effect on many women."

"She appears to have the same effect on him."

Rhianna answered archly, "You should be the first to understand if Evaric enjoys a brief flirtation with a girl as lovely as Lyriel."

"I would indeed understand: Mistress Lyriel is beautiful and obviously infatuated. Your son cannot have encountered too many attractive, intelligent young women who could forgive him his profession for more than the span of an evening."

"State your point, Ineuil, without your courtier's circumlocution."

"In my humble courtier's opinion, your son is a true romantic, confronted by a cunning siren of exceptional determination. She will conquer him."

Rhianna laughed with mordant humor. "Of all the problems confronting my son, Lyriel seems hardly the most menacing."

"You underestimate her, I think."

"And you are the romantic, I think. The differences between Evaric and Lyriel encompass far too vast an array to overcome."

"Your son, however, does not know that the salient difference exists."

"He knows," replied Rhianna. Ineuil raised his brows. "In the heart of him, he knows."

"I still think that you wrong him by withholding the truth."

"It is not yet time."

"Why not? And do not allude obscurely to matters of Power incomprehensible to a mere mortal like myself. I understand, my dear Rhianna, a great deal more than you choose to credit."

Rhianna regarded him with a wrenchingly lonely and wist-ful expression. "Evaric's Power is tangled with the Rending. Every mote of his self-realization frees him a little and frees the 'Rendies' a little more. Ineuil, I do not know how to free him without destroying this world."

"He will learn his Power eventually and free himself," said Ineuil soberly. "Surely it would be better, however dangerous, if you controlled his learning."

"You are not hearing me: If I free him by telling him his heritage, I give the world irrevocably to the Rending crea-tures. No slightest chance exists of other outcome."

Ineuil replied sharply, "Forgive me, Rhianna, but your prophecy of certain doom does not persuade me to sit placidly and accept. An alternative must exist."

"Indeed," concurred Rhianna grimly, "an alternative does exist: Horlach has offered to free Evaric if I will 'lend' my Power to the operation."

"Horlach? He still survives?"

"He survives. He is imprisoned in the Taormin, and his Power is nearly null, but he retains his serpent's tongue. I know his legacy of treachery; I know how foully he has behaved throughout his history. I would not listen to him, but all other voices have abandoned me. I say to you: Destruction approaches. You listen, my friend, but you do not comprehend, for you have never walked in that other world. I know, and Horlach knows, and I fear—Ineuil, you cannot imagine how much I fear—that I shall have no other option but to accept my enemy's help."

"Loan Horlach your Power? What insanity has beset you? Did Kaedric and so many others die that you might now surrender to the very foe we dreaded?" Rhianna closed her eyes in pain and would not face Ineuil's incredulous fury. "Rhianna, my fair and wise Infortiare, you have convinced me that Horlach still exists: I recognize this brand of mad-ness, having heard its like before from Hrgh. Horlach is possessing you."

"You cannot understand, Ineuil," she pleaded in a for-lorn voice.

"Then summon Ixaxis or the monarchs of the Seriin Alli-ance. Summon a Wizards' Circle, or summon Kaedric's ghost, but listen to someone's voice beyond the vile one in your head!"

"Can you know how alone I feel!"

"I know how you terrify me with this talk of yours! You mourn Kaedric: I understand. But do not condemn the world to die because you lost your one great love. Find the options that Horlach hides. You might begin by trusting your own son; he cannot be more a devil than the one you fight within you. Work through the girl, Lyriel, if you cannot face your son yourself."

Rhianna shook her head in silence. Her pale hair caught the light; she wore it like an aureole of heaven. Demon or divinity? mused Ineuil in deep frustration; Kaedric, what have you bequeathed to her and to us all?

*　　*　　*

"He is here in D'hai."

"You assured me that he could never come so far. I cannot have assassins slaying one another in the holy city."

"Pilgrims do not note the death of a K'shai."

"Those he Protects will take note of it, and that will bring trouble with the locals. I paid your Guild well to eliminate him, and you have failed abominably. I must attend to him myself, which is precisely the situation I wished to avoid."

The K'shai called Circle stiffened. He seldom received criticism of his Guild's efficiency, but he had seldom competed with his own Guild-mates for the death of a pretender. "I must remind you, Shrine Keeper, that your information to us was significantly less than complete. Your contract is not the only one aimed against this man." Too many Guild-mates had accepted contracts against this target; too many of those Guild-mates had underestimated the target and given the target warning.

"I want him dead and proven so. You may collect for the deed all the contracts that you find, but bring the body to me." The Shrine Keeper drove his finger against the K'shai's chest, startling Circle into anger.

"You are a rash man, Shrine Keeper." A blade had appeared in the K'shai's hand, and he laid it against the Shrine Keeper's arm.

The Shrine Keeper closed his hand, smiling lightly. "I am a man of faith."

The K'shai hesitated, impressed despite himself by the coolly confident man who owned D'hai. Many K'shai had served this master's ruthless ambition. Many K'shai had abandoned large fees when asked to assassinate the K'shai imposter, Fire. Circle had never failed in a contract, but neither had Straw until the last.

*   *   *

The Shrine Keeper sat alone. "He knows where to find me," muttered the Shrine Keeper to himself. "Why has he not come? How does he survive every attack thrown against him? Is there no one able to kill him? He must come to me." The Shrine Keeper shook his head, as a shudder coursed through his body. "Leave D'hai before I can kill you, Evaric," he pleaded. The deep pain assaulted him. "No. He must die. He will die, my lord. He is the devil's own son, and he must not live. He has lived too long already and endangers us. I am your servant, my lord, and I obey you." The pain returned and intensified as the Shrine Keeper said tightly, "Damn you, Gorng."

Chapter 18

On the third day after arriving in D'hai, six of us headed bravely from Vale's Inn to give our season's first performance at the amphitheater at the city's edge. One of the Shrine Keeper's overbearing priests accosted us before we had walked half the distance. The priest was a gaunt man, and the gray robes made him look sickly. A dozen lesser officials of the Shrine accompanied him, all of them attired in gray robes and gloom.

Ardasian natives of D'hai, who had populated the street moments before, vanished. Even the constable disappeared. Beyond our little group of brightly hued players, everything and everyone looked gray and ominous.

"Your ways are evil!" declared the priest. "Your women are licentious." He pointed his finger directly at Alisa, which amused me in an acrid way. One of the officials actually jabbed Alisa, and she jumped away from him hastily. Quietly, I told Zel, Solomai's youngest, to find Fog. The old K'shai had accompanied us when we departed the inn, though I could not see him now. Rubi had sent Evaric ahead with Denz to establish our stage.

Someone began to shout in competition with the zealous priest. When I recognized the source as Zakari, leaping to his precious Alisa's defense, vexation made me want to strangle him. "Sands, Zakari," I muttered to myself, "you are only meant to be heroic in the play. Leave reality to those who are better equipped to face it."

Zakari marched toward the Shrine official who had dared to touch Alisa. The man squeaked with indignation when Zakari caught him by the collar. The man flailed helplessly, as Zakari began to beat him. The other Shrine officials watched in disquieting calm. A few pilgrims had gathered to gaze aghast and mutter ineffectual protests. The priest stood grimly straight and triumphant. Alisa looked more stricken than I had ever seen her.

As Rayn and Eolh tried to pry Zakari from the unfortunate Shrine official, a group of unusually substantial pilgrims emerged purposefully from one of the nearby buildings. They drew swords from the folds of their pilgrim robes, and they pressed their swords against Rayn and Eolh as well as Zakari. One sword was aimed toward Alisa and myself, and its wielder lacked even the grace to look apologetic.

The man who seemed to lead the sword-bearing pilgrims addressed us. He resembled a soldier more than a humble pilgrim, despite his pilgrim gray. "The Shrine Keeper wishes you to accompany us."

"We have a play to present," I retorted. "When it is done, we shall be happy to present ourselves to Tanist Firo's delegate."

"The Tanist has conveyed his full authority to us, the Shrine Keeper's Guard. You have caused a disturbance. It is our duty to arrest you."

"There has been a misunderstanding," announced Fog gruffly. The old K'shai came among us calmly, his thumbs tucked into his belt. He studied the swords of the Shrine Keeper's Guard with the detached air of a man appraising a possible purchase. "That man," he said, pointing at Zakari, "will pay the proper fine to the Tanist, as will that man." Fog pointed at the priest, who affected shock. "The rest of these people are blameless, and no one will be detained."

To my astonishment, the representatives of the Shrine Keeper's Guard lowered their swords without perceptible hesitation. They retreated by slow, deliberate steps into the featureless pilgrim building from which they had issued; the priest and his entourage followed, half dragging the battered official, who was nearly unconscious. A K'shai is always menacing but seldom so promptly effective against an army. I had a curious suspicion that Fog's eyes would seem blue, if I could see them.

Fog preceded us through the streets to the amphitheater, and most pilgrims stepped well away from us. The Ardasian inhabitants proceeded about their daily tasks but gave us a wide berth. Only Anni's pilgrim cousin, who hovered near the amphitheater, made no effort to avoid us; he smiled broadly at us and waved exuberantly. I wondered if we would have an audience.

* * *

The amphitheater was one of D'hai's numerous oddities. It appeared on cursory glance to be a natural formation, augmented by the mix of stone and wooden benches which lined its tiers. Low, slender trees sprang from an old irrigation canal behind the level circle on which Denz had fastened the pieces of our stage. The amphitheater appeared quite natural in its grandeur, so long as one did not delve beneath the layers of encrusting dirt and discover its impervious foundation: smooth, yellow, and molded into odd circles of irregular, lumpish forms. A few of the lumps resembled proper chairs, but the benches served far better. The dirt smoothed the surface enough to support the benches with only an occasional mishap due to instability.

I leaned against the side of Denz's stage wall, part of the assembly which comprised our portable theater, and watched the play inattentively. An audience had materialized, after all; Taf was counting the profits with a nod of mild satisfaction. Rubi stood near me, oblivious to everything but the play's rendition. Evaric sat just behind me, scarcely visible among the shadows of lacy trees and tall grasses. Something singed the air beside me in a rush of heated fury. Evaric had jerked me to his side before I saw the fire explode from the wooden stage wall.

"Denz!" Rubi was shouting. The members of our audience vied to leave us, treading upon one another in their haste to exit the amphitheater. The wooden benches were old, dry, and flammable, but the panicked departure posed more danger than the fire. Taf and Rayn led the sensible contingent in beating at the fire, curtailing its spread to the first tiers and nearest grasses. The stage itself was not faring well; the wall against which I had leaned was gone, caught quickly by the incendiary substance that had struck it.

I tried to reach Taf, but Evaric dragged me from the area. Most of the crowd had fled toward the rear of the amphitheater, and the Troupe members were all occupied in rescuing what they could of our stage and their personal property. Those who did try to escape through the brush behind the stage kept warily clear of Evaric's sword.

Evaric did not let me stop until we were well into the native quarter. Some of the fleeing audience had begun to spread word of the fire, and many of the curious were now returning to the site so recently abandoned. "Did you see who cast the fire-lamp?"

"No." He sounded angry with himself. "I was watching for intelligent attacks. A fire-lamp is a senselessly destructive weapon."

"Not every attacker has the finesse of a K'shai," I remarked caustically. Evaric might not have heard me; he sheathed his sword, but he remained vibrantly attentive to all that occurred around us. "The Shrine Keeper obviously does not want us in D'hai." When Evaric still did not respond, I added dryly, "Audiences are not usually so dissatisfied as to set us afire."

Evaric answered absently, "Fog will find the miscreant." We had reached Vale's Inn. Evaric inspected the courtyard as well as the common room; he acknowledged Vale evenly, but he studied strangers with a care that made several of them cringe. He held me firmly at his left, carefully keeping his sword hand free from interference. Vale's wife watched us curiously. I greeted her with defiant good cheer.

Evaric did not relax a bit until he had closed the door of my room, which he insisted upon searching. I grumbled at him from the chair in which he had placed me, "What do you expect to find here?"

"There are many weapons, Mistress Lyriel, and not all of them are obvious." He was lifting one of my costumes from its trunk, and I held my breath until he replaced it. "I have too long neglected certain unpleasant possibilities. I shall apologize profusely for invading the privacy of your possessions, but only after assuring myself that you are not endangered by them." He had lifted another costume, when he paused. He laid it aside wordlessly, but his lips were tight.

"Spare me your disapproval, K'shai."

He continued his dispassionate search. "Is the drug Zakari's?" he asked tonelessly. "You need not pretend surprise, Mistress Lyriel. A K'shai's education encompasses many fields of doubtful kind."

I responded sharply, "Without Zakari, we have no marketable play by which to earn enough to pay the exorbitant fees of the K'shai. Without the drug, we have no Zakari. I allow him only enough of his beastly virol to keep him functional."

Apparently satisfied with his search, Evaric brought the room's other chair to a position opposite me. Having done so, he did not occupy it, standing behind it instead, pensively running his hands over the chair's roughly carved back. "You take too many risks, Lyriel—for Taf, for Zakari, for me. One of these days, you may realize that the risks are real. That fire-lamp was thrown at you."

"By the Shrine Keeper himself, I suppose."

He did not react to my cynical interjection. "By someone who means to exchange your safety for my life. You really should be more careful as to whom you kiss on a public road."

I wished he would look at me instead of the chair. I could only focus on his hands and the unnatural brand. "I thought that you eliminated your Guild problems in Arahinos," I said weakly.

"Only one of them."

I tried studying my own hands, but my eyes kept returning to the K'shai. "How many lethal enemies do you have?"

"An unlimited supply, it would seem. They have never previously inconvenienced my clients."

My reactions to this Seriin K'shai conflicted in a drastic and unnerving manner. "Are you K'shai or K'shai target?"

"Both, I think, though the dual status does hold some inherent inconsistencies."

Rubi entered without knocking. "The stage is ruined," she announced in a tragic tone, which was not quite credible. She did look the part of a sufferer: She was sooty and scorched, and her rusty hair stood on end, stiffened by the pasty glop she applies to it. She was enjoying her tragedy.

She snapped at Evaric instead of at me, which pleased me. "How could you permit this to happen?" Her indignation was affecting.

Evaric bestowed a lopsided grimace on me and offered to Rubi the chair he still held. Rubi sank into it grandly, which constituted a difficult gesture in a chair of such intimidating hardness. She pretended to languish in exhaustion and despair. Her fingers betrayed her: She was making a mental tally.

"Your K'shai wages will reflect this disaster," she told Evaric firmly. She watched him, as did I, wondering if she could actually bluff a K'shai into subsidizing the new stage that she had long been wanting.

"I think the perpetrator would be a better choice for reparations," replied Evaric dryly.

"The perpetrator whom you allowed to escape."

"Fog will find him."

"You have great confidence in your partner's abilities."

"Implicit confidence, Mistress Rubi."

"You had best be right."

Or you will do what to him, Rubi dear? I wondered. She was taking advantage of his Seriin courtesy, which was fine if that courtesy actually penetrated beneath the polished surface. I was wishing that Rubi would leave, for there were questions I wanted to ask the K'shai. I wanted to ask if he had found his brother, if he had learned what he hoped to learn in D'hai. I wanted him to stay on any pretext, but he left graciously when Rubi stared at him in obvious dismissal. He seemed to be contrary only with me.

"Taf will need your help in replacing our equipment." Rubi was enjoying remarkably good spirits, all things considered. "I shall want you to present the bill to the Shrine Keeper, since he claims responsibility for all that transpires in D'hai." She was positively glowing now.

"If you wanted to antagonize the Shrine Keeper, why did we delay for his useless holiday?"

"He had not attacked my players then."

"We do not know who instigated the fire, and I thought you blamed me for the other incident. You did say something about my failure to keep Zakari out of trouble?"

"I changed my mind."

"You choose a fine time to become sensitive to my perspective. Do you intend to seek restitution from the K'shai and the Shrine Keeper both?"

"They are not likely to communicate with one another."

Sometimes greed overwhelms Rubi's common sense. "And you complain about me looking for trouble."

Fog brought the silver to Rubi that afternoon. He informed her in a grimly affable way that the former owner had no further need of silver serisni. To questions regarding said owner's identity, Fog simply shrugged, "A pilgrim."

I steadfastly refused to deliver Rubi's demands to the Shrine Keeper. I had almost persuaded her to forget that foolish plan, when Vale informed us that citizens of D'hai had been offered the choice of our patronage or the Shrine Keeper's. "It is not you in particular, Rubi," Vale told her. "The Shrine Keeper wants no one in D'hai whom he cannot control. He is bright enough to know that itinerant players with strong K'shai Protection are not about to worship his kind."

Taf muttered, "I suppose he persuaded Tanist Firo to agree."

"First thing," agreed Vale glumly. "This Shrine Keeper only came to D'hai a couple of years back, but he has taken over the temples, sent the old Shrine Keeper into retirement in Ardas, and garnered the blessing of Tanist, constables, and anyone of influence in the nearest six domains. He speaks, and these pilgrims fall all over themselves to do his holy bidding."

"Sounds like the pilgrims are not the only ones," I suggested.

Vale rubbed his big hands on his apron, delaying his answer. "The Shrine Keeper is a rich man," he said finally, which I suspected was not what he originally intended to say. "You know your business is still welcome here, Rubi." Someone called him to fetch ale to another table, and he left us.

"Without supplies, we cannot replace our stage," said Taf glumly.

"We have managed without such luxury before," retorted Rubi.

"Can we survive without an audience?" I asked.

Rubi frowned, but she raised her head defiantly. "We pack tomorrow," she said briskly. "We leave the following morning."

The packing required little time, for the fire had decimated some of our bulkiest possessions. When Noryne and Anni invited me to observe the Shrine blessing with them, I agreed for no better reason than unaccustomed idleness. Anni's cousin materialized as an overly eager escort, which made me glad that I had chosen to accompany the party; I did not want either Anni or Noryne to desert us due to Master Ineuil's glib tongue.

We had neared the Shrine. We traversed a crowded part of the city, packed with pilgrims, pressing to reach their goal. A cluster of gray figures broke free of the mass, ran, and pushed past us roughly. The shouting began. I felt myself shoved from behind. Noryne gave a startled yelp. Her hand let go of my arm, and she was pulled away from me. I could see neither Anni nor Ineuil. The pressing crowd reached me, and I could not move save by the throes of the bodies squeezed against me from every side.

Faces passed me: hollow cheeks, a drooping jowl, narrow shoulders, a bony neck. Grunting and crying, the mob whisked their many faces past me. I sensed no motion on my own part. The Shrine marched to me, and the crowd seeped away. I saw one face then: pinched lips, a satisfied and smiling face above strong shoulders, darkly clad in a tunic embroidered in white. His breath burned my face. The K'shai brought forward his short sword. He raised it; the edgewise blade looked innocuous.

The blood seemed to well very slowly from his throat, startled by the thin dagger which protruded from it. The dead K'shai's short sword grazed my cheek as its stubborn wielder slumped. Jarred by the fall, the dagger sliced a ragged rent, and the straining blood escaped him into a pool. I winced and averted my eyes.

"How much alike death makes them," remarked Fog with ironic wonder. He stooped to retrieve his dagger. For so coarse and big a man, he moved with unlikely elegance and grace.

"You killed him?" I asked stupidly. "He was K'shai."

"He was K'shai," agreed Fog, "endeavoring to effect a paid obligation. You think he did not deserve death?" The question was impersonally curious.

"I suppose I would not have enjoyed the alternative."

How strangely Fog smiled. "What will a man not offer to survive? If one man will forsake infinity in a mere hope of mortality, surely another should not regret the murder of a wretched tool."

I had no idea what he meant, or if he were even sane. "You view his death as murder?" It seemed an odd judgment from a K'shai.

"Do you not?" He nodded toward the knotted mob, which had ebbed from us. A few members had strayed free of the throng, as had we, and several of these had observed our grisly companion. "We would do well to leave guilty verdicts to uncertain renderings."

We circled behind the Shrine, and Fog found a clear path for our escape. We left, knowing nothing of Noryne, seeing no hint of Anni or her cousin, asking no one about the cause or reason for the initial turmoil. We had given the

Shrine a bloody offering, which the pilgrims and their Shrine Keeper could interpret as they wished.

Fog and I did not speak again until we had regained the safer city of Ardasian souls. "Shall I speak of the incident at the Shrine?" I asked him, for it was he who had betrayed K'shai practice by so bloodily preventing his fellow from completion of contract.

"Riots and death go together," replied Fog. "Not much news in them." I took his gruff statement as a suggestion to ignore the death of the K'shai. Fog sounded utterly unlike the calmly calculating executioner at the Shrine: a man no less cavalier about death but less philosophically engrossed by it. I almost felt that my pensive rescuer had been some demonic entity, known to the Fog we paid but entirely distinct from him.

Lyriel, I told myself scathingly, you will soon start buying pilgrim icons and talismans against evil auras if you persist in this vein. It came of mixing with foreigners. Sorcery, wizardry, Rendies: look at them too long, and you begin to imagine them everywhere. Nothing mystical had occurred. A pilgrim riot had separated me from my companions, making me vulnerable to a K'shai who had overestimated my significance to Evaric. The idea was not palatable, but neither was it unnatural. What could be more prosaic than violence, coercion, and misunderstanding? I ought to feel satisfied that the assassin no longer stalked me. I certainly owed a debt of gratitude to Fog.

Anni returned to the inn with her cousin, both of them apparently unmoved by the afternoon's events. Evaric returned Noryne, a little battered but safe. She had been caught and dragged by a man she could not identify. The man had dropped her and fled before Evaric located her. I could have suspected that the man had been paid to draw Protection away from me. I could have believed that the K'shai assassin had concocted the riot; someone had purportedly murdered pilgrims in the crowd. Before the evening hour all D'hai had heard another version of the riot, and I no longer knew what to believe. The pilgrims who had been nearest to the Shrine claimed that Rendies had appeared to them: Rendies in daylight. I was glad that we were to leave D'hai in the morning.

* * *

Rhianna studied the wall and the tangle. The trickle of darkness had become a narrow stream. *"We have very little time left to us,"* said Horlach urgently. *"The instability accelerates."* Rhianna did not reply. *"Lend me your Power! You have no other choice."* Rhianna touched the rent, bathing it in healing Power. The tangle stretched, achieving pattern for an instant. The rent recoiled, and the darkness spread.

Chapter 19

I sequestered myself in my room, curled myself in the corner and pondered. I seemed to hold many pieces of a great puzzle without discernible pattern, and my inability to resolve the design frustrated me. I had always understood the intricacies of those clever little Bethiin boxes that fit together so uniquely and so well: a single key piece holds all the rest in place; without it, one holds only random wedges of wood. I could not reconstruct the disassembled design of which I sensed that I was a lesser part. I had identified the key, but I could not define his proper placement in the whole. K'shai, target, or Rendie in the guise of a man: Evaric bewildered me.

"Lyriel, my girl, you are a fool," I told myself severely, "letting a crazy Seriin muddle your head." A rap at the door interrupted my self-recriminations, and I snapped at its unseen issuer, "I am not receiving!"

"Lyriel," said Evaric dimly, "please open the door." I had complied before he finished his request; I did not even pause to brighten the lamp. "I missed you at supper," he remarked prosaically, but he rubbed at the K'shai brand with a nervousness rare in him.

"I ate early. We shall leave before dawn, after all."

"I shall not be leaving D'hai with you," said Evaric slowly. "I told Mistress Rubi that I would follow the Troupe from a distance, so as to preclude any further attacks from D'hai, but I deceived her. Fog will provide you with Protection to Tayn, and he will ensure that you are well Protected subsequently. I wanted you to know, Lyriel."

"You wanted me to know?" I repeated incredulously. "You mean just to disappear and leave me to inform Rubi that you have broken contract? Is this the way you fulfill your obligations? No wonder your own Guild seeks to elimi-

287

nate you!" Torn between fury and devastating disappointment, my voice trembled.

"My Guild-mates mistake me for someone else," he replied, his expression resigned and miserable.

"You committed to a full season of Protection," I persisted. "Either complete your contract, K'shai, or I shall hire an assassin to seek you myself!" I fought to keep my tears inside of me. Evaric touched my hair, but I shook free of him and leaned my head heavily against the wall.

Lotin emerged from his mother's room and gave us a bluntly questioning look as he passed. He even turned at the stair to regard us once again before descending. Evaric said very softly, "I wish I could explain to you, Lyriel, but I have no rational reason to give. I could say that I must remain in D'hai to answer questions long sought, but I would be lying: I do not know why I must stay here. I know only that departure is impossible for me."

"Blast all foreigners," I whispered, when he had gone.

We packed the wagons quickly, for the fire had claimed our largest items. I searched for Evaric, but Fog joined us alone. I might have informed Rubi of our young K'shai's desertion, but I could not betray Evaric's implicit trust in me, though I felt sufficiently betrayed myself. Rubi would miss him soon enough.

Beyond D'hai, the desert rose in gentle hills, sparsely dotted with thorn trees and the worn, jutting crags of some ancient shift of the solid earth. The sky bloomed pink with dawn's innocence. I reined my mare and allowed three of the wagons to pass me. Alisa leaned from Chard's wagon, looking bored, and I flung my irritation at her. "You may quit searching for him," I told her sharply. "Zakari's rival has abdicated."

"Rubi!" shouted Taf urgently. I rode forward to join him, leaving Alisa's angrily insistent questions unanswered. Taf, alone in the lead wagon, had just mounted the first high hill beyond D'hai.

"What is it, Taf?" I began to ask, but he did not need to respond. "Sands," I murmured. The lovely pink sky did not brush the top of the next range of hills, for the sky melted into darkness somewhere near where the hills ought to have risen. The line of murky distortion cloaked the horizon. I could not look long into the rippling darkness, because my senses recoiled from the chaos of its twisting motion.

"We can circle back through Walier," announced Rubi, as if we might avoid some ordinary quirk of the landscape.

"Circle what?" muttered Rayn, rubbing pensively at the short bristles of his beard. Most of the Troupe had now gathered atop the hill to stare into bleak oblivion.

"Whatever it is," answered Denz, "I want no closer look."

"We certainly cannot leave D'hai by this route," agreed Taf.

"The Walier road will also be closed by the time you reach it," remarked Anni with unsettling calm. She reached her thin hand to Taf's lead mule, absently quieting the restless animal.

"What is that thing?" I asked her.

"A distortion of energy." Her face became dreamy and remote. "It reaches into infinities beyond me. It spreads itself into a sphere, surrounding that point which touches all infinities."

Noryne added nervously, "We must return to D'hai, before the barrier tightens and catches us."

Anni nodded very slightly. "Yes. There was never any question of leaving D'hai."

The Troupe members had begun to return mutely to their wagons. I detained Anni. "If you anticipated this phenomenon," I said, "you might have warned us."

She regarded me keenly. "Would you have believed me?"

"Perhaps," I replied, but I convinced neither of us. I had not believed Evaric, who had warned me of the obstacle in his own cryptic way. The eerie barrier might imprison us or strangle us, but neither prospect could dismay me. Nothing short of a second Rending could have overpowered my awareness that I was returning to my troublesome K'shai.

Vale accepted our return with equanimity; the mail carrier, who had confronted the obstacle shortly after dawn, had already spread news of the barrier surrounding D'hai's ancient valley. I saw Evaric approach Solomai to help her with the horses. Before I could escape my own efforts to unpack, Alisa had reached the K'shai's side. I saw Zakari throw his load to the ground and stalk into the city; I felt inclined to join him.

The day seemed interminable: we could neither depart

nor perform. We could make no purchases, for the Shrine Keeper had forbidden trade with us, nor could we even walk safely in the city. Minaro tried to begin a song in Vale's common room, where most of the Troupe sat dumbly, but the song quickly became dismal.

Rubi had seldom looked more mournful. Anni and Noryne had vanished with Anni's cousin. Taf, more comfortable with despondency than the rest of us, displayed his conjuring skills to an attentive Fog, but I knew the tricks too well to share the K'shai's fascination. When Evaric arrived with Alisa clinging possessively to his arm, my frustration erupted.

I marched purposefully to the door. Rubi demanded, "Lyriel, where are you going?"

"To visit the Shrine Keeper. Since we seem condemned to remain in D'hai, we had best try to resolve our position with him."

"We have enough trouble without you seeking more of it, girl," said Taf.

I glared at him. "Fire me," I told him, and I whirled to leave.

"You are not making my job easier," said Evaric.

"Then Protect Alisa instead," I snapped. He ignored my injunction and followed me, for which I felt much more grateful than I intended ever to let him know.

Chapter 20

The Shrine Keeper discouraged spontaneous visits. He surrounded himself with priests, pious servants, and his ubiquitously menacing Shrine guards. Consternation over the black barrier and the reputed appearance of Rendies in daylight compounded the obstacles: crowds of pilgrims had gathered in the entry yard to plead for enlightenment.

By employing bribery, trickery, and threat of the lean and dangerous K'shai beside me, I managed to procure an audience within a little over three hours. Guards led us to a cold, white room, sparsely furnished. Evaric remained near the entry columns in the shadow of the guards' company, as I strode forward to face the Shrine Keeper, whose cleanly carved stone chair conveyed the arrogant impression of a royal throne. Gray-robed priests bustled about their chosen liege, accomplishing nothing apparent but contributing considerable noise.

A large man of fair coloring and with a strong, square jaw, the Shrine Keeper did exude a potent presence, even in his falsely humble gray robes. "Mistress Lyriel," he commented with a proud, vaguely disdainful air, "you are a very forceful young woman. I seldom speak to those who have been unblessed by the Shrine's truth." His priests murmured approval of his words.

"A truth greater than yours seems determined to keep our Troupe in D'hai despite your diligent efforts to oust us. You have attacked us, threatened us, alienated us from D'hai's rightful citizens, and behaved altogether insufferably. The harassment must stop."

The Shrine Keeper remarked languidly, "You overestimate my interest in your little local squabbles. If D'hai's citizens shun you, the fact derives from troubles you have brought with you. I have always found D'hai to be a quiet city, until your recent arrival brought chaos to us."

I sensed motion behind me, as Evaric emerged from his self-imposed position of obscurity. Evaric said quietly, "You always did excel at eluding blame, Arvard."

The Shrine Keeper's blandly superior gaze darted from me to Evaric. "Lords of Serii," he whispered.

"Shrine Keeper," murmured several priests with varied blends of bewilderment and consternation, for their indomitable Shrine Keeper had begun to tremble like an ailing old man.

The Shrine Keeper commanded imperiously, "Leave us." Some of his devoted entourage hesitated, and the Shrine Keeper shouted, "Leave us!" The priests dispersed through various arched doorways amid a flurry of troubled glances.

I remained firmly immovable; I could feel the chill of the cold stone floor even though my sandals. The Shrine Keeper had forgotten me. He walked toward Evaric and touched the face of my K'shai escort with a tentative gentleness full of wonder. "I had forgotten how you affect me," he said delightedly. He clasped Evaric's arms with an enthusiasm that Evaric did not reciprocate. "I knew Conierighm would make a K'shai of you!"

"I left a message of explanation for you with Ylsa. You would have received it if you had ever returned to Tyntagel."

"I never returned, because I have not yet finished what I began. I sent a message to you that I was leaving Serii."

"I know. I received it only a year ago." Something cynical stirred in Evaric. "I came, as you expected."

Considering my own strongly ambivalent feelings toward the K'shai, I had little right to condemn another's obsession, but I did not consider the Shrine Keeper's fanatically hungry, almost tortured gaze a natural expression. I seated myself on the Shrine Keeper's throne and pondered the two men bemusedly. I resented deeply that Evaric had told me nothing of his acquaintance with the Shrine Keeper. Evaric had made such frantic issue of his nightmarish concern with Rendies and ancient artifacts that I had almost persuaded myself of his candor. I had actually begun to trust a K'shai.

"I am near to finding the Taormin, Evaric," said the Shrine Keeper fervently, and I became more attentive. "It is here in D'hai. Together we shall find it. I have missed you, little brother."

I began to laugh, ridiculously affected by thought of the holy Shrine Keeper, the man who had garnered more eco-

nomical influence in Ardasia than any Tanist, being the
elusive brother of my K'shai. The Shrine Keeper turned on
me like a fury. "Leave us, Ardasian whore!" he shouted.

Evaric said quietly, "Apologize to her, Arvard."

The Shrine Keeper wilted, which made an odd image
from a man so obviously capable and strong. "We don't
need her, Evaric. We don't need any of them. We need only
each other, just as we always have: the Lost Prince and his
devoted servant. We'll have our own world. Nothing can
stop us: not these narrow, useless Ardasians, not Ixaxis, not
Rendies, not . . ." He stopped and furrowed his face in
effort. "Not anyone. I am Immortal, and you are my loyal
ally, little brother."

The Shrine Keeper, I thought with the beginning of true
uneasiness, was entirely mad: Rendie madness, perhaps, but
of a kind more pervasive and deadly than any I had seen.
When Evaric came to me and reached for my hand, I gave it
to him with alacrity. "Mistress Lyriel is under my Protection, Arvard." Evaric's eyes burned with a starkly silver
light that seemed inhumanly bright, and he frightened me,
though his anger flared on my behalf. "Do you understand
me, Arvard?"

"I shall not harm her," promised the Shrine Keeper meekly.

"Neither you nor your people will harm her."

"My people obey me." The Shrine Keeper offered me a
brilliant smile. "Forgive my rudeness, Mistress Lyriel. Let
my clerk know your Troupe's needs, and I shall see that you
have all you require."

"Thank you." I distrusted the Shrine Keeper. I distrusted
the exchange between the two brothers, both of whom
seemed to keep secrets well buried.

Evaric drew me toward the main door. He told the Shrine
Keeper, "I shall return to talk to you later, Arvard."

"You'll understand, little brother, when I explain what
I've learned." The Shrine Keeper looked peculiarly forlorn
when we left him.

Evaric did not relinquish my hand as he led me through
the crowds of curious pilgrims. He remained forbiddingly
silent as we crossed the pilgrim city. I let my own specula-
tive thoughts carry me to the edge of the Ardasian district.
"So you came to D'hai to combat a Rendie's whisper about
the Taormin," I said archly.

"Yes."

"And you happened to discover that your brother, whom you had heard might possibly be in D'hai, just happens to be the Shrine Keeper, who has acquired more influence in the past year than anyone else in Ardasia."

"Arvard has always been quick to achieve the ambitions he sets for himself."

"Nothing that you told me about your brother was true."

"It was all true, as far as I know. Despite his show of delight and incredulity, Arvard was neither surprised nor pleased to see me."

"Why did you not try to see him before today? You obviously knew where to find him."

"I watched him give the Shrine blessing. That abolished any notions I entertained about discovering the brother I remembered."

"Why did he come here?"

"For the same reasons I came."

"To escape a nightmare?" I asked dryly.

"He came to escape a Rendie's madness. Please, Lyriel, I am not in the mood for an inquisition."

"You might have told me," I muttered.

He kissed the palm of my hand, which silenced me very effectively. My thoughts remained largely incoherent until we reached Vale's Inn. I felt very conscious of Solomai watching us enter together, even more aware of Alisa's unheeded voice calling to Evaric from the common room.

Only when we stood alone at the door of my room did Evaric speak again. "Why do we argue, Lyriel?"

"Because you are impossible."

"Then why do I continue to seek your approval?"

My approval? "Because you are a fool."

"Which of us is the more foolish, Lyriel? Me for seeking, or you for stubbornly refusing to admit approval of anything about me? I think you would do nearly anything for me, except confess that you might not dislike me as much as you pretend."

"If you want to earn my approval, Seriin, you might begin by leaving my room now."

"Yesterday, you cursed me for leaving."

"I cursed you for breaking contract."

"You wept for me."

"You have an active imagination." I tried to shut the

door against him, but he would not depart. I turned my back on him and walked to the window. The sky grew dusky; I closed the shutters.

"I nearly asked you to remain in D'hai with me yesterday. When I thought that I might not see you again, I realized how much you have come to matter to me."

"You recovered quickly: I hoped Alisa entertained you with the harrowing tale of our failed foray from D'hai."

"No, but she provided me with some enlightening insight into the differences between Ardasian customs and those with which I was raised."

"Have your interests migrated from ancient history to contemporary cultures?"

"Seriin courtship," he remarked blandly, "consists of elaborate rituals, carefully arranged by the families of the betrothed pair. Ardasians are apparently less regimented, generally pledging themselves to one another without any formal ceremony or public acknowledgment."

I began to feel noticeably warm. "An appreciation of privacy," I replied stiffly, "does not make us immoral."

"I agree, which is why my question emerges so slowly. I want your honest answer, not the product of some misunderstanding based on your father's prejudice against 'Foreigners.' "

I faced him, though I could not meet his eyes. "You Seriins talk in circles," I complained. "What are you asking me?"

"Would you accept my pledge?"

"Your pledge?" I repeated absurdly.

"I ask to love you," he explained patiently. "Lyriel?"

"Close the door," I told him sternly.

"From which side?" asked Evaric wryly.

"From inside, you ridiculous Seriin. Do you think I want everyone in the Troupe to know that I am foolish enough to love a K'shai?"

He laughed against my hair. "Why not? Everyone in your Troupe already suspects it."

I formed a retort, but I never managed to use it. I was otherwise occupied for a considerable number of hours.

*   *   *

"You did know that your brother was the Shrine Keeper."

"Yes. Arvard hired the man who tried to kill me in Ardas, the man who tried to kill me in Samth, the man who tried to kill me in Arahinos, and the man who tried to drive the Troupe from D'hai, so that he might kill me outside of the Shrine Keeper's city."

"Your brother wants to kill you?" The man who had greeted Evaric with devouring eagerness had hardly seemed replete with enmity. "Why?"

"Rendie madness. Or human madness. Something altered Arvard after Ixaxis refused him. A Seriin nobleman—Fog's contacts could not tell me which one, though I believe I know—captured Arvard and evidently enhanced his madness by using illegal sorcery. I spent a good part of five years tracing Arvard to that point. By that time, he had already come to Ardasia and already tried to kill me twice in Serii."

"At this mysterious nobleman's behest?"

"I prefer to believe that Arvard would not otherwise have turned on me so thoroughly." Evaric drew his finger along the line of my cheekbone. "I thought that I became K'shai to protect Arvard. Instead, I defend myself from him."

"Then it is not K'shai rivalry that pursues you. All the attacks and the warnings originate with the Shrine Keeper." I never had trusted pilgrims, I mused.

"Unfortunately, Arvard is not the only issuer of a contract against me. Or perhaps the multiplicity has saved me: Some of my more amateur attackers have destroyed one another in their eagerness to reach me."

"What does Fog do while you fight other assassins?"

"At his best, he protects me and those who matter to me; the K'shai who tried to kill you near the Shrine had pursued me from Walier, trying to fulfill a contract to Lord Borgor dur Sandoral. At Fog's worst, Fog takes contracts and drinks too much between them."

"You dislike him."

"Sometimes." He grimaced. "Most of the time. Dearest Lyriel, I do understand your dislike for the 'typical' K'shai, because I share it. I never wanted to kill, not even defensively. I never even wanted to kill Rendies, much as they torment me. Something pushes me to it. Every death haunts me, but it is so easy at the moment of killing. A life is such an easy thing to take." His voice ebbed.

I murmured tenderly, "How do you define this 'conscience' that you claim to lack?"

"As something independent of self-interest, which is all that motivates me."

"I think you overestimate the motives of the rest of us." He smiled but did not answer. "Why does this nobleman want to kill you?"

"He seeks vengeance against a man he believes was my true father, and he considers me a danger because of that supposed parentage. His contracts are not the only ones aimed at me, but his wealth makes his efforts the most professional and the most persistent. Fortunately, the very magnitude of the reward keeps assassins competing for me rather than joining forces in any effective manner."

"You told me that your father was a clerk."

"He is an accountant actually, though 'clerk' is commonly used to designate all Tyntagel Staff positions."

"Do Seriin accountants generally make such determined enemies?"

"No." Evaric said nothing for many moments. Voices and the sound of dishes clattered through the floorboards. "Vale's Inn prepares for another day caught between a blackening sky's despair and the futile hope of the Shrine Keeper's theatrics," murmured Evaric. "Arvard has always enjoyed domination. It soothes his insecurity."

"He also searches for the Taormin," I prompted.

"I suppose that part of Arvard still expects to have Power one day. Lord Gorng's manipulations did not change that old madness. Or Arvard could be baiting a trap for me by hinting at hidden secrets. He knows how the Rendies torment me. He would expect me to do anything to be free of them."

"Who is your father?"

"In the opinions of Lord Gorng dur Liin and a rather impressive roster of others, my father was Lord Venkarel dur Ixaxis."

Evaric felt warm against me, and nothing else mattered. "What do you believe?"

"Evram and Terrell of Tyntagel raised me, and they are my parents, whether by birth or fostering."

"Did you ever ask them?"

"I would not let them tell me if they tried. What would it change?"

"You are not even curious?"

"About people I have never met or ever will? No. I should like to be free of Rendies, but that is a problem only I can remedy."

"How can you be sure?"

"Because I have never met an Ixaxin whom I could not deceive."

"You are the Venkarel's son," I whispered, staring at him, so close to me.

"Possibly. Does the unlikely chance of it make you regret the love you have given me?"

"Only if it takes you from me."

"Not Rendies, assassins, nor even Arvard's schemes could effect such a schism as *that*, my Lyriel."

Chapter 21

I floated through the morning, so dizzily gleeful that everyone I met gave me looks of doubt, suspicion, or knowingness. Evaric had gone to see his brother, and I danced through busy, aimless chores, waiting for Evaric, listening and watching for him, though he had warned me that he would likely not return until late.

When the Shrine Keeper's Guard arrived to inform Rubi that the Troupe could resume performances until the peculiar barrier around the city dissipated, I positively beamed at the horrid little man. When Rubi screamed orders at me, I smiled and did her bidding without complaint. When Taf endeavored to lecture me on the idiocy of my behavior, I laughed at him, kissed his sour scowl, and pirouetted from the room.

I could not argue with anyone. I wanted to please everyone within reach, because euphoria had entirely conquered my sense of practicality. When Anni asked me to guide her to the old D'hai, I agreed without considering my answer for an instant.

Anni's cousin had readied three horses before Anni and I reached the stable. I ought to have suspected his certainty of my compliance, but I cared only about Evaric and the hours until I would be with him again. Noryne was at the theater, where Rubi had assembled an impromptu audience from the restless, worried populace of D'hai. Even a few pilgrims had paid admission to gain the distraction of the Troupe's performance.

Old D'hai did begin to penetrate my haze of happiness. On the brightest and best of days, old D'hai evoked disquiet. When the sky twisted and seethed from the horizon, old D'hai resembled a piece of pilgrim purgatory.

Three facets of the first, oldest D'hai invariably struck me at initial approach: the darkness, the silence, and the cold. All three impressions faded quickly, for it was chiefly contrast which engendered them. The glare of the open desert, the hurling wind in its uproar, and the burning sun on undefended shoulders folded into the city and failed. When the senses adjusted to old D'hai, the city could be seen as blandly smooth and stark in its pure, chaotic colors. The silence rose only of emptiness. The cold came only of shade. When the senses accepted old D'hai, the mind could begin to wonder and fear.

It lay not far from the newer cities, but old D'hai recalled nothing of the familiar. Old D'hai spread sterile and unbroken, more pure than pilgrim pretension, more impassioned than Ardas at the height of summer's humid heat. The same impervious substance which formed the Shrine coated the ground of old D'hai. Walls rose from the ground in unchanging texture. Color delineated one building from the next by exploiting illusions; the structures stood many times the height of sensible constructions. The first D'hai was at least as foreign as the last.

Horses refused to enter the city, as did every creature with any sense. We tied our mounts to a scrubby tree near the city's edge. For once, I did not worry about losing the animals to thieves, who would be as trapped as the rest of us by unnatural barriers. I hoped that Taf had the sense to restrain his light fingers until the barrier cleared.

"The street absorbs the sound of our steps," observed Ineuil. I could have added that his voice, too, would be absorbed at half a dozen paces distant. A shout would fall silent from one building to the next. "Have you entered any of these?" he asked me, gesturing toward an acridly green facade.

"Do you see any entrances?" I retorted.

"The arches?"

"Lie flush with the buildings, despite appearance. They are painted or dyed—all of one piece like the streets and most of the structures throughout the city." Nervousness had resurrected my sharpness. The city's colors blazed too garishly for calm. The colors offended the landscape, which cried for muted tones or at least for softer blendings. This shouting obtrusion of reds and purples, oranges and greens disturbed the dusty respect of time, making D'hai too bawdy to be dead, too vibrant to be deserted. A city of ghosts should keep to ghostly softness. Pilgrim gray belonged in dead D'hai, just as color should have populated the D'hai of the living.

Anni commented calmly, "You have entered the building to which you are leading us." I did not ask her how she had known my intention; she was a wizardess, and I was beginning to understand the Seriin obsession with the breed.

"The dome is different." I stopped and pointed, for a glimpse of it could be had if one sought it closely. The dome lay straight before us and loomed large enough to be clearly visible, but the towers behind it befuddled the view. Ineuil squinted and shook his head. "You will see it soon enough," I promised him. I have known no one who could discern it from afar before seeing it once closely.

I had first visited the oldest D'hai in the company of a citizen of Ardasian D'hai and a party of that young man's friends. I had been barely beyond childhood, but the youth had been enamored of me and eager to impress me. The prospect of seeing the haunted city had enticed me, especially since it comprised a forbidden pleasure. Taf and Silf had warned me against approaching it, though I suspect that Taf himself had visited it, as I first did, in the company of D'hai youths more daring than intelligent.

I remembered the disappointment of my first visit. Expecting ghostly glimpses, I found deserted desolation and a city which wore its lively color only on the surface. Nothing happened to us, though two of the native girls made a great show of fear for the sake of their swaggering beaux. We had played the games of testing the sounds and silences, trying the false doors and endeavoring (vainly) to inflict some pointless, lasting sign of our presence. The only one of us who felt truly nervous was the one boy who had come for a second time. That was the charm of old D'hai: Its specters multiplied with every glance. The first visit was almost always easy and dull; the second became nervous and peculiar; few visited more than twice. Escorting Anni and her cousin comprised my third.

Uneasiness rubbed my nerves. I sensed the wrongness, though I could not label it any better this time than on either previous occasion. The city's spirit had twisted awry. These were odd perceptions, and I disliked them. I trusted them only because the city was old D'hai, and odd things came to those who trespassed there too often. Rumor said that no one had ever visited old D'hai more than seven times and remained sane. Like Rendie madness, old D'hai was insidious. I concentrated on the recollection of Evaric's touch.

Ineuil struck a violet wall with the pommel of his dagger. "Peculiar," he murmured, which could have described color, form, or substance. I did not ask him to elaborate. The street ended at the wide band of the central circle, and I directed his attention toward it. Anni already studied D'hai's central building, the broken dome.

The dome itself was clear like amber, though its feel was like that of the rest of the city. A web of gold fragmented its base. More than a few trespassers had tried to free a strip of gold from its setting, but the ubiquitous, impenetrable substance of old D'hai encased the gold and made the effort futile.

I swayed with dizziness, and Ineuil steadied me. I shrugged away his concern and his hand. Only the city's ill ease, deepest at its heart, troubled me; I recalled how avidly I had derided such tremors when first I visited old D'hai. Anni watched me attentively.

The road drew us beneath the arch, where darkness faced us. I braced myself for the entry, but the abrupt illumination of those inner walls still startled me. Ineuil released his cloak and drew a sword, a weapon suspiciously reminiscent of those carried by the Shrine Keeper's Guard; those folds of foreign fabric concealed a multitude of possibilities.

"The walls brighten automatically," I remarked with supremely specious nonchalance. Some Ardasians would have added that the broken dome desired and demanded entry; they would have likened the dome to those bright plants of the coastal marshes down whose dew-bedecked throats eager insects march to death.

The interior did not maintain the color of the outer city, though precious ores patterned the building's floor in dizzy convolutions. Everything nonmetallic within the dome had an amber cast. Amber might have been the original hue; it might have been the product of age. When one entered the vast, misshapen central chamber, one could easily believe that the amber represented the color of calamity.

Great, solid amber tears dripped from the walls, looking liquid, though they were hard and brittle. Pieces from this one room could be broken, though all pieces of any potential value had long since been taken. "I call this room the stage chamber," I informed my audience of two, "due to the raised area in its center." I pointed to the mass of fused amber and melted metals. Brown streaked the amber near it, and the stage was largely black.

Ineuil accorded my description an ironic smile. "What happened here?"

"Fire."

He replied witheringly, "That much I could deduce for myself. When did the fire occur?"

"Years, maybe millennia ago. If you had ever tried to set fire to anything in old D'hai, you would realize that it was no campfire that burned here."

"Lightning?" suggested Ineuil with a glance at the sundered ceiling, opened to the patch of still-blue sky.

"Maybe." I shivered, wondering how long that cerulean morsel would remain untouched by the bleak and growing darkness. The rippling barrier seemed distressingly appropriate to old D'hai. I dropped my gaze to circle the stage, for treacherous amber bubbles pocked and bloated the floor. "You are a pilgrim. You must have heard the histories."

Ineuil probed the stage pensively with his sword's tip. "A Sorcerer King of Serii, stealing the D'hai Control, would likely wreak some damage. Horlach never was noted for his delicacy."

"Ineuil," reprimanded Anni, "this is neither the time nor the place to summon specters." Her cousin offered her a bland smile with an elegant, rather affected sweep of his hand. Anni's expression softened into forbearance; her cousin swayed her well.

" 'Hot as wizard's fire,' " I quoted dryly. The room had set my nerves to needles, and these two dubious pilgrims did not help. I wished for Evaric. "Is this what you wanted to see?"

"I think it is," replied Anni quietly. She stepped gingerly onto the stage, treading carefully among the jutting golden ridges, which marched in an irregular circle around the central point.

Ineuil had been tapping several of the stage formations with his sword, but he sheathed the weapon when Anni reached the central protuberance. The center was less obviously damaged than the surrounding areas of the room; it retained a distinctly cylindrical form extruding from a bubbling black sea at its base. The top of the cylinder was slightly hollowed and etched in a regular, radiating pattern.

"How long do you mean to stay here?" I asked, just as Anni extended her fine, dexterous fingers to touch the top of the cylinder.

Bright sheaths of light bathed the air around her. They danced and rippled and reached toward the nonexistent ceiling. I jumped toward the room's perimeter; the floor had certainly shifted beneath me. As I looked upward, I thought I saw a Rendie swirl and weave an incipient spell. The strange lights vanished, and the room solidified; Anni had removed her hand from the cylinder.

Anni stared at me as if I were the aberration. I slumped against the amber wall and complained, "Nothing is dull with you Seriins, is it?"

Anni turned from me to Ineuil. "What did you see?" she asked deliberately. Her voice chilled me more than the illusion I had just experienced. Anni seemed to address only her cousin, but her voice crawled into my ears and forced me to reply.

"The city awoke," I said without intending response. "The stage shifted around you. Curtains of light appeared. I think I saw a Rendie."

"Yes," approved Anni tersely. She circled the stage, which had become more regular along its circumference. I noted how carefully she avoided the metallic projections. "A construct existed here, connected by wire and light to other constructs throughout the city."

"And to the Rendies?" I asked uncomfortably.

"No. The Rendies came of subsequent meddling. Yet, they reflect the original function of this place: a place of gates to other worlds. I can still sense the pattern of the ancient energies, though the gates were sealed long ago."

"By Horlach?" asked Ineuil, assessing me as he spoke.

"No." Anni weighed her answer. "The gates were sealed because of him, I think. The Taormin was never meant to be a tool of sorcerous Power. Horlach warped it to that purpose by using it to intensify his own abilities. Because it possessed the faculty to learn, Horlach's example distorted it, even while it used his knowledge toward its own recovery."

"Then it was here that the Taormin originated," mused Ineuil.

"It was here," replied Anni slowly. "Did you doubt my assessment as well as my judgment?" she added with a quickly fleeting bit of arrogant humor. "This is where the

Taormin belongs. Its removal effected a Rending far more thorough than the latest. The two Rendings are connected by more than the commonality of Horlach's mischief." Anni's expression veered from placid distraction to painful emotion. "Someone has stood here recently. Someone has touched the patterns, as I have. The energies reverberate still from the echo of great Power."

"Whose?" demanded Ineuil, his supple body shifting into wariness.

"I am unsure." Even I could see that Anni lied, and I could not claim to know her well.

"You are still an abominable liar—Anni," said her cousin with a peculiar, rigid grin. "No matter. Whenever you assume that stubbornly defensive air, I know that you are thinking of Kaedric, and I am wise enough to delve no further. Shall we return to Master Vale's charming establishment, or would you prefer to provide further wonders for the lovely Mistress Lyriel's speculation?" He acknowledged me with a gallant flourish of his sweeping gray cloak.

"She is intrinsic to the pattern, Ineuil," said Anni, as if I could not retort for myself. "You were wiser than I in perceiving her importance. Lyriel is necessary to the restoration, and restoration must be effected soon if we are to preserve this infinity; in that much, Horlach has spoken truly. The barrier of distorted energy forming around D'hai bleeds from the Taormin's tangled realm; it flows from the instability, which is destruction. We have been brought here, Ineuil, all of us. Whatever we thought our reasons might have been, we are here because the pattern demands us."

"I have never liked being manipulated," said Ineuil with a shade of weary exasperation, "especially by Horlach."

Anni shook her head faintly. "Horlach is crippled. The manipulator is not Horlach." She added uncertainly, "Nor even Kaedric. Or perhaps both of them manipulate together. Perhaps the Taormin itself directs us."

I wanted to shake from Anni a great many answers that I thought she might be able to provide. I did not want to ask in the presence of her cousin with his sword and his deceptively innocent charm. I did not want to remain any longer in old D'hai with its haunts of old terror and its empty, silent streets. I felt very ready to return to Vale's Inn.

Chapter 22

Evaric strode easily through the corridors to the Shrine Keeper's rooms, while even his gray-robed escort endeavored to ignore him. The sight of a K'shai walking boldly into the Shrine Keeper's Hall had unsettled many pilgrims. Most of the priests who placated those pilgrims felt at least equally distraught. Only a select few of the priests knew how often K'shai entered the Shrine Keeper's Hall in pilgrim guise. None of the priests had quite dared to ask Evaric to leave his weapons at the entry.

The escort led him to the Shrine Keeper's private suite rather than to the more formal reception room which he had visited with Lyriel. Arvard kept his private rooms sparse of furnishings, as a token of the simplicity befitting the Shrine Keeper, but the rooms opened to a magnificent view of D'hai's golden valley. Arvard entered grandly, newly returned from giving a mass blessing to the hundreds of troubled pilgrims at the Shrine. He dismissed his entourage summarily. He shed his outer robe with a grimace. "I may never adjust to this beastly climate." Arvard slapped Evaric's arm boisterously. "I am glad you came. We have so much to discuss, little brother." Arvard filled a goblet from the decanter on the marble-topped table; the table and eight chairs of wrought iron constituted the room's only furniture. Arvard drank deeply of the potent liquor, made from a small local fruit, before offering a goblet to Evaric.

"No. Thank you." Evaric had not moved since Arvard entered. "Why did you send for me, Arvard? A K'shai brother can only be an embarrassment to you."

"We are brothers who have not seen each other in eight years. Do I need a better reason?" Arvard drank again and began to refill his goblet.

Evaric paced to the window and back, no longer bothering to disguise his restlessness. "We are strangers who were

brothers once. I watched you give blessing to your followers: a very spiritual performance from someone who once
scorned religion as a crutch for the weak and inadequate.''

"And you argued with me," mused Arvard, staring for a
moment into the past. He roused himself with a start, shaking his yellow hair. "So we have both changed. But the
bond between us is stronger than ideologies or position in
the world's affairs. You must work with me, Evaric." Arvard
raised his hand in a powerful gesture at once supplicating
and inspirational; he had practiced the gesture extensively.

"Assuming for the moment that I believe in your sincerity, toward what goal should we strive so devotedly? Toward the conquest of your troubled followers with this
emotional display of false miracles and fanatical ravings that
you call religion? These unhappy pilgrims are a sorry substi-
tute for the Ixaxin Guild of Wizards and the Lords of Serii,
whom I think you meant to conquer when we parted in
Tyntagel. Even the petty intrigues of Tyntagel Keep must
have offered you more challenge than these pilgrims, who
will believe anything told with fervor, and their Ardasian
hosts, who will sell anything if they sense some immediate
profit to themselves.''

"I comfort the pilgrims, and I pay the Ardasians. All
derive satisfaction from the result. Of what can you possibly
disapprove, little brother?''

"I disapprove of hypocrisy. Would the Shrine Keeper
continue to give so generously of his spiritual largess if his
long-vaunted, imaginary Power ever became real?''

Arvard threw his goblet at the wall, smashing the delicate
glass and staining the buff wall with the liquor that ran like
thin blood. He mastered himself by slow increments, while
Evaric wondered how even Rendies and abusive sorcery
could have molded Arvard into such a stranger. The tension
in this man who was Shrine Keeper made Evaric's own
muscles tighten defensively. Even Arvard's voice sounded
thick with conflict.

"I want you to come with me to old D'hai, little brother,
and then you will see for yourself why I am trapped here.
That accursed place holds the key to all that it is my right to
be and have. I have come so close to it, and it sits there,
mocking me. Look at it." Arvard pointed across the desert
toward the barren hills so unlike Serii's splendid mountains.
Old D'hai lay between the Shrine Keeper's Hall and the

hills; the hills were not far, but only a shimmering of the ancient city could be seen, with blackness rising grimly behind it. "There lies the means to prove my heritage to the Ixaxins who rebuffed me and to the great Infortiare, who refused even to acknowledge her own son. There lies the answer to Rendies, Evaric. The answers to barriers of dark Power and to all a mortal's insurmountable obstacles lie there, if only a man could reach them."

"You have not changed in one thing, Arvard. You still talk more to yourself than to me."

"We can leave for old D'hai immediately. I must show you what I have discovered."

"I have obligations elsewhere, Arvard, and you appear to be very well tended."

Arvard spoke sharply. "I control this city, little brother."

"So I have seen. But you do not control me. That was Lord Gorng's primary mistake in selecting you as his tool of vengeance. He trusted in your mistaken self-confidence. You never controlled me, Arvard, except by my choice."

Arvard took another goblet and poured again from the decanter. His hands shook only slightly, but Evaric observed the sign of weakness with mixed regret. Evaric doubted that Arvard would try to harm him directly in the Shrine Keeper's Hall, but clever K'shai instincts whispered sly words of warning, vying with nostalgic sympathy. The layers of this unfamiliar Arvard's deception made Evaric glad of the sword at his side.

Arvard remarked coldly, "That Ardasian actress of yours is rather pretty in a sultry, primitive way. I am told that these Ardasian women possess a very potent physical allure, if one is susceptible to that sort of blatant sensuality. I had hoped that your standards would have risen higher."

"No, Arvard, you really have not changed." Except, thought Evaric bitterly, to become my attacker instead of my defender. But Gorng did not fabricate your mad jealousy of anyone whom I might love beyond you. The sad, isolated traces of the familiar Arvard made the situation both easier and more difficult to accept.

Evaric touched the carefully balanced door, and it opened soundlessly. Two flustered priests straightened hurriedly from positions suspiciously near to the door. Evaric ignored both the priests and the guards, as well as Arvard's anxious commands to return. Evaric employed his laboriously cultivated, unhurried K'shai grace to depart without approaching any Shrine guard or priest closely. He wanted no further proof of the death of the brother whom he had loved.

* 　 * 　 *

Arvard slammed both hands flat against the marble table. "Kritz!" he shouted, and a handsome young man in pilgrim robes emerged from the inner chamber. "See that he is watched. I want to know every move he makes."

Kritz bowed low and complied. Arvard seated himself before the table. The needles in his head grew more painful with every thought of his brother. He could not hurt Evaric, he insisted to himself; he could never hurt Evaric. The needles seared him, until his eyes burned and he recanted, begging the unseen Lord whose command drove him. He needed to plan. He needed to act. He needed to destroy Evaric. He could not hurt Evaric. The needles made him shudder with pain.

He had tried to comply, he pleaded. He had done more than any reasonable man could expect of him. The target could not be killed. Evaric could not be killed. Evaric was his brother and his friend.

Arvard tried to forget the needles, and he failed. He had already tried all of the tricks he could devise, and he had always failed. The only solution was compliance. Or Power. But his Power was trapped in the Taormin—in old D'hai. If he could reach the Taormin with Evaric, then the Power could save them both.

The needles intensified. Arvard repented aloud to them, "I shall kill him. I shall kill him in old D'hai." The needles eased just a little to a pain that was merely bearable. Not even the Power of a Caruillan sorceress could quite determine which parts of Arvard's schemes held true to Power's dictates, Rendie madness, or a deep, obstinate loyalty to a brother who had always been special.

"Shrine Keeper?" asked a hesitant priest, when his repeated knocks had failed to elicit response.

Arvard straightened painfully, donning pride which was only a remembered mask. "What is it, Lefner?"

"Another member of that acting group," announced Lefner, "insists upon seeing you, sir. You did ask that we accommodate them." Lefner's stilted disapproval afforded Arvard a sorry amusement. "He is a Master Zakari."

"Permit him to enter, Lefner." Arvard felt exhausted, but that was a feeling to which he had inured himself. He posed himself for his visitor, emulating the cool austerity of the Ixaxin who had destroyed his hopes. Arvard appraised the actor indifferently: a fine looking man, albeit a swaggerer. "Master Zakari," said Arvard with just the right mixture of weariness and forbearance. Zakari's swagger faltered a bit. Lefner retreated with a smirk. "You have something to tell me," prompted Arvard carelessly. The Shrine Keeper had impressed the pathetic, ignorant Ardasian and could afford to become condescendingly gracious.

Zakari spoke clearly. That rich voice would serve well in a Shrine blessing, thought Arvard idly. "I heard that you wanted information about a K'shai named Evaric."

Who had talked to a member of that troupe? "I am a religious leader, Master Zakari. Why should I interest myself in a K'shai?"

Zakari's confidence was reviving. "The reason is your concern. I have my own reasons to wish no good to that K'shai. The word I hear is that you would be glad enough to see the last of this K'shai as well. As a member of the Troupe he Protects, I could assist you. Fifty serisni, and the K'shai is yours."

The needles in Arvard's head retreated, replaced by the pleasure of reward for proper thinking. "Where did you acquire this fantastic notion of yours?"

"Gariman," replied Zakari confidently, and the Shrine Keeper's acknowledging grimace did not disappoint him. Gariman was a reliable reference: a man who dealt in information, such as open kill contracts or illegal drug sources.

"If someone performs a valued service for me, Master Zakari, I can be generous." Circle might well make use of the stupid Ardasian.

"I can deliver him to you."

"No, Master Zakari. You will deliver him to a man named Circle, who will himself apprise you of any further details. Ten serisni will await your success."

"You are a wealthy, important man, Shrine Keeper, and forty serisni would remind me much more effectively to keep silent."

"My word would certainly overcome your unsubstantiated claims. However, twenty serisni would express the level of my gratitude properly."

"Twenty-five."

"Acceptable. Master Lefner will show you to the door." This Zakari does not even bargain well, thought Arvard disparagingly.

"It has been a pleasure, Shrine Keeper."

Arvard grunted to himself, wondering if Master Zakari comprehended even dimly the magnitude of the task he had assumed for such a pittance. Knowing that he needed to keep his own wits sharp, Arvard resolved, nonetheless, to imbibe as much strong liquor as D'hai could supply.

*   *   *

"Turn inward, Noryne. Gather peace unto yourself. Become the softness of the morning, the gentleness of a cool breeze."

"There is so much turmoil, Anni."

"Do not address me! Do not focus on me or on the turmoil but on the calm, clear light within yourself."

Noryne's breathing became smooth and slow. Rhianna allowed herself one wisp of Power by which to verify the young actress' control. Rhianna dared exert no more Power than that wisp, for she did not want her pattern to be associated with Noryne's. She did not want her own pattern to provide the warning by which Kaedric would elude her yet again.

Rhianna said softly, "Study the K'shai, Noryne."

"Evaric frightens me."

"Not Evaric." Not this time. "Sense Fog. Define him to me."

"Dead."

Rhianna caught her breath. She maintained her shell of calm with difficulty. "Fog died?"

"Yes. More than once."

"He was restored."

Noryne answered hesitantly, "Yes. Something veils my sight."

"Do not try to pierce the shadow, Noryne," said Rhianna softly. "You have done well." And you would never dent Kaedric's personal barrier. A stronger, harsher Power than yours could not have approached him even so closely, for he would have perceived the threat and repulsed it, as he has denied me repeatedly. But I analyzed correctly. I understand your scheme now, Kaedric, my obstinate love, and I perceive my proper role at last.

When Noryne roused from her trance of Power, she discovered Anni stitching quietly, as ever. A difference, however, which Noryne could only define distantly, had come: anticipation. Noryne wondered, feeling uncertain, awed and frightened by the patterns she could not quite discern; this Power was an uncomfortable gift.

* * *

"You are deceived!" shouted Horlach, but he could not pierce the barrier of Rhianna's Power. He sensed the muted essence of Noryne, but that tentative sort of Power had always eluded him, and Rhianna had added extra shields to thwart him. *"Where are you, Venkarel?"* But only emptiness replied. Horlach tried to reach into the mind of Arvard, but Horlach could not touch a mortal save with pallid, voiceless prods of pain; a Lord of Liin might be manipulated by his own precarious Power, but the laws of Zerus, the sole inescapable truths of Power, forbade Horlach from molding a mortal directly.

Horlach turned to face the flood of darkness cloaking the Taormin's silent plain. The tangle burned both bright and black amid the inky tide. Horlach hesitated, but he stepped into the darkness' midst. His image ebbed and faltered; his twisted pattern blurred and dimmed. *"Rending-born,"* hissed Horlach. The tangle did not stir. *"Fire-child, heed me!"* Horlach's pattern nearly failed, as he dredged all lingering motes of Power from his hidden, faded store: all focused, all desperate, he cast it all into one final, fierce attempt. *"Son of the Taormin, hear me!"*

Something in the tangle moved minutely. Horlach smiled; his pattern firmed; but as he tried to grasp the tangle, a rush of darkness burst from the rest. Horlach leaped free of its path and cursed it; Horlach knew its deadliness. Patiently (for Horlach had learned patience through the millennia of helpless, anguished waiting), Horlach recommenced his search for any means to claim the one, entangled limit point of both the dark world and the light.

Chapter 23

I heard him speak to Fog, though the sound came softly overshadowed by more raucous, careless voices returning to the inn as evening neared. I dropped the scripts in Rubi's lap. I did not care how many watched me. I did not care how many of Vale's customers I aggravated in my effort to reach Evaric. When I located him in the courtyard with Fog, I stopped just to delight in the sight of him.

He felt me watch him, left Fog, and came to me. We stood a pace apart. "I never knew how long a day could be," he said, "until today."

"I thought you would never return."

"I cannot sit across the common room from you through the evening, pretending to enjoy anyone else's company."

"Can you reach my room without being seen?"

"Of course." He smiled his miraculous smile. "I am K'shai."

"I shall meet you there in ten minutes."

"Five minutes."

"Five minutes," I agreed blissfully.

* * *

Rendies came to him when he slept. I held to him tightly, calling to him as hungrily as did the Rendies, and he woke to me and not to them. "Lyriel," he whispered again and again, "you are all that I need. The Rendies have no more power over me. All the emptiness and anger within me have become nothing, for I have you, and nothing else matters."

I had been taught from a tender age: never let a man know you need him. The first time the advice applied, I forgot it, all for the sake of a foreigner who was K'shai. "Never let go of me, Evaric."

"Not though all the forces of the world try to part us."

"We could escape your enemies in Ardas. I know every useful official in the city. No one, not the Shrine Keeper, not K'shai, not Seriin lords, not even Rendies, will find us."

His laughter against my skin rippled with warmth. "I am more concerned about keeping my enemies from you, my dear firebrand. I am rather practiced in preserving myself."

"Would you fight your brother?"

"I can manage Arvard without fighting him."

"We need to leave D'hai."

"We have a few obstacles," he said, even as he moved to make me forget them.

"We must concentrate on keeping you alive," I insisted.

"Yes, my lady," he agreed with amused irony.

"There must be a way to leave here. This barrier must be a thing of Power. Anni knew that it existed before we saw it." As Evaric had known, I thought, in his own way. "She must know a way through it."

"Anni?"

"She is an Ixaxin."

Evaric became absolutely still. "Are you certain?"

"I have only her word for it, but I never thought to doubt her claim. She certainly has some odd abilities if she is not a wizardess."

"I never sensed it in her. I have never felt the danger in her."

"Anni is not a danger to you." He was troubled again, in much the same way as the Rendies made him.

"Why is she here?"

"She is a pilgrim."

"No."

"Forget about her, Evaric. She does not matter to us." I should have known not to speak to him of Power during the night, when the Rendie voices still rang in him. "Nothing matters, dearest Evaric, except that you are with me, and we shall never be apart again."

I did not try again until morning to broach with Evaric any plans to escape D'hai. I opened the shutters to reinforce the light; most of the sky was dark with turmoil. "By tomorrow, there will be no sunlight," said Evaric from behind me.

"Will the Rendies come?"

"Probably, though not because the sky is dark. The gate between their world and ours is widening."

"Anni spoke of gates yesterday. I took her and her cousin to old D'hai. She said that the Taormin once controlled gates between worlds." I wrapped my arms around Evaric as I spoke. I felt reassured when my words did not make him flinch.

"Arvard wants me to visit old D'hai with him."

"Will you go?"

"No."

"You did come here to learn about the Taormin, as much as to see your brother. I think Anni may know at least a part of the answers you seek."

"None of it matters any longer. I have found what I need, Lyriel, and it is you."

"Your flattery may turn my head, Seriin."

"My love for you is no more than the truth."

"How are we to leave here, Evaric?"

"We shall find a way." He raised his head from me to gaze at the menacing sky. "I shall take a closer look at that barrier."

"Shall we leave now, or shall we eat first?"

"I shall eat as I ride. You are staying here, my love, until I have a better idea of what we are facing."

I tried to scowl at him, but I failed; I enjoyed the novelty of being protected. "Take Fog with you, at least."

"And leave the Troupe undefended?"

"No one will bother with us. It is you whom everyone trails with malicious intent. In any case, we shall all be at the theater, in clear view of most of D'hai. Impending catastrophe stimulates attendance miraculously. We have recovered all the season's losses and more."

"Try not to take too much advantage of the populace until I return. I should hate to lose you to an irate shopkeeper."

"I have been outmaneuvering merchants and city officials since I could talk." I felt happier and easier than circumstances warranted, but when Evaric reached the door, I ran to him, stopping him before he could open it. "Be careful, Evaric," I beseeched him. I tried to fix in my mind the sweetness of touching him, knowing him, and feeling his love. I was not prescient; the dangers around us simply mocked me.

* * *

Our play sparkled, enthralling our audience, packed five
to a bench. The performance of every player exceeded
anything we had done all season. It was a fitting cap of
glory, a final brightness in the closing darkness. I watched it
in silent entrancement with Taf beside me. Taf almost smiled
at me when the play was done.

We walked slowly and circuitously together to Vale's Inn.
Most of D'hai, Ardasians and pilgrims both, strolled the
streets with us, clustered in twos or threes, all of us aware
that the slender column of hot sun would not likely bless us
beyond this day. Many pilgrims still crowded and moaned
their fears at the Shrine, but many more had discovered
greater courage in the last day's light. It was an eerily
beautiful day.

"You have been with that K'shai," said Taf dourly, just
as we approached Vale's courtyard.

"I love him, Taf, as thoroughly as ever you loved Silf."

"You have seen what comes of such love," Taf growled.

"I shall never leave Evaric, whatever he is or does."

"Will he be as constant to you, girl?"

"Yes." I was utterly confident of my love. As I spoke, I
saw him, and my joy made me hasten, leaving Taf to trail
behind me.

Vale and many of the Troupe members had gathered in
the courtyard, and all watched Evaric and the man who
cowered before him; no one intervened between a K'shai
and his victim. My limbs became leaden. The victim was
Zakari, and he pressed himself against the stable wall, shrinking from my K'shai in whose blue-silver eyes fury burned.
Evaric hissed, "You placed your filthy drug in the water bag
that you knew I would take. How much were you paid for
my life, Zakari?"

"Nothing," whimpered Zakari, so terrified that his makeup
ran with the tears of his fear. "I did nothing."

"How many virol addicts came to the stable this morning,
as I was leaving? You hoped the drug would weaken me too
much to fight the assassin with whom you conspired. The
plan was excellent. Was it yours? No matter. It failed. Fog
exchanged horses with me; Fog drank the tainted water; it
was Fog whom the assassin struck through the heart." Evaric
gripped Zakari's wrist and squeezed it cruelly. "You did not
expect Fog to accompany me today, did you? Not after the

quantities and varieties of Ardasian liquor that you encouraged him to imbibe last night."

"Is it a crime to drink with a man?" asked Zakari weakly.

Evaric, I wanted to cry, stop torturing him, but I remained mute with fright. "This is Fog's blood that I wear, Zakari," said Evaric fiercely. "He continues to bleed, and there are no drugs to heal such a wound, even if your wretched virol would allow another drug to take effect. Fog dies, Zakari, but you die first."

The deadliness made a mask of Evaric's perfect face. Zakari tried to break free and run, but Evaric twisted and struck Zakari's neck. Blood began to spurt from Zakari's wrist, where Evaric had crushed it. Zakari wavered and grew limp. Evaric discarded him, releasing Zakari to the courtyard's dirty cobbles. Hard and predatory, Evaric stalked away from his kill. He did not even see me.

Noryne burst from the inn and screamed. She sank to Zakari's side and cradled his head against her breasts. "You cannot leave me, Zakari," she implored him. A deeply violet light flowed along her slender arms and covered him. "You must not die."

"My dear," whispered Zakari so dimly that I barely heard him.

"I am here, Zakari," said Noryne with desperation.

"I only wanted you to be safe from him, my dear," whispered Zakari, and Noryne crooned frantic encouragement. We could not drag her from him, even when he had died. She stroked his fine, tranquil face, and she grieved.

"He thought he spoke to me," said Alisa in a shaken voice.

"He made his own choice," I told her gruffly. I had blamed her often enough for taunting Zakari into folly, but her grief compelled me to console her. "He thought he played the hero's role. He did not understand." He did not know that his rival was not mortal.

"Zakari looks nobly peaceful," Alisa answered vaguely. "He always did enjoy a good death scene." I took Alisa's tiny hand to lead her to the inn. We leaned on one another, both sickened by death.

Rubi hailed me unsteadily. "You had better make it right with the constables," she said, and I nodded. The constables would need bribing to ignore a murder; even a K'shai was expected to pay if his kills were not discreetly done.

"I am sorry, Rubi," I apologized, as if I had killed her lead actor or felt less touched by his death than she.

"Lyriel, no," protested Alisa weakly. It was odd to feel comforted by Alisa.

Rubi grumbled roughly, "At least he died quickly, which is better than the rest of us are likely to do in this unholy place. Taf, make arrangements for the burial as soon as possible." Taf was staring at Anni's cousin, who had pried Noryne from her dead gallant. Ineuil carried Noryne into Vale's Inn, and Noryne wept in his arms like a lost child. Ineuil's expression had grown flat. I wondered where Anni had gone. I wondered the more where Evaric's bitter mood had taken him. I was not sure that I wanted either answer.

Chapter 24

The common room was dark and empty with the night. Alisa sat alone, too cold and forlornly tired to make the journey to her chamber. She heard the outer door open and close. When the inner door opened, she heard no sound of other movement from the K'shai who entered. She could not see him well, though dim lamplight filtered through the curtain from the kitchen.

Alisa began to giggle, a high, loud, erratic sound. "I told Zakari that he could never hope to compete with a man like you."

Evaric responded coolly, "You should get some sleep, Alisa. The hour is late."

"Sleep?" Alisa pushed at her hair, and a blonde curl fell loose across her face. She had not removed the silver pins worn for the role she had played opposite Zakari. When she discovered one of the pins in her hand, she stared at it, as it caught the fragile remnant of light. "There is a very old play, as I remember, which comments lengthily on the elusiveness of sleep among the guilty." Alisa dropped the pin onto the floor, where it clattered and lay still. She composed her face as she watched it fall. When she raised her face to Evaric, she was smiling and seductive.

"Let me take you to your room, Alisa."

"Did you kill Zakari for me, Evaric? Or did I kill him for you?" She did not resist when Evaric drew her to her feet. "I want you, Evaric."

"To forget?" asked Evaric crisply.

"Why not?" demanded Alisa with sudden harshness. She wanted to consume this K'shai with passion and then dismiss him. She wanted to eradicate images of Zakari. She wanted to escape all thought.

The accusations of the Shrine priest kept circling in her head. "You are damned," the priest assured her repeatedly.

"You belong to us." No, that was wrong; that was not what the priest had said. "Come with us." Why was her haunt changing his words?

Evaric propelled her toward the stairs. She stumbled. Evaric stopped to help her. She no longer felt him. A chill had replaced him, and the room was empty of all but mist. "You belong to us," sang a thing which was gray and nebulous. "Come with us, Fire-child," whispered a cloud that hung before her and around her.

Something very hot and very cold drew a line across Alisa's throat. She could not speak nor move. The tendrils of a Rendie's form slithered against her, and they burned with cold. A tendril began to twine around her legs. She experienced a sensation of sliding through a ragged gap in the floor. She looked downward. The skirt of her gown had turned dark, and the stiff white fabric clung limply to a shape which resembled her legs. There was something wrong with the image, but she could not identify the problem.

"Time ends soon for this sorry world you claim, Fire-child. Come with us before it is too late to escape the endings."

A piece of trailing cloud stung Alisa's face. She touched her cheek and felt the sticky hollow where flesh had been. She looked at Evaric, standing motionless amid the swirls of terrible mist that lashed at her and hurt her. His eyes did not see her, and he did not respond when she screamed at him. She tried to run from the clouds, but they pursued her. They pressed her to the stairs. She could not climb nor escape.

Her throat was opened to air; she began to gag. The retching turned to torment, as her body tried to evict the sweet, sick taste of Rendie. When something hard and hot touched her, she began to scream aloud. The hardness slapped her, but Alisa refused to stop her screams. She would never stop, for pain would never stop.

The light spilled from above her. "Zakari," Alisa cried, and she croaked his name in a shrill shriek of madness, which she knew would never end.

Chapter 25

I was deeply asleep, dreaming of the previous day's horror. Most of the players enacted simple chorus roles. Minaro upheld his part with a quiet, careless conversation. Zakari was shrieking hysterically, though none of us seemed to notice. He shrieked as he drew a dagger and leaped wildly upon a K'shai. He shrieked while Evaric spun and danced the death blow. Zakari continued shrieking, though he lay dead and staring.

I tossed restlessly, awoke, and heard the shrieking still. "The pitch is too high for Zakari," I muttered to myself, but some sense penetrated. I snatched my cloak, for it came first to hand, and the dry, early dawn air felt cold.

Others had heard also and reacted more quickly. Every door along the hall had opened. The timid peered into the dim hall from behind shields of doors; the more bold had gathered around the room from which the screams emerged.

It was Alisa's room, and Minaro stood at the door trying to keep the curious from entering. He was not succeeding well at the task, for craning heads still sought to see the source of chaos. Taf dispersed the mob with a gesture and a curse. Reluctantly, the onlookers retreated to their room, but few doors were reclosed. Rubi's head emerged from Alisa's room. She saw me and beckoned urgently.

The screams sounded much worse inside the cramped room. Noryne and Miria stood shivering beside the door, looking starkly frightened. I knelt by Alisa, who was huddled in the corner of the room. She had been dreadfully mauled; she would never heal cleanly. Hers were Rendie wounds, deep and ragged.

I tried speaking her name calmly. Failing to effect any change in noise level by kindness, I shook her very soundly. She choked for a moment but continued at a piercing volume. I shook her repeatedly, until she sobbed herself from screams to loud weeping.

Rubi helped me pull Alisa to her feet, and we saw the

wretched state of Alisa's legs. Rubi and I tried to coax her, mostly carrying her, toward the bed. Alisa began to shake her head violently, and we finally settled her into a chair. I dropped my cloak around her, for she seemed to need it more than I. She tugged the heavy fabric close to her skin, and the gesture seemed to calm her slightly.

"I heard her scream," chattered Miria nervously.

"Evaric was carrying her up the stairs," added Noryne. "He brought her here."

"Why did he not Protect her?" demanded Rubi roughly. Her wildly uncombed hair made her look all the more ferocious. "My poor, sweet little girl."

"Alisa," I asked gently, "where is Evaric?" Alisa only shivered, her pretty eyes wide and fixed.

Rubi shouted irritably, "Will somebody find the accursed K'shai and bring him here!" The command received an uneasily dismayed response of silence.

"I shall go, Rubi," I answered calmly, though I could appreciate the general reluctance to leave one another's company and seek a man who left destruction in his wake. Rubi only betrayed approval of my offer by a tight nod and the gesture which sent Noryne scurrying to replace me at Alisa's side. Taf eyed me as if he found my behavior idiotic.

Most of the doors had closed in the face of uncertainty. I headed for my room, intending to pause only long enough to pull a skirt and jacket over my sleeping gown; the sun might have risen, but neither heat nor light could seep well through a barrier of black turmoil. Finding Evaric required no great skill or effort. He awaited me in a chair in my room. "Careless of you to leave your door open," he murmured ironically. "Any sort of monster might enter."

Carefully, I closed the door behind me. Evaric had dropped into solemn silence. I circled around him, gathered some scattered garments and hung them in the armoire; I devoted an excessive number of minutes to inconsequential activities. I seated myself on the end of the bed, forcing Evaric to twist his head in order to see me. "The Rendies paid you another visit tonight," I commented, as if discussing an old friend's social call.

"You have seen Alisa."

"I have seen and heard her. The Rendies attacked her in your presence, I suppose. How else could they have entered a solid building, sealed for the night, save by following the beacon of your presence?"

"I told you that the Rendie gates were widening," retorted Evaric acridly. He rose and began to pace, which irritated me unreasonably.

"Will you settle a moment and let me think!" He settled, and I began to pace instead. "Ardasians might tolerate the killing of a jealous lover, who may have tried to kill you. Pilgrims could scarcely bother to disapprove of the death of an Ardasian actor. But not even your Shrine Keeper brother can manufacture forgiveness for a Rendie lodestone. When Alisa begins to talk, as she will, the very wildness of her accusations will make them insidious. There will be nowhere in Ardasia for us to hide, even if we do escape D'hai."

"Would you like to know what happened tonight?"

"I think I can guess enough," I replied sharply. "The Rendies sought you again. But this time they preferred to dine on Alisa. I was more fortunate than I knew. I assumed that you could Protect even while they spoke to you."

Evaric asked wearily, "Do you want me to leave?"

"We have no Protection now, do we? Nothing exists between us and the Rendies? Even Fog is dead. How long can we survive, Evaric, those of us who are not adored by Rendies but merely devoured by them, merely trapped with them in a city of endless night?"

"I shall not let them harm you, Lyriel."

"Can you stop them if they try?"

He closed his eyes. I wondered what he was trying not to see. "Yes. I can stop them from hurting you."

"You failed to help Alisa. Your brother is Rendie mad; I suppose you failed to help him, too."

"It is not that easy, Lyriel!" His anger felt sharp. His eyes glowed coldly silver, and his jaw was tightly clenched. "I wanted to believe that I could forget everything but you. I was wrong. I am sincerely sorry about Alisa, Zakari, Fog, Arvard, that mad wizard in Tyntagel, and all of the other victims of whatever wrongness makes me Rendie kin. I love you, Lyriel." He left before I could resolve my fear and hurt with my longing for him.

*   *   *

The Shrine Keeper's Guard came for me less than an

hour later. They wanted to question me, they said. They wanted me to accompany them.

Rubi started to become indignant about this disruption of our grief and mourning. Vale said nothing, as he continued to polish the tavern glasses, doubtless debating the nature of this latest disturbance to his establishment. I had lost interest in arguing somewhere between my fight with Evaric and my morning visit to Alisa, who lay battered and bandaged in her bed, staring at the ceiling and clinging to Noryne. Noryne had tended her alone; no one had seen Anni since the previous day.

"Give me a moment to fetch my shawl," I told the guards.

"Of course, Mistress," their captain responded politely, but the guards escorted me to my room, waited while I collected my shawl, and did not let me leave their sight. I began to feel like a prisoner, but I did not worry greatly. The Shrine Keeper had promised my safety for his brother's sake. The company of the Shrine Keeper could seem no more menacing than the arms of my lover.

"Where is my brother, Mistress Lyriel?" The Shrine Keeper looked worse than I felt. His face had become haggard and as gray as a pilgrim's robes. His hands shook, and I suspected that the libation he poured from the decanter was not by any means his first of the day.

"You are the man who controls the city. Why ask me?"

"My brother has always had a lamentable weakness for women of your type."

I ignored the typical foreigner's insult. "I do not know where he has gone, Master Arvard. I do know that you paid to have him killed."

"No!" he cried, his square, strong face contorting. "Yes," he said calmly. "He is an enemy of all mortal kind. It is the Shrine's will that he die. Lenzl, bring her."

Three guards came toward me; they caught and took me before I realized their intent. I kicked all three soundly and bit one, but they tied me. I called them several choice names, but I divided the best epithets between the Shrine Keeper and myself.

The guards gagged me when I made a particularly disrespectful comment to their holy Shrine Keeper, whose own reaction was remarkably like approval. The guards dropped a rough sack over my head, and one of the burlier men threw me over his shoulder. I squirmed and struggled as he carried me. When I landed over a horse's rump, I abandoned my futile effort.

I felt furious and frightened. I could do nothing to resolve either emotion. I had the meager consolation that our destination must lie within the D'hai valley, for I expected no miracle of the Shrine to abolish a barrier built of some sorcerous abomination. The guards had not killed me yet. I did not know why they would want me, alive or otherwise, unless I was a pawn to use against Evaric. I did not place the odds in such a contest with the Shrine Keeper, but my own prospects did not seem good.

We paused once, and someone unseen checked my bonds. I tried to strike him, but hands tied tightly behind one's back do not move well. I did inspire a reaction, however. "Hold still," he whispered. "It is hard enough to loosen these surreptitiously."

"Ineuil?" I hissed, though his aristocratic voice was unmistakable.

"Hush."

The tightness at my wrists eased, and I felt the prickle of returning circulation. He had barely touched the ropes at my ankles when another voice shouted, "Ho, there. You, come hold this wheel steady." My ankles remained as closely bound as they had begun, but at least I had a chance to free my hands. I began to work slowly at the loosened bonds as the journey resumed. Wherever we were headed, I preferred not to be entirely defenseless. I wished that Anni's cousin had managed to restore my dagger to me; it was too small to help significantly against even one armed professional, but any weapon would have boosted my flagging confidence.

The horse stepped into a hollow, and my nose struck the animal's side with a painful thud. My eyes watered. Only yesterday morning, I had been happy.

Chapter 26

Fog's body failed him. The blood escaped too quickly to be staunched. The lungs rasped. He had grown too old and too tired to maintain the agility and alertness mandatory for a K'shai's survival. Ordinary men had caught him unaware. He had grown too old for his profession.

"Where have you gone, devil?" he demanded.

"I am here, Fog."

"You promised me life."

"I have repaired you three times from death."

"I want my life, devil. That was our bargain."

"I did not promise eternity."

"Save me now!"

"Once more, Fog. I shall not guarantee another healing."

"Heal me!"

When the Ardasian medic returned to the death ward, he discovered the burly K'shai struggling to sit upright. The medic felt astonished that the man still lived. The K'shai had drifted in the coma of death since the younger K'shai had delivered him. The young K'shai had departed in despair; the old K'shai had been pierced through the chest and could not possibly survive.

The medic tried to prevent Fog from rising. "Let go of me, fool man," said Fog gruffly, shaking free of the medic with the ease of K'shai strength and skill. "Where is my partner?" The boy was a good partner, admitted Fog reluctantly, despite his peculiarities and the devil's attention to him. The boy had almost made Fog regret the stubborn years of working alone.

"We told him that you would not regain consciousness," stammered the medic.

"Fool man," grumbled Fog, but he could not blame the medic for failing to anticipate intervention by the devil. Fog

himself believed in the devil only when he was very drunk
or nearly dead.

Someone had entered the death ward, which stood empty
of patients but for Fog and an elderly, dying man whose
heart had been too stressed by the blackening sky. The
medic turned from Fog to the intruder. "You ought not to
be here, Mistress," said the medic. "No visitors are allowed
in this ward."

Fog recognized the Troupe's seamstress and wondered
why she should have come to the hospital. He wondered
still more when she approached him, disregarding the medic's protests. She stared at Fog, disconcerting him, even as
her proximity stirred his renewed body. Pilgrim or no, Fog
acknowledged to himself, she was a pretty thing in her own
way; she might please him.

Sharp lines of fire ran through his head on the thought.
Fog felt his newly healed body waver. The medic jumped
away from Fog, as if the man could feel the fire, too.

"Kaedric," whispered Anni uncertainly.

Fog shivered only in his skull, for the devil had taken
hold. "No more than the shadow of a shadow, beloved,"
said the devil through Fog's mouth.

"You cannot evade me this time."

"You are a stubborn woman, Rhianna. You realize what
you have brought upon yourself by following me?"

"Yes, my darling. I must hold the Taormin until this
pattern ends."

"We must go to the old city."

"He will await us."

"As he must. As must all of the players. *Horlach!*"

A cold breath of bitter age made the medic shiver and
flee from the ward. In the minds of the Immortals, a little
man spoke. *"Your way will not succeed, Venkarel. You can
touch the past, but you cannot recover its pattern. You must
use my memory. You must permit me to mold the restoration, or it will surely fail."*

"If I fail, then we shall adapt to another Rending," answered Kaedric dryly, *"of my choosing."*

"We shall not fail," asserted Rhianna coldly. *"Horlach!"*
She extended her mind to the image of a little man who had
been old ten thousand years before her birth. He argued
with the desperation of sincerity, but she did not listen to his
pleas. She absorbed the Sorcerer King and bound him within

herself with his ancient knowledge and his terrible, hurtful evils. She learned by stealing pieces of his mind, and she saw the past, which was the future. "Let us hurry, dearest Kaedric. I cannot contain him long without destroying my own sanity."

"We require him only a little longer, my darling. I would not have asked this of you. I hoped you would not discover me so soon."

"Have you still not realized, my omnipotent love, that you cannot protect me from that which manipulates us both?" Her husband laughed with rueful tenderness. The frail pilgrim seamstress and the grizzled K'shai left the hospital with their arms entwined and their hands clasped together.

Chapter 27

We had finally stopped. My hands moved freely within the circles of loose ropes, but I could not run nor even see. Anni's cousin had spoken to me; Ineuil was here. Did he mean to rescue me, or was he merely one of the Shrine's more merciful fanatics?

I could not entrust my fate to a pilgrim. I knew better than to rely on anyone but myself; Silf had taught me that lesson by abandoning me. I yearned to trust Evaric, who had promised to protect me from his enemies. Stop it, Lyriel, I chided myself. Evaric cannot help you now. No one can help you but yourself.

When an unknown guard dragged me from the horse's back, I sank heavily, dropping my head in a futile attempt to free it of the stale-smelling sack. The guard steadied me, and I drooped, clutching at his waist until I found his belt. I grasped his knife while he fumbled with my dragging weight.

I stabbed upward blindly, meeting fleshy resistance. I tore the sack from my head and hacked the ropes from my feet. The guard, a mediocre man of innocuous appearance, had fallen; blood gurgled from a deep gash in his throat.

I had no time to feel squeamish. I tried to leap to the back of the horse, but my feet were numb and uncooperative. I heard shouts. I did not look to identify them. I tried again to mount the horse, and I succeeded. I kicked the animal's sides as hard as my sandals allowed. The horse leaped forward, startled into a gallop. The shouts intensified, but I was free. I jerked the gag from my mouth.

The horse stopped short, skidding on the slick edge of old D'hai's polished road. I clung to his mane and barely kept from being thrown. I might as well have fallen; the guards pulled me from the horse and threw me down on the road. I felt glad of the resiliency of old D'hai, but my eyes overflowed with useless tears.

The guards did not speak to me. Whatever hope I had known dissolved at sight of their number. Guards, priests, and the Shrine Keeper himself, lofty in his fine curricle, opposed me. I could not run from them in old D'hai, where there were only straight lines and no concealing shelters. The guards did not even trouble themselves to tie me again.

The priests wore hoods, as did the guards. I could not identify Ineuil among the Shrine Keeper's entourage, nor could I discern any sympathetic expression. The Shrine Keeper had selected his zealots carefully, or he had paid them well to serve him blindly.

They dragged me to the central building, the broken dome. My fourth visit, I thought: over half the way to insanity. "What can you hope to achieve, Arvard?" I demanded, for my tongue was the only weapon left to me.

"He will come for you. He must come for you." Arvard spoke calmly. He had lost the look of madness, which had overcome him when sight of Evaric brought fever to his eyes; rather, the Shrine Keeper wore the tightly ashen mask of protracted pain or illness. I could not help thinking how remarkably strong and talented he must once have been, before Rendies and unnatural commands from a Seriin Lord overwhelmed him, to have retained such force of presence. He must once have loved Evaric, too. I shivered.

"Why here?" I asked him, though I could guess at many reasons. "You own D'hai. Why must you bring him here to die?"

"Because the Shrine revealed the way to me!" He had designed his emotional statement to impress an audience, and he succeeded; the Shrine Keeper was a fine orator.

His inspired priests jerked my arms in opposing directions. I snapped at them, "How can you listen to this man? You should be working to find a way to destroy the barrier that imprisons us, not sitting in a dead city, waiting to fulfill the vengeance of some Seriin nobleman."

"Destroy the K'shai," proclaimed Arvard, "and the barrier falls. The Rendies will be driven from this world."

"It is the Voice of the Shrine," murmured several of the priests.

"It is the voice of a man who would slay his own brother." I poured fervor into my speech; I could rant quite as eloquently as the Shrine Keeper.

"Arvard," called Evaric, and the name echoed beneath the damaged dome. A small part of me rejoiced to hear him, but most of me despaired.

"You have come," announced Arvard. His ragged expression smoothed; the lines of anguish vanished. For an instant, the serenity of his demeanor impressed even me. "I knew that you would come to me, little brother."

Evaric walked through the ranks of Shrine guards, apparently indifferent to the swords poised against him. The guards stepped away from him, but the circle closed behind him. "Release her, Arvard," said Evaric softly. "She has no part in the argument that Lord Gorng has manufactured between us."

"She is the tool of evil," replied the Shrine Keeper soberly. "She taints you, Evaric." He pointed at one of his nearest guards and then at me. "Slay the Rendie daughter," he ordered with placid confidence, "that her evil blood may become pure in the chamber of our salvation."

The guard approached me; brown eyes in a round, smooth face observed me indifferently. He raised his sword to strike me, and I could only stare at the large, dark mole on his wrist at the joining of his sword hand. I continued to watch the mole, as it fell with the hand and the wrist, severed by the bright flash of K'shai steel. Blood spattered me, and the grips that had restrained me jerked, became limp, and released me.

I leaped from the path of the swords that slashed at Evaric, and I raced to the dais. Two guards reached for me, but they tripped on the uneven floor of the stage, and Evaric slew them. Evaric's sword pierced another guard, as the shorter blade in his left hand thwarted a stroke from a source behind him. Six guards lay bleeding in crumpled hillocks, as Evaric moved slowly to my side, and the Shrine Keeper's Guard encircled us cautiously.

"I am the tool of holy destiny," announced Arvard grandly. He spread his arms as if to summon some elemental force to strike us. His sand-colored hair stood awry, but it seemed to shine like a halo when he spoke. "I shall cleanse the affliction from my brother, and he will be made pure."

The circle of enemies tightened around us, flowing to the Shrine Keeper's command. I retreated a pace involuntarily, and the central cylinder bruised my thigh. The cylinder felt colder than the floor, even colder than my hands. Anni had touched it and summoned the slumbering city; I touched it and felt only the reflection of my own chill dread. I was not prepared to die for a madman's vengeance nor for the holy cause in which most of these deadly men believed. "Touch the cylinder, Evaric," I entreated my perilous love.

"No." He studied each of his enemies, pressing around us from all directions. He watched his brother with a bitter regret and a mournful sorrow. "I cannot touch it, Lyriel." The only fear in him sprang from me and my request. "I shall not touch it," he insisted, though I had not argued with him. He no longer spoke to me. "I am Evaric, son of Evram and Terrell. I am not the one you seek!"

From the darkness of the open dome poured wraiths. Arvard covered his ears with his hands and cried, "Never listen to Rendies, little brother!" Rendie wails captured the chant of the Shrine Keeper's priests, as the Shrine Keeper's guards began to shout and stumble in their haste to flee. "You must kill *him*," wailed the Shrine Keeper, but his vigor fled with his panicked troop. "I cannot kill you, Evaric."

A Shrine guard shook the hood from his golden head. Ineuil seemed taller and finer than I had remembered, or perhaps the difference lay in his manner. "Touch the pillar, Evaric," he implored, "for Lyriel. You must save her."

Evaric turned his gaze from Arvard to Ineuil, and the Rendie hunger lay in Evaric's eyes. I thought that he would hurl his short sword at the pilgrim's throat. A wraith wailed, and the mists passed across my arm, leaving uneven, bloody scores. I cried aloud. Evaric cast both of his weapons to the floor, whirled to the cylinder, and struck it with both hands.

The room groaned and cracked. The floor shook, or the ground beneath it moved. The rocking motion thrust me to my knees. Arvard and his remaining followers scrambled on the rough floor. Rendies broke into frightened fragments. Only Evaric continued to stand, for the room did not shudder beneath him, as beneath the rest of us. All shifted and shuddered around him, who alone remained steady and solid.

The floor began to flow into molten smoothness. With a roar, a clear blue shell snapped across the open dome and sealed it, severing Rendies. The riven wraiths drifted to the floor, slow and soft as ashes. "Fire-child," they howled forlornly. The air moaned with them, and the light grew red and warped. The circle of enemies became a circle of rippling emptiness encompassing the lonely stage.

I blinked, and Anni stood with us on the dais. Around her neck hung the stone like starlight, and her hair glowed like a pale gold sunrise. In her outstretched hand, she held a spindle: no true tool of spinning but a thing of amber and gold filigree. "You must take it, Evaric," she said gently, and she was crying. "You must return it."

"You have no choice," said Fog, but he was not Fog, for an image overlaid his: an image of a man as fine and dark as Evaric himself, save that Fog's image eyes were as blue as the cold, expensive crystal on Marlund's elegant Diarmon table. Evaric's eyes had lost all trace of color.

Someone took my hand. I blinked to see the room beyond the three figures standing before me. Rendies had dismembered many of the Shrine priests and guards, and Rendies still fed upon the dying. A few priests and guards huddled against the dome wall. Arvard sat hunched upon the floor, clutching at his head as if it pained him terribly.

The insistent hand pulled me. I tried to jerk free of it, for the arm was clothed in gray. The man was strong, and he would not release me. "Movement attracts undesirable attention," he whispered with barely a discernible motion.

"Are you a Shrine guard, Ineuil?"

"Only as an actor, fair Lyriel. It was a convenient pose and an informative one."

The room shuddered again. I felt nothing but Ineuil's rigid grip. The circle of dreadful emptiness sharpened; it resembled the barrier around the city, but it spewed a thicker turbulence. I looked at Anni's golden-haired cousin, trapped with me between the barrier and the stage. His attention was concentrated upon the trio near the cylinder.

"You must be the focus," said Anni and Fog as one. "You are the limit point."

"It must occur now," said another voice, entwined with Anni's but emerging from a wider, less definable source.

"She has bound Horlach within herself," Ineuil informed me, though I think he talked only to disperse his restlessness, "that the necessary knowledge of the Sorcerer King be immediately available to Kaedric. Evaric must be the focus, Kaedric the force, and Rhianna the stabilizing continuity."

The shape of Evaric's hands blurred against the cylinder. The muscles of his arms showed sharply as he pressed; he embedded the cylinder's edges in his flesh. His hands became fire, hot and intangible. Those same unearthly hands had touched me with love.

Evaric raised one arm slowly, and the hand became solid

as it separated from the rippling cylinder. I could even discern the brand, as he accepted the spindle that Anni offered him. Evaric's strong, lean hand shook. The brand upon it grew hazy.

My vision doubled, producing two rooms and two cylinders, distinct and superimposed. One was bright and frantic; one was dim and frightened. Patches of shrinking and expanding emptiness dashed around me, consuming what they touched. One caught the Shrine Keeper, and he was gone, wailing his brother's name in utter despair.

A stranger in odd, slick clothing occupied the second dais, addressing a little man beside the second cylinder. The little man, who held a spindle like that in Evaric's grasp, laughed and vanished. The sourceless voice spun from Anni, laughing in crazy echo.

The stranger gazed frantically at a glowing band upon his arm. The stranger's face wore bewilderment and shock, but calculation and intelligence stirred there as well. I could not understand his words, but I could sense his revulsion and his fear.

"Recall the pattern!" commanded Fog's voice, which was everywhere and inescapable.

The stranger slumped to the floor. Softly ringing tones issued from the band at his wrist. Anni crossed to him, knelt and touched him. The healing Power that she poured into him was visible even to me.

"Recall the pattern!" repeated Fog.

Evaric alternately studied the stranger and the spindle. The spindle glowed brilliantly. The shape of light around it shifted each time Evaric looked upon it. The air pulsed with the changes. Everywhere was silence.

Evaric grew pale, and I made a motion toward him. Ineuil restrained me, hissing, "You cannot touch raw Power and survive." His words made the only sound in all of that gaping, empty space.

"I love him," I whispered in a breath of loss.

"He is his father's son." Ineuil added bitterly, "And his mother's."

Anni went to Evaric's side, and Evaric let her arms draw him from the shuddering cylinder; I envied her. "He is not yet finished," declared Fog sternly.

Anni stood as tall and adamant as any queen, defending my love. "He cannot bear more alone, Kaedric. I shall not lose him now, having finally gained him."

The cold and heat of Rendies broke upon me. *"Give him to me,"* pleaded the sourceless voice, *"and I shall save him."*

"No, Horlach," replied Anni irrevocably. "Your part is played. Your era is ended. I can protect my son now, for you have shown me how to untangle his energies and make him whole. It was never your pattern that bound him; it was the Taormin itself."

Angry lightning exploded from the black barrier that had contracted to this single room's dimensions. The lightning hurled itself at Anni. A crackling of fire burst from Fog and met the lightning. I shut my eyes against the brightness. When I reopened them, the old K'shai had crumpled. Ineuil started when the K'shai's dark shade stepped free of its fallen host. Ineuil whispered with something of wry respect in his voice, "I should have known you could not die, O Immortal Venkarel."

Lord Venkarel spoke, and the sense of him rattled me to the marrow. "Concede to us, Horlach, as you must, and spare me this waste of time. You knew from the day you stole the Taormin that restoration must be made. You have lived this moment before, Horlach, and you know that it is your last."

Evaric stepped free of Anni's arms, and she let him go, though her thin hand drifted after him in a tremulous gesture. Evaric raised the spindle once and lowered it, until it hovered just above the blackened cylinder.

"The wait has grown long," said the sourceless voice, sounding suddenly tired and ancient beyond belief. *"Dr. Terry has the final word, after all. He condemned us, Venkarel. You know only this time and this space. You do not know what he stole from us with his 'topological closure.'"*

"You stole it from yourself, Horlach, by desiring it for yourself alone."

"I yield my kingdom, Venkarel. Not even I—nor you—can cheat the past."

Evaric rammed the spindle into the blackened cylinder before him. The second cylinder exploded with amber light, as a golden fury enveloped Evaric. The doubled images merged. The body of the stranger vanished in a rippling wake of air.

The light expanded in blinding vehemence, and the force of it made me stagger against Ineuil. We clung to each other, as wave upon wave of coldly burning Power buffeted us. Rendie mists tore past us, splattered against the light, and disappeared. The wind of Power roared.

And it ended. The light dimmed. The wind failed. The dais storm returned to calm, and no one remained on the dais at all. Nothing remained on the dais but a silver cylinder, empty light, and motes of quietly drifting dust.

Ineuil dragged me from the dais' edge. The barrier had gone. Everything that mattered to me had gone.

My gaze drooped. I stared at the floor. I took each slow step cautiously, though the surface now extended in a smoothly golden plane beneath me. I waited for the floor to fall from beneath my feet, as my prosaic world had fallen from my expectations.

Ineuil stopped abruptly. A body lay before us: dried, as if an eternity of unkind suns had stolen all its moisture and its life. Ineuil knelt beside it and examined its hollowed clothing gingerly. "Fog," he informed me roughly. "It was the K'shai, Fog."

I quipped with raw brightness, "We two must be sturdier than K'shai. Do you suppose we are the last to live upon the world?"

Ineuil grimaced only a little wanly. "I am reassured, at least, to have a beautiful woman as my sole companion."

The dais drew my desolate eyes. The light had darkened to the smoky haze of shattered crystal, and a rainbow smear within it hid the cylinder. I caught my breath raggedly, for a shadow stirred.

Anni emerged, beautiful and joyful, reft of her veil of sorrow. I did not breathe again until my strange, bewildering Evaric appeared behind her. I ran to him, weeping from my heart, but more than blurry tears made his figure seem ethereal and unreal. He looked emptied of all spirit, as he crossed the once-ruined floor with a dutiful deference to the vanished pocks and furrows.

He approached me cautiously and stared at me lengthily before he seemed to see me. He nodded toward Anni. "She is the Lady Rhianna dur Ixaxis," he remarked softly, "my mother."

"You have a peculiar family," I responded with brittle care, recalling the Venkarel's shade with an unwilling shudder.

"I once deplored the prosaic nature of my parents: a Tyntagel clerk and an embittered former governess." Evaric

resembled marble, artfully carved but lifeless. He rubbed
his chin; the everyday motion shocked me unreasonably. "It
is the queerest feeling," he murmured in a voice both casual
and calm. He locked on me his eyes of cold silver, and I saw
what he saw: strength extending in all directions, ensnaring
the unattainable, capturing all desires. By a careless thought,
he could take, create, destroy, and conquer; if this was
Power, I wondered that the Sorcerer Kings had ever met
defeat. He gave me his wonderful smile, and I wanted to fly
to his arms and forget.

I clenched my hands at my sides and did not touch him.
His smile tightened painfully, and his Power bathed me in
compassionate understanding. I shrank from him, for his
Power terrified me. Ineuil caught me as I tried to flee, and I
burrowed my head against pilgrim gray.

"We are only mortal," Ineuil told me gently, "and they
are not."

"She is not your cousin, is she?"

"Hardly."

*   *   *

The sky had cleared to pristine blue, unmarred by any
turbulence. The streets of old D'hai felt empty but warm.
Arvard was gone with his priests, Shrine Guard, and tortured, ambivalent schemes. A Lord of Serii had been thwarted
in his vengeance; a Sorcerer King had surrendered to his
past; and I felt quite sure that no one could harm the
Venkarel's son now. Behind us, the broken dome had become whole; it emitted a sound like crackling fire, but its
unseen smoke was scented more of sweetness than of death.
"The node renews itself," said Anni, who was Rhianna,
Lady of Ixaxis. She moved forward strongly with Evaric at
her side.

Ineuil and I followed slowly. We did not speak; we both
watched the figures that preceded us. I no longer cared who
saw me cry.

OPENING

Chapter 1

Only long lessons would persuade a conditioned world that the-night dangers had retreated to their own sealed realm. Not even Taf and Rubi believed me. They had determined that I, like Alisa, who struggled to recover mind and body both, had been unbalanced by events.

Noryne believed, but she had always been too trusting. She had even trusted Zakari. She also had Power. She was becoming a little like Anni—Lady Rhianna.

The weather might convince the skeptics: Rain had fallen each evening of the past week. Weeds of strange, unfamiliar kind had begun to rise in great patches of the Ardasian desert, where nothing had grown for long years. Eventually, the changes would prove themselves. Just as the world adjusted to the Rending, so it would adapt to the Rending's repair. Mortals had regained the night, though most of us remained too bound by old fear to face the stars as yet. The histories would explain the changes badly. Pilgrims already claimed a miracle of the Shrine, achieved by the martyrdom of the Shrine Keeper, Arvard.

At least D'hai had forgotten the crimes of Evaric and the part of Rubi's Troupe in bringing him to the city; we were free again to leave or stay, to trade or perform. True, we had lost our two leading players, for Alisa would not fill any major role for a long while. Rubi had already begun to seek substitutes in local, untapped talent. Rubi despaired aloud, inwardly inspired by the obstacles she cursed.

Rubi never considered that the Troupe's sole surviving K'shai might have lost interest in the mundane business of Protecting a sorry group of struggling players, any more than she recognized that Protection against Rendies had become unnecessary. The fact that her seamstress was the Infortiare of Serii never penetrated Rubi's narrow focus. When Serii's Adjutant, the Lord Arineuil dur Ven, offered

Protection to the Troupe in exchange for passage to Ardas, both Rubi and Taf haggled with him lengthily over the precise terms of the arrangement. Titles did not intimidate my Taf, and Rubi remained oblivious to anything but her ailing Troupe.

Lady Rhianna seemed to feel indebted to me, though I knew not why. The good will of the Infortiare could only be considered a rare and priceless boon. I was free of enemies, terrors, and awkward entanglements with mysterious K'shai. I ought to have felt delighted, or I ought to have felt devastated. I felt nothing.

I received sympathy from likely and unlikely sources. Taf fretted for me; even Vale patted my shoulder as he brought my supper to my room. I received offers of a willing ear to listen (though I did not know what I might say) from at least three quarters of the Troupe. I received great kindness; my voice gave thanks. My mind tallied friends and blessings I had never suspected that I owned; I felt nothing.

My skull developed a chronic ache at its base, and I did not care. Vale's wife, Epra, prepared her finest meals for me, but I scarcely ate, because the effort seemed excessive and futile. Sleep eluded me, but I could not settle to any useful task. The feelings that assaulted me huddled deeply within me, afraid to emerge into truth; I could not free them, for I could not find them. I had not thought that I could love a man so much nor miss him so sorely.

In lucid moments, I cried uncontrollably. I sobbed and shivered in fear of the Power that had always existed, but of which I had always been blissfully ignorant. I clung to Taf, and I ached for Silf, and I missed Sanston of my childhood dreams with an anguish that nearly shattered me. I had not despaired when the world threatened to fail and darken; I had not despaired when my proud Ardasia seemed likely to crumble into desolate sand. My fears had never seemed so strong, until I faced them in the eyes of my love.

I had not imagined the horror which eroded my spirit; I had seen the dire, infinite calamity that Evaric had faced and conquered. Anni/Rhianna, her Venkarel, Evaric: they were not human. They could not even perceive that the forces they battled were impossible for the rest of us. My Evaric had never left old D'hai: I did not know the man who rode beside our wagons now and wore my lover's face. Ineuil was right; they were beyond me.

During a midday halt on our long-delayed journey away from D'hai, Ineuil approached me, as I attempted to expunge my despair with furious scribbling. "Does it do you any good?" he asked me.

"It might." I did not pause in my hasty scrawl.

"Have you another quill?"

"In the wagon."

He found the quill and took a scrap of paper from my stack. He sat beside me, using a sand-tumbled stone as table. I never saw what he wrote, nor did he request details of my writing. As the Troupe began to stir for departure, he asked me, "Do you ever wonder, lovely Lyriel, why you are subjected to so much of what wise cynics label 'interesting times?' Do you wonder if the fates have truly embroiled you more deeply in drama than the rest of the world's pathetic masses, or if you only magnify your own perspective? Are we special, fair Lyriel, lucky or unfortunate? Or are we no more than common souls, whose individual trials and triumphs emit no greater sound than any plodder's dirge of life?"

"You are poetic today."

"Discouragement makes me so."

"Discouragement?" I tasted the word. "Is that what you feel?"

"It is less sharp than despair, less sanguine than phlegmatism. Yes, I think it is discouragement."

"Why?"

"They are beyond me. They are Immortal, and I am not. They have worlds to walk which I can never see. They cannot care for me."

"You mean that Rhianna cannot love you."

"Just as I cannot truly love her. I do finally realize my absurdity in hoping otherwise."

"Can you cease to love so easily?"

"Nothing about it has been easy. The effort has taken me half a lifetime, and in the process of learning my painful lesson, I have probably destroyed what love I might have earned from the very beautiful, enchanting woman who is my wife."

"You give me little hope."

"There is none if you think to have Evaric."

I looked toward the farthest wagon, where Evaric sat, listening thoughtfully to Rhianna. Noryne listened also, which made me feel unjustly envious. "I love him, blast you," I said, cursing myself more than Ineuil.

"You love a man who no longer exists. Power has consumed him."

"His own Power."

"Ultimately, yes."

"I loved him though he was K'shai and pursued by Rendies. I loved him without knowing or caring what danger he might bring to me. Why should I stop loving him because he becomes a wizard?"

Ineuil answered dryly, "He could destroy you with a thought."

"But he would never harm me knowingly. He loves me." I added, as if in proof, "He has remained with the Troupe."

"He has inherited his mother's obsession with duty. If you are so certain of him, then go to him. You have not spoken with him since he restored the Taormin, have you?" Ineuil folded the paper on which he had written and concealed it in a recess of his tunic, an Ardasian tunic of green and not of gray. "You will grow old, and he will not age."

"I am not old yet," I snapped, rising in a whirl that scattered my papers to the ground. The Adjutant of Serii saluted me wryly.

Evaric met me before I had crossed half the distance to where he had sat with Rhianna and Noryne. "If I touch you now," I asked him roughly, "will your Power destroy me?"

"No," he answered slowly, "not if I am controlling that Power."

"Are you controlling it?"

"If I were not, you would already be as lost to me as Arvard."

"Sands," I muttered, still terrified despite his ressurance. I felt startled to sense no shock but his own when I encircled him with my arms. I murmured his name repeatedly, holding him and touching him as I had done to combat Rendies for him.

"Lyriel," he whispered with a shade of warning and a shade of hungry hope, "do you understand what I am?"

I placed my hands on each side of his too-perfect face.

"You are a man who loves me and who has pledged himself to me."

"You will not allow me to forget it, will you?" His expression only hinted at the wonderful smile, but the promise had returned.

"Not a chance, Seriin. We Ardasians do not take our pledges lightly."

He still tasted like my Evaric.

Chapter 2

Jon Terry spoke suddenly, startling his wife. "I think I understand."

Beth raised her head from her work. "What?"

"The second controller, the man who held it, and the voice in my head."

Beth searched his eyes for the fever brightness which frightened her. Jon had closed in upon himself so much since closing the DI ports, as if he had remained part of that strangely altered world they had abandoned. Network psychologists acknowledged that he was troubled, but Jon would not accept their advice to confess the source of his guilt or seek more specialized treatment. Beth felt sure that Jon had not told even her the full account of that dreadful day's events. "Do you feel like telling me, Jon?"

Jon smiled at her, and her hope surged into her throat. He spoke rapidly, but a very rational excitement marked him. "The controller performed its primary function of preserving topological integrity by readjusting the aberrations. It discovered a way to redefine the nodal limit point." Jon sounded almost giddy with delight. He took Beth's hands and kissed her solemnity from her face. "I designed better than I ever guessed."

"You're being a bit incoherent, my dear and brilliant husband."

"The Immortal stole the controller before the destruct sequence could commence. The closure was effected; all the limit points were removed from intersecting worlds, including the node, which was the only active limit point at the time. Trapped in a closed world, the controller's function as gatekeeper became meaningless, but it continued to exist because the Immortal impeded the energies of implosion." Jon Terry whistled softly, considering his own statement.

"That must have taken some doing. These Immortals of yours are an impressive people, Beth."

"They are mindlessly destructive, Jon," she reminded him gently.

"Not all of them. Not any longer. The controller escaped its genetically aberrant captor by performing its own genetic manipulation. The Immortal who took it was influenced unconsciously; select individuals within his reach could have been influenced equally: The changes could be subtle, because even a marginally stable system could have been maintained for a few thousand years with a little care. The controller needed only to tap a few of the most basic human instincts to breed its own savior. The Immortal who held the controller was restoring it."

Beth did not want to argue with him and watch him retreat again into his shell of fear. "Your controller managed all that without external keying?" She knew her comment sounded weak and doubtful.

"The controller merely fulfilled its underlying requirement to stabilize."

"Past tense?"

"Past and future both. They—the future Immortals—understood the need for topological correction, but they lacked adequate reference by which to define a stable space. So they returned to the source of the last acceptable topological configuration, absorbed the pattern from me, and rebuilt their world's stability."

"Are you suggesting that our home world has existed for several thousand years during the six months since we left it?"

"During the minute that we left it. If they kept decent histories, they would have known which moment to seek. They connected past and future space with a mapping that some of our Network geniuses would sell their souls to understand. I can prove it, Beth."

"Jon, where are you going?" He had not left the apartment voluntarily since they arrived.

"To my office."

"You are on medical leave."

"I need to reopen the DI ports."

"Reopen!" Beth eyed the security alarm; the guards could arrive in a few seconds; they had observed Jon closely since Tom Davison and a world were lost.

Jon kissed her again. "Don't worry, my Beth. I shall use all the proper channels this time. I know what I'm doing."

"Jon, the Immortals are still there, still a deadly danger."

"But they are not mad any longer, Beth, my darling. They have had twenty thousand years to master their Power. Think of what a thesis you can make of them now. My controller has tamed them!"

Even amid his exhilaration, Jon Terry could hear the echoes of Immortal voices laughing in his head with deep delight.

Definitions

I. Let X be a set. Let T be a collection of subsets of X. T is a *topology* for X if and only if:
(1) The null set and X are elements of T;
(2) If D and E are elements of T, then the intersection of D and E is an element of T;
(3) If U is an arbitrary subcollection of T, then the union of U is an element of T.

II. If T is a topology for X, then (X, T) comprises a *topological space*. A subset S of X is an *open* subset of (X,T) if S is an element of T.

III. If each open set containing an element p of X intersects a subset S of X in at least one point distinct from p, then p is a *limit point* of S with respect to the toplogical space (X,T).

IV. A subset S of X is *closed* if it contains all its limit points. The union of a subset S of X and the set of all its limit points is called the *closure* of S.

DAW

Magical Tales of the Taormin
Cheryl J. Franklin

☐ **FIRE GET: Book 1** (UE2231—$3.50)

In a kingdom where magic was hated and feared, Lady Rhianna had been taught to deny the Power she herself possessed. Fleeing the marriage her father had planned for her, she was drawn to Lord Venkarel, a master sorcerer who could save her world from the Evil that threatened—if he himself, did not become its portal through which to invade mortal lands.

☐ **FIRE LORD: Book 2** (UE2354—$3.95)

The dread legacy of the Taormin war has fallen on the land of Serii—the Rendies, creatures of soul fire that prey upon the living, bringing insanity and death. With Lord Venkarel gone, the Lady Rhianna has no choice but to send their son into hiding, to be raised as a commoner ignorant of both his noble and magical heritage. Yet even Rhianna can't protect her son from the siren call of the Rendies and of the Taormin matrix itself—nor from the destiny that will lead him to a confrontation with a Power his world was never meant to contain.

DAW

New Worlds of Fantasy

STEPHANIE A. SMITH

☐ SNOW EYES   (UE2286—$3.50)
When the mysterious mother who abandoned her returns to claim Snow-Eyes for the goddess known as Lake-Mother, Snow-Eyes is compelled to go with her to the goddess' citadel—there to face betrayal and a confrontation with her own true nature.

☐ THE BOY WHO WAS THROWN AWAY   (UE2320—$3.50)
The spell-binding sequel to SNOW-EYES! Gifted with a musical magic and a shape-changing talent he can scarcely control, Amant struggles to rescue his cousin caught in a terrifying spell halfway between life and the realm of Lord Death.

MELANIE RAWN

☐ DRAGON PRINCE   (UE2312—$4.50)
☐ THE STAR SCROLL   (UE2349—$4.95)
In a land on the verge of war, Rohan and his Sunrunner bride would face the challenge of the desert, the dragons—and the High Prince's treachery! *"Marvelous . . . impressive . . . fascinating . . . I completely and thoroughly enjoyed DRAGON PRINCE."* —Ann McCaffrey

TANYA HUFF

☐ CHILD OF THE GROVE   (UE2272—$3.50)
☐ THE LAST WIZARD   (UE2331—$3.95)
Magic's spell was fading, but one wizard had survived to wreak madness and destruction. And though the Elder Races had long withdrawn from mortals, they now bequeathed them one last gift—Crystal, the Child of the Grove!

NEW AMERICAN LIBRARY
P.O. Box 999, Bergenfield, New Jersey 07621

Please send me the DAW BOOKS I have checked above. I am enclosing $_____ (check or money order—no currency or C.O.D.'s). Please include the list price plus $1.00 per order to cover handling costs. Prices and numbers are subject to change without notice. (Prices slightly higher in Canada.)

Name_____

Address_____

City _____ State _____ Zip Code _____
Please allow 4-6 weeks for delivery.